THE GUN SELLER

Hugh Laurie was born in 1959. At Cambridge University he took part in a number of undergraduate revues, the last of which won the Perrier Award at the Edinburgh Fringe in 1981. He also rowed for Cambridge in the 1980 Boat Race.

Since university he has made his living as a writer, actor, director and musician, appearing in, amongst others, series of *Blackadder*, *A Bit of Fry & Laurie*, *Jeeves and Wooster* and *House*.

He lives in London with his wife and three children, and is utterly devoted to motorcycling.

THE
GUN SELLER

HUGH LAURIE

arrow books

Reissued in 2009 by Arrow Books

11 13 15 17 19 20 18 16 14 12

First published in the United Kingdom in 1996 by William Heinemann
This edition first published in 1997 by Mandarin Paperbacks
First edition in Arrow Books published in 1997

Arrow Books
Random House, 20 Vauxhall Bridge Road,
London SW1V 2SA

www.rbooks.co.uk

Addresses for companies within The Random House Group Limited
can be found at: www.randomhouse.co.uk/offices.htm

The Random House Group Limited Reg. No. 954009

A CIP catalogue record for this book
is available from the British Library

ISBN 9780099469391

The Random House Group Limited supports The Forest Stewardship
Council (FSC), the leading international forest certification organisation.
All our titles that are printed on Greenpeace approved FSC certified paper
carry the FSC logo. Our paper procurement policy can be found at:
www.rbooks.co.uk/environment

Printed and bound in Great Britain by
CPI Cox & Wyman, Reading, RG1 8EX

For my father

I am indebted to the writer and broadcaster
Stephen Fry for his comments;
to Kim Harris and Sarah Williams for their
overpowering good taste and intelligence;
to my literary agent Anthony Goff, who has been
unstinting in his support and encouragement;
to my theatrical agent Lorraine Hamilton,
for not minding that I also have a literary agent,
and to my wife Jo, for things that would
fill a longer book than this.

PART ONE

One

I saw a man this morning
Who did not wish to die;

P. S. STEWART

Imagine that you have to break someone's arm.

Right or left, doesn't matter. The point is that you have to break it, because if you don't . . . well, that doesn't matter either. Let's just say bad things will happen if you don't.

Now, my question goes like this: do you break the arm quickly – snap, whoops, sorry, here let me help you with that improvised splint – or do you drag the whole business out for a good eight minutes, every now and the ʼncreasing the pressure in the tiniest of increments, until the pain becomes pink and green and hot and cold and altogether howlingly unbearable?

Well exactly. Of course. The right thing to do, the ̍ *only* thing to do, is to get it over with as quickly as possible. Break the arm, ply the brandy, be a good citizen. There can be no other answer.

Unless.

Unless unless unless.

What if you were to hate the person on the other end of the

3

arm? I mean really, *really* hate them.

This was a thing I now had to consider.

I say now, meaning then, meaning the moment I am describing; the moment fractionally, oh so bloody fractionally, before my wrist reached the back of my neck and my left humerus broke into at least two, very possibly more, floppily joined-together pieces.

The arm we've been discussing, you see, is mine. It's not an abstract, philosopher's arm. The bone, the skin, the hairs, the small white scar on the point of the elbow, won from the corner of a storage heater at Gateshill Primary School – they all belong to me. And now is the moment when I must consider the possibility that the man standing behind me, gripping my wrist and driving it up my spine with an almost sexual degree of care, hates me. I mean, really, *really* hates me.

He is taking for ever.

His name was Rayner. First name unknown. By me, at any rate, and therefore, presumably, by you too.

I suppose someone, somewhere, must have known his first name – must have baptised him with it, called him down to breakfast with it, taught him how to spell it – and someone else must have shouted it across a bar with an offer of a drink, or murmured it during sex, or written it in a box on a life insurance application form. I know they must have done all these things. Just hard to picture, that's all.

Rayner, I estimated, was ten years older than me. Which was fine. Nothing wrong with that. I have good, warm, non-arm-breaking relationships with plenty of people who are ten years older than me. People who are ten years older than me are, by and large, admirable. But Rayner was also three inches taller than me, four stones heavier, and at least eight however-you-measure-violence units more violent. He was uglier than a car park, with a big, hairless skull that dipped and bulged like a balloon full of spanners, and his flattened,

4

fighter's nose, apparently drawn on his face by someone using their left hand, or perhaps even their left foot, spread out in a meandering, lopsided delta under the rough slab of his forehead.

And God Almighty, what a forehead. Bricks, knives, bottles and reasoned arguments had, in their time, bounced harmlessly off this massive frontal plane, leaving only the feeblest indentations between its deep, widely-spaced pores. They were, I think, the deepest and most widely-spaced pores I have ever seen in human skin, so that I found myself thinking back to the council putting-green in Dalbeattie, at the end of the long, dry summer of '76.

Moving now to the side elevation, we find that Rayner's ears had, long ago, been bitten off and spat back on to the side of his head, because the left one was definitely upside down, or inside out, or something that made you stare at it for a long time before thinking 'oh, it's an ear'.

And on top of all this, in case you hadn't got the message, Rayner wore a black leather jacket over a black polo-neck.

But of course you would have got the message. Rayner could have swathed himself in shimmering silk and put an orchid behind each ear, and nervous passers-by would still have paid him money first and wondered afterwards whether they had owed him any.

As it happened, I didn't owe him money. Rayner belonged to that select group of people to whom I didn't owe anything at all, and if things had been going a little better between us, I might have suggested that he and his fellows have a special tie struck, to signify membership. A motif of crossed paths, perhaps.

But, as I said, things weren't going well between us.

A one-armed combat instructor called Cliff (yes, I know – he taught unarmed combat, and he only had one arm – very occasionally life is like that) once told me that pain was a thing you did to yourself. Other people did things to you – they hit you, or stabbed you, or tried to break your arm – but

5

pain was of your own making. Therefore, said Cliff, who had spent a fortnight in Japan and so felt entitled to unload dogshit of this sort on his eager charges, it was always within your power to stop your own pain. Cliff was killed in a pub brawl three months later by a fifty-five-year-old widow, so I don't suppose I'll ever have a chance to set him straight.

Pain is an event. It happens to you, and you deal with it in whatever way you can.

The only thing in my favour was that, so far, I hadn't made any noise.

Nothing to do with bravery, you understand, I simply hadn't got round to it. Up until this moment, Rayner and I had been pinging off the walls and furniture in a sweatily male silence, with only the occasional grunt to show that we were both still concentrating. But now, with not much more than five seconds to go before I passed out or the bone finally gave way – now was the ideal moment to introduce a new element. And sound was all I could think of.

So I inhaled deeply through my nose, straightened up to get as close as I could to his face, held the breath for a moment, and then let out what Japanese martial artists refer to as a *kiai* – you'd probably call it a very loud noise, and that wouldn't be so far off – a scream of such blinding, shocking, what-the-fuck-was-that intensity, that I frightened myself quite badly.

On Rayner, the effect was pretty much as advertised, because he shifted involuntarily to one side, easing the grip on my arm for about a twelfth of a second. I threw my head back into his face as hard as I could, feeling the gristle in his nose adjust itself around the shape of my skull and a silky wetness spreading across my scalp, then brought my heel up towards his groin, scraping the inside of his thigh before connecting with an impressive bundle of genitalia. By the time the twelfth of a second had elapsed, Rayner was no longer breaking my arm, and I was aware, suddenly, of being drenched in sweat.

I backed away from him, dancing on my toes like a very old St Bernard, and looked around for a weapon.

The venue for this pro-am contest of one fifteen-minute round was a small, inelegantly furnished sitting-room in Belgravia. The interior designer had done a perfectly horrible job, as all interior designers do, every single time, without fail, no exceptions – but at that moment his or her liking for heavy, portable *objets* happened to coincide with mine. I selected an eighteen-inch Buddha from the mantelpiece with my good arm, and found that the little fellow's ears afforded a satisfyingly snug grip for the one-handed player.

Rayner was kneeling now, vomiting on a Chinese carpet and improving its colour no end. I chose my spot, braced myself, and swung at him back-handed, plugging the corner of the Buddha's plinth into the soft space behind his left ear. There was a dull, flat noise, of the kind that only human tissue under attack can make, and he rolled over on to his side.

I didn't bother to see whether he was still alive. Callous, perhaps, but there you go.

I wiped some of the sweat from my face and walked through into the hall. I tried to listen, but if there was any sound from the house or from the street outside I would never have heard it, because my heart was going like a road drill. Or perhaps there really was a road drill outside. I was too busy sucking in great suitcase-sized chunks of air to notice.

I opened the front door and immediately felt cool drizzle on my face. It mingled with the sweat, diluting it, diluting the pain in my arm, diluting everything, and I closed my eyes and let it fall. It was one of the nicest things I've ever experienced. You may say that it's a pretty poor life I've been leading. But then, you see, context is everything.

I left the door on the latch, stepped down on to the pavement and lit a cigarette. Gradually, grumpily, my heart sorted itself out, and my breathing followed at a distance. The pain in my arm was terrible, and I knew it would be with me for days, if not weeks, but at least it wasn't my smoking arm.

I went back into the house and saw that Rayner was where I'd left him, lying in a pool of vomit. He was dead, or he was grievously-bodily-harmed, either of which meant at least five years. Ten, with time added on for bad behaviour. And this, from my point of view, was bad.

I've been in prison, you see. Only three weeks, and only on remand, but when you've had to play chess twice a day with a monosyllabic West Ham supporter, who has 'HATE' tattooed on one hand, and 'HATE' on the other – using a set missing six pawns, all the rooks and two of the bishops – you find yourself cherishing the little things in life. Like not being in prison.

I was contemplating these and related matters, and starting to think of all the hot countries I'd never got around to visiting, when I realised that that noise – that soft, creaking, shuffling, scraping noise – was definitely not coming from my heart. Nor from my lungs, nor from any other part of my yelping body. That noise was definitely external.

Someone, or something, was making an utterly hopeless job of coming down the stairs quietly.

I left the Buddha where it was, picked up a hideous alabaster table lighter and moved towards the door, which was also hideous. How can one make a hideous door? you may ask. Well, it takes some doing, certainly, but believe me, the top interior designers can knock off this kind of thing before breakfast.

I tried to hold my breath and couldn't, so I waited noisily. A light switch flicked on somewhere, waited, then flicked off. A door opened, pause, nothing there either, closed. Stand still. Think. Try the sitting-room.

There was a rustle of clothing, a soft footfall, and then suddenly I found I was relaxing my grip on the alabaster lighter, and leaning back against the wall in something close to relief. Because even in my frightened, wounded state, I was ready to stake my life on the fact that Nina Ricci's Fleur de Fleurs is just not a fighting scent.

She stopped in the doorway and looked around the room. The lights were out, but the curtains were wide open and there was plenty of light coming in from the street.

I waited until her gaze fell on Rayner's body before I put my hand over her mouth.

We went through all the usual exchanges dictated by Hollywood and polite society. She tried to scream and bite the palm of my hand, and I told her to be quiet because I wasn't going to hurt her unless she shouted. She shouted and I hurt her. Pretty standard stuff, really.

By and by she was sitting on the hideous sofa with half a pint of what I thought was brandy but turned out to be Calvados, and I was standing by the door wearing my smartest and best 'I am psychiatrically A1' expression.

I'd rolled Rayner on to his side, into a kind of recovery position, to stop him from choking on his own vomit. Or anyone else's, if it came to that. She'd wanted to get up and fiddle with him, to see if he was all right – pillows, damp cloths, bandages, all the things that help to make the bystander feel better – but I told her to stay where she was because I'd already called an ambulance, and all in all it would be better to leave him alone.

She had started to tremble slightly. It started in the hands, as they clutched the glass, then moved to her elbows and up to her shoulders, and it got worse every time she looked at Rayner. Of course, trembling is probably not an uncommon reaction to discovering a mixture of dead person and vomit on your carpet in the middle of the night, but I didn't want her getting any worse. As I lit a cigarette with the alabaster lighter – and yes, even the flame was hideous – I tried to take in as much information as I could before the Calvados booted her up and she started asking questions.

I could see her face three times in that room: once in a silver-framed photograph on the mantelpiece, with her in Ray Bans, dangling from a ski-lift; once in a huge and terrible oil portrait, done by someone who can't have liked her all that much, hanging by the window; and finally, and definitely the best of all, in a sofa ten feet away.

She couldn't have been more than nineteen, with square

shoulders and long brown hair that waved and cheered as it disappeared behind her neck. The high, round cheek-bones implied Orientalness, but that disappeared as soon as you reached her eyes, which were also round, and large, and bright grey. If that makes any sense. She was wearing a red silk dressing-gown, and one elegant slipper with fancy gold thread across the toes. I glanced around the room, but its mate was nowhere to be seen. Maybe she could only afford one.

She cleared some husk from her throat.

'Who is he?' she said.

I think I'd known she was going to be American before she opened her mouth. Too healthy to be anything else. And where do they get those teeth?

'His name was Rayner,' I said, and then realised that this sounded a little thin as an answer, so I thought I'd add something. 'He was a very dangerous man.'

'Dangerous?'

She looked worried by that, and quite right too. It was probably crossing her mind, as it was crossing mine, that if Rayner was dangerous, and I'd killed him, then that, hierarchically-speaking, made me very dangerous.

'Dangerous,' I said again, and watched her closely as she looked away. She seemed to be trembling less, which was good. Or maybe her trembling had just fallen into sync with mine, so I noticed it less.

'Well . . . what is he doing here?' she said at last. 'What did he want?'

'It's difficult to say.' Difficult for me, at any rate. 'Maybe he was after money, maybe the silver . . . '

'You mean . . . he didn't tell you?' Her voice was suddenly loud. 'You hit this guy, without knowing who he was? What he was doing here?'

Despite the shock, her brain seemed to be coming along pretty nicely.

'I hit him because he was trying to kill me,' I said. 'I'm like that.'

I tried a roguish smile, then caught sight of it in the mirror over the mantelpiece and realised it hadn't worked.

'You're like that,' she repeated, unlovingly. 'And who are you?'

Well now. I was going to have to wear some very soft shoes at this juncture. This was where things could suddenly get a lot worse than they already were.

I tried looking surprised, and perhaps just a little bit hurt.

'You mean you don't recognise me?'

'No.'

'Huh. Odd. Fincham. James Fincham.' I held out my hand. She didn't take it, so I converted the movement into a nonchalant brush of the hair.

'That's a name,' she said. 'That's not who you are.'

'I'm a friend of your father's.'

She considered this for a moment.

'Business friend?'

'Sort of.'

'Sort of.' She nodded. 'You're James Fincham, you're a sort of business friend of my father's, and you've just killed a man in our house.'

I put my head on one side, and tried to show that yes, sometimes it's an absolute bugger of a world.

She showed her teeth again.

'And that's it, is it? That's your CV?'

I reprised the roguish smile, to no better effect.

'Wait a second,' she said.

She looked at Rayner, then suddenly sat up a little straighter, as if a thought had just struck her.

'You didn't call anybody, did you?'

Come to think of it, all things considered, she must have been nearer twenty-four.

'You mean . . . ' I was floundering now.

'I mean,' she said, 'there's no ambulance coming here. Jesus.'

She put the glass down on the carpet by her feet, got up and walked towards the phone.

11

'Look,' I said, 'before you do anything silly . . . '

I started to move towards her, but the way she spun round made me realise that staying still was probably the better plan. I didn't want to be pulling bits of telephone receiver out of my face for the next few weeks.

'You stay right there, Mr James Fincham,' she hissed at me. 'There's nothing silly about this. I'm calling an ambulance, and I'm calling the police. This is an internationally approved procedure. Men come round with big sticks and take you away. Nothing silly about it at all.'

'Look,' I said, 'I haven't been entirely straight with you.'

She turned towards me and narrowed her eyes. If you know what I mean by that. Narrowed them horizontally, not vertically. I suppose one should say she shortened her eyes, but nobody ever does.

She narrowed her eyes.

'What the hell do you mean "not entirely straight"? You only told me two things. You mean one of them was a lie?'

She had me on the ropes, there's no question about that. I was in trouble. But then again, she'd only dialled the first nine.

'My name is Fincham,' I said, 'and I do know your father.'

'Yeah, what brand of cigarette does he smoke?'

'Dunhill.'

'Never smoked a cigarette in his life.'

She was late-twenties, possibly. Thirty at a pinch. I took a deep breath while she dialled the second nine.

'All right, I don't know him. But I am trying to help.'

'Right. You've come to fix the shower.'

Third nine. Play the big card.

'Someone is trying to kill him,' I said.

There was a faint click and I could hear somebody, somewhere, asking which service we wanted. Very slowly she turned towards me, holding the receiver away from her face.

'What did you say?'

'Someone is trying to kill your father,' I repeated. 'I don't know who, and I don't know why. But I'm trying to stop them. That's who I am, and that's what I'm doing here.'

She looked at me long and hard. A clock ticked somewhere, hideously.

'This man,' I pointed at Rayner, 'had something to do with it.'

I could see that she thought this unfair, as Rayner was hardly in a position to contradict me; so I softened my tone a little, looking around anxiously as if I was every bit as mystified and fretted-up as she was.

'I can't say he came here to kill,' I said, 'because we didn't get a chance to talk much. But it's not impossible.' She carried on staring at me. The operator was squeaking hellos down the line and probably trying to trace the call.

She waited. For what, I'm not sure.

'Ambulance,' she said at last, still looking at me, and then turned away slightly and gave the address. She nodded, and then slowly, very slowly, put the receiver back on its cradle and turned to me. There was one of those pauses that you know is going to be long as soon as it starts, so I shook out another cigarette and offered her the packet.

She came towards me and stopped. She was shorter than she'd looked on the other side of the room. I smiled again, and she took a cigarette from the packet, but didn't light it. She just played with it slowly, and then pointed a pair of grey eyes at me.

I say *a* pair. I mean her pair. She didn't get a pair of someone else's out from a drawer and point them at me. She pointed her own pair of huge, pale, grey, pale, huge eyes at me. The sort of eyes that can make a grown man talk gibberish to himself. Get a grip, for Christ's sake.

'You're a liar,' she said.

Not angry. Not scared. Just matter-of-fact. You're a liar.

'Well, yes,' I said, 'generally speaking, I am. But at this particular moment, I happen to be telling the truth.'

She kept on staring at my face, the way I sometimes do when I've finished shaving, but she didn't seem to get any more answers than I ever have. Then she blinked once, and the blink seemed to change things somehow. Something had been released, or switched off, or at least turned down a bit. I started to relax.

'Why would anyone want to kill my father?' Her voice was softer now.

'I honestly don't know,' I said. 'I've only just found out he doesn't smoke.'

She pressed straight on, as if she hadn't heard me.

'And tell me Mr Fincham,' she said, 'how you came by all this?'

This was the tricky bit. The really tricky bit. Trickiness cubed.

'Because I was offered the job,' I said.

She stopped breathing. I mean, she actually stopped breathing. And didn't look as if she had any plans to start again in the near future.

I carried on, as calmly as I could.

'Someone offered me a lot of money to kill your father,' I said, and she frowned in disbelief. 'I turned it down.'

I shouldn't have added that. I really shouldn't.

Newton's Third Law of Conversation, if it existed, would hold that every statement implies an equal and opposite statement. To say that I'd turned the offer down raised the possibility that I might not have done. Which was not a thing I wanted floating round the room at this moment. But she started breathing again, so maybe she hadn't noticed.

'Why?'

'Why what?'

Her left eye had a tiny streak of green that went off from the pupil in a north-easterly direction. I stood there, looking into her eyes and trying not to, because I was in terrible trouble at this moment. In lots of ways.

'Why'd you turn it down?'

'Because . . . ' I began, then stopped, because I had to get this absolutely right.

'Yes?'

'Because I don't kill people.'

There was a pause while she took this in and swilled it round her mouth a few times. Then she glanced over at Rayner's body.

'I told you,' I said. 'He started it.'

She stared into me for another three hundred years and then, still turning the cigarette slowly between her fingers, moved away towards the sofa, apparently deep in thought.

'Honestly,' I said, trying to get a hold of myself and the situation. 'I'm nice. I give to Oxfam, I recycle newspapers, everything.'

She reached Rayner's body and stopped.

'So when did all this happen?'

'Well . . . just now,' I stammered, like an idiot.

She closed her eyes for a moment. 'I mean you getting asked.'

'Right,' I said. 'Ten days ago.'

'Where?'

'Amsterdam.'

'Holland, right?'

That was a relief. That made me feel a lot better. It's nice to be looked up to by the young every now and then. You don't want it all the time, just every now and then.

'Right,' I said.

'And who was it offered you the job?'

'Never seen him before or since.'

She stooped for the glass, took a sip of Calvados and grimaced at the taste of it.

'And I'm supposed to believe this?'

'Well . . .'

'I mean, help me out here,' she said, starting to get louder again. She nodded towards Rayner. 'We have a guy here, who isn't going to back up your story, I wouldn't say, and I'm supposed to believe you because of what? Because you have a nice face?'

I couldn't help myself. I should have helped myself, I know, but I just couldn't.

'Why not?' I said, and tried to look charming. 'I'd believe

anything you said.'

Terrible mistake. Really terrible. One of the crassest, most ridiculous remarks I've ever made, in a long, ridiculous-remark-packed life.

She turned to me, suddenly very angry.

'You can drop that shit right now.'

'All I meant . . . ' I said, but I was glad when she cut me off, because I honestly didn't know what I'd meant.

'I said drop it. There's a guy dying in here.'

I nodded, guiltily, and we both bowed our heads at Rayner, as if paying our respects. And then she seemed to snap the hymn book shut and move on. Her shoulders relaxed, and she held out the glass to me.

'I'm Sarah,' she said. 'See if you can get me a Coke.'

She did ring the police eventually, and they turned up just as the ambulance crew were scooping Rayner, apparently still breathing, on to a collapsible stretcher. They hummed and harred, and picked things up off the mantelpiece and looked at the underneath, and generally had that air of wanting to be somewhere else.

Policemen, as a rule, don't like to hear of new cases. Not because they're lazy, but because they want, like everyone else, to find a meaning, a connectedness, in the great mess of random unhappiness in which they work. If, in the middle of trying to catch some teenager who's been nicking hub-caps, they're called to the scene of a mass murder, they just can't stop themselves from checking under the sofa to see if there are any hub-caps there. They want to find something that connects to what they've already seen, that will make sense out of the chaos. So they can say to themselves, this happened because that happened. When they don't find it – when all they see is another lot of stuff that has to be written about, and filed, and lost, and found in someone's bottom drawer, and lost again, and eventually chalked up against no one's name – they get, well, disappointed.

They were particularly disappointed by our story. Sarah

and I had rehearsed what we thought was a reasonable scenario, and we played three performances of it to officers of ascending rank, finishing up with an appallingly young inspector who said his name was Brock.

Brock sat on the sofa, occasionally glancing at his fingernails, and nodded his youthful way through the story of the intrepid James Fincham, friend of the family, staying in the spare-room on the first floor. Heard noises, crept downstairs to investigate, nasty man in leather jacket and black polo-neck, no never seen him before, fight, fall over, oh my god, hit head. Sarah Woolf, d.o.b. 29th August, 1964, heard sounds of struggle, came down, saw the whole thing. Drink, Inspector? Tea? Ribena?

Yes, of course, the setting helped. If we'd tried the same story in a council flat in Deptford, we'd have been on the floor of the van in seconds, asking fit young men with short hair if they wouldn't mind getting off our heads for a moment while we got comfortable. But in leafy, stuccoed Belgravia, the police are more inclined to believe you than not. I think it's included in the rates.

As we signed our statements, they asked us not to do anything silly like leave the country without informing the local station, and generally encouraged us to abide at every opportunity.

Two hours after he'd tried to break my arm, all that was left of Rayner, first name unknown, was a smell.

I let myself out of the house, and felt the pain creep back to centre stage as I walked. I lit a cigarette and smoked my way down to the corner, where I turned left into a cobbled mews that had once housed horses. It'd have to be an extremely rich horse who could afford to live here now, obviously, but the stabling character of the mews had hung about the place, and that's why it had felt right to tether the bike there. With a bucket of oats and some straw under the back wheel.

The bike was where I'd left it, which sounds like a dull remark, but isn't these days. Among bikers, leaving your machine in a dark place for more than an hour, even with padlock and alarm, and finding it still there when you come back, is something of a talking point. Particularly when the bike is a Kawasaki ZZR 1100.

Now I won't deny that the Japanese were well off-side at Pearl Harbor, and that their ideas on preparing fish for the table are undoubtedly poor – but by golly, they do know some things about making motorcycles. Twist the throttle wide open in any gear on this machine, and it'd push your eyeballs through the back of your head. All right, so maybe that's not a sensation most people are looking for in their choice of personal transport, but since I'd won the bike in a game of backgammon, getting home with an outrageously flukey only-throw 4-1 and three consecutive double sixes, I enjoyed it a lot. It was black, and big, and it allowed even the average rider to visit other galaxies.

I started the motor, revved it loud enough to wake a few fat Belgravian financiers, and set off for Notting Hill. I had to take it easy in the rain, so there was plenty of time for reflection on the night's business.

The one thing that stayed in my mind, as I jinked the bike along the slick, yellow-lit streets, was Sarah telling me to drop 'that shit'. And the reason I had to drop it was because there was a dying man in the room.

Newtonian Conversation, I thought to myself. The implication was that I could have kept on holding that shit, if the room hadn't had a dying man in it.

That cheered me up. I started to think that if I couldn't work things so that one day she and I would be together in a room with no dying men in it at all, then my name isn't James Fincham.

Which, of course, it isn't.

Two

For a long time I used to go to bed early.

MARCEL PROUST

I arrived back at the flat and went through the usual answerphone routine. Two meaningless bleeps, one wrong number, one call from a friend interrupted in the first sentence, followed by three people I didn't want to hear from who I now had to ring back.

God, I hated that machine.

I sat down at my desk and went through the day's mail. I threw some bills into the bin, and then remembered that I'd moved the bin into the kitchen – so I got annoyed, stuffed the rest of the post into a drawer, and gave up on the idea that doing chores would help me to get things straight in my mind.

It was too late to start playing loud music, and the only other entertainment I could find in the flat was whisky, so I picked up a glass and a bottle of The Famous Grouse, poured myself a couple of fingers, and went into the kitchen. I added enough water to turn it into just a Vaguely Familiar Grouse, and then sat down at the table with a pocket dictaphone, because someone had once told me that talking out loud helps clarify things. I'd said would it work with butter? and they'd said no, but it would work with whatever is troubling your spirit.

I put a tape in the machine and flicked the record switch.

'*Dramatis personae*,' I said. 'Alexander Woolf, father of Sarah Woolf, owner of dinky Georgian house in Lyall Street, Belgravia, employer of blind and vindictive interior designers, and Chairman and Chief Executive Officer of Gaine Parker. Unknown male Caucasian, American or Canadian, fiftyish. Rayner. Large, violent, hospitalised. Thomas Lang, thirty-six, Flat D, 42 Westbourne Close, late of the Scots Guards, honourable discharge with rank of Captain. The facts, insofar as they are known, are these.'

I don't know why tape recorders make me talk like this, but they do.

'Unknown male attempts to secure employment of T. Lang for the purpose of committing unlawful killing of A. Woolf. Lang declines position on grounds of being nice. Principled. Decent. A gentleman.'

I took a mouthful of whisky and looked at the dictaphone, wondering if I was ever going to play this soliloquy back to anyone. An accountant had told me it was a sensible thing to buy because I could get the tax back on it. But as I didn't pay any tax, have any need for a dictaphone, or trust the accountant as far as I could spit him, I looked upon this machine as one of my less sensible purchases.

Heigh ho.

'Lang goes to Woolf's house, with the intention of warning him against possible assassination attempt. Woolf absent. Lang decides to instigate enquiries.'

I paused for a while, and the while turned into a long while, so I sipped some more whisky and laid aside the dictaphone while I did some thinking.

The only enquiry I had instigated had been the word 'what' – and I'd barely managed to get that out of my mouth before Rayner had hit me with a chair. Beyond that, all I'd done was half-kill a man and leave, wishing, pretty fervently, that I'd other-half-killed him too. And you don't really want that sort of thing lying around on magnetic tape unless you know what you're doing. Which, amazingly enough, I didn't.

However, I'd just about known enough to recognise Rayner, even before I knew his name. I couldn't say he'd been following me exactly, but I've a good memory for faces – which makes up for being utterly pathetic with names – and Rayner's was not a difficult face. Heathrow airport, the public bar of some Devonshire Arms on the King's Road, and the entrance to Leicester Square tube had been enough of an advertisement, even for an idiot like me.

I'd had the feeling that we were going to meet eventually, so I'd prepared myself for the rainy day by visiting Blitz Electronics on the Tottenham Court Road, where I'd shelled out two pounds eighty for a foot of large-diameter electrical cable. Flexible, heavy, and, when it comes to beating off brigands and footpads, better than any purpose-built cosh. The only time it doesn't work as a weapon is when you leave it in the kitchen drawer, still in its wrapping. Then it's really not very effective at all.

As for the unknown male Caucasian who'd offered me a killing job, well, I didn't hold out much hope of ever tracing him. Two weeks ago I'd been in Amsterdam, escorting a Manchester bookmaker who desperately wanted to believe that he had violent enemies. He'd hired me to bolster the fantasy. So I'd held car doors open for him, and checked buildings for snipers that I knew weren't there, and then spent a gruelling forty-eight hours sitting with him in night-clubs, watching him throw money in every direction but mine. When he'd finally wilted, I'd ended up loafing about my hotel room watching blue movies on television. The phone had rung – during a particularly good bit, as I remember – and a male voice had asked me to the bar for a drink.

I'd checked to make sure that the bookmaker was safely tucked up in bed with a nice warm prostitute, then sidled downstairs in the hope of saving myself forty quid by wringing a couple of drinks out of some old army friend.

21

But, as it turned out, the voice on the phone belonged to a short fat body in an expensive suit who I definitely didn't know. And didn't particularly want to know either, until he reached into his jacket and pulled out a roll of bank notes about as thick as I am.

American bank notes. Exchangeable for goods and services at literally thousands of retail outlets worldwide. He pushed a one hundred dollar bill across the table to me, so I spent five seconds quite liking the little chap, and then, almost immediately, love died.

He gave me some 'background' on a man named Woolf – where he lived, what he did, why he did it, how much he did it for – and then he told me that the bank note on the table had a thousand little friends, who would find their way into my possession if Woolf's life could be discreetly brought to an end.

I had to wait until our part of the bar was empty, which I knew wouldn't take long. At the prices they were charging for liquor, there were probably only a couple of dozen people in the world who could afford to stick around for a second drink.

When the bar had cleared, I leant across to the fat man and gave him a speech. It was a dull speech, but even so, he listened very carefully, because I'd reached under the table and taken hold of his scrotum. I told him what kind of a man I was, what kind of a mistake he'd made, and what he could wipe with his money. And then we'd parted company.

That was it. That was all I knew, and my arm was hurting.

I went to bed.

I dreamt a lot of things that I won't embarrass you with, and ended up imagining that I was having to hoover my carpet. I kept hoovering and hoovering, but whatever was making the mark on the carpet just wouldn't go away.

Then I realised that I was awake, and that the stain on the carpet was sunlight because someone had just yanked open the curtains. In the twinkling of an eye I whipped my body into a coiled, taut, come-and-get-it crouch, the electrical cable in my fist and bloody murder in my heart.

But then I realised that I'd dreamt that too, and what I was actually doing was lying in bed watching a large, hairy hand very close to my face. The hand disappeared, leaving a mug with steam coming out of it, and the smell of a popular infusion, sold commercially as PG Tips. Perhaps in that twinkling of an eye I'd worked out that intruders who want to slit your throat don't boil the kettle and open the curtains.

'Time is it?'

'Thirty-five minutes past the hour of eight. Time for your Shreddies, Mr Bond.'

I pulled myself up from the bed and looked over at Solomon. He was as short and cheerful as ever, with the same ghastly brown raincoat that he'd bought from the back pages of the *Sunday Express*.

'I take it you've come to investigate a theft?' I said, rubbing my eyes until white dots of light started appearing.

'What theft would that be, sir?'

Solomon called everyone 'sir' except his superiors.

'The theft of my doorbell,' I said.

'If you are, in your sarcastic fashion, referring to my silent entrance to these premises, then may I remind you that I am a practitioner of the black arts. And practitioners, in order to qualify for the term, have to practise. Now be a good lad and jump into some kit will you? We're running late.'

He disappeared into the kitchen and I could hear the clicking and buzzing of my fourteenth-century toaster.

I hauled myself out of bed, wincing as my left arm took some weight, slung on a shirt and a pair of trousers and took the electric razor into the kitchen.

Solomon had laid a place for me at the kitchen table, and set out some toast in a rack that I didn't even know I had. Unless he'd brought it with him, which seemed unlikely.

'More tea, vicar?'

'Late for what?' I said.

'A meeting, master, a meeting. Now, have you got a tie?'

His large, brown eyes twinkled hopefully at me.

'I've got two,' I said. 'One of them's the Garrick Club, which I don't belong to, and the other one's holding the lavatory cistern to the wall.'

I sat down at the table and saw that he'd even found a pot of Keiller's Dundee marmalade from somewhere. I never really knew how he did these things, but Solomon could rootle around in a dustbin and pull out a car if he had to. A good man to go into the desert with.

Maybe that was where we were going.

'So, master, what's paying your bills these days?' He parked half his bottom on the table and watched me eat.

'I hoped you were.'

The marmalade was delicious, and I wanted to make it last, but I could tell Solomon was anxious to be off. He glanced at his watch and disappeared back into the bedroom, where I could hear him rattling his way through the wardrobe, trying to find a jacket.

'Under the bed,' I called. I picked up the dictaphone from the table. The tape was still inside.

As I gulped down the tea, Solomon came in carrying a double-breasted blazer with two buttons missing. He held it out like a valet. I stayed where I was.

'Oh master,' he said. 'Please don't be difficult. Not before the harvest is in, and the mules are rested.'

'Just tell me where we're going.'

'Down the road, in a big shiny car. You'll love it. And on the way home you can have an ice-cream.'

Slowly, I got to my feet and shrugged on the blazer.

'David,' I said.

'Still here, master.'

'What's happening?'

He pursed his lips and frowned slightly. Bad form to ask questions like that. I stood my ground.

'Am I in trouble?' I said.

He frowned a little more, and then looked up at me with his calm, steady eyes.

'Seems like it.'

'Seems like it?'

'There's a foot of heavy cable in that drawer. The young master's weapon of choice.'

'So?'

He gave me a small, polite smile.

'Trouble for somebody.'

'Oh come off it, David,' I said. 'I've had that for months. Been meaning to wire up two things that are very close to each other.'

'Yes. Receipt's from two days ago. Still in the bag.'

We looked at each other for a while.

'Sorry, master,' he said. 'Black arts. Let's go.'

The car was a Rover, which meant it was official. Nobody drives these idiotically snobbish cars, with their absurd bundles of wood and leather, badly glued into every seam and crevice of the interior, unless they absolutely have to. And only the government and the board of Rover have to.

I didn't want to interrupt Solomon as he drove, because he had a nervous relationship with cars, and didn't even like it if you switched on the radio. He wore driving gloves, a driving hat, driving glasses and a driving expression, and he fed the wheel through his hands in the way everyone does until four seconds after they've passed their test. But as we trickled past Horseguards Parade, more or less flirting with twenty-five miles an hour, I thought I'd risk it.

'Don't suppose there's any chance of me knowing what it is I'm supposed to have done?'

Solomon sucked his teeth and gripped the wheel even harder, concentrating furiously as we negotiated a particularly awkward stretch of wide, empty road. When he'd checked the speed, the revs, the fuel, the oil pressure, the temperature, the time, and his seatbelt, twice, he decided he could afford an answer.

'What you were supposed to have done,' he said, through clenched teeth, 'is stay good and noble, master. As you always were.'

We pulled into a courtyard behind the Ministry of Defence.

'Haven't I done that?' I said.

'Bingo. Parking space. We've died and gone to heaven.'

In spite of a large security notice proclaiming that all Ministry of Defence installations were in a state of Bikini Amber alert, the guards at the door let us through with no more than a glance.

British security guards, I've noticed, always do this; unless you happen actually to work in the building they're guarding, in which case they'll check everything from the fillings in your teeth to your trouser turn-ups to see if you're the same person who went out to get a sandwich fifteen minutes ago. But if you're a strange face, they'll let you straight through, because frankly, it would just be too embarrassing to put you to any trouble.

If you want a place guarded properly, hire Germans.

Solomon and I travelled up three sets of stairs, down half a dozen corridors and in two lifts, with him signing me in at various points along the way, until we reached a dark green door labelled C188. Solomon knocked, and we heard a woman's voice shout 'wait', and then 'okay'.

Inside there was a wall three feet away. And between the wall and the door, in this unbelievably tiny space, a girl in a lemon-coloured shirt sat at a desk, with word processor, potted plant, mug of pencils, furry gonk, and wadges of orange paper. It was incredible that anyone or anything could function in such a space. It was like suddenly discovering a family of otters in one of your shoes.

If you've ever done that.

'He's expecting you,' she said, nervously holding both her arms out across the desk in case we dislodged anything.

'Thank you, madam,' said Solomon, squeezing past the desk.

'Agoraphobic?' I asked, following him, and if there'd been enough room I would have kicked myself, because she must

26

have heard that fifty times a day.

Solomon knocked on the inner door and we walked straight through.

Every square foot the secretary had lost, this office had gained.

Here, we had a high ceiling, windows on two sides hung with government-issue net curtains and, between the windows, a desk about the size of a squash court. Behind the desk, a balding head was bowed in concentration.

Solomon headed for the central rose of the Persian carpet, and I took up a position just off his left shoulder.

'Mr O'Neal?' said Solomon. 'Lang for you.'

We waited.

O'Neal, if that really was his name, which I doubted, looked like all men who sit behind large desks. People say that dog-owners resemble their dogs, but I've always thought the same is true, if not truer, of desk-owners and their desks. It was a large, flat face, with large, flat ears, and plenty of useful places for keeping paper-clips. Even his lack of any beard growth corresponded with the dazzling French polish. He was in expensive shirt sleeves, and I couldn't see a jacket anywhere.

'I thought we said nine-thirty,' said O'Neal without looking up or at his watch.

This voice was not believable at all. It strained for a patrician languor, and missed it by a mile. It was tight and reedy, and in other circumstances I might have felt sorry for Mr O'Neal. If that really was his name. Which I doubted.

'Traffic, I'm afraid,' said Solomon. 'Got here as fast as we could.'

Solomon looked out of the window, as if to say he'd done his bit. O'Neal stared at him, glanced at me, and then went back to his performance of Reading Something Important.

Now that Solomon had delivered me safely, and there was no chance of getting him into any trouble, I decided it was time to assert myself a little.

'Good morning, Mr O'Neal,' I said, in a stupidly loud voice. The sound bounced back from the distant walls. 'Sorry to see this isn't a convenient time. It's not that good for me either. Why don't I have my secretary make another appointment with your secretary? In fact, why don't our secretaries have lunch together? Really put the world to rights.'

O'Neal ground his teeth together for a moment, and then looked up at me with what he obviously thought was a penetrating stare.

When he'd overdone that, he put down the papers and rested his hands on the edge of the desk. Then he took them off the desk and put them on his lap. Then he got annoyed with me for having seen him carry out this awkward procedure.

'Mr Lang,' he said. 'You realise where you are?' He pursed his lips in a practised fashion.

'Indeed I do, Mr O'Neal. I am in room C188.'

'You are in the Ministry of Defence.'

'Mmm. Jolly nice too. Any chairs about?'

He glared at me again, and then flicked his head at Solomon, who went over to the door and dragged a reproduction Regency thing to the middle of the carpet. I stayed where I was.

'Do sit down, Mr Lang.'

'Thanks, I'd rather stand,' I said.

Now he was genuinely thrown. We used to do this kind of thing to a geography teacher at school. He'd left after two terms to become a priest in the Western Isles.

'What do you know, please, about Alexander Woolf?' O'Neal leant forward with his forearms on the desk, and I caught a glimpse of a very gold watch. Much too gold to be gold.

'Which one?'

He frowned.

'What do you mean, "which one?" How many Alexander Woolfs do you know?'

I moved my lips slightly, counting to myself.

'Five.'

He sighed irritably. Come along, 4B, settle down.

'The Alexander Woolf to whom I am referring,' he said, with that particular tone of sarcastic pedantry that every Englishman behind a desk slides into sooner or later, 'has a house in Lyall Street, Belgravia.'

'Lyall Street. Of course.' I tutted to myself. 'Six, then.'

O'Neal shot a look at Solomon, but didn't get any help there. He turned back to me, with a creepy smile.

'I'm asking you, Mr Lang, what do you know about him?'

'He has a house in Lyall Street, Belgravia,' I said. 'Is that any help?'

This time, O'Neal tried another tack. He took a deep breath and exhaled slowly, which was meant to make me think that beneath that chubby frame there lurked an oiled killing machine, and for two pins he'd be over that desk and beating the life out of me. It was a pathetic performance. He reached into a drawer and pulled out a buff folder, then started angrily flicking through its contents.

'Where were you at ten-thirty last night?'

'Windsurfing off the Ivory Coast,' I said, almost before he'd finished speaking.

'I'm asking you a serious question, Mr Lang,' said O'Neal. 'I advise you, most strongly, to give me a serious answer.'

'And I'm telling you it's none of your business.'

'My business . . . ' he began.

'Your business is defence.' I was suddenly shouting, genuinely shouting, and out of the corner of my eye I could see that Solomon had turned to watch. 'And the thing you're being paid to defend is my right to do whatever I want without having to answer a lot of fucking questions.' I dropped back into a normal gear. 'Anything else?'

He didn't answer, so I turned and walked towards the door.

'Cheerio, David,' I said.

Solomon didn't answer either. I had my hand on the door-knob when O'Neal spoke.

'Lang, I want you to know that I could have you arrested the second you leave this building.'

I turned and looked at him.

'For what?'

I suddenly didn't like this. I didn't like this because, for the first time since I came in, O'Neal looked relaxed.

'Conspiracy to murder.'

The room was very quiet.

'Conspiracy?' I said.

You know how it is when you're caught up in the flow of things. Normally, words are sent from the brain towards the mouth, and somewhere along the line you take a moment to check them, see that they are actually the ones you ordered and that they're nicely wrapped, before you bundle them on their way towards your palate and out into the fresh air.

But when you're caught up in the flow of things, the checking part of your mind can fall down on the job.

O'Neal had uttered three words: 'Conspiracy to murder'.

The correct word for me to repeat in an incredulous tone of voice would have been 'murder'; a very small, and psychiatrically disturbed, section of the population might have opted for the 'to'; but the one word out of the three I most definitely should not have chosen to repeat was 'conspiracy'.

Of course, if we'd had the conversation again, I'd have done things very differently. But we didn't.

Solomon was looking at me, and O'Neal was looking at Solomon. I busied myself with a verbal dustpan and brush.

'What the hell are you talking about? Have you really got nothing better to do? If you're talking about that business last night, then you should know, if you've read my statement, that I'd never seen that man before in my life, that I was defending myself against an illegal assault, and that in the course of the struggle he . . . hit his head.'

I was suddenly conscious of how limp a phrase that is.

30

'The police,' I continued, 'declared themselves fully satisfied, and . . . '

I stopped.

O'Neal had leaned back in his chair and put both hands behind his head. A patch of sweat the size of a ten pence piece showed at each armpit.

'Well, of course, they *would* declare themselves satisfied, wouldn't they?' he said, looking horribly confident. He waited for me to say something, but nothing came to mind so I let him go on. 'Because they didn't know then what we know now.'

I sighed.

'Oh God, I am just so fascinated by this conversation I think I might have a nosebleed. What do you know now that is so fucking important that I have to be dragged here at this frankly ridiculous time of day?'

'Dragged?' he said, eyebrows shooting towards his hairline. He turned to Solomon. 'Did you *drag* Mr Lang here?'

O'Neal had suddenly gone camp and playful, and it was a nauseating sight. Solomon must have been as appalled by it as I was, because he didn't answer.

'My life is ebbing away in this room,' I said, irritably. 'Please get to the point.'

'Very well,' said O'Neal. 'We know now, but the police didn't know then, that a week ago you had an assignation with a Canadian arms dealer by the name of McCluskey. McCluskey offered you a hundred thousand dollars if you would . . . terminate Woolf. We know now that you turned up at Woolf's London house and that you were confronted by a man named Rayner – aka Wyatt, aka Miller – legitimately employed by Woolf in the capacity of bodyguard. We know that Rayner was severely injured as a result of this confrontation.'

My stomach seemed to have contracted to the size and density of a cricket ball. A drop of sweat abseiled amateurishly down my back.

O'Neal went on. 'We know that in spite of your story to

31

the police, not one but two 999 calls were made to the operator last night; the first one being for an ambulance only, the second for the police. The calls were made fifteen minutes apart. We know that you gave a false name to the police, for reasons we have not yet established. And finally,' he looked up at me like a bad magician with a rabbit-filled hat, 'we know that the sum of twenty-nine thousand, four hundred pounds, equivalent to fifty thousand US dollars, was transferred to your bank account at Swiss Cottage four days ago.' He snapped the file shut and smiled. 'How's that for starters?'

I was sitting on the chair in the middle of O'Neal's office. Solomon had gone to make some coffee for me and camomile tea for himself, and the world was slowing down slightly.

'Look,' I said, 'it's perfectly obvious that for some reason I'm being set up.'

'Explain to me please, Mr Lang,' said O'Neal, 'why that conclusion is obvious.'

He'd gone camp again. I took a deep breath.

'Well, I'm telling you first of all that I don't know anything about that money. Anyone could have done that, from any bank in the world. That's easy.'

O'Neal made a big show of removing the top of his Parker Duofold and jotting something down on a pad of paper.

'And then there's the daughter,' I said. 'She saw the fight. She vouched for me to the police last night. Why haven't you got her in here?'

The door opened and Solomon backed in, balancing three cups. He'd got rid of his brown raincoat somewhere, and was now sporting a zip-up cardigan of the same colour. O'Neal was obviously annoyed by it, and even I could see that it didn't live up to the rest of the room.

'We do, I assure you, intend to interview Miss Woolf at some convenient juncture,' said O'Neal, as he sipped gingerly at his coffee. 'However, the immediate concern of this department's operation is you. You, Mr Lang, were asked to perform an assassination. With or without your consent, money was transferred to your bank account. You present yourself at the target's house and very nearly kill his bodyguard. You then . . . '

'Wait a minute,' I said. 'Just wait one cotton-fucking minute here. What's all this bodyguard stuff? Woolf wasn't even there.'

O'Neal gazed back at me in a nastily unruffled way.

'I mean how,' I went on, 'does a bodyguard guard a body who isn't in the same building? By phone? This is digital bodyguarding, is it?'

'You searched the house, did you, Lang?' said O'Neal. 'You went to the house, and searched it for Alexander Woolf?' A smile played clumsily about his lips.

'She told me he wasn't there,' I said, annoyed at his pleasure. 'And anyway, fuck off.'

He flinched slightly.

'Nevertheless,' he said eventually, 'under the circumstances, your presence in the house makes you worthy of our valuable time and effort.'

I still couldn't work this out.

'Why?' I said. 'Why you and not the police? What's so special about Woolf?' I looked from O'Neal to Solomon. 'If it comes to that, what's so special about me?'

The phone on O'Neal's desk chirped, and he snatched it up with a practised flourish, flicking the wire behind his elbow as he brought the receiver to his ear. He looked at me as he talked.

'Yes? Yes . . . Indeed. Thank you.'

The receiver was back in its cradle and fast asleep in an instant. Watching him handle it, I could tell that the telephone was O'Neal's one great skill.

He scribbled something on his pad and beckoned Solomon over to the desk. Solomon peered at it, and then they both looked at me.

'Do you own a firearm, Mr Lang?'

O'Neal asked this with a cheerful, efficient smile. Would

you prefer an aisle or a window seat?

I started to feel sick.

'No, I do not.'

'Had access to firearms of any sort?'

'Not since the army.'

'I see,' said O'Neal, nodding to himself. He left a long pause, checking the pad to see that he'd got the details absolutely right. 'So the news that a nine millimetre Browning pistol, with fifteen rounds of ammunition, has been found in your flat would come as a surprise to you?'

I thought about this.

'It's more of a surprise that my flat is being searched.'

'Never mind that.'

I sighed.

'All right then,' I said. 'No, I'm not particularly surprised.'

'What do you mean?'

'I mean that I'm starting to get the hang of how today is going.' O'Neal and Solomon looked blank. 'Oh do come on,' I said. 'Anyone who's prepared to spend thirty thousand pounds to make me look like a hired gun presumably wouldn't stop at another three hundred to make me look like a hired gun who has a gun he can hire.'

O'Neal played with his bottom lip for a moment, squeezing it on either side between thumb and forefinger.

'I have a problem here, don't I, Mr Lang?'

'Do you?'

'Yes, I rather think I do,' he said. He let go of the lip, and it hung there in a bulbous pout, as if it didn't want to go back to its original shape. 'Either you are an assassin, or someone is trying to make you look like one. The problem is that every piece of evidence I have applies equally well to both possibilities. It really is very difficult.'

I shrugged.

'That must be why they gave you such a big desk,' I said.

Eventually they had to let me go. For whatever reason, they didn't want to involve the police with an illegal firearm charge, and the Ministry of Defence is not, so far as I know, equipped with its own detention cells.

O'Neal asked me for my passport, and before I could spin a yarn about having lost it in the tumble-dryer, Solomon produced it from his hip-pocket. I was told to remain contactable, and to let them know if I received any further approaches from strange men. There wasn't much I could do but agree.

As I left the building and strolled through St James's Park in some rare April sunshine, I tried to work out whether I felt any different, knowing that Rayner had only been trying to do his job. I also wondered why I hadn't known that he was Woolf's bodyguard. Or even that he had one.

But much, much more to the point, why hadn't Woolf's daughter?

Three

God and the doctor we like adore
But only when in danger, not before;

JOHN OWEN

The truth is I was feeling sorry for myself.

I'm used to being broke, and unemployment is more than a nodding acquaintance. I've been left by women I loved, and had some pretty fierce toothache in my time. But somehow, none of these things quite compares with the feeling that the world is against you.

I started to think of friends I could lean on for some help, but, as always happened when I attempted this kind of social audit, I realised that far too many of them were abroad, dead, married to people who disapproved of me, or weren't really my friends, now that I came to think of it.

Which is why I found myself in a phone box on Piccadilly, asking for Paulie.

'I'm afraid he's in court at the moment,' said a voice. 'May I take a message?'

'Tell him it's Thomas Lang, and if he's not there to buy me lunch at Simpson's on the Strand at one o'clock sharp, his legal career is over.'

'Legal career . . . over,' recited the clerk. 'I shall give him that message when he rings in, Mr Lang. Good morning.'

Paulie, full name Paul Lee, and I had an unusual relationship.

It was unusual in that we saw each other every couple of months, in a purely social way – pubs, dinner, theatre, opera, which Paulie loved – and yet we both freely admitted that we had not the slightest liking for each other. Not a shred. If our feelings had run as strong as hatred, then you might interpret that as some twisted expression of affection. But we didn't hate each other. We just didn't like each other, that's all.

I found Paulie an ambitious, greedy prig, and he found me lazy, unreliable, and a slob. The only positive thing you could say about our 'friendship' was that it was mutual. We would meet, pass an hour or so in each other's company, and then part with that all-important 'there but for the grace of God' sensation in precisely equal measures. And in exchange for giving me fifty quids-worth of roast beef and claret, Paulie admitted that he got exactly fifty quids-worth of superior feeling, paying for my lunch.

I had to ask to borrow a tie from the *maître d'hôtel,* and he punished me for it by giving me the choice between a purple one and a purple one, but at twelve forty-five I was sitting at a table in Simpson's, melting some of the unpleasantness of the morning in a large vodka and tonic. A lot of the other diners were American, which explained why the joints of beef were selling faster than the joints of lamb. Americans have never really caught on to the idea of eating sheep. I think they think it's cissy.

Paulie arrived bang on one, but I knew he'd apologise for being late.

'Sorry I'm late,' he said. 'What's that you've got there? Vodka? Gimme one of those.'

The waiter coasted away, and Paulie looked round the room, stroking his tie down the front of his shirt and shooting his chin out from time to time to ease the pressure of his collar on the folds of his neck. As always, his hair was fluffy and squeaky clean. He claimed this went down well with juries, but for as long as I'd known him, love of hair had always been a weakness with Paulie. In truth he was not physically blessed, but as a consolation for his short, round, runty body, God had given him a fine head of hair which he would probably keep, in varying shades, until he was eighty.

'Cheers Paulie,' I said, and threw back some vodka.

'Hiya. How's things?' Paulie never looked at you when he spoke. You could be standing with your back to a brick wall, he would still look over your shoulder.

'Fine, fine,' I said. 'You?'

'Got the bugger off, after all that.' He shook his head, wonderingly. A man constantly amazed by his own abilities.

'I didn't know you did buggery cases, Paulie.'

He didn't smile. Paulie only really smiled at weekends.

'Nah,' he said. 'The bloke I told you about. Beat his nephew to death with a garden spade. Got him off.'

'But you said he'd done it.'

'He had.'

'So how did you manage that?'

'I lied like fuck,' he said. 'What are you having?'

We swapped career progress as we waited for the soup, with every one of Paulie's triumphs boring me, and every one of my failures delighting him. He asked me if I was all right for money, although we both knew he hadn't the slightest intention of doing anything about it if I wasn't. And I asked him about his holidays, past and future. Paulie set a lot of store by holidays.

'Group of us are hiring this boat in the Med. Scuba diving, windsurfing, you name it. Cordon bleu cook, everything.'

'Sail or motor?'

'Sail.' He frowned for a moment, and suddenly looked twenty years older. 'Although, come to think of it, it's probably got a motor. But there's a crew who do all that stuff. You getting a holiday?'

'Hadn't thought about it,' I said.

'Well, you're always on holiday, aren't you? Got nothing to take a holiday from.'

'Nicely put, Paulie.'

'Well, have you? Since the army, what have you done?'

'Consultancy work.'

'Consult my arse.'

'Don't think I could afford it, Paulie.'

'Yeah, well. Let's ask our catering consultant what the fuck's happened to the soup.'

As we looked round for the waiter, I saw my followers.

Two men, sitting at a table by the door, drinking mineral water and turning away as soon as I looked towards them. The older one looked as if he'd been designed by the same architect that had done Solomon, and the younger one was trying to head in that direction. They both seemed solid, and for the time being I was happy enough to have them around.

After the soup arrived, and Paulie had tasted it, and judged it to be just about acceptable, I shifted my chair round the table and leaned towards him. I hadn't actually planned on picking his brains, because, to be honest, they weren't properly ripe yet. But I couldn't see that I had anything to lose by it.

'Does the name Woolf mean anything to you, Paulie?'

'Person or company?'

'Person,' I said. 'American, I think. Businessman.'

'What's he done? Drink-driving? I don't do that kind of thing now. And if I do, it's for a sack of money.'

'As far as I know, he hasn't done anything,' I said. 'Just wondered if you'd heard of him. Gaine Parker is the company.'

Paulie shrugged and ripped a bread roll to pieces.

'I could find out for you. What's it for?'

'About a job,' I said. 'I turned it down, but I'm just curious.'

He nodded, and pushed some bread into his face.

'I put you up for a job a couple of months ago.'

I stopped my soup spoon half-way from bowl to mouth. It

was unlike Paulie to take any sort of hand in my life, never mind a helping one.

'What sort of job?'

'Canadian bloke. Looking for someone to do some strong arm stuff. Bodyguard, that kind of thing.'

'What was his name?'

'Can't remember. Began with J, I think.'

'McCluskey?'

'McCluskey doesn't begin with a J now, does it? No, it was Joseph, Jacob, something like that.' He quickly gave up trying to remember. 'Did he get in touch?'

'No.'

'Pity. Thought I'd sold him on the idea.'

'And you gave him my name?'

'No, I gave him your fucking shoe size. Course I gave him your name. Well, not straight away. I put him on to some private dicks we use a bit. They've got some big blokes who do bodyguard stuff, but he didn't take to them. Wanted someone upmarket. Ex-army, he said. You were the only person I could think of. Apart from Andy Hick, but he's earning two hundred grand a year in a merchant bank.'

'I'm touched, Paulie.'

'You're welcome.'

'How did you meet him?'

'He'd come to see Toffee, and I got roped in.'

'Toffee being a person?'

'Spencer. The guv'nor. Calls himself Toffee. Don't know why. Something to do with golf. Teeing-off, maybe.'

I thought for a while.

'You don't know what he was seeing Spencer about?'

'Who says I don't?'

'Do you?'

'No.'

Paulie had fixed his gaze somewhere behind my head and I turned to see what he was doing with it. The two men at the door were standing now. The older one said something to the *maître d'*, who aimed a waiter in the direction of our table. A few of the other lunchers watched.

'Mr Lang?'

'I'm Lang.'

'Phone call for you, sir.'

I shrugged at Paulie, who was now licking his finger and picking crumbs off the tablecloth.

By the time I reached the door, the younger of the two followers had disappeared. I tried to catch the eye of the older one, but he was studying a nameless print on the wall. I picked up the phone.

'Master,' said Solomon, 'all is not well in the state of Denmark.'

'Oh, what a shame,' I said. 'And things were going so nicely before.'

Solomon started to answer but there was a click and a bang, and O'Neal's reedy tones came on the line.

'Lang, is that you?'

'Yup,' I said.

'The girl, Lang. Young woman, I should say. Have you any idea where she might be at this moment?'

I laughed.

'You're asking *me* where she is?'

'Indeed I am. We are having problems locating her.'

I glanced at the follower, still staring at the print.

'Sadly, Mr O'Neal, I can't help you,' I said. 'You see, I don't have a staff of nine thousand and a budget of twenty million pounds with which to find people and keep track of them. Tell you what though, you might try the security people at the Ministry of Defence. They're supposed to be very good at this kind of thing.'

But he'd hung up half-way through the word 'Defence'.

I left Paulie to pay the bill, and hopped on a bus to Holland Park. I wanted to see what kind of a mess O'Neal's lot had made of my flat, and also to see if I'd had any more approaches from Canadian arms dealers with Old Testament names.

41

Solomon's followers got on to the bus with me, and peered out of the windows as if it was their first visit to London.

When we got to Notting Hill, I leaned over to them.

'You may as well get off with me,' I said. 'Save yourselves having to run back from the next stop.' The older one looked away, but the younger one grinned. In the event, we all got off together, and they hung around on the other side of the street while I let myself back into the flat.

I'd have known that the place had been searched without being told. I hadn't exactly expected them to change the sheets and run a hoover over the place, but I thought they might have left it in better shape than this. None of the furniture was in the right place, the few paintings I had were skewed, and the books on the shelves were in a pathetically different order. They'd even put a different CD in the stereo. Or maybe they just felt that Professor Longhair was better flat-searching music.

I didn't bother moving things back to how they were. Instead, I walked through into the kitchen, flicked on the kettle and said in a loud voice, 'Tea or coffee?'

There was a faint rustle from the bedroom.

'Or do you fancy a Coke?'

I kept my back to the door while the kettle wheezed its way towards boiling, but I still heard her as she moved into the kitchen doorway. I dumped some coffee granules into a mug and turned round.

Instead of the silk dressing-gown, Sarah Woolf was currently filling a faded pair of jeans and a dark-grey cotton polo-neck shirt. Her hair was up, tied loosely back in a way that takes some women five seconds, and others five days. And as a colour-matching accessory to the shirt, she wore a Walther TPH .22 automatic in her right hand.

The TPH is a pretty little thing. It has a straight blowback action, a six-round box magazine and two-and-a-quarter-inch barrel. It's also utterly useless as a firearm, because unless you can guarantee hitting either the heart or the brain first time, you're only going to annoy the person you're shooting at. For most people, a wet mackerel is the better choice of weapon.

'Well, Mr Fincham,' she said, 'how did you know I was here?' She sounded the way she looked.

'Fleur de Fleurs,' I said. 'I gave some to my cleaning lady last Christmas but I know she doesn't use it. Had to be you.'

She threw a sceptically-raised eyebrow over the flat.

'You have a cleaning lady?'

'Yeah, I know,' I said. 'Bless her. She's knocking on a bit. Arthritis. She doesn't clean anything below the knee or above the shoulder. I try to get all my dirty stuff at waist height, but sometimes . . . ' I smiled. She didn't smile back. 'If it comes to that, how did you get in here?'

'Wasn't locked,' she said.

I shook my head in disgust.

'Well that is frankly shoddy. I'm going to have to write to my MP.'

'What?'

'This place,' I said, 'was searched this morning by members of the British Security Services. Professionals, trained at the taxpayers' expense, and they can't even be bothered to lock the door when they're done. What sort of service do you call that? I've only got Diet Coke. That okay?'

The gun was still pointing in my general direction, but it hadn't followed me to the fridge.

'What were they looking for?' She was staring out of the window now. She really did look like she'd had a hell of a morning.

'Beats me,' I said. 'I've got a cheesecloth shirt in the bottom of my cupboard. Maybe that's an offence against the realm now.'

'Did they find a gun?' She still wasn't looking at me. The kettle clicked and I poured some hot water into the mug.

'Yes, they did.'

'The gun you were going to use to kill my father.'

I didn't turn round. Just kept on with my coffee-making.

'There is no such gun,' I said. 'The gun they found was put

43

here by someone else so it would look as if I was going to use it to kill your father.'

'Well, it worked.' Now she was looking straight at me. And so was the .22. But I've always prided myself on the froidness of my sang, so I just poured milk into the coffee and lit a cigarette. That made her angry.

'Cocky son-of-a-bitch, aren't you?'

'Not for me to say. My mother loves me.'

'Yeah? Is that a reason for me not to shoot you?'

I'd hoped she wouldn't mention guns, or shooting, as even the British Ministry of Defence could afford to bug a room properly, but since she'd raised the subject I could hardly ignore it.

'Can I just say something before you fire that thing?'

'Go ahead.'

'If I meant to use a gun to kill your father, why didn't I have it with me last night, when I came to your house?'

'Maybe you did.'

I paused and took a sip of coffee.

'Good answer,' I said. 'All right, if I had it with me last night, why didn't I use it on Rayner when he was breaking my arm?'

'Maybe you tried to. Maybe that's why he was breaking your arm.'

For heaven's sake, this woman was tiring me out.

'Another good answer. All right, tell me this. Who told you that they'd found a gun here?'

'The police.'

'Nope,' I said. 'They may have said they were the police, but they weren't.'

I'd been thinking of jumping her, maybe throwing the coffee first, but there wasn't much point now. Over her shoulder, I could see Solomon's two followers moving slowly through the sitting-room, the older one holding a large revolver out in front of him in a two-handed grip, the younger one just smiling. I decided to let the wheels of justice do some grinding.

'It doesn't matter who told me,' said Sarah.

'On the contrary, I think it matters a lot. If a salesman tells you that a washing machine's great, that's one thing. But if the Archbishop of Canterbury tells you it's great, and that it removes dirt even at low temperatures, that's quite different.'

'What are you . . . '

She heard them when they were only a couple of feet away, and as she turned, the younger one grabbed her wrist and turned it down and outwards in a highly competent manner. She gave out a short yelp, and the gun slid from her hand.

I picked it up and passed it, butt first, to the older follower. Keen to show what a good boy I was really, if only the world would understand.

By the time O'Neal and Solomon arrived, Sarah and I were comfortably plugged into the sofa, with the two followers arranged round the door, and none of us making much in the way of conversation. With O'Neal bustling about the place, there suddenly seemed to be an awful lot of people in the flat. I offered to nip out and get a cake, but O'Neal showed me his fiercest 'the defence of the Western world is on my shoulders' expression, so we all went quiet and stared at our hands.

After some whispering with the followers, who then quietly withdrew, O'Neal paced this way and that, picking things up and curling his lip at them. He was obviously waiting for something, and it wasn't in the room or about to come through the door, so I got up and walked across to the phone. It rang as I reached it. Very occasionally, life's like that.

I picked up the receiver.

'Graduate Studies,' said a harsh, American voice.

'Who is this?'

'That O'Neal?' There was a spot of anger in the voice now. Not a man you'd ask for a cup of sugar.

'No, but Mr O'Neal is here,' I said. 'Who's speaking?'

'Put O'Neal on the goddamn phone, will you?' said the voice. I turned and saw O'Neal striding towards me, hand outstretched.

'Go and get some manners somewhere,' I said, and hung up.

There was a brief silence, and then lots of things seemed to happen at once. Solomon was leading me back to the sofa, not very roughly but not very gently either, O'Neal was shouting to the followers, the followers were shouting at each other, and the phone was ringing again.

O'Neal grabbed it and immediately started fiddling with the flex, which didn't sit well with his previous attempts to convey masterly composure. It was obvious that, in O'Neal's world, there were many smaller cheeses than the harsh American on the other end of the line.

Solomon shoved me back down next to Sarah, who shrank away in disgust. It really is quite something to be hated by so many people in your own home.

O'Neal nodded and yessed for a minute or so, then delicately replaced the receiver. He looked at Sarah.

'Miss Woolf,' he said, as politely as he could manage, 'you are to present yourself to a Mr Russell Barnes at the American Embassy as soon as you can. One of these gentlemen will drive you.' O'Neal looked away, as if expecting her immediately to jump to her feet and be gone. Sarah stayed where she was.

'Screw you in the ass with an anglepoise lamp,' she said.

I laughed.

As it happens, I was the only one who did, and O'Neal fired off one of his increasingly famous looks in my direction. But Sarah was still glaring at him.

'I want to know what's being done about this guy,' she said. She jerked her head at me, so I thought it best to stop laughing.

'Mr Lang is our concern, Miss Woolf,' said O'Neal. 'You yourself have a responsibility to your State Department, by . . . '

'You're not the police, are you?' she said. O'Neal looked uneasy.

'No, we are not the police,' he said, carefully.

'Well I want the police here, and I want this guy arrested for attempted homicide. He tried to kill my father, and for all I know he's going to try again.'

O'Neal looked at her, then at me, then at Solomon. He seemed to want help from one of us, but I don't believe he got any.

'Miss Woolf, I have been authorised to inform you . . . '

He stopped, as if unable to remember whether he really had been authorised, and if he had, whether the author had really meant it. He wrinkled his nose for a moment, and decided to press on after all.

'I have been authorised to inform you that your father is, at this moment, the subject of an investigation by agencies of the United States government, assisted by my own department of the Ministry of Defence.' This clanged to the floor, and we all just sat there. O'Neal flicked a glance at me. 'It is in our joint discretion as to whether we charge Mr Lang, or indeed take any other action affecting your father or his activities.'

I'm no great reader of the human face, but even I could see that all of this was coming as something of a shock to Sarah. Her face had gone from grey to white.

'What activities?' she said. 'Investigated for what?' Her voice was strained. O'Neal looked uncomfortable, and I knew he was terrified that she was going to cry.

'We suspect your father,' he said eventually, 'of importing Class A prohibited substances into Europe and North America.'

The room went very quiet, and everybody was watching Sarah. O'Neal cleared his throat.

'Your father is trafficking in drugs, Miss Woolf.'

It was her turn to laugh.

Four

There's a snake hidden in the grass.

VIRGIL

Like all good things, and like all bad things too, it came to an end. The replica Solomons swept Sarah off towards Grosvenor Square in one of their Rovers, and O'Neal ordered a taxi, which took far too long to arrive and gave him more time to sneer at my belongings. The real Solomon stayed behind to wash up the mugs, and then suggested that the two of us put ourselves outside a quantity of warm, nourishing beer.

It was only five-thirty, but the pubs were already groaning with young men in suits and misjudged moustaches, sounding off on the state of the world. We managed to find a table in the lounge bar of The Swan With Two Necks, where Solomon made a lavish production out of rootling for change in his pockets. I told him to put it on expenses, and he told me to take it out of my thirty thousand pounds. We tossed a coin and I lost.

'Obliged to you for your kindness, master.'

'Cheers, David.' We both took a long suck, and I lit a cigarette.

I was expecting Solomon to kick off with some observation about the events of the last twenty-four hours, but he seemed happy to just sit and listen while a nearby gang of estate agents discussed car alarm systems. He'd managed to make me feel as if our sitting there was my idea, and I wasn't having that.

'David.'

'Sir.'

'Is this social?'

'Social?'

'You were asked to take me out, weren't you? Slap me on the back, get me drunk, find out whether I'm sleeping with Princess Margaret?'

It annoyed Solomon to hear the Royal family being taken in vain, which was why I'd done it.

'I'm supposed to stay close, sir,' he said eventually. 'I thought it might be more fun if we sat at the same table, that's all.' He seemed to think that answered my question.

'So what's going on?' I said.

'Going on?'

'David, if you're going to just sit there, wide-eyed, repeating everything I say as if you've lived your whole life in a Wendy house, it's going to be a pretty dull evening.'

There was a pause.

'Pretty dull evening?'

'Oh shut up. You know me, David.'

'Indeed I have that privilege.'

'I may be many things, but one of the things I am definitely not is an assassin.'

'Long experience in these matters,' he took another deep swallow of beer and smacked his lips, 'has led me to the view, master, that everybody is definitely not an assassin, until they become one.'

I looked at him for a moment.

'I'm going to swear now, David.'

'As you wish, sir.'

'What the fuck is that supposed to mean?'

The estate agents had moved on to the subject of women's breasts, from which they were extracting much humour. Listening to them made me feel about a hundred and forty years old.

'It's like dog-owners,' said Solomon. '"My dog wouldn't hurt anyone", they say. Until one day, they find themselves saying "well he's never done that before".' He looked at me and saw that I was frowning. 'What I mean is, nobody can ever really know anybody. Anybody or any dog. Not *really* know them.'

I banged my glass down hard on the table.

'Nobody can ever know anybody? That's inspired. You mean in spite of us spending two years practically in each other's pockets, you don't know whether I'm capable of killing a man for money?' I admit I was getting a little upset by this. And I don't normally get upset.

'Do you think I am?' said Solomon. The jolly smile still hung round his mouth.

'Do I think you could kill a man for money? No, I don't.'

'Sure of that?'

'Yes.'

'Then you're a clot, sir. I've killed one man and two women.'

I already knew that. I also knew how much it weighed on him.

'But not for money,' I said. 'Not assassination.'

'I am a servant of the Crown, master. The government pays my mortgage. Whichever way you look at it, and believe me I've looked at it lots of ways, the deaths of those three people put bread on my table. Another pint?'

Before I could say anything, he'd taken my glass and headed for the bar.

As I watched him carve a path through the estate agents, I found myself thinking back to the games of cowboys and Indians Solomon and I had played together in Belfast.

Happy days, dotted around some miserable months.

It was 1986, and Solomon had been drafted in, along with

a dozen others from the Metropolitan Police Special Branch, to supplement a temporarily buggered RUC. He'd quickly proved to be the only one of his group worth the air-ticket, so, at the end of his stint, some extremely hard-to-please Ulstermen had asked him to stay on and try his hand at the loyalist paramilitary target, which he did.

Half-a-mile away, in a couple of rooms above the Freedom Travel Agency, I was serving out the last of my eight years in the army on attachment to the snappily-titled GR24, one of the many military intelligence units that used to compete for business in Northern Ireland, and probably still do. My brother officers being almost exclusively Old Etonians, who wore ties in the office and flew to Scottish grouse moors at the weekend, I'd found myself spending more and more time with Solomon, most of it waiting in cars with heaters that didn't work.

But every now and then we got out and did something useful, and in the nine months we were together, I saw Solomon do a lot of brave and extraordinary things. He'd taken three lives, but he'd saved dozens more, mine included.

The estate agents were sniggering at his brown raincoat.

'Woolf's a bad lot, you know,' he said.

We were into our third pint, and Solomon had undone his top button. I'd have done the same if I'd had one. The pub was emptier now, as people headed home to wives, or out to cinemas. I lit my too-manyeth cigarette of the day.

'Because of drugs?'

'Because of drugs.'

'Anything else?'

'Does there need to be anything else?'

'Well yes.' I looked across at Solomon. 'There needs to be something else if all this isn't going to be taken care of by the Drug Squad. What's he got to do with your lot? Or is it just that business is slow at the moment, and you're having to slum it?'

'I never said a word of this.'

'Course you didn't.'

Solomon paused, weighing his words and apparently finding some of them a bit heavy.

'A very rich man, an industrialist, comes to this country and says he wants to invest here. The Department of Trade and Industry give him a glass of sherry and some glossy brochures, and he sets to work. Tells them he's going to manufacture a range of metal and plastic components and would it be all right if he built half a dozen factories in Scotland and the north-east of England? One or two people at the Board of Trade fall over with the excitement, and offer him two hundred million quid in grants and a residents' parking permit in Chelsea. I'm not sure which is worth more.'

Solomon sipped some beer and dried his mouth with the back of his hand. He was very angry.

'Time passes. The cheque is cashed, factories are built, and a phone rings in Whitehall. It's an international call, from Washington, DC. Did we know that a rich industrialist who makes plastic things also deals in large quantities of opium from Asia? Good heavens, no, we didn't know that, thanks ever so much for letting us know, love to the wife and kids. Panic. Rich industrialist is now sitting on a large lump of our money and employing three thousand of our citizens.'

At this point, Solomon seemed to run out of energy, as if the effort of controlling his fury was too much for him. But I couldn't wait.

'So?'

'So a committee of not particularly wise men and women put their fat heads together and decide on possible courses of action. The list includes doing nothing, doing nothing, doing nothing, or dialling 999 and asking for PC Plod. The only thing they are sure about is they do not like that last course.'

'And O'Neal . . . ?'

'O'Neal gets the job. Surveillance. Containment. Damage Control. Give it any flipping name you like.' For Solomon, 'flipping' constituted strong language. 'None of this, of course, has anything whatsoever to do with Alexander Woolf.'

'Of course not,' I said. 'Where is Woolf now?'

Solomon glanced at his watch.

'At this moment, he is in seat number 6C on a British Airways 747 from Washington to London. If he's got any sense, he'll have chosen the Beef Wellington. He may be a fish man, but I doubt it.'

'And the film?'

'While You Were Sleeping.'

'I'm impressed,' I said.

'God is in the detail, master. Just because it's a bad job doesn't mean I have to do it badly.'

We supped some beer in a relaxed silence. But I had to ask him.

'Now, David.'

'Yours to command, master.'

'Do you mind explaining where I come into all this?' He looked at me with the beginnings of a 'you tell me' expression, so I hurried on. 'I mean, who wants him dead, and why make it look as if I'm the killer?'

Solomon drained his glass.

'Don't know the why,' he said. 'As for the who, we rather think it might be the CIA.'

During the night I tossed a little, and turned a little more, and twice got up to record some idiotic monologues about the state of play on my tax-efficient dictaphone. There were things about the whole business that bothered me, and things that scared me, but it was Sarah Woolf who kept coming into my head and refusing to leave.

I was not in love with her, you understand. How could I be? After all, I'd only spent a couple of hours in her company, and none of those had been under very relaxing circumstances. No, I was definitely not in love with her. It takes more than a pair of bright grey eyes and pillows of dark-brown, wavy hair to get me going.

For God's sake.

*

At nine o'clock the next morning I was pulling on the Garrick tie and the under-buttoned blazer, and at half past nine I was ringing the enquiries bell at the National Westminster Bank in Swiss Cottage. I had no clear plan of action in mind, but I thought it might be good for morale to look my bank manager in the eye for the first time in ten years, even if the money in my account wasn't mine.

I was shown into a waiting-room outside the manager's office, and given a plastic cup of plastic coffee which was far too hot to drink until, in the space of a hundredth of a second, it suddenly became far too cold. I was trying to get rid of it behind a rubber plant when a nine-year-old boy with ginger hair stuck his head out of the door, beckoned me in, and announced himself as Graham Halkerston, Branch Manager.

'So, what can I do for you, Mr Lang?' he said, settling himself behind a young, ginger-haired desk.

I struck what I thought was a big business pose in the chair opposite him, and straightened my tie.

'Well, Mr Halkerston,' I said, 'I am concerned about a sum of money, recently transferred to my account.'

He glanced down at a computer print-out on the desk.

'Would that be a remittance on the seventh of April?'

'Seventh of April,' I repeated carefully, trying hard not to muddle it up with other payments of thirty thousand pounds I'd received that month. 'Yes,' I said. 'That sounds like the one.'

He nodded.

'Twenty-nine thousand, four hundred and eleven pounds and seventy-six pence. Were you thinking of transferring the money, Mr Lang? Because we have a variety of high-yielding accounts that would suit your needs.'

'My needs?'

'Yes. Ease of access, high interest, sixty day bonus, it's up to you.'

It seemed strange somehow, hearing a human being use phrases like that. Until that point in my life, I'd only ever seen them on advertising billboards.

'Great,' I said. 'Great. For the time being, Mr Halkerston, my needs are simply for you to keep the money in a room with a decent lock on the door.' He stared back at me blankly. 'I'm more interested to know the origins of this transfer.' His face went from blank to highly blank. 'Who gave me this money, Mr Halkerston?'

I could tell that unsolicited donations were not a regular feature of banking life, and it took a few more moments of blankness, followed by some paper-rustling, before Halkerston was back at the net.

'The payment was made in cash,' he said, 'so I have no actual record of the origin. If you'll hold on a second, I can get a copy of the credit slip.' He pressed an intercom button and asked for Ginny, who duly trundled in bearing a folder. While Halkerston browsed through it, I had to wonder how Ginny could hold her head up under the weight of cosmetics smeared all over her face. Underneath it all, she may have been quite pretty. Or she may have been Dirk Bogarde. I will never know.

'Here we are,' said Halkerston. 'The name of the payer has been left out, but there is a signature. Offer. Or possibly Offee. T Offee, that's it.'

Paulie's chambers were in the Middle Temple, which I remembered him telling me was somewhere near Fleet Street, and I got there eventually with the help of a black cab. It's not the way I usually travel, but while I was at the bank I decided there was no harm in withdrawing a couple of hundred pounds worth of my blood money for expenses.

Paulie himself was in court on a hit-and-run case, playing his part as a human brake-pad on the wheels of justice, so I had no special entrée to the chambers of Milton Crowley Spencer. Instead, I had to submit to the clerk's interrogation on the nature of my 'problem' and by the time he'd finished, I felt worse than I've ever done in any venereal clinic.

Not that I've been to a lot of venereal clinics.

Having passed the preliminary means test, I was then left

to cool my heels in a waiting-room filled with back numbers of *Expressions,* the journal for American Express card-holders. So I sat there and read about bespoke trouser-makers in Jermyn Street, and sock-weavers in Northampton, and hat-growers in Panama, and how likely it was that Kerry Packer would win the Veuve Cliquot Polo Championship at Smith's Lawn this year, and generally caught up on all the big stories happening behind the news, until the clerk came back and raised a pert couple of eyebrows at me.

I was ushered into a large, oak-panelled room, with shelves of Regina versus The Rest Of The World on three walls, and a row of wooden filing cabinets along the fourth. There was a photograph on the desk of three teenage children, who looked as if they'd been bought from a catalogue, and next to it, a signed picture of Denis Thatcher. I was chewing on the peculiar fact that both these photographs were pointing outwards from the desk, when a connecting door opened, and I was suddenly in the presence of Spencer.

And quite a presence it was. He was a taller version of Rex Harrison, with greying hair, half-moon spectacles and a shirt so white it must have been running off the mains. I didn't actually see him start the clock as he sat down.

'Mr Fincham, sorry to keep you, do have a seat.'

He gestured around the room, as if inviting me to take my pick, but there was only one chair. I sat down, and immediately jumped to my feet again as the chair let out a scream of creaking, tearing wood. It was so loud, and so agonised, that I could picture people in the street outside stopping, and looking up at the window, and wondering about calling a policeman. Spencer didn't seem to notice it.

'Don't think I've seen you at the club,' he said, smiling expensively.

I sat down again, to another roar from the chair, and tried to find a position which might allow our conversation to be more or less audible above the howling woodwork.

'Club?' I said, and then looked down as he gestured at my tie. 'Ah, you mean the Garrick?'

He nodded, still smiling.

'No, well,' I said, 'I don't get up to town as often as I'd like.' I waved my hand in a way that implied a couple of thousand acres in Wiltshire and plenty of labradors. He nodded, as if he could picture the place exactly, and might pop over for a spot of lunch the next time he was in the neighbourhood.

'Now then,' he said, 'how can I help?'

'Well, this is rather delicate . . . ' I began.

'Mr Fincham,' he interrupted smoothly, 'if the day ever comes when a client comes to me and says that the matter upon which he or she requires my advice is not delicate, I shall hang up my wig for good.' From the look on his face, I could see that I was meant to take this as a witticism. All I could think was that it had probably cost me thirty quid.

'Well, that's very comforting,' I said, acknowledging the joke. We smiled comfortably at each other. 'The fact is,' I went on, 'that a friend of mine told me recently that you had been extremely helpful in introducing him to some people with unusual skills.'

There was a pause, as I'd rather suspected there might be.

'I see,' said Spencer. His smile faded slightly, the glasses came off, and the chin lifted five degrees. 'Might I be favoured with the name of this friend of yours?'

'I'd rather not say just at the moment. He told me that he needed . . . a sort of bodyguard, someone who would be prepared to carry out some fairly unorthodox duties, and that you furnished him with some names.'

Spencer leaned back in his chair and surveyed me. Head to toe. I could tell that the interview was already over, and that now he was just deciding on the most elegant way of telling me. After a while, he took in a slow breath through his finely wrought nose.

'It is possible,' he said, 'that you have misunderstood the services we offer here, Mr Fincham. We are a firm of barristers. Advocates. We argue cases before the bench. That is our function. We are not, and this I think is where the confusion may have arisen, an employment agency. If your friend obtained satisfaction here, then I am glad. But I hope and believe that it had more to do with the legal advice we were able to offer than with any recommendations on the engagement of staff.' In his mouth, 'staff' had a rather nasty sound to it. 'Might it not be preferable for you to contact your friend in order to secure whatever information it is you require?'

'Well that's the problem,' I said. 'My friend has gone away.'

There was a pause, and Spencer blinked slowly. There is something strangely insulting about a slow blink. I know, because I use it myself.

'You are welcome to use the telephone in the clerk's office.'

'He didn't leave a number.'

'Then, alas, Mr Fincham, you are in difficulty. Now, if you will excuse me . . . ' He slid the glasses back on to his nose and busied himself with some papers on his desk.

'My friend wanted someone,' I said, 'who would be prepared to kill someone.'

Off came the glasses, up went the chin.

'Indeed.'

A long pause.

'Indeed,' he said again. 'That in itself being an unlawful act, it is highly improbable that he would have received any assistance from an employee of this firm, Mr Fincham . . . '

'He assured me that you were most helpful . . . '

'Mr Fincham, I shall be candid.' The voice had stiffened considerably, and I realised that Spencer would be good fun to watch in court. 'The suspicion has formed in my mind that you may be acting here in the capacity of *agent provocateur.*' The French accent was confident and immaculate. He had a villa in Provence, natch. 'From what motive, I cannot tell,' he continued. 'Nor am I particularly interested. I do, however, decline to say anything further to you.'

'Unless you're in the presence of a lawyer.'

'Good day to you, Mr Fincham.' Glasses on.

'My friend also told me that you handled the payment of

his new employee.'

No answer. I knew there weren't going to be any more answers from Mr Spencer, but I thought I'd press on anyway.

'My friend told me that you signed the credit slip yourself,' I said. 'In your own hand.'

'I am rapidly tiring of news of your friend, Mr Fincham. I repeat, good day to you.'

I got to my feet and moved towards the door. The chair screamed its relief.

'Does the offer of the telephone still stand?'

He didn't even look up.

'The cost of the call will be added to your bill.'

'Bill for what?' I said. 'You haven't given me anything.'

'I have given you my time, Mr Fincham. If you have no desire to make use of it, that is entirely your concern.'

I opened the door.

'Well, thanks anyway, Mr Spencer. By the way . . . ' I waited until he had looked up. 'There's some ugly talk at the Garrick that you cheat at bridge. I told the chaps that it was all rubbish and tommy-rot, but you know what these things are like. Chaps get an idea in their head. Thought you ought to know.'

Pathetic. But all I could think of at the time.

The clerk sensed that I was not a terribly *grata persona*, and warned me, peevishly, to expect a bill for services in the next few days.

I thanked him for his kindness and turned towards the staircase. As I did so, I noticed that someone else was now treading my path through back numbers of *Expressions*, the journal for American Express card-holders.

Short fat men in grey suits: this is a large category.

Short fat men in grey suits whose scrotums I have held in a hotel bar in Amsterdam: this is a very small category.

Tiny, in fact.

Five

Take a straw and throw it up into the air,
you shall see by that which way the wind is.

JOHN SELDEN

To follow somebody, without them knowing that you're doing it, is not the doddle they make it seem in films. I've had some experience of professional following, and a lot more experience of professional going back to the office and saying 'we lost him'. Unless your quarry is deaf, tunnel-sighted and lame, you need at least a dozen people and fifteen thousand quids-worth of short-wave radio to make a decent go of it.

The problem with McCluskey was that he was, in the jargon phrase, 'a player' – somebody who knows that they are a possible target, and has some idea of what to do about it. I couldn't risk getting too close, and the only way to avoid that was by running; hanging back on the straights, sprinting flat-out as he rounded corners, pulling up in time to avoid him if he doubled back. None of this would have been countenanced by a professional outfit, of course, because it ignored the possibility that he had someone else watching his back, who might begin to wonder at this sprinting, shuffling, window-shopping lunatic.

The first stretch was easy enough. McCluskey waddled his way from Fleet Street along towards the Strand, but when he reached the Savoy, he skipped across the road and headed north into Covent Garden. There he dawdled amongst the myriad pointless shops, and stood for five minutes watching a juggler outside the Actors Church. Refreshed, he set off at a brisk pace towards St Martin's Lane, crossed over on his way to Leicester Square, and then sold me a dummy by suddenly turning south into Trafalgar Square.

By the time we reached the bottom of the Haymarket, the sweat was pouring off me and I was praying for him to hail a taxi. He didn't do it until he got to Lower Regent Street, and I caught another one an agonising twenty seconds later.

Well, obviously it was another one. Even the amateur follower knows that you don't get into the same taxi as the person you're following.

I threw myself into the seat and shouted at the driver to 'follow that cab', and then realised what a strange thing that is to say in real life. The cabbie didn't seem to find it so.

'Tell me,' he said, 'is he sleeping with your wife, or are you sleeping with his?'

I laughed as though this was the grandest thing I'd heard in years, which is what you have to do with cabbies if you want them to take you to the right place by the right route.

McCluskey got out at the Ritz, but he must have told his driver to stay and keep the meter running. I left him for three minutes before doing the same with my cab, but, as I opened the door, McCluskey came scooting back out and we were off again.

We crawled along Piccadilly for a while, and then turned right into some narrow empty streets that I didn't know at all. This was the sort of territory where skilled craftspeople hand-build underpants for American Express card-holders.

I leaned forward to tell the driver not to get too close, but he'd done this sort of thing before, or seen it done on television, and he hung back a good distance.

McCluskey's cab came to rest in Cork Street. I saw him pay

his driver, and I told my man to trickle past and drop me two hundred yards further down the street.

The meter said six pounds, so I passed a ten pound note through the window and watched a fifteen-second production of 'I'm Not Sure I've Got Change For That', starring licensed cab driver 99102, before getting out and heading back down the street.

In those fifteen seconds, McCluskey had vanished. I'd just followed him for twenty minutes and five miles, and lost him in the last two hundred yards. Which, I suppose, served me right for being mean with the tip.

Cork Street is nothing but art galleries, mostly with large front windows, and one of the things I've noticed about windows is that they're just as good for seeing out of as they are for seeing in through. I couldn't go pressing my nose against every art gallery until I found him, so I decided to take a chance. I judged the spot where McCluskey had dismounted, and turned for the nearest door.

It was locked.

I was standing there looking at my watch, trying to work out what an art gallery's opening hours might be if twelve wasn't one of them, when a blonde girl wearing a neat black shift appeared out of the gloom and slipped the latch. She opened the door with a welcoming smile, and suddenly I seemed to have no choice but to step inside, my hopes of finding McCluskey ebbing away with every second.

Keeping one eye on the front window, I sank back into the relative darkness of the shop. Apart from the blonde, there didn't seem to be anyone else in the place, which wasn't all that surprising when I looked at the paintings.

'Do you know Terence Glass?' she asked, handing me a card and price list. She was a frightfully pukka young thing.

'Yes, I do,' I said. 'I've got three of his, as a matter of fact.'

Well, I mean. Sometimes you've just got to have a go, haven't you?

'Three of his what?' she said.

Doesn't always work, of course.

'Paintings.'

'Good heavens,' she said. 'I didn't know he painted. Sarah,' she called out, 'did you know that Terence painted?'

From the back half of the gallery, a cool American voice came back. 'Terry has never painted in his life. Hardly write his own name.'

I looked up just as Sarah Woolf came through the archway, immaculate in a dog-tooth skirt and jacket, and pushing that gentle bow wave of Fleur de Fleurs. But she wasn't looking at me. She was looking towards the front of the gallery.

I turned, followed her gaze, and saw McCluskey standing in the open doorway.

'But this gentleman claims he's got three . . . ' said the blonde, laughing.

McCluskey was moving quickly towards Sarah, his right hand sliding across his chest towards the inside of his coat. I pushed the blonde away with my right arm, heard her gasp something polite, and at the same moment McCluskey turned his head towards me.

As he swung his body round, I aimed a round-house kick to his stomach, and to block it, he had to pull his right hand down from his coat. The kick connected, and for a moment, McCluskey's feet left the floor. His head came forward as he gasped for breath, and I moved behind him and slipped my left arm around his neck. The blonde was screaming 'oh my God' in a very posh accent, and scrabbling for the phone on the table, but Sarah stayed where she was, arms rigid at her sides. I shouted at her to run, but she either didn't hear me, or didn't want to hear me. As I tightened my grip round McCluskey's neck, he fought to get his fingers between the crook of my elbow and his throat. No chance of that.

I put my right elbow on McCluskey's shoulder, and my right hand at the back of his head. My left hand slipped into the crook of my right elbow, and there I was, the model in diagram (c) in the chapter headed 'Neck-Breaking: The Basics'.

As McCluskey kicked and struggled, I eased my left

forearm back and my right hand forward – and he stopped kicking very quickly. He stopped kicking because he suddenly knew what I knew, and wanted him to know – that with a few extra pounds of pressure, I could end his life.

I'm not absolutely sure, but I think that was when the gun went off.

I don't remember the actual feeling of being hit. Just the flatness of the sound in the gallery, and the smell of burnt whatever it is they use nowadays.

At first I thought it was McCluskey she'd shot, and I started to swear at her because I had everything under control, and anyway, I'd told her to get out of here. And then I thought Christ, I must be sweating a lot, because I could feel it running down my side, trickling wetly into my waistband. I looked up, and realised that Sarah was going to fire again. Or maybe she already had. McCluskey had wriggled free and I seemed to be falling back against one of the paintings.

'You stupid bitch,' I think I said, 'I'm . . . on your side. This is him . . . the one . . . he's the one . . . to kill your father. Fuck.'

The fuck was because everything was starting to go strange now. Light, sound, action.

Sarah was standing right over me, and I suppose, maybe, if circumstances had been different, I'd have been enjoying her legs. But they weren't different. They were the same. And all I could look at now was the gun.

'That would be very strange, Mr Lang,' she said. 'He could do that at home.' I suddenly couldn't make anything of this. Lots of things were wrong, very wrong, the numbness down my left side being not the least of them. Sarah knelt down next to me and put the muzzle of the gun under my chin.

'This,' she jerked a thumb towards McCluskey, 'is my father.'

As I can't remember any more, I assume I must have blacked out.

'How are you feeling?'

It's a question you're bound to get asked when you're lying on your back in a hospital bed, but I wish she hadn't asked it all the same. My brain was scrambled to the point where you usually have to summon the waiter and ask for a refund, and it would have made more sense for me to be asking her how I felt. But she was a nurse, and therefore unlikely to be trying to kill me, so I decided to like her for the time being.

With a mighty effort, I ungummed my lips and croaked back at her, 'Fine.'

'That's good,' she said. 'Doctor will be along to see you shortly.' She patted the back of my hand and disappeared.

I closed my eyes for a few moments, and when I opened them it was dark outside. A white coat was standing over me, and despite the fact that its wearer looked young enough to be my bank manager, I could only assume he was a doctor. He gave me my wrist back, although I wasn't aware that he'd been holding it, and jotted something down on a clipboard.

'How are you feeling?'

'Fine.'

He kept on writing.

'Well you shouldn't be. You've been shot. Lost quite a bit of blood, but that's not a problem. You were lucky. Passed through your armpit.' He made it sound as if the whole thing was my own silly fault. Which, in a way, it was.

'Where am I?' I said.

'Hospital.'

He went away.

Later, a very fat woman came in with a trolley and put a plate of something brown and foul-smelling on a table beside me. I couldn't imagine what I'd ever done to her, but whatever it was, it must have been bad.

She obviously realised that she'd over-reacted, because half an hour later she came and took the plate away again. Before she left, she told me where I was. The Middlesex Hospital, William Hoyle Ward.

My first proper visitor was Solomon. He came in, looking

65

steady and eternal, sat down on the bed and chucked a paper bag of grapes on to the table.

'How are you feeling?'

A definite pattern was emerging here.

'I feel,' I said, 'almost exactly as if I've been shot, I'm now lying in a hospital trying to recover, and a Jewish policeman is sitting on my foot.' He shifted his weight slightly along the bed.

'They tell me you were lucky, master.'

I popped a grape.

'Lucky as in . . . ?'

'As in it being only a couple of inches away from your heart.'

'Or a couple of inches away from missing me altogether. Depends on your point of view.'

He nodded, considering this.

'What's yours?' he said, after a while.

'What's my what?'

'Point of view.'

We looked at each other.

'That England should play a flat back four against Holland,' I said.

Solomon lifted himself off the bed and started to unpeel his raincoat, and I could hardly blame him. The temperature must have been in the nineties, and there seemed to be far, far too much air in the room. It was bunched and crowded, and in your face and eyes, and it made you think the room was a rush-hour tube train, and a lot of extra air had managed to sneak in just as the doors were closing.

I'd asked a nurse if she could turn the temperature down a little, but she'd told me that the heating was controlled by a computer in Reading. If I was the sort of person who writes letters to *The Daily Telegraph*, I'd have written a letter to *The Daily Telegraph*.

Solomon hung his coat on the back of the door.

'Well now, sir,' he said, 'believe it or not the ladies and gentlemen who pay my wages have asked me to extract from you an explanation as to how you came to be lying on the floor of a prestigious West End art gallery, with a bullet hole in your chest.'

'Armpit.'

'Arm, if you prefer, pit. Now will you tell me, master, or am I going to have to hold a pillow over your face until you co-operate?'

'Well,' I said, thinking that we may as well get down to business, 'I presume you know that McCluskey is Woolf.' I hadn't presumed any such thing, of course. I just wanted to sound efficient. It was obvious from Solomon's expression that he hadn't known, so I pressed on. 'I follow McCluskey to the gallery, thinking he might be there to do something unpleasant to Sarah. I bop him, get shot by Sarah, who then tells me that the boppee was, in fact, her father, Alexander Woolf.'

Solomon nodded calmly, the way he always did when he heard weird stuff.

'Whereas you,' he said eventually, 'had him down as a man who had offered you money to kill Alexander Woolf?'

'Right.'

'And you assumed, master, as I'm sure many would in your position, that when a man asks you to kill someone, the someone is not going to turn out to be the man himself.'

'It's not the way we do it on planet Earth, certainly.'

'Hmm.' Solomon had drifted over to the window where he seemed captivated by the Post Office Tower.

'That's it, is it?' I said. '"Hmm"? The Ministry of Defence report on this is going to consist of "Hmm", bound in leather with a gold seal and signed by the Cabinet?'

Solomon didn't answer, but just kept staring at the Post Office Tower.

'Well then,' I said, 'tell me this. What's happened to Woolfs major and minor? How did I get here? Who rang the ambulance? Did they stay with me until it came?'

'Have you ever eaten at that restaurant, the one that goes round and round at the top . . . ?'

'David, for Christ's sake . . . '

'The person who actually rang for the ambulance was a Mr Terence Glass, owner of the gallery in which you were shot, and putter-in of a claim to have your blood removed from his floor at the Ministry's expense.'

'How touching.'

'Although the ones who saved your life were Green and Baker.'

'Green and Baker?'

'Been following you about a lot. Baker held a handkerchief over the wound.'

This was a shock. I'd assumed, after my beer session with Solomon, that the two followers had been called off. I'd been sloppy. Thank God.

'Hurrah for Baker,' I said.

Solomon appeared to be about to tell me something else when he was interrupted by the door opening. O'Neal was very quickly among us. He came straight over to the side of my bed, and I could tell from his expression that he thought my getting shot was a thoroughly splendid development.

'How are you feeling?' he said, almost managing not to smile.

'Very well, thank you Mr O'Neal.'

There was a pause, and his face fell slightly.

'Lucky to be alive is what I heard,' he said. 'Except that from now on, you might think that you're unlucky to be alive.' O'Neal was very pleased with that. I had a vision of him rehearsing it in the lift. 'Well this is it, Mr Lang. I don't see how we can keep this one away from the police. In the presence of witnesses, you made a clear attempt on Woolf's life . . . '

O'Neal stopped, and he and I both looked round the room, at floor level, because the sound we'd heard was definitely that of a dog being sick. Then we heard it again, and both realised that it was Solomon, clearing his throat.

'With respect, Mr O'Neal,' said Solomon, now that he had our attention, 'Lang was under the impression that the man he was assaulting was, in fact, McCluskey.'

O'Neal closed his eyes.

'McCluskey? Woolf was identified by . . . '

'Yes, absolutely,' said Solomon, gently. 'But Lang maintains that Woolf and McCluskey are one and the same man.'

A long silence.

'I beg your pardon?' said O'Neal.

The superior smile had disappeared from his face, and I suddenly felt like bounding out of bed.

O'Neal gave a fat little snort. 'McCluskey and Woolf are one and the same man?' he said, his voice cracking into a falsetto. 'Are you entirely sane?'

Solomon looked to me for confirmation.

'That's about the size of it,' I said. 'Woolf is the man who approached me in Amsterdam, and asked me to kill a man called Woolf.'

The colour had now completely dribbled out of O'Neal's face. He looked like a man who's just realised that he's posted a love letter in the wrong envelope.

'But that's not possible,' he stammered. 'I mean, it makes no sense.'

'Which doesn't mean it's not possible,' I said.

But O'Neal wasn't really hearing anything now. He was in an awful state. So I pushed on for Solomon's benefit.

'I know I'm only the parlour maid,' I said, 'and it's not my place to speak, but this is how my theory goes. Woolf knows that there are some parties around the globe who would like him to cease living. He does the usual sort of thing, buys a dog, hires a bodyguard, doesn't tell anyone where he's going until he's already got there, but,' and I could see O'Neal shake himself into concentrating, 'he knows that that isn't enough. The people who want him dead are very keen, very professional, and sooner or later they'll poison the dog and bribe the bodyguard. So he has a choice.'

O'Neal was staring at me. He suddenly realised that his mouth was open, and shut it with a snap.

'Yes?'

'He can either take the war to them,' I said, 'which for all we know, may not be feasible. Or he can ride the punch.' Solomon was chewing his lip. And he was right to, because this was all sounding terrible. But it was better than anything they could come up with just now. 'He finds someone who he knows isn't going to accept the job, and he gives them the job. He lets it be known that a contract is out on his own life, and hopes that his real enemies will slow up for a while because they think that the job will get done anyway without them having to take any risks or spend any money.'

Solomon was back on Post Office Tower duty, and O'Neal was frowning.

'Do you really believe that?' he said. 'I mean, do you think that's possible?' I could see that he was desperate for a handle, any handle, even if it came off with the first flush.

'Yes, I think it's possible. No, I don't believe it. But I'm recovering from a gunshot wound, and it's the best I can do.'

O'Neal started to pace the floor, running his hands through his hair. The heat in the room was getting to him too, but he didn't have time to get rid of his coat.

'All right,' he said, 'somebody may want Woolf dead. I can't pretend that Her Majesty's government would be heartbroken if he walked under a bus tomorrow. Granted, his enemies may be considerable, and normal precautions useless. So far, so good. Yes, he can't take the war to them,' O'Neal rather liked that phrase, I could tell, 'so he puts out a fake contract on himself. But that doesn't work.' O'Neal stopped pacing and looked at me. 'I mean, how could he be sure it would be fake? How could he know that you wouldn't go through with it?'

I looked at Solomon, and he knew I was looking at him, but he didn't look back.

'I've been asked before,' I said. 'Offered a lot more money. I said no. Maybe he knew that.'

O'Neal suddenly remembered how much he disliked me.

'Have you always said no?' I stared back at O'Neal, as

70

coolly as I could. 'I mean, maybe you've changed,' he said. 'Maybe you suddenly need the money. It's a ridiculous risk.'

I shrugged, and my armpit hurt.

'Not really,' I said. 'He had the bodyguard, and at least with me he knew where the threat would come from. Rayner was hanging around me for days before I got into the house.'

'But you went to the house, Lang. You actually . . . '

'I went there to warn him. I thought it was a neighbourly thing to do.'

'All right. All right.' O'Neal got stuck into some more pacing. 'Now how does he "let it be known" that this contract is out? I mean, does he write it on lavatory walls, put an advertisement in the *Standard*, what?'

'Well, you knew about it.' I was starting to get tired now. I wanted sleep and maybe even a plate of something brown and foul-smelling.

'We are not his enemies, Mr Lang,' said O'Neal. 'Not in that sense, at any rate.'

'So how did you find out that I was supposedly after him?'

O'Neal stopped, and I could see him thinking that he'd already said whole volumes too much to me. He looked over at Solomon crossly, blaming him for not being a good enough chaperon. Solomon was a picture of calm.

'I don't see why we shouldn't tell him that, Mr O'Neal,' he said. 'He's had a bullet through his chest through no fault of his own. Might make it heal quicker if he knows why it happened.'

O'Neal took a moment to digest this, and then turned to me.

'Very well,' he said. 'We received the information about your meeting with McCluskey, or Woolf . . . ' He was hating this. 'We received this information from the Americans.'

The door opened and a nurse came in. She might have been the one who patted my hand when I first woke up, but I couldn't swear to it. She looked straight through Solomon and O'Neal, and came over to fiddle with my pillows, plumping them up, pushing them about, making them considerably less comfortable than they had been.

I looked up at O'Neal.

'Do you mean the CIA?'

Solomon smiled, and O'Neal nearly wet himself.

The nurse didn't even flicker.

Six

The hour is come, but not the man.

WALTER SCOTT

I was in hospital for seven meals, however long that is. I watched television, took painkillers, tried to do all the half-finished crosswords in the back numbers of *Woman's Own*. And asked myself a lot of questions.

For a start, what was I doing? Why was I getting in the way of bullets, fired by people I didn't know, for reasons I didn't understand? What was in it for me? What was in it for Woolf? What was in it for O'Neal and Solomon? Why were the crosswords half-finished? Had the patients got better, or died, before completing them? Had they come into hospital to have half their brain removed, and was this the proof of the surgeon's skill? Who had ripped the covers off these magazines and why? Can the answer to 'Not a woman (3)' really be 'man'?

And why, above all, was there a picture of Sarah Woolf pasted on the inside of the door of my mind, so that whenever I yanked it open, to think of anything – afternoon television, smoking a cigarette in the lavatory at the end of the ward, scratching an itchy toe – there she was, smiling and scowling at me simultaneously? I mean, for the hundredth time, this was a woman I was quite definitely *not* in love with.

I thought Rayner might be able to answer at least some of these questions, so when I judged myself well enough to get up and shuffle around, I borrowed a dressing-gown and headed upstairs to the Barrington Ward.

When Solomon had told me that Rayner was also in the Middlesex Hospital, I'd been, for a moment at least, surprised. It seemed ironic that the two of us should end up getting repaired in the same shop, after all we'd been through together. But then, as Solomon pointed out, there aren't many hospitals left in London these days, and if you hurt yourself anywhere south of the Watford Gap, you're liable to end up in the Middlesex sooner or later.

Rayner had a room to himself, directly opposite the nurses' desk, and he was wired up to a lot of bleeping boxes. His eyes were closed, either from sleep or coma, and his head was wrapped in a huge, cartoon bandage, as if Road Runner had dropped that safe just once too often. And he wore blue flannelette pyjamas, which, perhaps for the first time in a lot of years, made him look child-like. I stood by his bed for a while, feeling sorry for him, until a nurse appeared and asked me what I wanted. I said I wanted a lot of things, but would settle for knowing Rayner's first name.

Bob, she said. She stood at my elbow, with her hand on the door-knob, wanting me to leave, but deferring to my dressing-gown.

I'm sorry, Bob, I thought.

There you were, just doing what you were told, what you were paid to do, and some arse comes along and hits you with a marble Buddha. That's rough.

Of course, I knew that Bob wasn't exactly a choirboy. He wasn't even the boy who bullies the choirboy. At the very best, he was the older brother of the boy who bullies the boy who bullies the choirboy. Solomon had looked Rayner up in the MoD files, and found that he'd been chucked from the Royal Welch Fusiliers for black-marketeering – anything from army boot laces to Saracen armoured cars had gone through the barrack gates under Bob Rayner's jersey – but even so, I was the one who'd hit him, so I was the one who felt sorry for him.

I put what was left of Solomon's grapes on the table by his bed, and left.

Men and women in white coats tried to get me to stay in hospital for a few more days, but I shook my head and told them I was fine. They tutted, and made me sign a few things, and then they showed me how to change the dressing under my arm and told me to come straight back if the wound started to feel hot or itchy.

I thanked them for their kindness, and refused their offer of a wheelchair. Which was just as well, because the lift had stopped working.

And then I limped on to a bus and went home.

My flat was where I'd left it, but seemed smaller than I remembered. There were no messages on the answering machine and nothing in the fridge besides the half-pint of natural yoghurt and stick of celery that I'd inherited from the previous tenant.

My chest was hurting, as they'd said it would, so I took myself off to the sofa and watched a race meeting at Doncaster, with a large tumbler of I'm Sure I've Seen That Grouse Somewhere Before at my elbow.

I must have dozed off for a while, and it was the phone that woke me. I sat up quickly, gasping at the pain from my armpit, and reached for the whisky bottle. Empty. I felt really terrible. I looked at my watch as I lifted the receiver. Ten past eight, or twenty to two. I couldn't tell which.

'Mr Lang?'

Male. American. Click, whirr. Come on, I know this one.

'Yes.'

'Mr Thomas Lang?' Got it. Yes, Mike, I'll name that voice in five. I shook my head to try and wake myself up, and felt something rattling.

'How do you do, Mr Woolf?' I said.

Silence at the other end. And then: 'A lot better'n you, from what I hear.'

'Not so,' I said.

'Yeah?'

'My biggest worry in life has always been having no stories to tell my grandchildren. My time with the Woolf family should last them until they're about fifteen, I'd say.'

I thought I heard him laugh, but it could have been a crackle on the line. Or it could have been O'Neal's lot, tripping over their bugging equipment.

'Listen, Lang,' said Woolf, 'I'd like us to meet up some place.'

'Of course you would, Mr Woolf. Let me see. This time you'd like to offer me money to perform a vasectomy on you without you noticing. Am I close?'

'I'd like to explain, if that's okay by you. You like to eat Italian?'

I thought of the celery and the yoghurt and realised that I like to eat Italian very much indeed. But there was a problem here.

'Mr Woolf,' I said, 'before you name a place, make sure you can book it for at least ten people. I've a feeling this may be a party line.'

'That's okay,' he said, cheerfully. 'You got a tourist guide right by your phone.' I looked down at the table and saw a red paperback. *Ewan's Guide to London*. It looked new, and I certainly hadn't bought it. 'Listen carefully,' said Woolf, 'I want you to turn to page twenty-six, fifth entry. See you there in thirty minutes.'

There was a kerfuffle on the line, and I thought for a moment he'd hung up, but then his voice came back.

'Lang?'

'Yes?'

'Don't leave the guide-book in your apartment.'

I took a deep and weary breath.

'Mr Woolf,' I said, 'I may be stupid, but I'm not stupid.'

'That's what I'm hoping.'

The line went dead.

The fifth entry on page twenty-six of Ewan's comprehensive guide to losing dollars in the Greater London Area was 'Giare, 216 Roseland, WC2, Ital, 60 pp air con, Visa, Mast, Amex' followed by three sets of crossed spoons. One glance through the book told me that Ewan was pretty sparing with his three spoon motif, so at least I had a reasonable supper to look forward to.

The next problem was how to get there without towing along a dozen brown-raincoated civil servants behind me. I couldn't be sure that Woolf would be able to do the same, but if he'd gone to the trouble of the guide-book trick, which I have to admit I liked, he must have been fairly sure that he could move around without being bothered by strange men.

I let myself out of the flat and went down to the street door. My helmet was there, resting on top of the gas meter, along with a pair of battered leather gloves. I opened the front door and stuck my head out into the street. No felt-hatted figure straightened up from a lamppost and tossed away an unfiltered cigarette. But then again, I hadn't really expected that.

Fifty yards to the left I could see a dark green Leyland van with a rubber aerial sticking out of the roof, and to the right, on the far side of the street, a red and white striped roadmenders tent. Both of them could have been innocent.

I slipped back inside, put on the helmet and gloves and dug out my key-ring. I eased open the letter-box on the front door, brought the remote control switch for the bike alarm level with the slot, and pressed the button. The Kawasaki blipped back at me once to tell me that its alarm was now off, so I threw open the door and ran down to the street as fast as my armpit would let me.

The bike started first time, as Japanese bikes tend to do, so I slid it to half-choke, popped it into first gear, and eased out the clutch. I also got on it, in case you were worried. By the time I passed the dark-green van I must have been doing forty miles an hour, and I amused myself for a moment with the thought of a lot of men in anoraks banging their elbows on things and saying shit. When I reached the end of the street, I could see, in the mirror, the lights of a car pulling out after me. It was a Rover.

I turned left on to the Bayswater Road within shouting distance of the speed limit, and stopped at a traffic light that's never once been green in all the years I've been coming up to it. But I wasn't bothered. I fiddled with my gloves and visor for a while, until I sensed the Rover crawling up on the inside, and then I glanced across at the moustachioed face behind the wheel. I wanted to tell him to go home, because this was about to become embarrassing.

As the light switched to amber, I closed the choke fully and eased the throttle to around five thousand revs, then shifted my weight forward over the petrol tank to keep the front wheel down. I dropped the clutch as the light turned green and felt the Kawasaki's gigantic rear wheel thrash madly from side to side like a dinosaur's tail, until it found the grip it needed to sling me forwards down the road.

Two-and-a-half seconds later I was doing sixty, and two-and-a-half seconds after that the street lamps were melting into one, and I'd forgotten what the Rover driver looked like.

Giare was a surprisingly cheerful place, with white walls and an echoing tile floor that turned every whisper into a shout and every smile into a howling belly-laugh.

A Ralph Lauren blonde with huge eyes took my helmet and showed me to a table by the window, where I ordered a tonic water for myself and a large vodka for the pain in my armpit. To pass the time before Woolf arrived, I had a choice between Ewan's guide-book or the menu. The menu looked slightly longer, so I started on that.

The first item was fighting under the name 'Crostini of Mealed Tarroce, with Benatore Potatoes' and weighed in at an impressive twelve pounds sixty-five. The Ralph Lauren blonde came over and asked me if I needed any help with the menu, and I asked her to explain what potatoes were. She didn't laugh.

I'd just started to unravel the description of the second dish, which could have been poached Marx Brother for all I know, when I caught sight of the Woolf at the door, clinging determinedly to a briefcase while a waiter peeled off his coat.

And then, at exactly the same moment that I noticed our table was laid for three, I saw Sarah Woolf step out from behind him.

She looked – and I hate to say this – sensational. Absolutely sensational. I know it's a cliché, but there are times when you realise why clichés become clichés. She wore a plain-cut dress in green silk, and it hung on her in a way that all dresses would like to hang if they got the chance – staying still at the bits where it ought to have stayed still, and moving at the bits where movement was exactly what you wanted. Just about everybody watched her travel to the table, and there was a hush in the room while Woolf pushed the chair in behind her as she sat down.

'Mr Lang,' said Woolf major, 'good of you to come.' I nodded at him. 'You know my daughter?'

I glanced across at Sarah, and she was looking down at her napkin, frowning. Even her napkin looked better than anyone else's.

'Yes of course,' I said. 'Now let me see. Wimbledon? Henley? Dick Cavendish's wedding? No, I've got it. Down the barrel of a gun, that's where we last met. How nice to see you again.'

It was supposed to be friendly, a joke even, but when she still didn't look at me, the line seemed to curdle into something aggressive, and I wished I'd shut up and just smiled. Sarah adjusted the cutlery into what she obviously thought was a more pleasing formation.

'Mr Lang,' she said, 'I've come here at my father's suggestion to say that I'm sorry. Not because I think I did anything wrong, but because you got hurt and you shouldn't have. And I'm sorry for that.'

Woolf and I waited for her to go on, but it seemed as if that was all we were going to get for now. She just sat there, rummaging in her bag for a reason not to look at me. Apparently she found several, which was odd, because it was quite a small bag.

Woolf gestured for a waiter, and turned to me.

'Had a chance to look at the menu yet?'

'Glanced at it,' I said. 'I hear that whatever you're having is excellent.'

The waiter arrived and Woolf loosened his tie a little.

'Two martinis,' he said, 'very dry, and . . . '

He looked at me and I nodded.

'Vodka martini,' I said. 'Incredibly dry. Powdered, if you've got it.'

The waiter pushed off, and Sarah started looking round the place, as if she was bored already. The tendons in her neck were beautiful.

'So, Thomas,' said Woolf. 'Mind if I call you Thomas?'

'Okay with me,' I said. 'It's my first name, after all.'

'Good. Thomas. First of all, how's your shoulder?'

'Fine,' I said, and he looked relieved. 'A lot better than my armpit, which is where I got shot.'

At last, at long last, she turned her head and looked at me. Her eyes were much softer than the rest of her pretended to be. She bowed her head slightly, and her voice was low and cracked.

'I told you, I'm sorry,' she said.

I wanted desperately to say something back, something nice, and gentle, but I came up empty-headed. There was a pause, which might somehow have turned nasty if she hadn't smiled. But she did smile, and a lot of blood suddenly seemed to be crashing about in my ears, dropping things and falling over. I smiled back, and we kept on looking at each other.

'I suppose we have to say it could have been worse,' she said.

'Of course it could,' I said. 'If I was an international armpit model, I'd be off work for months.'

This time she laughed, actually laughed, and I felt like I'd won every Olympic medal that had ever been struck.

We started with some soup, which came in a bowl about the size of my flat and tasted delicious. The talk was small. It turned out that Woolf was also a fan of the turf, and that I'd been watching one of his horses race at Doncaster that afternoon, so we chatted a little about racing. By the time the second course arrived, we were putting the finishing touches to a nicely-rounded three-minuter on the unpredictability of the English climate. Woolf took a mouthful of something meaty and sauce-covered, and then dabbed his mouth.

'So, Thomas,' he said, 'I guess there are one or two things you'd like to ask me?'

'Well, yes.' I dabbed my mouth in return. 'I hate to be predictable, but what the fuck do you think you're doing?'

There was an intake of breath from a nearby table, but Woolf didn't flinch and neither did Sarah.

'Right,' he said, nodding. 'Fair question. First of all, in spite of whatever you may have been told by your Defence people, I have nothing whatsoever to do with drugs. Nothing. I've taken some penicillin in my time, but that's it. Period.'

Well, that obviously wasn't good enough. Not by a long shot. Saying period at the end of something doesn't make it incontrovertible.

'Yes, well,' I said, 'forgive my tired old English cynicism, but isn't this a case of "you would say that wouldn't you"?' Sarah looked at me crossly, and I suddenly thought I might have overdone it. But then I thought heck, beautiful tendons or not, there were some things that needed to be straightened out here.

'Sorry to bring it up before you've even got started,' I said, 'but I assume we're here for plain talking, so I'm talking plainly.'

Woolf had another bite at his food and kept his eyes on his plate, and it took me a moment to realise that he was leaving it to Sarah to answer.

'Thomas,' she said, and I turned to look at her. Her eyes were big and round, and went from one side of the universe to the other. 'I had a brother. Michael. Four years older than me.'

Oh cripes. Had.

'Michael died half-way through his first year at Bates University. Amphetamines, qualudes, heroin. He was twenty years old.'

She paused, and I had to speak. Something. Anything.

'I'm sorry.'

Well, what else do you say? Tough? Pass the salt? I realised I was hunching down towards the table, trying to blend with their grief, but it was no good. On a subject like this, you're an outsider.

'I tell you that,' she said eventually, 'for one reason only. To show you that my father,' and she turned to look at him while he kept his head bowed, 'could no more get involved in the traffick of drugs than he could fly to the moon. It's that simple. I'd bet my life on that.'

Period.

For a while, neither of them would look at each other, or at me.

'Well, I'm sorry,' I said again. 'I'm very, very sorry.'

We sat like that for a moment, a little kiosk of silence in the middle of the restaurant din, and then suddenly Woolf switched on a smile, and seemed to get all brisk.

'Thanks, Thomas,' he said. 'But what's done is done. For Sarah and me, this is old stuff, and we dealt with it a long time ago. Right now, you want to know why I asked you to kill me?'

A woman at the next table turned and looked at Woolf, frowning. He can't have said that. Can he? She shook her head and went back to her lobster.

'In a nutshell,' I said.

'Well it's very simple,' he said. 'I wanted to know what kind of person you were.'

He looked at me, his mouth closed in a nice, straight line.

'I see,' I said, not seeing anything at all. This is what happens, I suppose, when you ask for things in a nutshell. I blinked a few times, then sat back in my chair and tried to look cross.

'Anything wrong with ringing my headmaster?' I said. 'Or an ex-girlfriend? I mean, that all seemed too dull, I suppose?'

Woolf shook his head.

'Not at all,' he said. 'I did all of that.'

That was a shock. A real shock. I still get hot flushes about having cheated in Chemistry O-Level and scoring an A when experienced teachers had anticipated an F. I know one day it's going to come out. I just know it.

'Really,' I said. 'How did I do?'

Woolf smiled.

'You did okay,' he said. 'A couple of your girlfriends reckon you're a pain in the ass, but otherwise you did okay.'

'Nice to know,' I said.

Woolf continued, as though reading from a list. 'You're smart. You're tough. You're honest. Good career in the Scotch Guards.'

'Scots,' I said, but he ignored me, and went on.

'And best of all, from my point of view, you're broke.'

He smiled again, which irritated me.

'You missed out my watercolour work,' I said.

'That too? Hell of a guy. The one thing I needed to know was whether you could be bought.'

'Right,' I said. 'Hence the fifty thousand.'

Woolf nodded.

This was starting to get out of hand. I knew that at some point I ought to have been making some kind of hard man speech about who I was, and who the hell did they think they were, prodding around in who I was, and just as soon as I'd had the pudding I was going right back to who I was – but somehow the right moment never seemed to come along. In spite of the way he'd treated me, and for all his nosing around in my school reports, I still couldn't bring myself to dislike Woolf. He just had something I liked. And as for Sarah, well, yes. Nice tendons.

Even so, a glint of the old steel wouldn't do any harm.

'Let me guess,' I said, giving Woolf a hard look. 'Once you've found out that I can't be bought, you're going to try and buy me.'

He didn't even falter.

'Exactly,' he said.

There. That was it, and this was the right moment. A gentleman has his limits, and so do I. I tossed my napkin on to the table.

'Well this is fascinating,' I said, 'and I suppose if I was a different sort of person I might even think it was flattering. But right now I really have to know what this is all about. Because if you don't tell me, now, I'm leaving the table, your lives, and possibly even this country.'

I could see that Sarah was watching me, but I kept my eyes fixed on Woolf. He chased the last potato round his plate and ran it down in a pool of gravy. But then he put down his fork and started to speak very quickly.

'You know about the Gulf War, Mr Lang?' he said. I don't know what happened to Thomas, but the mood certainly seemed to have changed somewhat.

'Yes, Mr Woolf,' I said, 'I know about the Gulf War.'

'No, you don't. I'll bet everything I have that you don't know the first damn thing about the Gulf War. Familiar with the term military-industrial complex?'

He was talking like a salesman, trying to bulldoze me somehow, and I wanted to slow things down. I took a long sip of wine.

'Dwight Eisenhower,' I said eventually. 'Yes, I'm familiar. I was part of it, if you remember.'

'With respect, Mr Lang, you were a very small part of it. Too small – forgive me for saying it – too small to know what you were a part of.'

'As you like,' I said.

'Now take a guess at the single most important commodity in the world. So important, that the manufacture and sale of every other commodity depends on it. Oil, gold, food, what would you say?'

'I've a feeling,' I said, 'that you're going to tell me it's arms.'

Woolf leaned across the table, too quickly and too far for my liking.

'Correct, Mr Lang,' he said. 'It is the biggest industry in the world, and every government in the world knows it. If you're a politician, and you take on the arms industry, in whatever form, then you wake up the next day and you're no longer a politician. Some cases, you might not even wake up the next day. Doesn't matter whether you're trying for a law on a gun ownership registration in the state of Idaho, or trying to stop the sale of F-16s to the Iraqi Air Force. You step on their toes, they step on your head. Period.'

Woolf sat back in his chair and wiped some sweat from his forehead.

'Mr Woolf,' I said, 'I realise it must be strange for you, being here in England. I realise that we must strike you as a nation of hicks, who only got hot and cold running water the day before you flew in, but even so, I have to tell you that I've heard a lot of this before.'

'Just listen, will you?' said Sarah, and I jumped slightly at the anger in her voice. When I looked at her, she just stared back at me, her lips pressed tightly together.

'Did you ever hear of the Stoltoi Bluff?' said Woolf.

I turned back to him.

'The Stoltoi . . . no, I don't believe so.'

'Doesn't matter,' he said. 'Anatoly Stoltoi was a Red Army General. Chief-of-Staff under Khrushchev. Spent his whole career convincing the US that the Russians had thirty times as many rockets as they had. That was his job. His life's work.'

'Well it worked, didn't it?'

'For us, yeah.'

'Us being . . . ?'

'Pentagon knew it was bullshit from start to finish. Knew it. But that didn't stop them using it to justify the biggest arms build-up the world has ever seen.'

Maybe it was the wine, but I felt I was being awfully slow to get the point of all this.

'Right,' I said. 'Well let's do something about it, shall we? Now, where did I leave my time-machine? Oh I know, next Wednesday.'

Sarah made a slight hissing noise and looked away from the table, and maybe she was right – maybe I was being flippant – but for God's sake, where were we going with all this?

Woolf closed his eyes for a moment, gathering some patience from somewhere.

'What would you say,' he said slowly, 'the arms industry needs more than anything else?'

I scratched my head dutifully.

'Customers?'

'War,' said Woolf. 'Conflict. Trouble.'

Well, here we go, I thought. Here comes the theory.

'I've got it,' I said. 'You're trying to tell me that the Gulf War was started by arms manufacturers?' Honestly, I was being as polite as I could.

Woolf didn't answer. He just sat there, with his head slightly tilted to one side, watching me and wondering if he'd got the wrong man after all. I didn't even have to wonder.

'No, seriously,' I said. 'Is that what you're telling me? I mean, I really want to know what you think. I want to know what this is all about.'

'You saw the footage they showed on TV?' said Sarah, while Woolf just kept on watching. 'Smart bombs, Patriot missile systems, all that stuff?'

'I saw it,' I said.

'The makers of those weapons, Thomas, are using that footage in promotional videos at arms fairs around the world. People dying, and they're using the stuff for commercials.

It's obscene.'

'Right,' I said. 'Agreed. The world is a pretty terrible place, and we'd all much rather live on Saturn. How does this affect me, specifically?'

As the Woolfs traded some meaningful looks, I tried desperately to conceal the enormous pity I now felt for the pair of them. Obviously, they had embarked on some ghastly conspiracy theory which would, in all probability, consume the best years of their lives with the cutting-out of articles from newspapers, and the attending of seminars on the subject of grassy knolls, and nothing I could say would divert them from their chosen course. The best thing would be to slip them a couple of quid towards their sellotape costs and be on my way.

I was thinking hard, trying to phrase a decent excuse for leaving, when I realised that Woolf had been tugging at his briefcase – and now he had it open and was pulling out a handful of ten-by-eight glossy photographs.

He passed the top one to me, so I took it.

It was a picture of a helicopter in flight. I couldn't judge its size, but it was nothing like any type I had seen or heard of. It had two main rotors, running a couple of feet apart off a single mast, and there was no tail rotor. The fuselage looked short compared to the main body, and there were no identifying letters anywhere. It was painted black.

I looked at Woolf for an explanation, but he simply handed me the next photograph. This one had been taken from above, so it showed a background, and what surprised me was that it was urban. The same aircraft, or one like it, was hovering between a pair of faceless tower blocks, and I could see that the machine was definitely small, possibly a single-seater.

The third photograph was a much closer shot, and showed the helicopter on the ground. Whatever else it was, it was definitely military, because there was a mess of very nasty-looking kit hanging from the armaments rack that ran through the fuselage behind the cabin. Hydra 70mm rockets, Hellfire air-to-ground missiles, .50 calibre machine guns, and heaps more besides. This was a big toy, for big boys.

'Where did you get these?' I said.

Woolf shook his head.

'That's not important.'

'Well, I think it is important,' I said. 'I have the very strong feeling, Mr Woolf, that you ought not to have these photographs.'

Woolf tilted his head back, as if he was finally starting to lose patience with me.

'It doesn't matter where they came from,' he said. 'What matters is the subject. This is a very important aircraft, Mr Lang. Believe me. Very, very important.'

I believed him. Why wouldn't I?

'The Pentagon's LH programme,' said Woolf, 'has been running for twelve years now, trying to find a replacement for the Cobras and Super-Cobras the USAAF and the Marine Corps have been using since the Vietnam War.'

'LH?' I said, tentatively.

'Light helicopter,' Sarah answered, with an 'imagine not knowing that' expression. Woolf senior pressed on.

'This aircraft is a response to that programme. It's a product of the Mackie Corporation of America, and is designed for use in counter-insurgency operations. Terrorism. The market for it, outside of the Pentagon's procurement, is among police and militia forces around the world. But at two-and-a-half million dollars each, they're going to be hard to shift.'

'Yes,' I said. 'I can see that.' I glanced at the pictures again and scrabbled for something intelligent to say. 'Why the two rotors? Looks a bit complicated.' I caught them looking at each other, but couldn't tell you what the look meant.

'You don't know anything about helicopters, do you?' said Woolf, eventually.

I shrugged.

'They're noisy,' I said. 'They crash a lot. That's about it.'

'They're slow,' said Sarah. 'Slow, and therefore vulnerable on a battlefield. The modern attack helicopter can travel at around two-hundred-and-fifty miles an hour.'

I was about to say that that sounded pretty slippy to me, when she continued: 'A modern fighter airplane will cover a mile in four seconds.'

Without summoning a waiter and asking for a pencil and paper, there was not the remotest chance of my working out whether this was faster or slower than two hundred and fifty miles an hour, so I just nodded and let her carry on.

'What limits the speed of a conventional helicopter,' she said slowly, sensing my discomfort, 'is the single rotor.'

'Naturally,' I said, and settled back in my seat for Sarah's impressively expert lecture. A lot of what she had to say passed comfortably over my head, but the gist of it, if I've got it right, seemed to be as follows:

The cross-section of a helicopter blade, according to Sarah, is more or less the same as the wing of an aeroplane. Its shape creates a pressure differential in the air passing over its upper and lower surfaces, producing a consequent lift. It differs from an aeroplane wing, however, in that when a helicopter moves forward, air starts passing over the blade that's coming forward faster than it passes over the blade that's going backwards. This produces unequal lift on the two sides of the helicopter, and the faster it goes, the more unequal the lift becomes. Eventually the 'retreating' blade stops producing any lift at all, and the helicopter flips on to its back and drops out of the sky. This, according to Sarah, was a negative aspect.

'What the Mackie people did was put two rotors on a coaxial shaft, spinning in opposite directions. Equal lift on both sides, possibility of nearly twice the speed. Also, no torque reaction, so no need for a tail rotor. Smaller, faster, more manoeuvrable. It's likely this machine will be capable of over four hundred miles an hour.'

I nodded slowly, trying to show that I was impressed, but not *that* impressed.

89

'Well, fine,' I said. 'But the Javelin surface-to-air missile will do damn near a thousand miles an hour.' Sarah stared back at me. How dare I challenge her on this technical stuff? 'What I mean is,' I said, 'things haven't changed that much. It's still a helicopter, and it can still be shot down. It's not invincible.'

Sarah closed her eyes for a second, wondering how to phrase this so that an idiot could understand.

'If the SAM operator is good,' she said, 'and he's trained, and he's ready, then he has a chance. One chance only. But the point of this machine is that the target will have no time to prepare. It'll be down his throat while he's still rubbing the sleep out of his eyes.' She stared at me hard. Now have you got it? 'Believe me, Mr Lang,' she continued, punishing me for my insolence, 'this is the next generation of military helicopter.' She nodded towards the photographs.

'Right,' I said. 'Okay. Well then, they must be jolly pleased.'

'They are, Thomas,' said Woolf. 'They are very, very pleased with this machine. Right now, the guys at Mackie have only one problem.'

Somebody obviously had to say 'which is?'

'Which is?' I said.

'Nobody at the Pentagon believes it will work.'

I pondered for a while.

'Well can't they ask for a test ride? Take it round the block a few times?'

Woolf took a deep breath, and I sensed that, at long last, we were approaching the main business of the evening.

'What will sell this machine,' he said slowly, 'to the Pentagon, and to fifty other air forces around the world, is the sight of it in action against a major terrorist operation.'

'Right,' I said. 'You mean they've got to wait for a Munich Olympics to come along?'

Woolf took his time, drawing out the punchline for all it was worth.

'No, I don't mean that, Mr Lang,' he said. 'I mean they're

going to *make* a Munich Olympics come along.'

'Why are you telling me all this?'

We were on to the coffee now, and the photographs were back in their folder.

'I mean, if you're right,' I said, 'and personally I'm stuck in the middle of that "if" with a flat tyre and no spare – but if you're right, what do you plan to do about it? Write to the Washington *Post*? Esther Rantzen? What?'

Both the Woolfs had gone very quiet, and I wasn't absolutely sure why. Perhaps they'd thought that just laying out the theory was going to be enough – that as soon as I heard it, I'd be up on my feet, sharpening the butter dish and shouting death to arms manufacturers – but for me it wasn't anything like enough. How could it be?

'Do you think of yourself as a good man, Thomas?'

This was from Woolf, but he still wasn't looking at me.

'No, I don't,' I said.

Sarah looked up.

'Then what?'

'I think of myself as a tall man,' I said. 'As a poor man. A man with a full stomach. A man with a motorcycle.' I paused, and felt her eyes on me. 'I don't know what you mean by "good".'

'I guess we mean on the side of the angels,' said Woolf.

'There are no angels,' I said quickly. 'I'm sorry, but there aren't.'

There was a lull, while Woolf nodded his head slowly as if conceding that, yes, that was a point of view, it just happened to be a massively disappointing one, and then Sarah sighed and got to her feet.

'Excuse me,' she said.

Woolf and I scrabbled at our chairs, but Sarah was half-way across the restaurant floor before we'd managed to get any meaningful standing-up done. She drifted over to a waiter, whispered something to him, then nodded at his reply and headed towards an archway at the back of the room.

'Thomas,' said Woolf. 'Let me put it this way. Some bad people are getting ready to do some bad things. We have a chance of stopping them. Are you going to help us?' He paused. And kept on pausing.

'Look, the question still stands,' I said. 'What are you planning to do? Just tell me. What's wrong with the press? Or the police? Or the CIA? I mean come on, we'll get a phone book and some coins and sort this out.'

Woolf shook his head in irritation, and rapped his knuckles on the table.

'You haven't been listening to me, Thomas,' he said. 'I'm talking about interests here. The biggest interests in the world. Capital. You don't take on capital with a telephone and a couple of polite letters to your Congressman.'

I stood up, swaying slightly from the effect of the wine. Or the talk.

'You leaving?' said Woolf, without lifting his head.

'Maybe,' I said. 'Maybe.' I didn't really know what I was going to do. 'But I'm going to the lavatory first.' And that's certainly what I meant to do at that moment, because I was confused, and because I find porcelain helps me think.

I walked slowly across the restaurant towards the archway, my brain rattling with all kinds of badly-stowed personal items which may fall out and injure a fellow passenger – and what was I doing even thinking about take-off, and runways, and the beginnings of long journeys? I had to get out of this, and get out quickly. Just handling those photographs had been stupid enough.

I turned into the archway, and saw that Sarah was standing in an alcove by a pay phone. She had her back to me, and her head was tipped forward, until it was almost resting against the wall. I stood there for a moment, watching her neck, and her hair, and her shoulders, and yes, all right, I believe I may have glanced at her bottom.

'Hi,' I said, stupidly.

She spun round, and for the tiniest instant I thought I saw real fear in her face – of what, I hadn't the slightest idea – and then she smiled and replaced the receiver.

'So,' she said, taking a pace towards me. 'You on the team?'

We looked at each other for a while, and then I smiled back, and shrugged, and started to say the word 'well', which is what I always do when I'm stuck for words. And you'll find, if you try this at home, that to form the 'w' sound, you have to pucker your lips into a kind of pout – very similar in shape to the one you'd use for whistling, say. Or, perhaps, even kissing.

She kissed me.

She kissed *me*.

What I mean is, I was standing there, lips puckered, brain puckered, and she just stepped up and threw her tongue into my mouth. For a moment, I thought maybe she'd tripped on a floorboard and stuck out her tongue as a reflex – but that didn't seem very likely somehow, and anyway, once she'd got her balance back, wouldn't she have put her tongue away again?

No, she was definitely kissing me. Just like in the movies. Just like not in my life. For a couple of seconds I was too surprised, and too out of practice, to know what to do about it, because it had been a very long time since something like this had happened to me. In fact, if I remember correctly, I was an olive-picker in the reign of Rameses III when it did, and I'm not sure how I dealt with it then.

She tasted of toothpaste, and wine, and perfume, and heaven on a nice day.

'You on the team?' she said again, and I realised from the clarity of her words that at some point she must have taken her tongue back, although I could still feel it, in my mouth, on my lips, and I knew that I'd always be able to feel it. I opened my eyes.

She was standing there, looking up at me, and yes, it was definitely her. It wasn't a waiter, or a hatstand.

'Well,' I said.

*

We were back at the table, and Woolf was signing his name on a credit card slip, and perhaps some other things were happening in the world too, but I'm not sure.

'Thanks for the supper,' I said, like a robot.

Woolf waved his hand at me and grinned.

'My pleasure, Tom,' he said.

He was pleased I'd said yes. Yes as in yes, I'd think about it.

Precisely *what* I was to think about, nobody seemed able to say exactly, but it was enough to satisfy Woolf, and for the time being we all had our reasons for feeling good. I picked up the folder and started leafing through the photographs again, one by one.

Small, fast, and violent.

Sarah was pleased too, I think, although she was now behaving as if nothing much had happened besides a decent meal and a bit of a chat about the new times.

Violent, fast and small.

Perhaps, underneath all that composure, there was a seething maelstrom of emotion, and she was only keeping a lid on it because her father was sitting there.

Small, fast, and violent.

I stopped thinking about Sarah.

As each image of this nasty-looking device passed before my eyes, I seemed to feel myself gradually waking up from something, or somewhere. To something or somewhere else. It sounds fanciful, I know, but the starkness of this machine – its ugliness, its stripped-down efficiency, its sheer pitilessness – seemed to seep from the paper into my hands, cooling my blood. Perhaps Woolf sensed what I was feeling.

'It has no official name,' he said, gesturing towards the pictures. 'But it's temporarily designated as an Urban Control and Law-enforcement Aircraft.'

'UCLA,' I said, pointlessly.

'You spell too?' said Sarah, with a kind of almost smile.

'Hence the working name given to this prototype,' said Woolf.

'Which is?'

Neither of them answered, so I looked up, and saw that Woolf was waiting until I met his gaze.

'The Graduate,' he said.

Seven

*One hair of a woman can draw more
than a hundred pair of oxen.*

JAMES HOWELL

I swung the Kawasaki along Victoria Embankment just for
the hell of it. To clear its pipes and mine.

I hadn't told the Woolfs about the phonecall to my flat and
the nasty American voice at the other end. 'Graduate studies'
could have meant anything – graduate studies, even – and the
caller could have been anybody. When you're dealing with
conspiracy theorists – and kiss or no kiss, that's definitely
what I *was* dealing with – there's no point in feeding them
extra coincidences to get excited about.

We'd left the restaurant in an amiable state of truce. Out
on the pavement, Woolf had squeezed my arm and told me to
sleep on it, which gave me a nasty jolt because I'd been
watching Sarah's bottom as he spoke. But as soon as I realised
what he meant I promised I would indeed, and out of
politeness asked where I could get hold of him if I needed to.
He'd winked and said he'd find me, which I didn't much care
for.

There was, of course, one extremely good reason for me to

stay on the right side of Woolf. He may have been a flake and a crank, and his daughter may have been nothing more than a very attractive back-to-front jacket case, but I couldn't deny that the two of them had a certain charm.

What I'm trying to say, is that they'd gone and put quite a large amount of that charm into my bank account.

Please don't misunderstand me. I don't care greatly for money, as a rule. I mean, I'm not one of these people who works for free, or anything like that. I charge for my services, such as they are, and I get cross when I think I'm owed by somebody. But at the same time, I think I can honestly say that I've never really chased money. Never done anything that I didn't enjoy, at least a little, just for the sake of having more of the stuff. Someone like Paulie, for example – and he's told me this himself, many times – spends most of his waking hours either getting hold of money, or thinking about getting hold of it. Paulie could do unpleasant things – immoral things, even – and if there was a plumpness about the cheque at the end of it, he wouldn't mind a bit. Bring it on, Paulie would say.

But me, I'm just not made that way. Different mould altogether. The only good thing I've ever noticed about money, the only positive aspect of an otherwise pretty vulgar commodity, is that you can use it to buy things.

And things, on the whole, I do quite like.

Woolf's fifty thousand dollars was never going to be the key to everlasting happiness, I knew that. I couldn't buy a villa in Antibes with it, or even rent one for more than about a day and a half. But it was handy, nonetheless. Comforting. It put cigarettes on my table.

And if, in order to keep hold of some of that comfort, I had to spend a couple more evenings in the chapters of a Robert Ludlum novel, getting periodically kissed by a beautiful woman, well, I could just about bear that.

It was after midnight and there wasn't much traffic on the Embankment. The road was dry and the ZZR needed a gallop, so I eased open the throttle in third gear and replayed some lines of Captain Kirk to Mr Chekhov in my head as the universe rearranged itself round my back wheel. I was probably brushing the cheek of a hundred and ten as Westminster Bridge came into view, and I dabbed the brakes and shifted my weight slightly, ready to crank the bike over for the right turn. The lights into Parliament Square were turning green and a dark-blue Ford was starting to move off, so I dumped another wedge of speed and prepared to ease round it on the outside of the bend. As I came level, my right knee getting down towards the tarmac, the Ford started drifting to the left, and I straightened up to take a wider line.

At that point, I thought he simply hadn't seen me. I thought he was an average car driver.

Time is a funny thing.

I once met an RAF pilot who told me how he and his navigator had had to eject from their very expensive Tornado GR1, three hundred feet above the Yorkshire dales, because of what he called a 'bird strike'. (This, rather unfairly in my view, made it sound as if it was the bird's fault; as if the little feathered chap had deliberately tried to head-butt twenty tons of metal travelling in the opposite direction at just under the speed of sound, out of spite.)

Anyway, the point of the story is that, after the accident, the pilot and navigator had sat in a de-briefing room and talked to investigators, uninterrupted, for an hour and fifteen minutes about what they'd seen, heard, felt and done, at the moment of contact.

An hour and fifteen minutes.

And yet the black box flight-recorder, when it was eventually pulled from the wreckage, showed that the time elapsed between the bird entering the engine intake and the crew ejecting, was a fraction under four seconds.

Four seconds. That's bang, one, two, three, fresh air.

I didn't really believe this story when I heard it. Apart from anything else, the pilot was a wiry little runt, with those creepily blue eyes that physically talented people often have.

And besides, I couldn't stop myself from siding with the bird in the story.

But I do believe it now.

I believe it because the driver of the Ford never took the right turn. And I lived several lives, not all of them pleasant and fulfilling, while he ran me off the road and into the railings along the side of the House of Commons. When I braked, he braked. When I accelerated, he accelerated. When I leaned the bike over to take the turn, he kept on going, straight for the railings, nudging me in the shoulder with the glass of his passenger window.

Yes, I could definitely talk for an hour about those railings. And a good deal longer about the moment I realised that the driver of the Ford was not an average driver at all. He was actually very good indeed.

It wasn't a Rover, which meant something. He must have had a radio set to get him into position, because nobody had passed me on the Embankment. The passenger was looking at me as I came alongside, and plainly not saying 'mind that motorcyclist' as the car drifted towards me. They had two rear-view mirrors, which has never been standard equipment on any Ford. And my testicles hurt. That's what woke me up.

You've probably noticed on your travels that motorcyclists don't wear seat-belts, which is both good and bad. Good because nobody wants to be tied to five hundred pounds of very hot metal when they're sliding down the road. Bad because when the brakes are applied severely, the bike stops and the rider doesn't. He carries on in a northerly direction until his genitals interface with the petrol tank and tears come to his eyes, preventing him from seeing the very thing he's braking to try to avoid.

The railings.

Those sturdy, no-nonsense, finely turned railings. Railings worthy of the task of encircling the mother of parliaments. Railings that, in the spring of 1940, they'd have been tearing down to make Spitfires and Hurricanes and Wellingtons and

Lancasters, and what was the other one with the split tail-plane? Was it a Blenheim?

Except of course the railings weren't there in 1940. They'd been put up in 1987 to stop mad Libyans from interrupting Parliamentary business with a quarter of a ton of high explosive wedged into the back of a family Peugeot.

These railings, my railings, were there to do a job. They were there to defend democracy. They were hand-built by craftsmen called Ted or Ned, or possibly Bill.

They were railings fit for heroes.

I slept.

A face. A very big face. A very big face with only enough skin to cover a very small face, so that everything about it looked tight. Tight jaw, tight nose, tight eyes. Every muscle and tendon on the face bulged and rippled. It looked like a crowded lift. I blinked, and the face was gone.

Or maybe I slept for an hour and the face stayed for fifty-nine minutes. I'll never know. Instead of the face there was only a ceiling. Which meant a room. Which meant I'd been moved. I started thinking about the Middlesex Hospital, but I knew straight away that this was a very different fish-kettle.

I tried flexing bits of my body. Gently, not daring to move my head in case my neck was broken. The feet seemed okay, if a little far away. As long as they weren't further than six feet and three inches I wasn't going to complain. The left knee answered my letter by return of post, which was nice, but the right felt wrong. Thick and hot. Come back to that. Thighs. Left okay, right not so good. Pelvic girdle seemed all right, but I wouldn't know for sure until I put some weight on it. Testicles. Ah, there was another matter entirely. I didn't have to put weight on those to know they were in a poor state. There were too many of them and they hurt too much. Abdomen and chest got a B-minus, and my right arm failed altogether. Just wouldn't move. Neither would the left, although I could just about move the hand, which is how I knew I wasn't in the William Hoyle Ward. Things can be rough and ready in NHS hospitals these days, but even so they tend not to tie your hands to the bed without a good reason. I left the neck and head for another day, and fell into as deep a sleep as I could manage with seven testicles.

The face was back, tighter than ever. This time he was chewing something, and the muscles in his cheeks and neck were standing out like a diagram from *Gray's Anatomy*. There were crumbs around his lips and every now and then a very pink tongue shot out and carried one off to the cave of his mouth.

'Lang?' The tongue was working round the inside of his mouth now, running over his gums and puckering his lips so that for a moment I thought he was going to kiss me. I let him wait.

'Where am I?' I was pleased to hear that there was a thoroughly ill-sounding croak to my voice.

'Yeah,' said the face. If it had enough skin, I think it might have smiled. Instead, it moved away from whatever I was lying on, and I heard a door open. But it didn't shut.

'He's up,' said the same voice, quite loud, and the door still didn't shut. Which meant that whoever controlled the room controlled the corridor too. If it was a corridor. For all I knew, it could have been the gantry to a space shuttle. Or from it. Maybe I was in a shuttle, about to leave the world very far behind.

Footsteps. Two pairs. One rubber, one leather. Hard floor. Leather steps are slower. Leather's in charge. Rubber's a flunky, holding the door, making way for leather. Rubber's the face. Rubber Face. Easy to remember.

'Mr Lang?' Leather had stopped by the bed. If it was a bed. I kept my eyes closed, a little frown of pain on my face.

'How're you feeling?' American. A lot of Americans in my life at the moment. Must be the exchange rate.

He started to move round the bed, and I could hear the crunch of dust under his shoes. And the aftershave. Much too strong. If we became friends, I'd tell him. But not now.

101

'I always wanted a bike when I was a kid,' said the voice. 'A Harley. My dad said they were dangerous. So when I learnt to drive I crashed the car four times in the first year just to get back at him. He was an asshole, my dad.'

Time passed. Which I couldn't do anything about.

'I think my neck is broken,' I said. I kept my eyes closed and the croak was coming along nicely.

'Yeah? Sorry to hear that. Now tell me about yourself, Lang. Who are you? What do you do? You like movies? Books? Ever had tea with the Queen? Talk to me.'

I waited until the shoes turned, and slowly opened my eyes. He was out of vision, so I fixed on the ceiling.

'Are you a doctor?'

'I'm not a doctor, Lang, no,' he said. 'I'm surely not a doctor. A son-of-a-bitch is what I am.' There was a snigger somewhere in the room, and I guessed that Rubber Face was still by the door.

'I beg your pardon?'

'A son-of-a-bitch. That's what I am. That's my job, that's my life. But hey, let's talk about you.'

'I need a doctor,' I said. 'My neck . . . ' Tears started in my eyes, and I let them come. I sniffed a bit, choked a bit, put on a cracking good show, if I say so myself.

'If you want to know the truth,' said the voice, 'I don't give any kind of shit about your neck.'

I decided I was never going to tell him about his aftershave. Not ever.

'I want to know other things,' said the voice. 'Lots and lots of other things.'

The tears kept coming.

'Look, I don't know who you are, or where I am . . . ' I faltered, straining to get my head off the pillow.

'Fuck away, Richie,' said the voice. 'Get some air.'

There was a grunt from over by the door, and two shoes left the room. I had to assume that Richie was in them.

'See, that's kind of the idea, Lang. You don't have to know who I am, and you don't have to know where you are. The

102

idea is that you tell me things, I don't tell you.'

'But what . . . '

'Did you hear what I said?' There was suddenly another face in front of mine. Smooth, scrubbed skin, and hair like Paulie's. Fluffily clean, and combed to ridiculous perfection. He was about forty, and probably spent two hours a day on an exercise bike. There was only one word for him. Groomed. He examined me closely, and from the way his gaze hung over my chin I guessed that I had a reasonably spectacular injury there, which cheered me up a bit. Scars are always handy for breaking the ice.

Finally his eyes met mine, and the four of them didn't get on at all. 'Good,' he said, and moved away.

It had to be early in the morning. The only excuse for that strength of perfume was that he'd only just shaved.

'You met Woolf,' said Groomed. 'And his air-head daughter.'

'Yes.'

There was a pause and I could tell that I'd pleased him, because the smile changed the sound of his breathing. If I'd denied it, wrong number, no speakee Engleesh, he'd have known I was a player. If I came clean, he might take me for an idiot. All the evidence pointed that way, after all.

'Good. Now. Mind telling me what you talked about?'

'Well,' I said, frowning in concentration, 'he asked me about my army record. I was in the army, by the way.'

'No shit. He knew that, or you tell him?'

Another big think from the idiot.

'I'm not sure. Now that you mention it, I think he must have known it already.'

'Girl knew it too?'

'Well, I can't be sure of that, can I? I didn't pay much attention to her.' Good thing I wasn't wired to a machine for that one. The needle would have gone into the next room for a lie-down. 'He asked about my plans, what sort of work I was up to. Which isn't much, to be honest.'

'You in intelligence?'

'What?'

The way I said it was supposed to answer his question, but he kept going.

'In the army. You fought terrorists in Ireland. Were you involved with intelligence.'

'Good God, no.' I smiled, as if I was flattered by the idea.

'What's funny?'

I stopped smiling.

'Nothing, it's just . . . you know.'

'No, I don't. That's got a lot to do with why I'm asking. Were you in military intelligence?'

I took a painful breath before answering.

'Ulster was a system,' I said. 'That's all. Everything that happened there had happened a hundred times already. System was everything. People like me just, you know, make up the numbers. I slogged around. Played some squash. Had a few laughs. Good fun, really.' I thought I might have overdone it with that, but he didn't seem to mind. 'Look, my neck . . . I don't know, there's something wrong. I really need to see a doctor.'

'He's a bad guy, Tom.'

'Who is?' I said.

'Woolf. Real bad. I don't know what he's told you about himself. I'm kind of guessing that he didn't tell you about the thirty-six tons of cocaine he's brought into Europe in the last four months. He tell you that?' I tried to shake my head. 'Nah, I figured he'd forget to mention that. But that's bad with a capital B, wouldn't you say, Tom? I'd say it was. The Devil's alive on earth, and he's selling crack cocaine. Yeah. Sounds like a song. What rhymes with cocaine?'

'Pain,' I said.

'Yeah,' said Groomed. He enjoyed that. 'Pain.' The leather shoes went for a stroll. 'Ever noticed how bad guys mix with bad guys, Tom? I've noticed that. Happens all the time. I don't know, they like to feel at home, shared interests, same star sign, whatever. See it a thousand times. A thousand times.' The shoes stopped. 'So when a guy like you starts holding hands with a guy like Woolf, I got to say that makes me not like you very much.'

'Look, that's it,' I said, petulantly. 'I'm not going to say one more word to you until I've seen a doctor. I haven't the faintest idea what you're talking about. I know as much about Woolf as I know about you, which is nothing, and I think there's every chance that my neck is broken.' No answer. 'I demand to see a doctor,' I repeated, trying to sound as much like a British tourist in a French customs shed as I could.

'No, Tom. I don't think we want to waste a doctor's time.' His voice was even, but I could tell that he was excited. The leather crunched, and the door opened. 'Stay with him. Every minute. You have to use the bathroom, you call me.'

'Wait a minute,' I said. 'What do you mean waste time? I'm injured. I'm in pain, for Christ's sake.'

The shoes turned towards me.

'That may be, Tom. That may very well be. But who the hell washes up paper plates?'

There weren't many good things to be said or felt about my situation. Not many at all. But the rule is that after any engagement, won or lost, you replay it in your mind to see how much you can learn. So that's what I did, while Richie slumped against the wall by the door.

First, Groomed knew a lot and he'd known it quickly. So he had manpower, or good communications, or both. Second, he didn't say 'you call Igor or one of the other boys'. He said 'you call me'. Which probably meant there was only Groomed and Richie in the space shuttle.

Third, and at that moment the most important, I was the only one who knew for certain that my neck wasn't broken.

Eight

For a soldier I listed, to grow great in fame,
And be shot at for sixpence a day.

CHARLES DIBDIN

Some time passed. It might have been a lot of time, and probably was, but after the bike crash I'd started being a bit suspicious about time and how it behaved. Patted my pockets after every meeting, that kind of thing.

There was no way of measuring anything in this room. The light was artificial, on constantly. And the noise-level didn't do anything at all. Hearing some milk-bottles rattling in a crate, or somebody yelling 'Evening Standard, five o'clock edition only just arrived' would have helped a bit. But you can't have everything.

The only chronometering device I had about my person was my bladder, which told me that roughly four hours had elapsed since the restaurant. Which didn't tally with the aftershave reckoning from Groomed. But then again, these cheap modern bladders can be hellishly unreliable.

Richie had left the room only once, to fetch a chair. While he was gone I tried to break free, knot the sheet together, and abseil to the ground, but only made it as far as scratching my thigh before he came back. Once he'd got himself comfortable he didn't make another sound, which made me think that he'd probably brought something to read as well. But there was no noise of any pages turning, so he was either a very slow reader or just happy to sit and stare at the wall. Or me.

'I need to go to the lavatory,' I croaked.

No answer.

'I said I need . . . '

'Shut the fuck up.'

This was good. This made me feel much better about what I was going to have to do to Richie.

'Look, you have to . . . '

'You hear what I said? Shut the fuck up. You gotta piss, piss where you are.'

'Richie . . . '

'Who the fuck told you to call me Richie?'

'What should I call you?' I closed my eyes.

'Don't call me anything. Don't call. Stay there and piss. Understand?'

'I don't want to piss.'

I could almost hear his brain grinding away.

'What?'

'I need to crap, Richie. Old British tradition. Now if you want to sit in the same room while I crap, that's up to you. I just thought it would be fair to warn you.'

Richie thought about this for a while, and I was sure I could hear his nose wrinkling. The chair scraped, and the rubber shoes made their way towards me.

'You don't go to the toilet, and you don't crap yourself.' The face came into view, tight as ever. 'Hear me? You stay where you are, you shut the fuck up . . . '

'You haven't got children, have you, Richie?'

He frowned, which looked like a gigantic effort on his face. Eyebrows, muscles, tendons, everything called into action for this single, faintly stupid, expression.

'What?'

'I don't actually have any myself, to tell the truth, but I have god-children. And you can't just tell them not to. It doesn't work.'

The frown deepened.

'The fuck are you talking about?'

'I mean, I've tried it. You've got children in the car, and one of them wants to crap, and you tell them to hold on, put a cork in it, wait until we reach somewhere, but it doesn't work. When the body has to crap, it has to crap.'

The frown eased slightly, which was nice, because I was starting to feel tired just looking at it. He bent down towards me, bringing his nose in line with mine.

'Listen to me, you piece of shit . . . '

That was as far as he got, because on the word 'shit' I brought my right knee up as hard as I could and caught him on the cheek. He froze for a second, part surprise, part concussion, and I lifted my left leg and hooked it round the back of his neck. As I dragged him down on to the bed, he managed to get his left hand out in front of him to try and keep himself up. But he had no idea how strong legs are. Legs are very strong indeed.

Much stronger than throats.

He lasted pretty well, I have to admit. He tried the usual stuff, grabbing at my groin, thrashing his foot towards my face, but to do that kind of thing effectively you need air, and I just wasn't in the mood to let him have it in any useful quantities. His resistance curved upwards through angry, to wild, to terrified, peaked and then drifted all the way down to unconscious. I held him for a good five minutes after his last kick, because if I'd been him I would have tried playing dead as soon as I realised the game was up.

But Richie definitely wasn't playing dead.

My hands had been tied with straps, which took a while. The only tools available were my teeth, and by the time I'd finished I felt like I'd eaten a couple of Portakabins. I also got

108

some solid confirmation of the injury to my chin, because the first time it brushed against a buckle, I thought I was going to go through the ceiling. Instead, I looked down and saw a mess of blood on the leather strap, some dark and old, some red and very new.

When it was over I fell back, panting with the effort, and tried rubbing some life back into my wrists. Then I sat up again and gently swung my feet over the edge of the bed and on to the floor.

It was the sheer variety of the pain that stopped me from crying out. It came from so many places, spoke so many languages, wore so many dazzling varieties of ethnic costume, that for a full fifteen seconds I could only hang my jaw in amazement. I gripped the side of the bed and screwed my eyes shut until the roar had eased to a babble, then took another inventory. Whatever I'd hit first, I'd hit with my right side. The knee, thigh and hip were screaming at me, and their screams were all the keener for the recent contact with Richie's head. My ribs felt as though they'd been taken out and put back in the wrong order, and my neck, though definitely not broken, was hardly movable. And then there were the testicles.

They'd changed. I simply couldn't believe that they were the same testicles I'd carried around with me all my life, and yes, treated as my friends. They were bigger, much bigger, and completely the wrong shape.

There was only one thing for it.

There is a technique, known to practitioners of the martial arts, for relieving scrotal discomfort. It is often used in Japanese *dojos*, whenever your training-partner has got a little over-eager and actually landed one in the genital neighbourhood.

What you do is this: jump six inches in the air, and land on your heels with your legs as stiff as you can make them, to increase, just for an instant, the gravitational pull on the scrotum. I don't know why it should work, but it does. Or rather it doesn't. So I had to try it a few times, pogoing around the room as hard as my right leg would let me, until gradually, infinitesimally, the howling pain began to subside.

Then I bent down to examine Richie's body.

The label in his suit proclaimed the gifts of Falkus, The Fine Tailors, but nothing else; he had six pounds and twenty pence in his right trouser pocket, and a camouflage-patterned penknife in his left. His shirt was white nylon, and the shoes were four-hole Baxter half-brogues in oxblood leather. That was more or less it. There was nothing else to mark Richie out from the crowd and set the keen-eyed investigator's pulse racing. No bus ticket. No library card. No page of personal ads from a local newspaper with one entry ringed in red felt-tip pen.

All I could find that was even remotely out of the ordinary was a Bianchi cross-draw holster, containing one brand new nine millimetre Glock 17 self-loading pistol.

You may have read, at one time or another, some of the nonsense that's been written about the Glock. The fact that its body is made from a fancy polymer material got one or two journalists very excited a while back about the possibility that the gun might not register on airport X-ray machines – which happens to be so much hooey. The slide, barrel, and a fair portion of its innards are metal, and if that weren't enough, seventeen rounds of Parabellum ammunition are pretty hard to pass off as lipstick refills. What it does have is a high magazine capacity for a low weight, great accuracy, and virtually unequalled reliability. All of which have made the Glock 17 the choice of housewives everywhere.

I worked the slide, pushing a round into the breech. There's no safety catch on the Glock. You just point, shoot, and run like hell. My kind of gun.

I eased open the door to the corridor, and there was no space shuttle. It was a plain, white corridor, with seven other doors leading off it. All shut. At the end of the corridor was a window, looking out at a skyline that could have been any

110

one of fifty cities. It was daylight.

Whatever the building was built for, it hadn't been doing it for a long time. The corridor was dirty and lined with rubbish – cardboard boxes, mounds of paper, bin-liners, and half-way down, a mountain bike without wheels.

Now, clearing a hostile building is really a game for three or more players. Six is a good number. The player to the left of the dealer checks the rooms, with two more as understudies, while the other three watch the corridor. That's how it works. If you really must play it on your own, the rules are entirely different. You open every door very slowly, checking your back as you do it, squinting through the hinges and taking about an hour to cover ten yards of corridor. That's what it says in every manual ever written on the subject.

My feeling about manuals is that the other fellow's probably read them too.

I zig-zagged down the corridor as fast as I could go, gun outstretched, flinging open all seven of the doors until I reached the other end where I threw myself down beneath the window, braced to empty the magazine at anyone who might pop their head out. Nobody did.

But now the doors were open, and the first one on the left led on to a staircase. I could see a few feet of banister, and above it, a mirror. I got up into a crouch and ran through the door, waving the gun up and down the stairs in as threatening a fashion as I could manage. Nothing.

I drew back my right hand and drove the butt of the Glock into the middle of the mirror, shattering the glass. I picked out a hefty-looking piece and cut my left hand on it. Which was an accident, in case you're wondering.

I held up the broken mirror and squinted at the reflection of my chin. The wound was less than pretty.

Back in the corridor, I reverted to the slow method of clearance, creeping to the edge of each door-frame, sticking the mirror out across the doorway, turning its gaze slowly across the room. It was a clumsy method, and since the walls were no more than an inch of Gyproc plaster board, and probably couldn't have stopped a cherry-stone squeezed from the fingers of a tired three-year-old, it was also fairly useless. But it felt better than standing in the doorway shouting 'yoohoo?'

The first two rooms were in the same state as the corridor. Dirty, and piled with junk. Dead typewriters, telephones, three-legged chairs. I was reflecting on the fact that there is nothing in any of the world's great museums that looks quite as ancient as a ten-year-old photocopier, when I heard a noise. A human noise. A groan.

I waited. It didn't repeat, so I replayed the noise in my head. It was the next room down the corridor. It was male. It was someone having sex, or in a bad state. Or it was a trap.

I eased back out into the corridor and along to the next doorway, and lay down along the wall. I pushed the mirror out in front of me and adjusted its position. Sitting in a chair in the middle of the room, his head slumped forward on to his chest, was a man. Short, fat, middle-aged, and tied to the chair. With leather straps.

There was blood on the front of his shirt. A lot of it.

If it was a trap, this was the moment when the opposition would expect me to leap up and say, 'good heavens, may I be of any assistance?'. So I stayed where I was and watched. The man and the corridor.

He didn't make any other noise, and the corridor didn't do anything that corridors don't normally do. After a solid minute of watching, I tossed the mirror aside and crawled round the door-jamb into the room.

I think maybe I'd known it was Woolf, from the moment I first heard the moan. Either I'd recognised the voice, or I'd been thinking all along that if Groomed had been able to catch me, he'd have had no trouble getting hold of Woolf.

Or Sarah, come to that.

I closed the door and propped a chair on two legs under the handle. It wouldn't stop anyone, but it would give me a

112

chance to get off three or four rounds before the door opened. I knelt down in front of Woolf, and immediately swore at a new pain in my knee. I shifted back and looked at the floor. Seven or eight oily-looking nuts and bolts lay at Woolf's feet, and I leant down to brush them away.

But they weren't nuts and bolts, and it wasn't oil. I was kneeling on his teeth.

I undid the straps and tried lifting his head. Both eyes were closed, but I couldn't tell whether that was because he was unconscious or because the tissue round his cheeks and eye sockets was horribly swollen. Bubbles of blood and saliva hung round his mouth and his breathing sounded terrible.

'You're going to be fine,' I said. But I didn't believe me, and I doubt whether he did. 'Where's Sarah?'

He didn't answer, but I could see he was struggling to open his left eye. He tilted his head back and a low grunt burst some of the bubbles round his lips. I leaned forward and took hold of his hands.

'Where's Sarah?' I repeated, with a thick, hairy fist of worry gripping at my larynx. He didn't move for a while, and I began to think he'd passed out, but then his chest heaved and he opened his mouth as if he was yawning.

'What do you say, Thomas?' The voice was a thin rasp, and his breathing was getting worse by the second. 'Are you . . . ' He stopped to suck in some more air.

I knew he shouldn't keep talking. I knew I should tell him to keep quiet and save his strength, but I couldn't do it. I wanted him to talk. To say anything. About how bad he felt, about who had done this, about Sarah, about racing at Doncaster. Anything to do with life.

'Am I what?' I said.

'Are you a good man?'

I think he smiled.

I stayed like that for a while, watching him, trying to think what to do. If I moved him, he might die. If I didn't move him, he would die. I even think that part of me actually wanted

113

him to die, so that I could be free to do something. Take revenge. Run away. Get angry.

And then suddenly, almost before I knew it, I was letting go of his hands and picking up the Glock, moving sideways across the room in as low a crouch as I could manage.

Because someone was trying the door-handle.

The chair held firm for a push or two and then slid away from the handle as a foot crashed against it. The door swung wide and a man stood in its place, taller than I'd remembered, which is why I took a few tenths to realise that it was Groomed and that he was pointing a gun into the middle of the room. Woolf started to get up out of the chair, or perhaps he was just falling forward, and there was a long, loud crash which tailed off into a series of flat bangs as I fired six shots into Groomed's head and body. He fell back into the corridor and I followed him, firing another three into his chest as he went down. I kicked the gun away from his hand and pointed the Glock at the middle of his head. Cartridge cases trickled across the floor of the corridor.

I turned back into the room. Woolf was six feet away from where I'd last seen him, lying on his back in a thickening black pool. I couldn't understand how his body had travelled so far, until I looked down and saw Groomed's weapon.

It was a MAC 10. A nasty, pocket-sized sub-machine gun, that didn't really mind who it hit, capable of emptying its thirty-round magazine in under two seconds. Groomed had managed to hit Woolf with most of the thirty, and they'd torn him to pieces.

I bent forward and fired another round into Groomed's mouth.

It took me an hour to go over the whole building from top to bottom. By the time I'd finished, I knew that it backed on to High Holborn, had once housed a largish insurance firm, and was now as empty as buildings ever get. Which I'd sort of guessed. Gunfire without subsequent police sirens generally

114

means there's no one home.

I had no choice but to leave the Glock behind. I dragged Richie's body into the room with Woolf, laid him across the floor, wiped the butt and trigger of the Glock on my shirt and pressed it into Richie's hand. I picked up the MAC and fired the last three rounds into Richie's body, before putting it back beside Groomed.

The tableau, as I'd left it, didn't make much sense. But then real life doesn't either, and a confusing scene is often easier to believe than a straightforward one. That's what I hoped, anyway.

I then retired to The Sovereign, a grubby bed and breakfast in King's Cross, where I spent two days and three nights while my chin dried up and the bruises on my body turned to beautiful colours. Outside my window, the British public traded crack, slept with itself for money, and fought drunken battles it couldn't remember in the morning.

While I was there, I thought about helicopters, and guns, and Alexander Woolf, and Sarah Woolf, and a whole lot of interesting stuff.

Am I a good man?

Nine

Boot, saddle, to horse, and away!

BROWNING

'Graduate what?'

The girl was pretty, in a stunningly beautiful kind of way, and I wondered how long she'd stay in her present job. I dare say being a receptionist at the American Embassy in Grosvenor Square gets you a reasonable salary and all the nylon stockings you can eat, but it must also be duller than last year's Budget speech.

'Graduate Studies,' I said. 'Mr Russell Barnes.'

'Is he expecting you?'

She wouldn't last six months, I decided. She was bored with me, bored with the building, bored with the world.

'I certainly hope so,' I said. 'My office telephoned earlier today to confirm. They were told that there would be someone to meet me.'

'Solomon, right?'

'Right.' She scanned a couple of lists. 'One M,' I said, helpfully.

'And your office is?'

'The one that telephoned this morning. I'm sorry, I thought I'd mentioned that.'

She was even too bored to repeat the question. She shrugged and started to fill in a visitor's pass for me.

'Carl?'

Carl wasn't just Carl. He was CARL. He was an inch-and-a-half taller than me, and he lifted weights in his spare time, of which he obviously had quite a lot. He was also a United States Marine, and wore a uniform so new I half expected to see someone still finishing off a hem down by his ankles.

'Mr Solomon,' said the receptionist. 'Room 5910. To see Barnes, Russell.'

'Russell Barnes,' I corrected her, but neither of them took any notice.

Carl took me through a series of expensive security checks, where some other Carls ran metal-detectors over my body and ruffled my clothes a lot. They were particularly interested in my briefcase, and worried by the fact that all it contained was a copy of the *Daily Mirror*.

'I only use the case as a prop,' I explained cheerfully, which for some reason seemed to satisfy them. Maybe if I'd told them I only used it to take secret documents out of foreign embassies, they would have slapped me on the back and offered to carry it for me.

Carl took me to a lift and stood aside while I entered. Music was being piped in at a maddeningly low volume, and if it hadn't been an embassy, I would have sworn that it was Johnny Mathis covering 'Bat Out Of Hell'. Carl followed me in and swiped a plastic card through an electronic reader, then jabbed a number into the keypad beneath with an immaculately-gloved finger.

As the lift flung us upwards, I steadied myself for what was likely to be a tricky kind of an interview. I kept telling myself that I was only doing what they tell you to do when you're swept out to sea by a strong current. Swim with it, they say, not against it. You'll hit land eventually. We dismounted at the fifth floor and I followed Carl along a well-waxed corridor to 5910 – Deputy Director European Research, Barnes, Russell P.

Carl waited while I knocked, and when the door opened I came within an ace of slipping a couple of pound coins into his gloved hand and asking him to book me a table at L'Epicure. Luckily, he stopped me by saluting violently, then turned on his heel and set off back down the corridor at a hundred and ten paces to the minute.

Russell P. Barnes had knocked around the world a bit. I may not be the greatest reader of men, but I know that you don't get to look like Russell P. Barnes by sitting behind a desk for half your life, and swilling cocktails at embassy receptions for the other half. He was nearly fifty, tall and lean, and with a scrum of scars and wrinkles fighting each other to see who could get control of his sunburned face. All I could think was that he was everything that O'Neal was trying so hard to be.

He looked over some half-moon glasses at me as I came in, but carried on reading, running an expensive fountain pen down the margin as he went. Every fibre of his body said dead Viet Cong, well-armed Contras and General Schwarzkopf calls me Rusty.

He flipped over a page and barked at me: 'Yeah.'

'Mr Barnes,' I said, setting my briefcase down by the chair opposite him and holding out my hand.

'What it says on the door.' He kept on reading. I kept my hand out.

'How do you do, sir?'

A pause. I knew the 'sir' would get him. He sniffed the air, picked up the scent of brother officer, and slowly raised his head to me. Then he looked down at my hand for a long moment before extending his own. Dry as dust.

He flicked his eyes down at the chair and I sat, and as I did so I caught sight of the photograph on the wall. Sure enough, it was Stormin' Norman, dressed in camouflage pyjamas,

118

with a long handwritten inscription under the face. The writing was too small for me to read, but I'd have bet everything I owned on it containing the words 'kick' and 'ass' somewhere in its text. Next to it, there was a larger photograph of Barnes in some kind of jump-suit, with a flying-helmet tucked under his arm.

'British?' He unpeeled his glasses and flopped them on the desk.

'To the core, Mr Barnes,' I said. 'To the core.' I knew that what he meant was British army. We exchanged wry military grins that told each other how much we hated those fly-blown pieces of shit who tied the hands of decent men and called it politics. When we'd had enough of that, I said: 'David Solomon.'

'What can I do for you, Mr Solomon?'

'As I think your secretary mentioned, sir, I come from Mr O'Neal's Ministry. Mr O'Neal has one or two questions that he hopes you might be able to answer.'

'Shoot.' The word fell easily from his lips, and I wondered how many times and in how many different contexts he'd said it.

'It concerns Graduate Studies, Mr Barnes.'

'Yup.'

That was it. Yup. No 'you mean the scheme whereby an unspecified group of people conspire to sponsor a terrorist action with the aim of boosting sales of anti-terrorist military equipment?' Which, I must admit, I'd sort of been banking on. If not that, then a guilty start would have sufficed. But 'yup', on its own, was no help at all.

'Mr O'Neal was hoping that you might care to enlighten us with your latest thinking on the subject.'

'Was he now?'

'Indeed he was,' I said firmly. 'He was hoping you might favour us with your interpretation of recent events.'

'What recent events might those be?'

'I'd rather not go into any details at this juncture, Mr Barnes. I'm sure you understand.'

He smiled, and there was a flash of gold from somewhere at the back of his mouth.

'You have anything to do with Procurement, Mr Solomon?'

'Absolutely not, Mr Barnes.' I tried a dollop of ruefulness. 'My wife won't even trust me to do the supermarket shopping.'

His smile faded. In the circles Russell P. Barnes moved in, marriage was a thing decent fighting men did in private. If they did it at all.

A phone on his desk buzzed softly, and he yanked the receiver to his ear.

'Barnes.' He picked up the fountain pen and clicked the top on and off a few times while he listened. He nodded and yeahed a few times, then hung up. He kept looking at the pen, and it seemed to be my turn to speak.

'I think I can say, however, that we are concerned as to the safety,' I paused to acknowledge the euphemism, 'of two American citizens presently residing on British soil. Woolf is their given name. Mr O'Neal wondered whether you had come by any information that might assist our Ministry in ensuring their continued protection.'

He folded his arms across his chest and sat back in his chair.

'I'll be goddamned.'

'Sir?'

'They say that if you sit still for long enough, the whole world will come by.'

I tried to look confused.

'I'm terribly sorry, Mr Barnes, but I think you may have lost me.'

'Been a long time since I've taken this amount of bullshit in one glass.'

Somewhere a clock ticked. Quite fast. Too fast, it seemed to me, to be counting seconds. But then this was an American building, and maybe Americans had decided that seconds were just too goddamned slow, and how's about a clock that can do a minute in twenty seconds? That way, we get more goddamned hours in a goddamned day than these faggot limeys.

'Do you have any information, Mr Barnes?' I asked, doggedly.

But he wasn't going to be rushed anywhere.

'How would I come by that information, Mr Solomon? You're the one with the foot-soldiers. I just hear what O'Neal tells me.'

'Well now,' I said, 'I wonder if that's strictly true.'

'Do you?'

Something was wrong. I hadn't the faintest idea what it was, but there was something very badly wrong here.

'Leaving that aside, Mr Barnes,' I said, 'let us suppose that my Ministry is slightly under-staffed with foot-soldiers just at the moment. Lot of 'flu about. Summer holidays. Let's suppose that our foot-soldiers, owing to their depleted numbers, had momentarily lost track of these two individuals.'

Barnes cracked some knuckles and leaned forward over the desk.

'Well, I don't see how that could happen, Mr Solomon.'

'I'm not saying it's happened,' I said. 'I'm offering it as a hypothesis.'

'All the same, I don't agree with your premise. Seems to me that, if anything, you're over-staffed just now.'

'I'm sorry, I'm not with you.'

'Seems to me you've got staff all over the place, chasin' your own tails.'

The clock ticked.

'What do you mean, exactly?'

'What I mean exactly is that if your department can afford to employ two David Solomons to do the same job, then you got a budget I wouldn't mind having.'

Whoops.

He got to his feet and started moving round the desk. Not threatening anything, just stretching his legs.

'Maybe you got more? Maybe you got a whole division of David Solomons. Is that it?' He paused. 'I put a call into O'Neal. David Solomon is on a flight to Prague right now, and O'Neal seems to think that's the only David Solomon he's got. So maybe all you David Solomons just share the one salary.' He reached the door and opened it. 'Mike, get an E team up here. Now.'

He turned and leaned against the jamb, arms folded, watching me.

'You got about forty seconds.'

'All right,' I said. 'My name isn't Solomon.'

The E team consisted of two Carls, one either side of my chair. Mike had taken the place at the door and Barnes was back at his desk. I was playing the dejected loser.

'My name is Glass. Terence Glass.' I tried to make it sound as dull as possible. So boring that no one would ever think to make it up. 'I run an art gallery in Cork Street.' I dug into my top pocket and found the card the well-brung-up blonde had given me. I handed it to Barnes. 'Here. Last one. Anyway, Sarah works for me. Used to work for me.' I sighed and slumped a little lower. A man who'd gambled everything and lost. 'The last few weeks, she's been behaving . . . I don't know. She seemed worried. Frightened, even. She'd started talking about some strange things. Then one day, she just didn't show up. Disappeared. I rang round. Nothing. I tried ringing her father a couple of times, but he seems to have disappeared too. I went through some things in her desk, odds and ends, and I found a file.'

Barnes stiffened very slightly at this, so I thought I'd try stiffening him some more.

'Graduate Studies. On the cover. I thought to begin with it was History of Art stuff, but it wasn't. I didn't really understand it, to be honest. Business. Manufacturing or whatever. She'd made some notes. Man called Solomon. And your name. American Embassy. I . . . Can I be honest with you?'

Barnes looked back at me. There was nothing on his face but scars and wrinkles.

'Don't tell her this,' I said. 'I mean, she doesn't know it, but . . . I'm in love with her. Have been for months. That's why I gave her the job, really. Didn't need anyone else working at the gallery, but I wanted to be close to her. It's all I could think of. I know it sounds feeble, but . . . do you know her? I mean have you seen her?'

Barnes didn't answer. He just fingered the card I'd given him, and looked up at Mike with a raised eyebrow. I didn't turn round, but Mike must have been busy.

'Glass,' said a voice. 'It checks.'

Barnes sucked his teeth for a moment and then looked out of the window. Apart from the clock, the room was astonishingly quiet. No phones, no typewriters, no traffic noise. The windows must have been quadruple-glazed.

'O'Neal?'

I looked as defeated as I could.

'What about him?'

'Where'd you get the stuff about O'Neal?'

'The file,' I shrugged. 'I told you, I read her file. I wanted to know what had happened to her.'

'Any reason why you didn't tell me this from the beginning? Why all this bullshit?'

I laughed and glanced up at the Carls.

'You're not an easy man to see, Mr Barnes. I've been trying to get you on the phone for days. They kept putting me through to the Visa Section. I think they thought I was trying to wangle a Green Card. Marrying an American.'

There was a long pause.

It really was one of the silliest stories I've ever told; but I was gambling – heavily, I have to admit – on Barnes' machismo. I read him as an arrogant man, trapped in a foreign country, and I hoped that most of him would want to believe that everyone he dealt with was as silly as my story. If not sillier.

'You try all this with O'Neal?'

'According to the Ministry of Defence, there is no one of that name working there, and I'd be better off making a missing persons report at my local police station.'

'Which you did?'

'Which I tried to do.'

'Which station?'

'Bayswater.' I knew they wouldn't check that. He just wanted to see how quickly I could answer. 'The police told me to wait a few weeks. They seemed to think she might have found another lover.'

I was pleased with that. I knew he'd go for it.

'"Another" lover?'

'Well . . . ' I tried to blush. 'All right. A lover.'

Barnes chewed his lip. I was looking so pathetic he didn't have much choice but to believe me. I would have believed me, and I'm very hard to please.

He came to a decision.

'Where's the file now?'

I looked up, surprised that the file was of any interest to anybody.

'Still at the gallery. Why?'

'Description?'

'Well, it's just a sort of . . . gallery, really. Fine art.'

Barnes took a deep breath. He was really hating having to deal with me.

'What does the file look like?'

'Like a file. Cardboard . . . '

'Jesus and Mary,' said Barnes. 'What colour?'

I thought for a moment.

'Yellow, I think. Yes. Yellow.'

'Mike. Saddle up.'

'Wait a minute . . . ' I started to get up but one of the Carls leaned on my shoulder and I decided to sit down again. 'What are you doing?'

Barnes was already heading back to his paperwork. He didn't look at me.

'You will accompany Mr Lucas to your place of business,

and you will hand the file over to him. Is that understood?'

'And why the hell should I do that?' I don't know how art gallery owners ought to sound, but I plumped for petulant. 'I came here to find out what's happened to one of my employees, not to have you meddling around with her private property.'

It was as if he'd suddenly glanced down and seen that the last item on the agenda was 'showing everybody what a tough piece of work I am' – even though Mike was out of the door and the Carls were already starting to back away.

'Listen to me, you fucking fairy,' he said. Which I thought was overdoing it, frankly. The Carls dutifully stopped to admire the testosterone. 'Two points. One. We don't know until we see it whether it's her private property or ours. Two. The more you do what the fuck I tell you to do, the better the chance you'll have of seeing this freak bitch again. Do I make myself understood?'

Mike was a nice enough lad. Late twenties, Ivy League, and smart as a whip. I could see that he wasn't comfortable with this heavy stuff, and I liked him all the more for that.

We were heading south down Park Lane in a light-blue Lincoln Diplomat, chosen from thirty identical ones in the embassy car park. It seemed to me a trifle obvious for diplomats to use a car called a Diplomat, but maybe Americans like those sort of signposts. For all I know, the average American insurance salesman drives around in something called a Chevrolet Insurance Salesman. I suppose it's one less decision in a man's life.

I sat in the back, playing with the ashtrays, while a plain-clothes Carl sat beside Mike in the front. The Carl had an earpiece with a wire disappearing inside his shirt. God knows where it went.

'Nice man, Mr Barnes,' I said eventually.

Mike looked at me in the rear-view mirror. The Carl turned his head an inch, and judging by the size of his neck, that was about all he could manage. I wanted to apologise for having cut into his weight-training time. 'Good at his job too, I would think. Mr Barnes. Efficient.'

Mike shot a glance across at the Carl, wondering whether to answer me.

'Mr Barnes is indeed a remarkable man,' he said.

I think that Mike probably hated Barnes. I'm pretty sure I would have done, if I'd worked for him. But Mike was a nice, honourable, professional man who was trying hard to be loyal, and I didn't think it fair to try and get any more out of him in front of the Carl. So I went back to fiddling with the electric windows.

Basically, the car wasn't equipped for the job it had to do – which is to say it had ordinary locks on the back doors, so that I could have stepped out at any traffic-light I chose. But I didn't do that, and didn't even want to do it. I don't know why, but I was suddenly feeling very cheerful.

'Remarkable, yes,' I said. 'That's the word I'd use. Well, no, it's the word you'd use, but do you mind if I use it as well?'

I really was enjoying myself. It doesn't happen often.

We turned into Piccadilly, and then up towards Cork Street. Mike pulled down the sun-visor, where he'd tucked Glass's card, and read out the number. I was mightily relieved he didn't ask me for it.

We pulled up outside number forty-eight, and the Carl had his door open and was out of the car before we'd come to a stop. He wrenched open the back door and looked up and down the street as I got out. I felt like a President.

'Forty-eight, right?' said Mike.

'Right,' I said.

I rang the bell and the three of us waited. After a few moments a shortish, dapper-looking chap appeared and busied himself with the bolts and locks on the door.

'Good morning, gentlemen,' he said. Very far back voice.

'Morning, Vince. How's the leg?' I said, and stepped into the gallery.

The dapper fellow was much too English to say who's Vince? what leg? and by the way, what are you talking about? Instead he stood back, with a polite smile, and let Mike and Carl in behind me.

The four of us moved to the middle of the shop and surveyed the daubs. They really were awful. If he sold one a year, I'd be amazed.

'If you see anything you fancy, I might be able to do you ten per cent,' I said to the Carl, who blinked slowly.

The good-looking blonde, in a red shift this time, came through from the back and beamed. Then she saw me, and her well-bred chin dropped to her even-better-bred chest.

'Who are you?' Mike was addressing the dapper man. The Carl was staring at the paintings.

'I am Terence Glass,' said the dapper man.

It was a great moment. One I'll always remember. There were five of us standing there, and only Glass and I were able to keep our mouths from hanging open. Mike was the first to speak.

'Wait a minute,' he said. 'You're Glass.' He turned to me with a desperate look on his face. A forty-year career with pension and numerous postings to the Seychelles was starting to flash before his eyes.

'Sorry,' I said. 'Not strictly true.' I looked down at the floor to see if I could spot my blood stain, but there was nothing there. Glass had been very swift either with the Vim, or a fake expenses claim.

'Is there something amiss, gentlemen?' Glass had sensed unpleasantness in the air. Bad enough that we weren't Saudi Princes. Now it looked like we weren't buyers at all.

'You're the . . . killer. Man who . . . ' The blonde was struggling for her words.

'Nice to see you too,' I said.

'Jesus Christ,' said Mike, and he turned to the Carl, who turned to me.

He was a big chap.

'Well, sorry about that little misunderstanding,' I said. 'But now that you're here, why don't you go away?' The Carl started to move towards me. Mike caught his arm, and then looked at me, wincing.

'Wait a minute. If you're not . . . I mean, do you realise what you've done?' I think he really was at a loss for words. 'Jesus.'

I turned to Glass and the blonde.

'Just to set your mind at rest, because I know you must be wondering ever so slightly about what's going on here. I am not who you think I am. Neither am I who they think I am. You,' I jabbed a finger at Glass, 'are who they think I am, and you,' to the blonde, 'are who I would like to talk to when everyone else has gone. Clear?'

Nobody put their hand up. I moved towards the door with an ushering motion.

'We want the file,' said Mike.

'What file?' I said.

'Graduate Studies.' He was still a lap or two off the pace at this point. I couldn't blame him.

'Sorry to disappoint you, but there is no file. Called "Graduate Studies" or anything else.' Mike's face fell, and I genuinely felt sorry for him. 'Listen,' I said, trying to make it easier, 'I was on the fifth floor, the windows were double-glazed, it was United States territory, and the only way I could think to get out was talking about a file. I thought it might appeal to you all.'

Another long pause. Glass started clicking his teeth, as if this kind of nuisance was just happening too often these days. The Carl turned to Mike.

'Do I take him?' His voice was surprisingly high, almost falsetto.

Mike chewed his lip.

'That's not really Mike's decision, actually,' I said. They both looked at me. 'What I mean is, it's up to me whether or not I'm taken, as you put it.'

The Carl stared at me, weighing me up.

'Look,' I said, 'I'll be honest with you. You're a big chap, and I'm sure you can do more press-ups than I can. And I admire you for it. This world needs people to be able to do press-ups. It's important.' He lifted his chin menacingly. Just keep talking, Mister. So I did. 'But fighting is a different thing. A very different thing, that I happen to be very good at. Doesn't mean I'm tougher than you, or more virile, or any of that stuff. It's just something I'm good at.'

I could see that the Carl wasn't comfortable with this kind of talk. He'd most likely been educated in the school of 'I'm gonna tear your heart out etc.' and knew how to respond to that, and only that.

'What I mean is,' I said, as kindly as I could, 'if you want to spare yourself a lot of embarrassment, you'll just walk away now and have yourselves a decent lunch somewhere.'

Which, after some whispering and staring, they eventually did.

An hour later, I was sitting in an Italian café with the blonde, who shall hereinafter be referred to as Ronnie because that's what her friends called her, and I'd apparently just become one.

Mike had left with his tail between his legs, and the Carl had had a 'one of these days fella' look about him. I'd given him a cheery wave in return, but I knew I wouldn't count my life a disaster if I never saw him again.

Ronnie had sat wide-eyed through my abridged version of events, leaving out the stuff about dead people, and had generally adjusted her opinion of me to the point where she now seemed to think I was a hell of a fellow, which made a nice change. I ordered another round of coffee and sat back to soak up some of her admiration.

She frowned a bit.

'So you don't know where Sarah is now?' she said.

'Not the faintest idea. She may be all right, just laying low, or she may be in quite a lot of trouble.'

Ronnie sat back and gazed out of the window. I could tell that she was fond of Sarah, because she was taking her worrying seriously. Then suddenly she shrugged and took a sip of coffee.

'At least you didn't give them the file,' she said. 'That's one thing.'

This of course is one of the hazards of lying to people. They start getting confused about what's true and what isn't. No great surprise, I suppose.

'No, you don't understand,' I explained gently. 'There is no file. I told them there was one, because I knew they'd have to check it out before they had me arrested or dumped in the river or whatever they do to people like me. You see, people who work in offices believe in files. Files are important to them. If you tell them you have a file, they want to believe it, because they set a lot of store by files.' Me, the great psychologist. 'But I'm afraid this one simply doesn't exist.'

Ronnie straightened up and I could see that she was suddenly excited. Two little red dots had appeared in her cheeks. It was rather a pleasant sight.

'But it does,' she said.

I shook my head once to check that my ears were where I'd left them.

'I beg your pardon?'

'Graduate Studies,' she said. 'Sarah's file. I've seen it.'

Ten

Yet in oure asshen olde is fyr weye.

CHAUCER

I arranged to meet Ronnie at four-thirty, when the gallery closed for the day and the thundering stampede of customers had been safely locked out for another night to drool on the pavement with their camp-beds and open cheque-books.

I didn't actively try to enlist her help, but Ronnie was a game young thing who, for some reason, sensed a combination of good deeds and high adventure and couldn't resist it. I didn't tell her that so far it had only involved bullet holes and mashed scrota, because I couldn't ignore the possibility that she would be extremely useful. For one thing I was now without transport, and for another, I find I often think better when there's someone else around to think for me.

I killed some hours at the British Library, trying to find out what I could about the Mackie Corporation of America. Most of the time was spent getting the hang of the index system, but in the last ten minutes before I had to leave, I managed to establish the following priceless information – that Mackie was a Scottish engineer who had worked with Robert Adams in producing a solid frame trigger-cocking cap-and-ball percussion revolver, which the two of them exhibited at the Great Exhibition in London in 1851. I didn't bother to write that down.

With one minute to go, I cross-referred my way into a crashingly dull volume called *The Teeth Of The Tiger*, by a Major J. S. Hammond (ret'd), where I discovered that Mackie had founded a company that had since grown to become the fifth largest supplier of defence 'materiel' to the Pentagon. The company's headquarters were currently in Vensom, California, and its last given annual pre-tax profit had more noughts on the end of it than I could fit on the back of my hand.

I was on my way back to Cork Street, weaving through the afternoon shoppers, when I heard the news vendor's cry, and it may well have been the first time in my life that I actually understood something a news vendor said. The other passers-by were almost certainly hearing 'Reeded In Silly Shut Up', but I hardly had to glance at the poster to know that he meant 'Three Dead In City Shoot-Up.' I bought a copy and read as I walked.

A 'massive police investigation' was under way following the discovery of the bodies of three men, all of whom had perished as the result of gunshot wounds, at a derelict office building in the heart of London's financial district. The bodies, none of which had yet been identified, were found by the security guard, Mr Dennis Falkes, 51 and father of three, returning to his post after a dental appointment. A police spokesman declined to speculate on the motive behind the killings, but was apparently unable to rule out drugs. There were no photographs. Just a rambly background story about the rise in the number of drug-related deaths in the capital in the last two years. I tossed the paper into a bin and kept walking.

Dennis Falkes had taken some folding money from

someone, that much was obvious. The chances were it was Groomed who paid him, so when Falkes got back and found his benefactor dead he didn't have much incentive not to call the police. I hoped for his sake that the dentist story was true. If it wasn't, the police were going to make his life extremely difficult.

Ronnie was waiting for me in her car outside the gallery. It was a bright red TVR Griffith, with a five litre V8 engine, and an exhaust note that could have been heard in Peking. It fell some way short of being the ideal car for a discreet surveillance operation, but (a), I wasn't in a position to quibble, and (b), there's an undeniable pleasure in stepping into an open-top sports car driven by a beautiful woman. It feels like you're climbing into a metaphor.

Ronnie was in high spirits, which didn't mean she hadn't seen the newspaper story about Woolf. Even if she had, and even if she'd known that Woolf was dead, I'm not sure it would have made much difference. Ronnie had what they used to call pluck. Centuries of breeding, some of it in, some of it out, had given her high cheek-bones and an appetite for risk and adventure. I pictured her at the age of five, careering over eight-foot fences on a pony called Winston, risking her life seventy times before breakfast.

She shook her head when I asked her what she'd found in Sarah's desk at the gallery, and then pestered me with questions all the way to Belgravia. I didn't hear a single one of them thanks to the howl of the TVR exhaust, but I nodded and shook my head whenever it seemed appropriate.

When we reached Lyall Street, I yelled at her to take a run past the house, and not to look at anything but the road ahead. I found a tape of AC/DC, slotted it into the cassette player, and turned the volume up as far as it would go. I was working on the principle, you see, that the more obvious you are, the less obvious you are. Given the choice, I'd usually say that the more obvious you are, the more obvious you are, but choice was one of the things I was short of at that moment.

Necessity is the mother of self-delusion.

As we passed the Woolf house, I put my hand up to my eye and prodded a bit, which allowed me to stare at the front of the house as hard as I could while apparently adjusting a contact lens. It looked empty. But then again, I'd hardly expected to see men with violin cases on the front steps.

We went round the block and I signalled to Ronnie to pull over a couple of hundred yards short of the house. She switched off, and for a few moments my ears rang with the sudden quiet. Then she turned to me, and I could see that the red spots were back in her cheeks.

'What now, boss?'

She really was getting into this.

'I'll take a stroll past and see what happens.'

'Right. What do I do?'

'Be great if you could stay here,' I said. Her face fell. 'In case I need to get out in a hurry,' I added, and her face picked itself up again. She reached into her handbag and brought out a small brass-coloured canister which she pressed into my hand.

'What's this?' I said.

'Rape alarm. Press the top.'

'Ronnie . . . '

'Take it. If I hear it, I'll know you need a lift.'

The street looked as ordinary as it could, given that every single house in it cost upwards of two million pounds. The value of the cars alone, lining both sides of the road, probably exceeded the wealth of many small countries. A dozen Mercedes, a dozen Jaguars and Daimlers, five Bentley saloons, a Bentley convertible, three Aston Martins, three Ferraris, a Jensen, a Lamborghini.

And a Ford.

Dark-blue, facing away from me, opposite the house on the other side of the street, which was why I hadn't noticed it the first time round. Two aerials. Two rear-view mirrors. A dent half-way up the nearside front wing. Sort of dent a large motorcycle might make in a side-to-side collision.

One man in the passenger seat.

My first feeling was relief. If they were staking out Sarah's house, there was a good chance that it was because they didn't have Sarah, and the house was the next best thing. But then again, they might already have Sarah and had just sent someone along to collect her toothbrush. If she still had any teeth, that is.

No point in worrying about that. I kept walking towards the Ford.

If you've ever had any training in military theory, it's possible that you had to sit through a lecture on a thing called the Boyd Loop. Boyd was a chap who spent a large amount of time studying air-to-air combat during the Korean war, analysing typical 'event sequences' – or, in layman's language, sequences of events – to see why pilot A was able to shoot down pilot B, and how pilot B felt about it afterwards, and which of them had had kedgeree for breakfast. Boyd's theory was based on the utterly facile observation that when A did something, B reacted, A did something else, B reacted again et cetera, forming a loop of action and reaction. The Boyd Loop. Nice work if you can get it, you may be thinking. But Boyd's 'Eureka' moment, which to this day causes his name to be bandied about military academies the world over, came when he hit upon the notion that if B could do two things in the space of time it normally took him to do one, he would 'get inside the loop', and the forces of right would thereby prevail.

Lang's Theory, which amounts to much the same thing at a fraction of the cost, is that you punch the other chap's face before he has a chance to get it out of the way.

I came up behind the Ford on the left-hand side, and stopped level with it, looking up at the Woolfs' house. The man in the Ford didn't look at me. Which he would have done if he'd been a civilian, because people do look at people when they've got nothing else to do. I bent down and knocked on his window. He turned and stared at me for a long moment before he wound it down, but I could tell he hadn't recognised me. He was in his forties and liked his whisky.

'Are you Roth?' I snapped, in the best American accent I could manage – which is actually pretty good, though I say so myself.

He shook his head.

'Roth been here?' I said.

'Who the fuck is Roth?' I'd expected him to be an American, but he sounded extremely London.

'Shit,' I said, standing up and looking towards the house.

'Who are you?'

'Dalloway,' I said, frowning. 'They tell you I was coming?' Again he shook his head. 'You been out of the car? Missed the call?' I was pushing hard, speaking fast and loud, and he was puzzled. But not suspicious. 'Heard the news? Seen a newspaper, for Christ's sake? Three dead men, and Lang wasn't one of them.' He stared up at me. 'Shit,' I said again, in case he hadn't heard me the first time.

'What now?'

Cigar for Mr Lang. I had him. I chewed my lip for a while, then decided to take a chance.

'You here alone?'

He nodded towards the house.

'Micky's inside.' He glanced at his watch. 'We change over in ten minutes.'

'You change over now. I have to get in. Anybody show so far?'

'Nothing.'

'Phone?'

'Once. Girl's voice, about an hour ago. Asking for Sarah.'

'Right. Let's go.'

I was inside his Boyd Loop, that was obvious. Amazing what you can make people do if you get the first note right. He clambered out of the car, eager to show how quickly he could clamber out of cars, and followed at my shoulder as I strode over to the house. I took the keys to my flat out of my pocket and then stopped myself.

'Have you got a knock?' I said as we reached the front door.

'Pardon?'

I rolled my eyes with impatience.

'A knock. Signal. I don't want Micky blowing a hole in my chest as we go through the goddamn door.'

'No, we just . . . I mean, I just shout "Micky".'

'Gee, that's really neat,' I said. 'Who worked that one out?' I laid it on a bit, trying to make him bristle so he'd be all the keener to show how efficient he was. 'Do it.'

He put his mouth to the letter-box.

'Micky,' he said, and then glanced up, apologetically. 'It's me.'

'Oh, I get it,' I said. 'That way he knows it's you. Cool.'

There was a pause, and then the latch turned and I pushed straight into the house.

I tried not to look at Micky much, so he'd know straightaway he wasn't the point at issue. But a quick glance told me he was also in his forties, and as thin as a very thin stick. He wore leather backless gloves and a revolver, and probably some clothes as well, but I wasn't really paying attention to them.

The revolver had a Smith & Wesson nickel finish, a short barrel, and an enclosed hammer, making it good for firing from inside a pocket. Probably a Bodyguard Airweight, or something similar. A sneaky kind of a gun. You may ask whether I could name an honest, decent, fair-minded kind of gun, and of course I can't. All guns throw lead at people with a view to causing harm, but, given that, they tend to have more or less distinct characters. And some are sneakier than others.

'You Micky?' I said, looking busily round the hall.

'I am.' Micky was a Scot, and was trying frantically to get some sign from his partner as to who the hell I was. Micky was going to be a problem.

137

'Dave Carter sends his regards.' I was at school with a Dave Carter.

'Oh. Yeah,' he said. 'Right.'

Bingo. Two Boyd Loops in five minutes. In a giddy whirl of triumph, I walked over to the hall table, and picked up the phone.

'Gwinevere,' I said, enigmatically. 'I'm in.'

I put the receiver back on the cradle and moved towards the stairs, cursing myself for having so massively overdone it. They couldn't have fallen for that one. But when I turned, they were both still standing there, meek as lambs, with a pair of 'you're the guv'nor' looks on their faces.

'Which one is the girl's bedroom?' I snapped. The lambs exchanged nervous glances. 'You checked the rooms, right?' They nodded. 'So which is the one with the lacy pillows and the poster of Stefan Edberg, for Chrissakes?'

'Second on the left,' said Micky.

'Thank you.'

'But . . . '

I stopped again.

'But what?'

'There's no poster . . . '

I gave them both a fair rendition of a withering look, and carried on up the stairs.

Micky was right, there was no poster of Stefan Edberg. There weren't even that many lacy pillows. Eight, maybe. But Fleur de Fleurs was in the air, one part per billion, and I felt a sudden, physical stab of worry and longing. For the first time I realised how much I wanted to protect Sarah from whatever it was, or whoever they were.

Now maybe this was just a lot of old damsel-in-distress nonsense, and perhaps, on another day, my hormones might have been busy on another subject entirely. But at that moment, standing in the middle of her bedroom, I wanted to rescue Sarah. Not just because she was good, and the bad guys weren't, but because I liked her. I liked her a lot.

Enough of that kind of talk.

I went to the bedside-table, lifted the phone receiver and tucked the mouthpiece under a lacy pillow. If either one of the lambs started to regain some courage, or just curiosity, and felt like trying Dial-An-Explanation, I'd hear it. But the pillow ought to stop them from hearing me.

I ran through the cupboards first, trying to guess whether a sizeable chunk of Sarah's clothes had gone. There were a few empty hangers here and there, but not enough to indicate an orderly departure to a far-away place.

The dressing-table had a scattering of pots and brushes on it. Face-cream, hand-cream, nose-cream, eye-cream. I wondered for a moment how serious it would be if you ever got home drunk and accidentally put face-cream on your hands or hand-cream on your face.

The drawers of the dressing-table contained more of the same. All the tools and lubricants necessary to keep a modern Formula 1 woman on the road. But definitely no file.

I closed them all and walked through to the adjoining bathroom. The silk dressing-gown Sarah had worn when I first saw her was hanging on the back of the door. There was a toothbrush in the rack over the basin.

I walked back through to the bedroom and looked around, hoping for a sign of something. I mean, not an actual sign – I wasn't expecting an address scrawled in lipstick on the mirror – but I'd hoped for something, something that should have been there and wasn't, or shouldn't have been there and was. But there was no sign, and yet something was wrong. I had to stand in the middle of the room and listen for a while before I realised what it was.

I couldn't hear the two lambs talking. That was wrong. They ought to have plenty of things to say to each other. After all, I was Dalloway, and Dalloway was a new element in their lives; they should have been talking about me.

I crossed to the window and looked down into the street. The door of the Ford was open, and it looked like the whisky lamb's leg sticking out of it. He was on the radio. I got the phone out of bed and put it back on the hook, and as I did so I automatically opened the draw of the bedside-table. It was a small drawer, but it seemed to contain more than the rest of the room. I rummaged through the packets of paper tissues, the cotton-wool, the paper tissues, the pairs of nail scissors, the half-eaten bar of Suchard chocolate, the paper tissues, the pens, the tweezers, the paper tissues, the paper tissues – do women eat these fucking things or what? – and there, at the bottom of the drawer, nestling on a bed of paper tissues, was a heavy bundle wrapped in a strip of chamois leather. Sarah's fetching little Walther TPH. I popped out the magazine and checked the slot down the side. Full.

I slipped the gun into my pocket, took another deep breath of Nina Ricci, and left.

Things had changed amongst the lambs since I'd last spoken to them. Definitely for the worse. The front door was open, Micky was leaning against the wall next to it with his right hand in his pocket, and I could see Whisky standing on the steps outside, looking up and down the street. He turned when he heard me on the stairs.

'Nothing,' I said, and then remembered I was supposed to be American. 'Not a goddamn thing. Shut the door will you?'

'Two questions,' said Micky.

'Yeah?' I said. 'Make it fast.'

'Who the fuck is Dave Carter?'

There didn't seem to be much point my telling him that Dave Carter had been under-sixteen fives champion at school, and that he'd gone on to work for his father's electrical engineering company in Hove. So I said, 'What's the second question?'

Micky glanced across at Whisky, who'd come up to the door and got himself very much in the way of my exit.

'Who the fuck are you?'

'Dalloway,' I said. 'Want me to write it down for you? What the hell is the matter with you guys?' I slipped my right hand into my pocket and saw Micky's right hand move in his.

If he decided to kill me, I knew I would never even hear the shot. Still, I'd managed to get my hand into my right pocket. Just a pity that I'd put the Walther in the left. I brought my hand out again, slowly, with my fist closed. Micky was watching me like a snake.

'Goodwin says he's never heard of you. He never sent anybody. Never told anybody we were here.'

'Goodwin is a lazy son-of-a-bitch who's way out of his depth,' I said, irritably. 'What the hell has he got to do with it?'

'Nothing at all,' said Micky. 'Want to know why?'

I nodded. 'Yes, I want to know why.'

Micky smiled. He had terrible teeth. 'Because he doesn't exist,' he said. 'I made him up.'

Well, there you are. I'd been Looped. As ye sew, so shall ye knit.

'I'm going to ask you again,' he said, starting towards me. 'Who are you?'

I let my shoulders slump. The game was up. I held my wrists out in front of me in a 'handcuff me, officer' gesture.

'You want to know my name?' I said.

'Yeah.'

The reason they never heard it was because we were interrupted by an ear-drum-splitting howl of incredible intensity. The sound bounced off the floor and ceiling of the hallway and came back twice as strong, rocking the brain and blurring the eyes.

Micky winced and backed away along the wall, and Whisky started to lift his hands to his ears. In the half second they gave me, I ran for the open door and hit Whisky in the chest with my right shoulder. He bounced back and fell against the railings, as I turned left and took off down the street at a speed I hadn't travelled at since I was sixteen. If I could get twenty yards away from the Airweight, I'd have a chance.

To be honest, I don't know if they fired at me. After the

unbelievable sound from Ronnie's little brass canister, my ears were in no state to process that kind of information.

All I know is they didn't rape me.

Eleven

There is no sin except stupidity.
OSCAR WILDE

Ronnie took us back to her flat off the King's Road, and we drove past it a dozen times in each direction. We weren't checking for surveillance, just looking for a place to park. This was the time of day when Londoners who own cars, and that's most of them, pay heavily for their indulgence – time stands still, or goes backwards, or does some fucking thing that doesn't correspond with the ordinary rules of the universe – and all those TV commercials showing sexy sportsters being flung about deserted country roads start to irritate you a little. They don't irritate me, of course, because I ride a bike. Two wheels good, four wheels bad.

When she'd finally managed to squeeze the TVR into a space, we discussed taking a taxi back to her flat, but decided that it was a nice enough evening and we both fancied the walk. Or rather, Ronnie fancied the walk. People like Ronnie always fancy the walk, and people like me always fancy people like Ronnie, so we each put on a stout pair of walking legs and set off. On the way, I gave her a brief account of the

Lyall Street session, and she listened in rapt near-silence. She hung on my words in a way that people, particularly women, don't usually hang. They usually let go, twist their ankle in the fall, and blame me for it.

But Ronnie was different somehow. Different because she seemed to think that I was different.

When we finally made it back to her flat, she unlocked the front door, stood to one side, and asked, in a strangely little-girl voice, if I wouldn't mind going in first. I looked at her for a moment. I think perhaps she wanted to gauge how serious the whole thing was, as if she still wasn't quite sure of it or me; so I put on a grim expression and went through the flat in what I hoped was a Clint Eastwoody sort of a way – pushing open doors with my foot, opening cupboards suddenly – while she stood in the corridor, her cheeks spotted with red.

In the kitchen, I said, 'Oh God.'

Ronnie gave a gasp, and then ran forward and peered round the door-jamb.

'Is this bolognese?' I said, and held up a wooden spoonful of something old and badly misjudged.

She tutted at me and then laughed with relief, and I laughed too, and we suddenly seemed like very old friends. Close, even. So obviously, I had to ask her.

'When's he coming back?'

She looked at me, and blushed a little, then went back to scraping bolognese from the saucepan.

'When's who coming back?'

'Ronnie,' I said. I moved round until I was more or less in front of her. 'You're very well put together, but you do not take a size forty-four chest. And if you did, you wouldn't take it in a lot of identical pin-stripe suits.'

She glanced towards the bedroom, remembering the cupboards, and then went to the sink and started to run hot water into the pan.

'Drink?' she said, without turning round.

She broke out a bottle of vodka while I threw ice-cubes over the kitchen floor, and eventually she decided to tell me that the boyfriend, who, as I think I could probably have guessed, sold commodities in the City, didn't stay at the flat every night, and when he did he never got there before ten. Honestly, if I'd had a pound for every time a woman has told me that, I'd have at least three by now. The last time it happened, the boyfriend came back at seven o'clock – 'He's never done that before,' – and hit me with a chair.

I deduced from her tone, and from her words too, that the relationship was not going as swimmingly as it might and, in spite of my curiosity, I thought it probably best to change the subject.

As we settled ourselves on the sofa, with the ice-cubes making sweet music inside the glasses, I started to give her a slightly fuller version of events – starting with Amsterdam, and ending with Lyall Street, but leaving out the bit about helicopters and Graduate Studies. Even so, it was a goodish yarn, with plenty of derring-do, and I added some derring-didn't-really-but-it-sounds-good, just to keep up her glowing opinion of me. When I'd finished, she wrinkled her brow slightly.

'But you didn't find the file,' she asked, looking disappointed.

'Nope,' I said. 'Which doesn't mean it isn't there. If Sarah really wanted to hide it in the house, it would take a team of builders about a week to search the place properly.'

'Well, I went over the gallery, and there's definitely nothing there. She's left some paperwork around, but it's all just work stuff.' She went over to the table and opened her briefcase. 'I did find her diary, if that's any good.'

I don't know if she was serious about this. She must have read enough Agatha Christies to know that finding diaries is almost always good.

But maybe not Sarah's. It was a leather-bound A4-sized affair, produced by a cystic fibrosis charity, and it didn't tell me much about its owner that I couldn't have guessed. She took her work seriously, lunched a little, didn't put circles instead of dots above her 'i's, but did doodle cats when she was on the phone. She hadn't made many plans for the months ahead, and the last entry simply said 'CED OK 7.30'. Looking back over the previous weeks, I saw that CED had also been OK three times before, once at 7.30 and twice at 12.15.

'Any idea who this is?' I said to Ronnie, showing her the entry. 'Charlie? Colin? Carl, Clive, Clarissa, Carmen?' I dried up on women's names beginning with 'C'.

Ronnie frowned.

'Why would she write a middle initial?'

'Beats me,' I said.

'I mean, if the name's Charlie Dunce, why not write CD?'

I looked down at the page.

'Charlie Etherington-Dunce? God knows. That's your patch.'

'What's that supposed to mean?' She was surprisingly quick to take offence.

'Sorry, I just mean . . . you know, I imagine you pass the time of day with double-barrelled sorts . . . ' I tailed off. I could see Ronnie didn't like this.

'Yes, and I've got a poncy voice, and a poncy job, and my boyfriend works in the city.' She got up and went to pour herself another vodka. She didn't offer me one, and I had the definite feeling that I was paying for someone else's crimes.

'Look, I'm sorry,' I said. 'I didn't mean anything by it.'

'I can't help the way I sound, Thomas,' she said. 'Or the way I look.' She took a belt of vodka and kept her back to me.

'What's to help? You sound great, you look even better.'

'Oh, shut up.'

'In a minute,' I said. 'Why are you so cross about it?'

She sighed and sat down again.

'Because it bores me, that's why. Half the people I meet never take me seriously because of the way I talk, and the other half *only* take me seriously because of the way I talk. Gets on your nerves after a while.'

'Well, I know this is going to sound pretty oily, but I take you seriously.'

'Do you?'

'Of course I do. Incredibly seriously.' I waited a bit. 'Doesn't bother me that you're a stuck-up bitch.'

She looked at me for a longish moment, in the course of which I started to think that maybe I'd got it wrong, and she was about to throw something. Then suddenly she laughed, and shook her head, and I felt a lot better. I hoped she did.

At about six o'clock the phone rang, and I could tell from the way Ronnie held the receiver that it was the boyfriend announcing his arrival time. She stared at the floor and said yeah a lot, either because I was in the room, or because their relationship had reached that stage. I picked up my jacket and carried my glass through to the kitchen. I washed and dried it, in case she forgot to, and was putting it back in the cupboard when Ronnie appeared.

'Will you call me?' She looked a bit sad. Perhaps I did, too.

'You bet,' I said.

I left her chopping onions in preparation for the commodity broker's return, and let myself out of the flat. Apparently the arrangement was that she made supper for him, and he made breakfast for her. Considering Ronnie was the sort of person to call a couple of grapefruit segments a major blow-out, I suspect that he'd got the better of the deal.

Honestly. Men.

A cab took me along the King's Road into the West End and by half past six I was loitering outside the Ministry of Defence. A couple of policemen watched me as I paced up and down, but I'd armed myself with a map and a disposable camera, and was taking pictures of pigeons in a gormless enough way to put their minds at rest. I'd had a lot more suspicion from the shopkeeper when I asked him for a map and said I didn't care which town it was of.

I'd made no other preparations for the trip, and I certainly hadn't wanted to have my voice logged on any incoming call to the Ministry. I was taking a chance on my reading of O'Neal as a swot and, from my first reconnaissance, it looked as if I'd got it right. Seventh floor, corner office, O'Neal's midnight oil was burning brightly. The regulation net curtains that hang in the windows of all 'sensitive' government buildings might defeat a telephoto lens, but they can't stop light from showing in the street.

Once upon a time, in the heady days of the Cold War, a twit in one of the supervising security branches had decreed that all 'targetable' offices should leave their lights on twenty-four hours a day, to prevent enemy agents from tracking who was at work where, and for how long. The idea was greeted at the time with nods of the head and pats on the back and many a murmured 'that fellow Carruthers will go a long way, mark my words' – until, that is, the electricity bills started flopping on to the mats of the relevant finance sections, whereupon the idea, and Carruthers, had been shown the door pretty smartly.

O'Neal emerged from the main door of the Ministry at ten minutes past seven. He gave a nod to the security guard, who ignored him, and stepped out into the Whitehall dusk. He was carrying a briefcase, which was odd – because nobody would have let him out of the building with anything more important than a few sheets of lavatory paper – so maybe he was one of those strange people who use a briefcase as a prop. I don't know.

I let him get a few hundred yards away from the Ministry before I started after him, and I had to work hard to keep my pace down, because O'Neal walked peculiarly slowly. One might have thought that he was enjoying the weather, if there'd been any to enjoy.

It wasn't until he crossed The Mall and started to speed up that I realised he'd been promenading; playing the part of the Whitehall tiger on the prowl, master of all he surveyed, privy to mighty secrets of state, any one of which would blow the socks off the average gawping tourist if he or she but knew. Once he'd stepped out of the jungle and on to the open savannah, the act wasn't really worth bothering with, so he walked normally. O'Neal was a man you could feel sorry for, if you had the time.

I don't know why, but I'd expected him to go straight home. I'd imagined a terraced house in Putney, where a long-suffering wife would feed him sherry and baked cod and iron his shirts while he grunted and shook his head at the television news, as if every word of it had an extra, darker, meaning for him. Instead, he skipped up the steps past the ICA, into Pall Mall and the Travellers Club.

There was no point in my trying anything there. I watched through the glass doors while O'Neal asked the porter to check his pigeon-hole, which was empty, and when I saw him shrug off his coat and move into the bar I judged it safe to leave him for a while.

I bought chips and a hamburger from a stall on the Haymarket and wandered a while, chewing as I went, watching people in bright shirts shuffle in to see musical shows that seemed to have been running for as long as I'd been alive. A depression started to drift down on to my shoulders as I walked, and I realised, with a jolt, that I was doing exactly the same thing as O'Neal – looking on my fellow man with a weary, cynical, 'you poor saps, if only you knew' feeling. I snapped myself out of it and threw the hamburger in a bin.

He came out at half past eight, and walked up the Haymarket to Piccadilly. From there he carried on up Shaftesbury Avenue, then took a left turn into Soho, where the tinkle of theatre-going chatter gave way to the bassier throbs of chic bars and strip joints. Huge moustaches with men hanging off the back loitered about in doorways, murmuring things about 'sexy shows' as I passed.

O'Neal was also being hustled by the doormen, but he seemed to know where he was going and didn't once turn his head to the advertised wares. Instead, he jinked left and right a few times, never looking back, until he reached his oasis, The Shala. He turned and walked straight in.

I kept going until the end of the street, dawdled for a minute, then headed back to admire The Shala's intriguing facade. The words 'Live', 'Girls', 'Erotic', 'Dancing' and 'Sexy' were painted round the door in a random fashion, as if inviting you to try and make a sentence out of them, and there were half-a-dozen faded snaps of women in their underwear pinned up in a glass case. A girl in a tight leather skirt lolled in the doorway, and I smiled at her in a way that said I was from Norway and yes, The Shala looked like just the place to refresh oneself after a hard day being Norwegian. I could just as easily have yelled that I was coming in there right now with a flamethrower, I doubt whether she would have batted an eyelid. Or could have batted it, under the weight of all that mascara.

I paid her fifteen pounds and filled in a membership form in the name of Lars Petersen, care of the Vice Squad, New Scotland Yard, and trotted down the steps into the basement to see just exactly how live, sexy, erotic, dancing and girls The Shala could really be.

It was a sorry sort of dive. Very, very sorry indeed. The management had long ago decided that turning the lights down was a cheap alternative to cleaning the place, and I had the constant feeling that the carpet-tiles were coming away with the soles of my shoes. Twenty or so tables were arranged around a small stage, on which three glassy-eyed girls bounced along to some loud music. The ceiling was so low that the tallest of them had to dance with a stoop; but surprisingly, considering all three were naked and the music was the Bee Gees, they were carrying the whole thing off with a fair degree of dignity.

O'Neal had a table at the front, and seemed to have taken a shine to the girl on the left, a pasty-faced creature who looked to me as if she could do with a large steak and kidney pie and a good night's sleep. She kept her eyes on the wall at the back of the club and never smiled.

'Drink.'

A man with boils on his neck was leaning over the bar at me.

'Whisky please,' I said, and turned to the stage.

'Five pounds.'

I looked back at him.

'I'm sorry?'

'Five pounds for the whisky. You pay now.'

'I don't think I do,' I said. 'You give me the whisky. Then I'll pay.'

'You pay first.'

'You fuck yourself with a garden fork first.' I smiled, to take the sting out of it. He brought the whisky. I paid him five pounds.

After ten minutes at the bar, I decided that O'Neal was here to enjoy the show and nothing else. He didn't look at his watch or the door, and he was drinking gin with enough abandon to convince me that he was definitely off the clock. I finished my own drink and sidled over to his table.

'Don't tell me. She's your niece and she's only doing this so she can get her Equity Card and join the Royal Shakespeare Company.' O'Neal turned and stared at me as I pulled out a chair and sat down. 'Hello,' I said.

'What are you doing here?' he said, crossly. I rather think he may have been a little embarrassed.

'Hang on,' I said. 'That's the wrong way round surely. You're supposed to say "hello" and I say "what are you doing here?"'

'Where the hell have you been, Lang?'

'Oh, hither and yon,' I said. 'As you know, I am a petal borne aloft on the autumn winds. It should say that in my file.'

'You followed me here.'

'Tut. Followed is such an ugly word. I prefer "blackmail".'

'What?'

'But, of course, it means something completely different. So all right, let's say I followed you here.'

He'd started looking round the room, trying to see if I had any large friends with me. Or maybe he was looking for large friends of his own. He leant forward and hissed at me. 'You

151

are in very, very serious trouble, Lang. It is only fair that I should warn you of that.'

'Yes, I think you're probably right,' I said. 'Very serious trouble is certainly one of the things I'm in. A strip club is another one. With a senior civil servant who shall remain nameless for at least an hour.'

He leaned back in his chair, a peculiar leer spreading across his face. The eyebrows raised, the mouth curled upwards. I realised it was the beginning of a smile. In kit form.

'Oh dear,' he said. 'You really are trying to blackmail me. That is terribly pathetic.'

'Is it? Well we can't have that.'

'I am meeting someone here. The choice of rendezvous was not mine.' He drained his third gin. 'Now I should be greatly obliged if you would take yourself off somewhere, so I don't have to call the doorman and have you ejected.'

The sound-track had moved seamfully into a loud but bland cover of 'War, What Is It Good For?' and O'Neal's niece moved down to the front of the stage and started shaking her vagina at us, almost in time to the music.

'Oh, I don't know,' I said. 'I think I like it here just fine.'

'Lang, I am warning you. You have at this moment very little credit in the bank. I have an important meeting here, and if you disrupt it, or inconvenience me in any way, I shall foreclose on you. Do I make myself plain?'

'Captain Mainwaring,' I said. 'That's who you remind me of.'

'Lang, for the last time . . . '

He stopped when he saw Sarah's Walther. I think I probably would have done the same, in his place.

'I thought you said you didn't carry firearms,' he said, after a while. Nervous, but trying not to show it.

'I'm a victim of fashion,' I said. 'Someone told me they're in this year, and I just had to have one.' I started to take off my jacket. The niece was only a few feet away, but she was still staring at the back wall.

'You are not going to fire a gun in here, Lang. I don't

believe you are entirely insane.'

I bundled the jacket into a tight ball and slipped the gun into one of the folds.

'Oh, I am,' I said. 'Entirely. Thomas "Mad Dog" Lang they used to call me.'

'I am beginning . . . '

O'Neal's empty glass exploded. Shards scattered across the table and on to the floor. He went very pale.

'My God . . . ' he stammered.

Rhythm's the thing. You've either got it or you haven't. I'd fired on one of the big crashing chords of 'War' and made no more noise than if I'd been licking an envelope. If the niece had been doing it, she would have fired on the upbeat and ruined everything.

'Another drink?' I said, and lit a cigarette to cover the smell of burnt powder. 'On me.'

'War' ended before Christmas and the three girls ambled off the stage, to be replaced by a couple whose act relied heavily on whips. They were pretty obviously brother and sister and couldn't have had less than a hundred years between them. The man's whip was only three feet long because of the low ceiling, but he wielded it as if it was thirty, lashing his sister to the tune of 'We Are The Champions'. O'Neal sipped chastely at a new gin and tonic.

'Now then,' I said, adjusting the position of the jacket on the table, 'I need one thing from you and one thing only.'

'Go to hell.'

'I certainly will, and I'll make sure your room is ready. But I need to know what you've done with Sarah Woolf.'

He stopped his glass amid sips, and turned to me, genuinely puzzled.

'What *I've* done with her? What on earth makes you think I've done anything with her?'

'She's disappeared,' I said.

'Disappeared. Yes. That's a melodramatic way of saying you can't find her, I assume?'

'Her father is dead,' I said. 'Did you know that?'

153

He looked at me for a long time.

'Yes, I did,' he said. 'What interests me is how you knew it.'

'You first.'

But O'Neal was starting to get bold, and when I moved the jacket closer to him he didn't flinch.

'You killed him,' he said, part angry, part pleased. 'That's it, isn't it? Thomas Lang, brave soldier of fortune, actually went through with it and shot a man. Well, my dear friend, you are going to have one hell of a job getting out of this one, I hope you realise that.'

'What are Graduate Studies?'

The anger, and the pleasure, gradually slipped out of his face. He didn't look as if he was going to answer, so I decided to press on.

'I'll tell you what I think Graduate Studies are,' I said, 'and you can give me points out of ten for accuracy.'

O'Neal sat, motionless.

'First of all, Graduate Studies means different things to different people. To one group, it means the development and marketing of a new type of military aircraft. Very secret, obviously. Very unpleasant, likewise. Very illegal, probably not. To another group, and this is where it all starts to get really interesting, Graduate Studies refers to the mounting of a terrorist operation that will allow the makers of this aircraft to show off their toy to advantage. By killing people. And make a genuinely huge sack of money from the resulting flow of enthusiastic buyers. Very secret, very unpleasant, and very, very, very to the power of ten, illegal. Alexander Woolf got wind of this second group, decided he couldn't let them get away with it, and started to make a nuisance of himself. So the second group, some of whom perhaps have legitimate positions in the intelligence community, start mentioning Woolf at drinks parties as a drugs trafficker, to blacken his name and undermine any little campaign he might want to get going. And when that didn't work, they threatened to kill him. And when *that* didn't work, they did kill him. And maybe they've killed his daughter as well.'

O'Neal still hadn't moved.

'But the people I really feel sorry for in all of this,' I said, 'besides the Woolfs, obviously, is anyone who *thinks* that they belong to the first group, not illegal, but all the time have been aiding, abetting and otherwise lending succour to the second group, very illegal, without even knowing it. Anyone in that position, I would say, has definitely got the skunk by the tail.'

He was looking over my shoulder now. For the first time since I'd met him, I couldn't tell what he was thinking.

'Well, that's it,' I said. 'Personally, I thought it was a wonderful routine, but now over to Judith and the opinion of the judges.'

But he still didn't answer. So I turned and followed his gaze towards the entrance to the club, where one of the doormen stood, pointing at our table. I saw him nod and step back, and the lean, powerful figure of Barnes, Russell P., strode into the room and headed towards us.

I shot them both dead there and then, and caught the next plane to Canada, where I married a woman called Mary-Beth and started up a successful pottery business.

At least, that's what I should have done.

Twelve

*He hath no pleasure in the strength of an horse:
neither delighteth he in any man's legs.*

BOOK OF PRAYER 1662

'My, you are a slippery bastard, Mr Lang. A real piece of work, if that expression means anything to you.'

Barnes and I were sitting in another Lincoln Diplomat – or maybe it was the same one, in which case someone had cleaned the ashtrays since I was last in it – parked underneath Waterloo Bridge. A large illuminated sign displayed the offerings at the National Theatre close by, a stage version of *It Ain't Half Hot, Mum* directed by Sir Peter Hall. Something like that.

O'Neal sat in the passenger seat this time, and Mike Lucas was once more at the wheel. I was surprised he wasn't in a canvas bag on a plane back to Washington, but Barnes had obviously decided to give him another chance after the Cork Street gallery débâcle. Not that it had been his fault, but fault has got very little to do with blame in these sorts of circles.

Another Diplomat was parked behind us, with whatever the collective noun for Carls is inside it. A neck of Carls, maybe. I'd given them the Walther, because they seemed to want it such an awful lot.

'I think I know what you're trying to say, Mr Barnes,' I said, 'and I take it as a compliment.'

'I don't give a rat's ass how you take it, Mr Lang. Not a rat's ass.' He gazed out through the side window. 'Jesus, do we have a mess of problems here.'

O'Neal cleared his throat and twisted round in the seat.

'What Mr Barnes is saying, Lang, is that you have stumbled upon an operation of considerable complexity here. There are ramifications about which you know absolutely nothing, yet you have, by your actions, made things extremely difficult for us.' O'Neal was chancing his arm a bit with that 'us', but Barnes let him get away with it. 'I think I can honestly say . . . ' he continued.

'Oh, do fuck off,' I said. O'Neal went a little pink. 'I have only one concern, and that is the safety of Sarah Woolf. Anything else, as far as I am concerned, is a lot of garnish.'

Barnes looked out of the window again.

'Go home, Dick,' he said.

There was a pause, and O'Neal looked hurt. He was being sent to bed without any supper, and yet he hadn't done anything wrong.

'I think I . . . '

'I said go home,' said Barnes. 'I'll call you.'

Nobody moved until Mike leaned across and opened O'Neal's door for him. In the circumstances, he had to go.

'Well, goodbye, Dick,' I said. 'It's been an unquantifiable pleasure. I hope you'll think nice thoughts about me when you see my body being dragged out of the river.'

O'Neal tugged his briefcase out behind him, slammed the door, and set off up the steps to Waterloo Bridge without looking back.

'Lang,' said Barnes. 'Let's walk.' He was outside the car and strolling down the Embankment before I could answer. I looked in the rear-view mirror and saw that Lucas was watching me.

'Remarkable man,' I said.

Lucas turned his head to watch Barnes' retreating back, then looked to the mirror again.

'Be careful, will you?' he said.

I paused, with my hand on the door lever. Mike Lucas didn't sound happy. Not at all.

'Careful of what, specifically?'

He hunched his shoulders slightly and put his hand up to his mouth, covering the movement of his lips as he spoke.

'I don't know,' he said. 'I swear to God, I don't know. But there's some shit going on here . . . ' He stopped at the sound of car doors opening and closing behind us.

I put my hand on his shoulder.

'Thanks,' I said, and climbed out. A couple of Carls ambled up alongside the car, and puffed their necks out at me. Twenty yards way, Barnes was watching, apparently waiting for me to catch him up.

'I think I prefer London at night,' he said, once we'd got ourselves in step.

'Me too,' I said. 'River's very pretty.'

'The fuck it is,' said Barnes. 'I prefer London at night because you can't see it so well.'

I laughed, and then stopped myself quickly because I think he meant it. He looked angry, and the notion suddenly hit me that his posting to London might have been a punishment for some past transgression, and that here he was, seething and smarting every day at the injustice of his treatment, and taking it out on the city.

He interrupted my notionalising.

'I hear from O'Neal that you got a little theory,' he said. 'A little idea you been working on. Is that right?'

'Certainly is,' I said.

'Take me through it, will you?'

And so, having no particular reason not to, I went ahead and repeated the speech I'd given O'Neal in The Shala, adding a bit here, subtracting a bit there. Barnes listened without showing much interest, and when I'd finished, he sighed. A long, tired, Jesus what am I going to do with you sort of sigh.

'To put it bluntly,' I said, not wanting there to be any misunderstanding about the way I felt, 'I think you're a dangerous, corrupt, lying piece of nine-day-old mosquito shit. I'd happily kill you now if I didn't think it would make Sarah's position even worse than it already is.' Even that didn't seem to bother him overmuch.

'Ah huh,' he said. 'And what you've just told me.'

'What about it?'

'Of course you wrote it all down? Gave a copy to your lawyer, your bank, your mother, the Queen, only to be opened in the event of your death. All that shit?'

'Naturally. We do have television programmes over here, you know.'

'That's fucking debatable. Cigarette?' He pulled out a packet of Marlboro and offered them to me. We smoked together for a while, and I reflected on how odd it was that two men who hated each other very deeply could, by sucking together on some burning paper, engage in a fairly companionable act.

Barnes stopped and leaned against the balustrade, gazing down into the slick, black water of the Thames. I stayed a few yards away, because you can take all this companionable nonsense too far.

'OK, Lang. Here it is,' said Barnes. 'I'll say it all once, because I know you're not an idiot. You're slap bang on the money.' He tossed his cigarette away. 'Big deal. So we're going to make a little noise, kick up some trade. Boo-hoo. How's that so terrible?'

I decided that I would try the calm approach. If that didn't work, I'd try the throwing him into the river and running like fuck approach.

'It's so terrible,' I said slowly, 'because you and I were both born and bred in democratic countries, where the will of the people is thought to count for something. And I believe it's the will of the people, at this time, that governments do not go around murdering their own or anyone else's citizens just

159

to line their own pockets. Next Wednesday, the people may say it's a great idea. But right now, it is their will that we should use the word "bad" when talking about this kind of activity.' I took a last drag and flicked my own dog-end out over the water. It seemed to fall a very long way.

'Two points occur to me, Lang,' said Barnes after a long pause, 'out of your nice speech. One, neither one of us lives in a democracy. Having a vote once every four years is not the same thing as democracy. Not at all. Two, who said anything about lining our own pockets?'

'Oh, of course.' I slapped my forehead. 'I hadn't realised. You're going to give all the money from the sale of these weapons to The Save The Children Fund. It's a gigantic piece of philanthropy, and I never even noticed. Alexander Woolf will be so thrilled.' I was beginning to stray from the calm approach. 'Oh, but wait a minute, his intestines are being scraped off a wall in the City. He may not be as fulsome with his thanks as he'd like. You, Mr Barnes,' and I even went so far as to point a finger, 'need your fucking head examined.'

I walked away from him, back down the river. Two Carls with ear-pieces were ready to cut me off.

'Where do you think it goes, Lang?' Barnes hadn't moved, he just talked a little louder. I stopped. 'When some Arab playboy drops into the San Martin valley and buys himself fifty M1 Abrams battle tanks and a half dozen F-16s. Writes a cheque for half-a-billion dollars. Where d'you think that money goes? You think I get it? You think Bill Clinton gets it? David fucking Letterman? Where does it go?'

'Oh tell me, do,' I said.

'I will tell you. Even though you know it already. It goes to the American people. Two hundred and fifty million people get a hold of that money.'

I did some not very quick arithmetic. Divide by ten, carry the two . . .

'They get two thousand dollars each, do they? Every man, woman and child?' I sucked my teeth. 'Now why doesn't that ring true?'

'A hundred and fifty thousand people,' said Barnes, 'have jobs because of that money. With those jobs they support another three hundred thousand people. And with that half-a-billion dollars those people can buy a lot of oil, a lot of wheat, a lot of Nissan Micras. And another half-million people will sell them the Nissan Micras, and another half-a-million will repair the Nissan Micras, and wash the windshields, and check the tyres. And another half-a-million will build the roads that the Nissan fucking Micras run on, and pretty soon, you've got two hundred and fifty million good democrats, needing America to go on doing the last thing it does well. Make guns.'

I stared down at the river because this man was making my head swim. I mean, where do you begin?

'So for the sake of those good democrats, a body here and a body there isn't such a terrible thing. Is that your drift?'

'Yip. And there isn't one of those good democrats who'd say any different.'

'I think Alexander Woolf would say different.'

'Big deal.'

I kept looking at the river. It looked thick and warm.

'I mean it, Lang. Big fucking deal. One man against many. He was out-voted. That's democracy. Want to know something else?' I turned to look at Barnes, and he was facing me now, his lined face caught in the flicker from the theatre sign. 'There's another two million US citizens I didn't get around to mentioning there. Know what they're going to do this year?'

He was walking towards me, slowly. Confidently.

'Become lawyers?'

'They're going to die,' he said. The idea didn't seem to disturb him all that much. 'Old age, auto accident, leukaemia, heart attack, fighting in bars, falling out of windows, who knows what fucking thing? Two million Americans are going to die this year. So tell me. You going to shed a tear for every one of them?'

'No.'

'Why the hell not? What's the difference? Dead is

dead, Lang.'

'The difference is I didn't have anything to do with their deaths,' I said.

'You were a soldier, for Chrissakes!' We were face to face now, him shouting as loud as he could go without getting people out of bed. 'You were trained to kill people for the good of your fellow countrymen. Isn't that the truth?' I started to answer, but he wouldn't have it. 'Is that, or is that not, the truth?' His breath smelled oddly sweet.

'This is very bad philosophy, Rusty. It really is. I mean read a book, for God's sake.'

'Democrats don't read books, Lang. The people don't read books. The people don't care a piece of blue shit about philosophy. All the people care about, all they want from their government, is a wage that keeps getting higher and higher. Year in, year out, they want that wage going up. It ever stops, they get themselves a new government. That's what the people want. It's all they've ever wanted. That, my friend, is democracy.'

I took a deep breath. In fact I took several deep breaths, because what I now wanted to do to Russell Barnes might result in me not breathing again for quite a while.

He was still watching me, testing me for some reaction, some weakness. So I turned and walked away. The Carls moved up to meet me, coming at each side, but I kept going because I reckoned they weren't going to do anything until they had the signal from Barnes. After a couple of paces, he must have given it.

The Carl on the left reached out and took hold of my arm, but I broke the grip easily, turning his wrist over and pushing down hard, so that he had to go with the movement. The other Carl got his arm round my neck for about a second, until I stamped hard on his instep and punched backwards at his groin. His hold broke, and then I was between the two of them as they circled me, and I wanted to hurt them so incredibly badly that they would never, ever forget me.

And then suddenly, as if nothing had happened, they were

162

backing away, and straightening their coats, and I realised that Barnes must have said something I never heard. He walked up between the Carls, coming very close to me.

'So, we get the idea, Lang,' he said. 'You're really pissed with us. You don't like me at all, and my heart is broken. But all that's kind of beside the point.'

He shook out another cigarette for himself and didn't offer me one.

'If you want to make trouble for us, Lang,' he said, gently exhaling smoke through his nose, 'best thing is for you to know what it's going to cost.'

He looked over at my shoulder and nodded at somebody.

'Murder,' he said.

Then he smiled at me.

Hello, I thought. This could be interesting.

We drove out on the M4 for about an hour, turning off, I would think, somewhere near Reading. I'd love to be able to tell you exactly which junction, and the numbers of the minor roads we took, but as I spent most of the journey on the floor of the Diplomat with my face being ground into the carpet, sensory data in-flow was a little restricted. The carpet was dark-blue and smelled of lemon, if that's any help.

The car slowed for about the last fifteen minutes of the ride, but that could have been for traffic, or fog, or giraffes on the road for all I know.

And then we reached a gravel drive, and I thought to myself – not long now. You could scrape up the gravel from most driveways in England, and come away with about enough to fill a sponge-bag. Any second now, I thought, I'll be outside, and within screaming distance of a public highway.

But this wasn't an average drive.

This one went on and on. And then it went on and on. And then, when I thought we were turning a corner and pulling over to park, it went on and on.

Eventually, we stopped.

And then we started again, and went on and on.

I had begun to think that maybe it wasn't a drive at all; it was simply that the Lincoln Diplomat had been designed, with fantastically precise manufacturing skill, to disintegrate into very small pieces as soon as it exceeded its warranty mileage; perhaps what I was listening to now, pinging and bouncing off the wheel arches, were bits of chassis.

And then, at last, we stopped. I knew we'd stopped for good this time, because the size twelve shoe that had been resting itself on the back of my neck was now sufficiently invigorated to slide off and get out of the car. I lifted my head and peered through the open door.

This was a grand house. A very grand house. Obviously, at the end of a drive like that, it was never going to be a two-up, two-down; but even so, this was grand. Late nineteenth-century, I reckoned, but copying earlier ones, with a lot of Frenchness thrown in. Well, not thrown, of course, but lovingly bonded and pointed, beaded and mitred, bevelled and chamfered, very possibly by the same blokes who did the House of Commons railings.

My dentist leaves back numbers of *Country Life* scattered around his waiting-room, so I had a rough idea of what a place like this must have cost. Forty bedrooms, within an hour of London. A sum of money beyond imagining. Beyond beyond imagining, in fact.

I had begun idly to calculate the number of lightbulbs you'd need to run a place like this, when a Carl took hold of my collar and plucked me out of the car, as easily as if I'd been a golf-bag, with not many clubs in it.

Thirteen

Every man over forty is a scoundrel.
GEORGE BERNARD SHAW

I was shown into a room. A red room. Red wallpaper, red curtains, red carpet. They said it was a sitting-room, but I don't know why they'd decided to confine its purpose just to sitting. Obviously, sitting was one of the things you could do in a room this size; but you could also stage operas, hold cycling races, and have an absolutely cracking game of frisbee, all at the same time, without having to move any of the furniture.

It could rain in a room this big.

I hung about by the door for a while, looking at paintings, the undersides of ashtrays, that kind of thing, then got bored and set off towards the fireplace at the other end. Half-way there I had to stop and sit down, because I'm not as young as I was, and as I did so, another set of double-doors opened, and some muttering took place between a Carl and a major-domo figure in striped grey trousers and black jacket.

Both of them glanced in my direction every once in a while, and then the Carl nodded his head and backed out of the room.

The major-domo started towards me, pretty casually I thought, and called out at the two hundred metre mark:

'Would you care for a drink, Mr Lang?'

I didn't have to think about this for very long.

'Scotch, please,' I called back.

That'd teach him.

At one hundred metres, he stopped at a frequent table and opened a small silver box, pulling out a cigarette without even looking down to see if there were any in there. He lit it, and kept on coming.

As he got nearer, I could see that he was in his fifties, good-looking in an indoor kind of way, and that his face had a strange sheen to it. The reflections of standard-lamps and chandeliers danced across his forehead, so that he seemed almost to sparkle as he moved. Yet somehow I knew it wasn't sweat, nor oil; it was just a sheen.

With ten yards still to go, he smiled at me and held out a hand, and kept it there as he came so that before I'd realised it, I was on my feet, ready to receive him like an old friend.

His grip was hot but dry, and he clasped me by the elbow and steered me back on to the sofa, sliding down next to me so that our knees were almost touching. If he always sat this close to visitors, then I have to say he was simply not getting his money's worth out of his room.

'Murder,' he said.

There was a pause. I'm sure you'll understand why.

'I beg your pardon?' I said.

'Naimh Murdah,' he said, then watched patiently while I readjusted the spelling in my head. 'A great pleasure. Great pleasure.'

His voice was soft, his accent educated. I had the feeling that he'd be just as good in a dozen other languages. He flicked some ash from his cigarette vaguely in the direction of a bowl, then leaned towards me.

'Russell has told me a lot about you. And I must say, I've been cheering for you very much.'

Close up, there were two things I could tell about Mr

166

Murdah: he was not the major-domo; and the sheen on his face was money.

It wasn't caused by money, or bought with money. It simply was money. Money that he'd eaten, worn, driven, breathed, in such quantities, and for so long, that it had started to secrete from the pores of his skin. You may not think this possible, but money had actually made him beautiful.

He was laughing.

'Very much indeed, yes. You know, Russell is a very considerable person. Very considerable indeed. But sometimes I think it does him good to become frustrated. He has a tendency, I would say, towards arrogance. And you, Mr Lang, I have the feeling that you are good for such a man.'

Dark eyes. Incredibly dark eyes. With dark edges to the lids, which ought to have been make-up but wasn't.

'You, I think,' said Murdah, still beaming, 'you frustrate many people. I think perhaps that is why God put you here among us, Mr Lang. Wouldn't you say?'

And I laughed back. Fuck knows why, because he hadn't said anything funny. But there I was, chuckling away like a drunk simpleton.

A door opened somewhere, and then suddenly a tray of whisky was between us, borne by a maid dressed in black. We took a glass each, and the maid waited while Murdah drowned his in soda, and I just got mine slightly damp. She left without a smile, or a nod. Without uttering a sound.

I took a deep slug of Scotch and felt drunk almost before I'd swallowed.

'You're an arms dealer,' I said.

I don't know quite what reaction I expected, but I expected something. I thought he might flinch, or blush, or get angry, or have me shot, tick any of the above, but there was nothing. Not even a pause. He continued as if he'd known for years what I was going to say.

'I am indeed, Mr Lang. For my sins.'

Wow, I thought. That was extremely cute. I am an arms

dealer for my sins. That was every bit as rich as he was.

He lowered his eyes with apparent modesty.

'I buy and sell arms, yes,' he said. 'I must say, I think, successfully. You, of course, disapprove of me, as do many of your countrymen, and this is one of the penalties of my profession. Something that I must bear, if I can.'

I suppose he was making fun of me, but it didn't sound that way. It really did sound as if my disapproval made him unhappy.

'I have examined my life, and my behaviour, with the help of many friends who are religious people. And I believe I can answer to God. In fact – if I can anticipate your questions – I believe I can *only* answer to God. So do you mind if we move on?' He smiled again. Warm, charmingly apologetic. He dealt with me like a man who's used to dealing with people like me – as if he was a polite film star, and I'd asked him for an autograph at a tricky moment.

'Nice furniture,' I said.

We were taking a tour of the room. Stretching our legs, filling our lungs, digesting some huge meal we hadn't eaten. To finish the picture, we really needed a couple of dogs mucking about at our ankles, and a gate to lean on. We didn't have them, so I was trying to make do with the furniture.

'It's a Boulle,' said Murdah, pointing at the large wooden cabinet under my elbow. I nodded, the same way I nod when people tell me the names of plants, and politely bent my head to the intricate brass inlay.

'They take a sheet of veneer and a sheet of brass, glue them together, then cut the pattern right through. That one,' he pointed towards an apparently related cabinet, 'is a *contre* Boulle. You see? An exact negative. Nothing wasted.'

I nodded thoughtfully, and looked back and forth at the two pieces, and tried to imagine how many motorbikes I'd need to own before I decided to start spending money on stuff like this.

Murdah had done enough walking, apparently, and peeled off back towards the sofa. The way he moved seemed to say that the pleasantries box was almost empty.

'Two opposite images of the same object, Mr Lang,' he said, reaching for another cigarette. 'You might say, if you like, that those two cabinets resemble our little problem.'

'I might, yes.' I waited, but he wasn't ready to expand. 'Of course, I'd need to know roughly what you're talking about first.'

He turned to me. The sheen was still there, and so were the indoor good-looks. But the chumminess was dying away, sputtering in the grate and warming nobody.

'I'm talking, Mr Lang, about Graduate Studies, obviously.' He looked surprised.

'Obviously,' I said.

'I have an involvement,' said Murdah, 'with a certain group of people.'

He was standing in front of me now, his hands held wide in that welcome-to-my-vision gesture that politicians like to use these days, while I lounged on the sofa. Otherwise little had changed, except that someone was cooking fishfingers near by. It was a smell that didn't quite belong in this room.

'These people,' he continued, 'are, in many cases, friends of mine. People with whom I have done business over many, many years. They are people who trust me, who rely on me. You understand?'

Of course, he wasn't asking me if I understood the specific relationship. He just wanted to know if words like Trust and Reliability still had any meaning down where I lived. I nodded to show that yes, I could spell them in an emergency.

'As an act of friendship towards these people, I have taken something of a risk. Which is rare for me.' This, I think, was a joke, so I smiled, which seemed to satisfy him. 'I have personally underwritten the sale of a quantity of merchandise.' He paused and looked at me, wanting some reaction. 'I think perhaps you are familiar with the nature of the product?'

'Helicopters,' I said. There didn't seem to be any point in playing stupid at this stage.

'Helicopters, precisely,' said Murdah. 'I must tell you that I dislike the things myself, but I am told that they perform some functions extremely well.' He was starting to go a little fey on me, I thought – affecting a distaste for the vulgar, oily machines that had paid for this house and, for all I knew, a dozen more like it – so I decided to try and blunt things up a bit, on behalf of the common man.

'They certainly do,' I said. 'The ones you're selling could destroy an average-size village in under a minute. Along with all its inhabitants, obviously.'

He closed his eyes for a second, as if the very thought of such a thing gave him pain, which, perhaps, it did. If so, it wasn't for long.

'As I said, Mr Lang, I don't believe I have to justify myself to you. I am not concerned with the use to which this merchandise is eventually put. My concern, for the sake of my friends, and for myself, is that the merchandise should find customers.' He clasped his hands together and waited. As if the whole thing was now my problem.

'So advertise,' I said, after a while. 'Back pages of *Woman's Own*.'

'Hm,' he said. Like I was an idiot. 'You are not a businessman, Mr Lang.'

I shrugged.

'I am, you see,' he continued. 'So I think you must trust me to know my own market-place.' A thought seemed to strike him. 'After all, I wouldn't presume to advise you on the best way . . . ' And then he realised he was in a jam, because there was nothing on my CV to indicate that I knew the best way to do anything.

'To ride a motorcycle?' I offered, gallantly.

He smiled.

'As you say.' He sat down on the sofa again. Further away,

this time. 'The product I am dealing with requires a more sophisticated approach, I think, than the pages of *Woman's Own*. If you are making a new mousetrap, then, as you say, you advertise it as a new mousetrap. If, on the other hand,' he held out his other hand, to show me what another hand looked like, 'you are trying to sell a snake trap, then your first task is to demonstrate why snakes are bad things. Why they need to be trapped. Do you follow me? Then, much, much later, you come along with your product. Does that make sense to you?' He smiled patiently.

'So,' I said, 'you're going to sponsor a terrorist act, and let your little toy do its business on the nine o'clock news. I know all this. Rusty knows that I know all this.' I glanced at my watch, trying to make it look as if I had another arms dealer to see in ten minutes. But Murdah was not a man to be hurried, or slowed down.

'That, in essence, is precisely what I intend to do,' he said.

'And I come into this where, exactly? I mean, now that you've told me, what am I supposed to do with the information? Put it in my diary? Write a song about it? What?'

Murdah looked at me for a moment, then took in a deep breath and pushed it out gently and carefully through his nose, as if he'd had lessons in how to breathe.

'You, Mr Lang, are going to carry out this terrorist act for us.'

Pause. Long pause. A feeling of horizontal vertigo. The walls of this massive room shooting inwards, then out again, making me feeling smaller, and punier, than I've ever felt.

'Aha,' I said.

Another pause. The smell of fishfingers was stronger than ever.

'Do I have a say in this, by any chance?' I croaked. My throat was giving me trouble, for some reason. 'I mean, if I were to say, for example, fuck you and all your relatives, roughly what could I expect to happen, at today's prices?'

It was Murdah's turn to do the glancing-at-the-watch bit. He seemed to have grown suddenly bored, and wasn't smiling at all any more.

'That, Mr Lang, is not an option that I think you should waste any time considering.'

I felt cooler air on my neck, and twisted round to see that Barnes and Lucas were standing by the door. Barnes looked relaxed. Lucas didn't. Murdah nodded, and the two Americans stepped forward, coming each side of the sofa to join him. Facing me. Murdah held out a hand, palm up, in front of Lucas, without looking at him.

Lucas slid back the flap of his jacket and pulled out an automatic. A Steyr, I think. 9mm. Not that it matters. He placed the gun gently in Murdah's hand, then turned towards me, his eyes widened by the pressure of some message that I couldn't decipher.

'Mr Lang,' said Murdah, 'you have the safety of two people to think about. Your own, of course, and Miss Woolf's. I don't know what value you place on your own safety, but I think it would be only gallant if you were to consider hers. And I want you to consider hers very deeply.' He beamed suddenly, as if the worst was over. 'But, of course, I don't expect you to do it without good reason.'

As he spoke, he cocked the hammer, and lifted his chin towards me, the gun loose in his hand. Sweat spurted from the palms of my hands and my throat wouldn't work. I waited. Because that was all I could do.

Murdah considered me for a moment. Then he reached out, pressed the muzzle of the gun to the side of Lucas's neck, and fired twice.

It happened so fast, was so unexpected, was so absurd, that for a tenth of a second I wanted to laugh. There were three men standing there, then there was a bang bang, and then there were two. It was actually funny.

I realised that I'd wet myself. Not much. But enough.

I blinked once, and saw that Murdah had handed the gun to Barnes, who was signalling towards the door behind my head.

'Why did he do that? Why would anyone do such a terrible thing?'

It should have been my voice, but it wasn't. It was Murdah's. Soft and calm, utterly in control. 'It was a terrible thing, Mr Lang,' he said. 'Terrible. Terrible, because it had no reason. And we must always try and find a reason for death. Don't you agree?'

I looked up at his face, but couldn't focus on it. It came and went, like his voice, which was in my ear and miles away at the same time.

'Well, let us say that although he had no reason to die, I had a reason to kill him. That is better, I think. I killed him, Mr Lang, to show you one thing. And one thing only.' He paused. 'To show you that I could.'

He looked down at Lucas's body, and I followed his gaze.

It was a foul sight. The muzzle had been so close to the flesh that the expanding gases had chased the bullet in, swelling and blackening the wound horribly. I couldn't look at it for long.

'Do you understand what I'm saying?'

He was leaning forward, with his head on one side.

'This man,' said Murdah, 'was an accredited American diplomat, an employee of the US State Department. He had, I'm sure, many friends, a wife, perhaps even children. So it would not be possible, surely, for such a man to disappear, just like that? To vanish?'

Men were stooping in front of me, their jackets rustling as they strained to move Lucas's body. I forced myself to listen to Murdah.

'I want you to see the truth, Mr Lang. And the truth is that if I wish him to disappear, then it is so. I shoot a man here, in my own house, I let him bleed on my own carpet, because it is my wish. And no one will stop me. No police, no secret agents, no friends of Mr Lucas's. And certainly not you. Do you hear me?'

I looked up at him again, and saw his face more clearly.

The dark eyes. The sheen. He straightened his tie.

'Mr Lang,' he said, 'have I given you a reason to think about Miss Woolf's safety?'

I nodded.

They drove me back to London, pressed into the carpet of the Diplomat, and chucked me out somewhere south of the river.

I went over Waterloo Bridge and along the Strand, stopping every now and then for no reason, occasionally dropping coins into the hands of eighteen-year-old beggars, and wanting this piece of reality to be a dream more than I've ever wanted any dream to become reality.

Mike Lucas had told me to be careful. He'd taken a risk, telling me to be careful. I didn't know the man, and I hadn't asked him to take the risk for me, but he'd done it anyway because he was a decent professional who didn't like the places his work was taking him, and didn't want me to be taken there too.

Bang bang.

No going back. No stopping the world.

I was feeling sorry for myself. Sorry for Mike Lucas, sorry for the beggars too, but very sorry indeed for myself, and that had to stop. I started to walk home.

I no longer had any reason to worry about being at the flat, since all the people I'd had breathing down my neck over the last week were now breathing in my face. The chance to sleep in my own bed was just about the only good thing to come out of all this. So I strode out for Bayswater at a good pace, and as I walked, I tried to see the funny side.

It wasn't easy, and I'm still not sure that I managed it properly, but it's just something I like to do when things aren't going well. Because what does it mean, to say that things aren't going well? Compared to what? You can say: compared to how things were going a couple of hours ago, or a couple of years ago. But that's not the point. If two cars are speeding towards a brick wall with no brakes, and one car hits the wall moments before the other, you can't spend those moments saying that the second car is much better off than the first.

Death and disaster are at our shoulders every second of our lives, trying to get at us. Missing, a lot of the time. A lot of miles on the motorway without a front wheel blow-out. A lot of viruses that slither through our bodies without snagging. A lot of pianos that fall a minute after we've passed. Or a month, it makes no difference.

So unless we're going to get down on our knees and give thanks every time disaster misses, it makes no sense to moan when it strikes. Us, or anyone else. Because we're not comparing it with anything.

And anyway, we're all dead, or never born, and the whole thing really is a dream.

There, you see. That's a funny side.

Fourteen

Thus freedom now so seldom wakes,
The only throb she gives,
Is when some heart indignant breaks,
To show that still she lives.

THOMAS MOORE

There were two things parked in my street that I hadn't expected to see when I turned into it. One was my Kawasaki, bruised and bloodied, but otherwise in reasonable shape. The other was a bright red TVR.

Ronnie was asleep at the wheel, with a coat pulled up to her nose. I opened the passenger door and slid in beside her. Her head came up and she squinted at me.

'Evening,' I said.

'Hello.' She blinked a few times and looked out at the street. 'God, what time is it? I'm freezing.'

'Quarter to one. Do you want to come in?'

She thought about it.

'That's very forward of you, Thomas.'

'Forward of me?' I said. 'Well, that depends, doesn't it?' I opened the door again.

'On what?'

'On whether you drove over here, or I rebuilt my street around your car.'

She thought a bit more.

'I'd kill for a cup of tea.'

We sat in the kitchen, not saying much, just sipping tea and smoking. Ronnie's mind was on other things, and at an amateurish guess I'd say that she'd been crying. Either that or she'd attempted a fancy rag-rolling effect with her mascara. I offered her some Scotch but she wasn't interested, so I helped myself to the last four drops in the bottle and tried to make them last. I was trying to concentrate on her, to put Lucas and Barnes and Murdah out of my mind, because she was upset and she was in the room. The others weren't.

'Thomas, can I ask you something?'

'Course.'

'Are you gay?'

I mean, really. First ball of the over. You're supposed to talk about films and plays, and favourite ski runs. All that kind of thing.

'No, Ronnie, I'm not gay,' I said. 'Are you?'

'No.'

She stared into her mug. But I'd used tea bags, so she wasn't going to find any answers there.

'What's happened to what's his name?' I said, lighting a cigarette.

'Philip. He's asleep. Or out somewhere. I don't really know. Don't much care, to be honest.'

'Now, Ronnie. I think you're just saying that.'

'No, really. I don't give a fuck about Philip.'

There's always something strangely thrilling about hearing a well-spoken woman swear.

'You've had a tiff,' I said.

'We've split up.'

'You've had a tiff, Ronnie.'

'Can I sleep with you tonight?' she said.

I blinked. And then, to make sure I hadn't just imagined it, I blinked again.

'You want to sleep with me?' I said.

'Yes.'

'You don't just mean sleep at the same time as me, you mean in the same bed?'

'Please.'

'Ronnie . . . '

'I'll keep my clothes on if you like. Thomas, don't make me say please again. It's terribly bad for a woman's ego.'

'It's terribly good for a man's.'

'Oh shut up.' She hid her face in the mug. 'I've gone right off you now.'

'Ha,' I said. 'It worked.'

Eventually we got up and went into the bedroom.

She did keep her clothes on, as it happens. So did I, as it also happens. We lay down side by side on the bed and stared at the ceiling for a while, and when I judged the while to be long enough, I reached out a hand and took hold of one of hers. It was warm and dry and a very nice thing to touch.

'What are you thinking?'

To be honest, I can't remember which one of us said this first. We both said it about fifty times before dawn.

'Nothing.'

We both said that a lot as well.

Ronnie wasn't happy, that was the long and the short of it. I can't say that she poured out her life story to me. It came in odd chunks, with long gaps in between, like belonging to a discount book club, but by the time the lark came on to relieve the nightingale, I'd learned quite a bit.

She was a middle child, which would probably make a lot of people go 'ah, well there you are, you see,' but I am too, and it's never bothered me that much. Her father worked in the City, grinding the faces of the poor, and the two brothers either side of her looked like they were headed in the same direction. Her mother had developed a passion for deep-sea fishing when Ronnie was in her teens, and since then had spent six months of every year indulging it in distant oceans while her father took mistresses. Ronnie didn't say where.

178

'What are you thinking?' Her, this time.

'Nothing.' Me.

'Come on.'

'I don't know. Just . . . thinking.'

I stroked her hand a bit.

'About Sarah?'

I'd sort of known she was going to ask this. Even though I'd deliberately kept my second serves deep and not mentioned Philip again, so she wouldn't be able to come into the net.

'Among other things. People, I mean.' I gave her hand a tiny squeeze. 'Let's face it, I hardly know the woman.'

'She likes you.'

I couldn't help laughing.

'That seems astronomically unlikely. The first time we met she thought I was trying to kill her father, and the last time, she spent most of the evening wanting to give me a white feather for cowardice in the face of the enemy.'

I thought it best to leave out the kissing thing, just for the moment.

'What enemy?' said Ronnie.

'It's a long story.'

'You've got a nice voice.'

I turned my head on the pillow and looked at her.

'Ronnie, in this country, when someone says something's a long story, it's a polite way of saying they're not going to tell it to you.'

I woke up. Which suggested the possibility that I'd fallen asleep, but I've no idea when that happened. All I could think was that the building was on fire.

I leapt out of bed and ran to the kitchen, and found Ronnie burning some bacon in a frying-pan. Smoke from the cooker frolicked about in the shafts of sunlight coming through the window, and Radio 4 burbled away somewhere nearby. She'd helped herself to my only clean shirt, which annoyed me a little because I'd been saving it for something special, like my grandson's twenty-first – but she looked good in it, so I let it pass.

'How d'you like your bacon?'

'Crispy,' I lied, looking over her shoulder. Not much else I could say.

'You can make some coffee if you like,' she said, and turned back to the frying-pan.

'Coffee. Right.' I started to unscrew a jar of instant stuff, but Ronnie tutted and nodded towards the sideboard where the shopping fairy had visited in the night and left all manner of good things.

I opened the fridge and saw someone else's life. Eggs, cheese, yoghurt, some steaks, milk, butter, two bottles of white wine. The sort of things I've never had in any fridge of mine in thirty-six years. I filled the kettle and switched it on.

'You'll have to let me pay you for all this,' I said.

'Oh, do grow up.' She tried cracking an egg one-handed on the edge of the pan and made a dog's breakfast of it. And I had no dog.

'Shouldn't you be at the gallery?' I asked, as I spooned Melford's Dark Roasted Breakfast Blend into a jug. This was all very strange.

'I rang. Told Terry my car was broken. Brakes had failed, and I didn't know how late I was going to be.'

I thought about this for a while.

'But if your brakes had failed, surely you ought to have got there early?'

She laughed and slid a plate of black, white and yellow stuff in front of me. It looked unspeakable and tasted delicious.

'Thank you, Thomas.'

We were walking through Hyde Park, going nowhere in particular, holding hands for a bit, then letting go as if holding hands wasn't one of life's big deals. The sun had come up to town for the day and London looked grand.

'Thank you for what?'

Ronnie looked down at the ground and kicked at something that probably wasn't there.

'For not trying to make love to me last night.'

'You're welcome.'

I really didn't know what she expected me to say, or even whether this was the beginning of a conversation or the end. 'Thank you for thanking me,' I added, which made it sound more like the end.

'Oh, shut up.'

'No, really,' I said. 'I appreciate it very much. I don't try and make love to millions of women every day, and never get a squeak out of most of them. It makes a nice change.'

We strolled on a bit. A pigeon flew towards us and then darted away at the last moment, as if he'd suddenly realised we weren't who he thought we were. A couple of horses trotted down Rotten Row, with tweed-jacketed men on their backs. Household Cavalry, probably. The horses looked quite intelligent.

'Do you have anybody, Thomas?' said Ronnie. 'At the moment?'

'You're talking about women, I would think.'

'That's the ticket. Are you sleeping with any?'

'By sleeping with, you mean . . . ?'

'Answer the question immediately, or I'll call a policeman.' She was smiling. Because of me. I'd made her smile, and it was a nice feeling.

'No, Ronnie, I'm not sleeping with any women at the moment.'

'Men?'

'Or any men. Or any animals. Or any types of coniferous tree.'

'Why not, if you don't mind me asking? And even if you do.'

I sighed. I didn't really know the answer to this myself, but saying that wasn't going to get me off the hook. I started talking without any clear idea of what was going to come out.

'Because sex causes more unhappiness than it gives

pleasure,' I said. 'Because men and women want different things, and one of them always ends up being disappointed. Because I don't get asked much, and I hate asking. Because I'm not very good at it. Because I'm used to being on my own. Because I can't think of any more reasons.' I paused for breath.

'All right,' said Ronnie. She turned and started walking backwards so she could get a good view of my face. 'Which of those is the real one?'

'B,' I said, after a bit of thought. 'We want different things. Men want to have sex with a woman. Then they want to have sex with another woman. And then another. Then they want to eat cornflakes and sleep for a while, and then they want to have sex with another woman, and another, until they die. Women,' and I thought I'd better pick my words a little more carefully when describing a gender I didn't belong to, 'want a relationship. They may not get it, or they may sleep with a lot of men before they do get it, but ultimately that's what they want. That's the goal. Men don't have goals. Natural ones. So they invent them, and put them at either end of a football pitch. And then they invent football. Or they pick fights, or try and get rich, or start wars, or come up with any number of daft bloody things to make up for the fact that they have no real goals.'

'Bollocks,' said Ronnie.

'That, of course, is the other main difference.'

'Do you honestly think I would want to have a relationship with you?'

Tricky. Straight bat, head over the ball.

'I don't know Ronnie. I wouldn't presume to guess what you want out of life.'

'Oh, other bollocks. Get a grip, Thomas.'

'On you?'

Ronnie stopped. And then grinned.

'That's more like it.'

We found a phone box and Ronnie called the gallery. She told them that she was feeling overwrought with the strain of dealing with her broken car, and that she needed to lie down for the rest of the afternoon. Then we got into the car and drove to Claridges for lunch.

I knew that eventually I was going to have to tell Ronnie something of what had happened, and something of what I thought was going to happen. It would probably involve a little lying, for my sake as well as hers, and it would also involve talking about Sarah. Which is why I put it off for as long as I could.

I liked Ronnie a lot. Maybe if she'd been the damsel in distress, held in the black castle on the black mountain, I would have fallen in love with her. But she wasn't. She was sitting opposite me, chattering away, ordering a rocket salad with her Dover sole, while a string quartet in Austrian national costume plucked and fiddled some Mozart in the lobby behind us.

I looked carefully round the room to see where my followers might be, knowing that there could be more than one team by now. There were no obvious candidates nearby, unless the CIA had taken to recruiting seventy-year-old widows with what looked like a couple of bags of self-raising flour tipped over their faces.

In any case, I was less concerned about being followed than about being heard. We'd chosen Claridges at random, so there'd been no chance to install any listening equipment. I had my back to the rest of the room, so any hand-held directional microphones wouldn't be getting much. I poured us each a large glass of perfectly drinkable Pouilly-Fuissé that Ronnie had chosen, and started to talk.

I began by telling her that Sarah's father was dead, and that I'd seen him die. I wanted to get the worst of it over with quickly, to drop her down a hole and then pull her up slowly, giving her natural pluck a bit of time to get to work. I also didn't want her to think that I was scared, because that wouldn't have helped either of us.

She took it well. Better than she took the Dover sole, which lay on her plate untouched, with a mournful 'did I say something wrong?' look in its eye, until a waiter swept it away.

By the time I'd finished, the string quartet had ditched Mozart in favour of the theme from *Superman,* and the wine bottle was upside down in its bucket. Ronnie stared at the tablecloth and frowned. I knew she wanted to go and ring somebody, or hit something, or shout out in the street that the world was a terrible place and how could everyone go on eating and shopping and laughing as if it wasn't. I knew that because that's exactly what I'd wanted to do ever since I'd seen Alexander Woolf blown across a room by an idiot with a gun. Eventually she spoke, and her voice was shaking with anger.

'So, you're going to do this, are you? You're going to do what they tell you?'

I looked at her and gave a small shrug.

'Yes, Ronnie, that's what I'm going to do. I don't want to do it, but I think the alternatives are slightly worse.'

'Do you call that a reason?'

'Yes I do. It's the reason most people do most things. If I don't go along with them, they will probably kill Sarah. They've killed her father already, so it's not as if they're crossing any big bridges from now on.'

'But people are going to die.' There were tears in her eyes, and if the wine waiter hadn't come and tried to flog us another bottle of the Pouilly at that moment, I probably would have hugged her. Instead I took her hand across the table.

'People are going to die anyway,' I said, and hated myself for sounding like Barnes's nasty little speech. 'If I don't do it, they'll find someone else, or some other way. The result will be the same, but Sarah will be dead. That's what they're like.'

She looked down at the table again, and I could see that she knew I was right. But she was checking everything all the same, like someone about to leave home for a long time. Gas off, TV disconnected, fridge defrosted.

'And what about you?' she said, after a while. 'If that's what they're like, what's going to happen to you? They're going to kill you, aren't they? Whether you help them or not, they're going to end up killing you.'

'They're probably going to have a go, Ronnie. I can't lie about that.'

'What can you lie about?' she said quickly, but I don't think she meant it the way it sounded.

'People have tried to kill me before, Ronnie,' I said, 'and they haven't managed it. I know you think I'm a slob who can't even do his own shopping, but I can look after myself in other ways.' I paused to see if she'd smile. 'If nothing else, I'll find some posh bint with a sports car to take care of me.'

She looked up, and nearly smiled.

'You've got one of those already,' she said, and took out her purse.

It had started raining while we'd been inside, and Ronnie had left the roof down on the TVR, so we had to pelt through Mayfair as fast as we could for the sake of her Connolly-hide seats.

I was scrabbling with the catches on the car's hood, trying to work out how I was going to fill the six-inch gap between the frame and the windscreen, when I felt a hand on my shoulder. I kept myself as loose as possible.

'And who the fuck might you be?' said a voice.

I straightened up slowly and looked round. He was about my height, and not far off my age, but he was considerably richer. His shirt was from Jermyn Street, his suit was from Savile Row, and his voice was from one of our more expensive public schools. Ronnie popped her head up from the boot where she'd been folding away the tonneau cover.

'Philip,' she said, which was pretty much what I'd expected her to say.

'Who the fuck is this?' said Philip, still looking at me.

'How do you do, Philip?'

I tried to be nice. Really I did.

'Fuck off,' said Philip. He turned to Ronnie. 'Is this the shit who's been drinking my vodka?'

A knot of tourists in bright anoraks stopped and smiled at the three of us, hoping that we were all good friends really. I hoped we were too, but sometimes hope isn't enough.

'Philip, please don't be boring.' Ronnie slammed the boot and came round to the side of the car. The dynamics shifted a little, and I tried to squirt myself out of the group and away. The last thing I felt like was getting involved in someone else's pre-marital row, but Philip wouldn't have it.

'The fuck do you think you're going?' he said, raising his chin a little higher.

'Away,' I said.

'Philip, come on.'

'You little shit. Who the hell do you think you are?' He put his right hand out and took hold of my lapel. He held it tight, but not so tight that he was committed to fighting me. Which was a relief. I looked down at his hand and then at Ronnie. I wanted to give her the chance to call this off.

'Philip, please, don't be stupid,' she said.

Which, obviously, was about as wrong a thing as she could have chosen to say. When a man's reversing himself flat out into a corner, the very last thing to make him slow down is a woman telling him he's being stupid. If it had been me, I'd have said I was sorry, or stroked his brow, or smiled, or done anything I could think of to dissipate the flow of hormones.

'I asked you a question,' said Philip. 'Who do you think you are? Drinking at my bar, cocking your leg in my house?'

'Please let go of me,' I said. 'You're creasing my jacket.' Reasonable, you see. Not facing him down, calling him out, squaring him up, or anything else involving odd prepositions. Just straightforward concern about my jacket. Man to man.

'I couldn't give a fuck about your jacket, you little tosser.'

Well, there you are. Every possible diplomatic channel having been tried and found wanting, I opted for violence.

I pushed towards him first, and he resisted, which is what people always do. Then I dropped back with his push, straightening his arm, and turned away so that he had to flip his wrist over to keep hold of the lapel. I put one hand on top of his, to make him keep the grip, and with my other forearm I leaned gently downwards on his elbow. If you're interested, this happens to be an Aikido technique called Nikkyo, and it causes a quite stupendous amount of pain with almost no effort.

His knees buckled and his face went white as he dropped down to the pavement, trying desperately to take the pressure off the wrist joint. I let him go before his knees touched the ground, because I reckoned that the more face I left him with, the less reason he'd have to try anything else. I also didn't want to have Ronnie kneeling over him saying there, there, who's a brave soldier? for the rest of the afternoon.

'Sorry,' I said, and smiled uncertainly, as if I didn't quite know what had happened either. 'Are you all right?'

Philip wrung his hand and shot me a pretty hateful look, but we both knew he wasn't going to do anything about it. Even though he couldn't be certain that I'd hurt him deliberately.

Ronnie moved in between us and gently put her hand on Philip's chest.

'Philip, you've got this very badly wrong.'

'Have I really?'

'Yes, you have really. This is business.'

'Fuck it is. You're sleeping with him. I'm not an idiot.'

That last remark ought to have had any decent prosecution counsel leaping to their feet, but Ronnie just turned to me and half-closed an eye.

'This is Arthur Collins,' she said, and waited for Philip to frown. Which he eventually did. 'He painted that triptych we saw in Bath, do you remember? You said you liked it.'

Philip looked at Ronnie, then at me, then back to Ronnie again. The world turned a little more while we waited for him to chew it over. Part of him was embarrassed at the possibility that he'd made a mistake, but a much bigger part was relieved that he now had the chance to seize on a respectable reason for not trying to hit me – there I was, don'cha know, ready to lay the blighter out, had him begging for mercy, and he turned out to be a wrong number. Different party altogether. Laughs all round. Philip, you're a scream.

'The one with the sheep?' he said, straightening his tie and shooting his cuffs in a well-practised movement. I looked at Ronnie, but she wasn't about to help me with this one.

'Angels, actually,' I said. 'But a lot of people see them as sheep.'

That seemed to satisfy him as an answer, and a grin spread across his face.

'God, I am so sorry. What can you think of me? I thought . . . well, it doesn't really matter, does it? There's a chap . . . oh, never mind.'

There was more in this vein, but I just spread my hands wide to show that I quite understood and that I made the same mistake myself three or four times a day.

'Will you excuse us, Mr Collins?' said Philip, as he took hold of Ronnie's elbow.

'Course,' I said. Philip and I were the best of pals now.

They moved a few feet away and I realised it had been at least five minutes since I'd smoked a cigarette, so I decided to put that right. The bright anoraks were still hovering anxiously further down the pavement and I waved to them to show that yes, London's a crazy place but they ought to go ahead and have a nice day all the same.

Philip was trying to make it up to Ronnie, that was obvious – but it looked as if he was playing the 'I forgive you card', instead of the much stronger 'please forgive me' one, which I've always found wins more tricks in the end. Ronnie's mouth was twisted into a half-accepting, half-bored shape, and she glanced at me every now and then to show how tiring all this was.

I smiled back at her, just as Philip reached into his pocket and pulled out a sheaf of paper. Long and thin. An airline ticket. A come away with me for the weekend and we'll have wheelbarrowsful of sex and champagne ticket. He handed it to Ronnie and kissed her on the forehead, which was another mistake, waved at Arthur Collins the distinguished West Country painter, and set off down the street.

Ronnie watched him go and then sauntered over to where I was standing.

'Angels,' she said.

'Arthur Collins,' I said.

She looked down at the ticket and sighed. 'He thinks we should have another go. Our relationship is too precious etc.'

I went ah, and we stared at the pavement for a while.

'So he's taking you to Paris, is he? On the corny side, I'd have said, if it was any of my business.'

'Prague,' said Ronnie, and a bell rang somewhere in my head. She opened the ticket. 'Prague's the new Venice, according to Philip.'

'Prague,' I said, and nodded. 'They tell me it's in Czechoslovakia at this time of year.'

'The Czech Republic, actually. Philip was very precise about that. Slovakia's gone to the dogs and isn't half as beautiful. He's booked a hotel near the town square.'

She looked down again at the open ticket and I heard the breath stop in her throat. I followed her gaze, but there didn't seem to be any tarantulas crawling up her sleeve.

'Something wrong?'

'CED,' she said, snapping the ticket shut.

I frowned.

'What about him?' I couldn't see what she was getting at, even though the bell was still ringing. 'D'you know who he is?'

'He's OK, isn't he?' said Ronnie. 'According to Sarah's diary, CED is OK, right?'

'Right.'

'Right.' She handed me the ticket. 'Look at the carrier.'

I looked.

Maybe I should have known it already. Maybe everybody knew it except Ronnie and me. But, according to Sunline Travel's printed itinerary for Ms R. Crichton, the national airline of the new Czech Republic goes by the letters CEDOK.

Fifteen

*In war, whichever side may call itself the victor,
there are no winners, but all are losers.*

N. CHAMBERLAIN

So the two strands of my life met in Prague.

Prague was where Sarah had gone, and Prague was where
the Americans were sending me for the first stage of what
they insisted on calling Operation Dead Wood. I told them
straight away that I thought it was a terrible name, but either
somebody important had chosen it, or they'd already had the
writing paper done, because they refused to budge. Dead
Wood is what it's called, Tom.

The operation itself, officially at least, was a standard, off-
the-shelf scheme to infiltrate a group of terrorists and, once
there, to muck up their lives, and the lives of their suppliers,
paymasters, sympathisers and loved ones, as far as was
practicable. Nothing remotely special about it. Intelligence
agencies all over the world are trying this kind of thing all the
time, with varying degrees of failure.

The second strand, the Sarah strand, the Barnes, Murdah,
Graduate Studies strand, was all about selling helicopters to
nasty despotic governments, and I gave this a name of my

190

own choosing. I called it Oh Christ.

Both strands met in Prague.

I was due to fly out on the Friday night, which meant six days of briefing from the Americans, and five nights of tea-drinking and hand-holding with Ronnie.

The boy Philip flew to Prague the day I nearly broke his wrist, to cut some high-powered deals with the velvet revolutionaries, and he left Ronnie confused and more than a little miserable. Her life may not have been a thrill-packed roller-coaster before I happened, but it wasn't exactly a rack of pain either, and this sudden jerk into the world of terrorism and assassination, coupled with a rapidly disintegrating relationship, didn't help to make a woman feel at her most relaxed.

I kissed her once.

The Dead Wood briefings took place in a red brick thirties mansion just outside Henley. It had about two square miles of parquet floor, every third board of which was curling up with damp, and only one of the lavatories flushed properly.

They'd brought furniture with them, a few chairs and desks and some camp beds, and slung them round the house without much thought. Most of my time was spent in the drawing-room, watching slide shows, listening to tapes, memorising contact procedures, and reading about life as a farm hand in Minnesota. I can't say it was like being back at school, because they made me work harder than I ever did as a teenager, but it was an oddly familiar atmosphere all the same.

I took myself down there every day on the Kawasaki, which they had arranged to have repaired for me. They wanted me to stay overnight, but I told them I needed to take a few deep draughts of London before I left, and they seemed to like that. Americans respect patriotism.

The cast changed constantly, and never dropped below six. There was a gofer called Sam, Barnes was in and out, and a few Carls hung around in the kitchen, drinking herbal tea and doing chin-ups in the doorways. And then there were the specialists.

The first called himself Smith, which was so unlikely that I believed him. He was a puffy little chap with glasses and a tight waistcoat, who talked a lot about the sixties and seventies, the great days of terrorism if you were in Smith's line of work – which seemed to consist of following Baaders and Meinhofs and assorted Red Brigaders round the world like a teenage girl tracking a Jackson Five tour. Posters, badges, signed photographs, the lot.

The Marxist revolutionaries were a big disappointment to Smith, most of them having packed it in and got themselves mortgages and life insurance in the early eighties, although the Italian Red Brigades occasionally re-formed to sing some of the old songs. The Shining Path and its like in Central and South America were not Smith's thing at all. They were as jazz to a Motown buff, and hardly worth mentioning. I dropped in what I thought were a couple of telling questions about the Provisional IRA, but Smith put on a Cheshire cat face and changed the subject.

Goldman came next, tall and thin and enjoying the fact that he didn't enjoy his work. Goldman's preoccupation seemed to be etiquette. He had a right way and a wrong way of doing everything, from hanging up a telephone receiver to licking a stamp, and he would brook no deviation. After a day of his tutoring I felt like Eliza Doolittle.

Goldman told me that henceforth I should answer to the name of Durrell. I asked him if I could pick my own name, and he said no, Durrell was already entered on the case file of Operation Dead Wood. I asked him if he'd heard of Tippex, and he said that was a silly name, and I'd better just get used to Durrell.

Travis was unarmed combat, and when they told him he only had an hour with me, he just sighed, said 'eyes and genitals', and left.

On the last day the planners arrived; two men and two women, dressed like bankers and carrying huge briefcases. I tried flirting with the women but they weren't having any of it. The shorter of the two men might have been on, though.

The tall one, Louis, was the friendliest of the four, and did most of the talking. He seemed to know his stuff, without ever really letting on what his stuff was, which sort of showed how well he knew it. He called me Tom.

One thing, and only one thing, was obvious from all of this. Dead Wood was not being improvised, and these people hadn't just sat down the day before with the Ladybird book of international terrorism. This train had been running for many months before I was dragged aboard.

'Kintex mean anything to you, Tom?' Louis crossed his legs and leaned towards me like some kind of David Frost.

'Nothing, Louis,' I said. 'I am a blank canvas.' I lit another cigarette just to annoy them all.

'That's just fine. First thing you should know, and I guess you know this already – there are no idealists left in the world.'

'Except for you and me, Louis.'

One of the women looked at her watch.

'Right, Tom,' he said. 'You and me. But freedom fighters, liberators, architects of the new dawn, all that stuff went the way of flared pants. Terrorists these days are businessmen.' A female throat cleared, somewhere at the back of the room. 'And businesswomen. And terror is a great-looking career for a modern kid. Really. Good prospects, lot of travel, expense account, early retirement. If I had a son, I'd say to him either law or terrorism. And let's face it, maybe terrorists do less harm.'

This was a joke.

'Maybe you wonder where the money comes from?' He raised his eyebrows at me, and I nodded like a Playschool presenter. 'Well there are the bad guys, the Syrians, the Libyans, the Cubans, who still look at terror as a state industry. They write big cheques now and then, and if an American Embassy gets a brick through the window as a result, they're happy. But in the last ten years, they've kind of taken a back seat. Nowadays, profit's the thing, and when it comes to profit, all roads lead to Bulgaria.'

He sat back in his seat, which was the cue for one of the women to step forward and read from a clipboard, although she obviously knew her speech by heart and just had the clipboard for comfort.

'Kintex,' she began, 'is ostensibly a state-run trading agency, based out of Sofia, where five hundred and twenty-nine personnel are employed on import-export activities. Covertly, Kintex handles upwards of eighty per cent of narcotics traffic from the Middle East into western Europe and North America, frequently in exchange for licit and illicit arms consignments resold to Middle Eastern insurgency groups. The heroin is similarly resold, to selected central and western European trafficking rings. Personnel involved in these operations are mostly non-Bulgarians, but are given storage and accommodation facilities in Varna and Burgas on the Black Sea. Kintex, under a new operating name of Globus, also participates in the laundering of drug profits from all over Europe, exchanging cash for gold and precious stones and redistributing funds to their clients via a chain of business operations in Turkey and eastern Europe.'

She looked up at Louis, to see whether he wanted to hear more, but Louis looked at me, saw that I had started to glaze over, and gave a tiny shake of his head.

'Nice guys, right?' he said. 'Also the folks who gave a gun to Mehmet Ali Agca.' That didn't mean a lot to me either. 'Took a shot at Pope John Paul in '81. Made a few headlines.'

I went ah yes, and wagged my head to show how impressed I was.

'Kintex,' he continued, 'is a regular one-stop shop, Tom. You want to make some trouble in the world, wreck a few countries, blight a few million lives, then just grab your credit card and head down to Kintex. Nobody beats their prices.'

Louis was smiling, but I could tell he was blazing with righteous anger. So I looked round the room, and sure enough, the other three had the same kind of zealous fire hanging round their heads.

'And Kintex,' I said, desperately hoping that they would answer no, 'are the people Alexander Woolf was dealing with.'

'Yes,' said Louis.

Which is when and why I realised, in a very horrible moment indeed, that none of these people, not even Louis, had the faintest idea of what Graduate Studies was really about – or what Operation Dead Wood was really supposed to achieve. These people actually thought they were fighting a straightforward battle against narco-terrorism, or terronarcotics, or whatever the hell they called it, on behalf of a grateful Uncle Sam and Auntie Rest Of The World. This was run-of-the-mill CIA business, with not a kink to be seen. They were putting me into a second division terrorist group in the simple, uncomplicated hope that I'd nip down to a phone box on my evening off and fill them in with a lot of names and addresses.

I was being taught how to drive by blind instructors, and the realisation shook me a bit.

They laid out the plan for the infiltration and made me repeat every stage of it a million times. I think that, because I was English, they were worried I wouldn't be able to hold more than one thought in my head at a time, and when they saw that I'd picked the whole thing up pretty easily, they slapped each other on the back and said 'good job' a lot.

After a revolting supper of meat balls and Lambrusco, served up by a harassed-looking Sam, Louis and his fellows packed up their briefcases, pumped my hand and nodded their heads meaningfully, before climbing into their cars and setting off back down the yellow brick road. I didn't wave.

Instead, I told the Carls that I was going for a walk and went through to the garden at the back of the house, where a lawn ran down to the river and a view of the most beautiful reach in the whole length of the Thames.

It was a warm night, and on the opposite bank young couples and elderly dog-walkers were still promenading. A few cabin-cruisers had moored nearby, water patting gently against their hulls, and the lights at their windows glowed a soft and welcoming yellow. People were laughing, and I could smell their tinned soup.

I was in deep shit.

Barnes arrived just after midnight, and he was a very different sight from our first meeting. The Brooks Brothers stuff had gone, and he now looked like he was ready to head into the Nicaraguan jungle at the drop of a bomb. Khaki trousers, dark-green twill shirt, Red Wing boots. A military-looking watch with canvas strap had taken the place of the dress Rolex. I had the feeling that for two pins he'd have been in front of a mirror, slapping camouflage paint on to his face. The lines were deeper than ever.

He dismissed the Carls and the two of us settled ourselves in the drawing-room, where he unpacked a half-bottle of Jack Daniels, a carton of Marlboro and a camouflage-painted Zippo lighter.

'How's Sarah?' I said.

It felt like a silly question, but it had to be asked. After all, she was the reason I was doing all this – and if it turned out that she'd stepped under a bus that morning, or died of malaria, I was definitely off the case. Not that Barnes would tell me if she had, but I might get something from his face when he answered.

'Fine,' he said. 'She's just fine.' He poured bourbon into two glasses, and skidded one of them across the parquet floor to me.

'I want to speak to her,' I said. He didn't flinch. 'I need to know she's all right. Still alive and still all right.'

'I'm telling you she's fine.' He took a suck at his glass.

'I know you're telling me that,' I said. 'But you're a psychopath, whose word isn't worth a flake of sick.'

'I don't like you much either, Thomas.'

We were sitting opposite each other now, drinking whisky and smoking cigarettes, but the atmosphere fell short of the ideal agent-handler relationship, and was falling shorter by the second.

'You know what your problem is?' said Barnes, after a while.

'Yes, I know perfectly well what my problem is. It buys its clothes from an L.L. Bean catalogue, and is sitting opposite me right now.'

He pretended he hadn't heard. Maybe he hadn't.

'Your problem, Thomas, is that you're British.' He started rotating his head in odd movements. Every now and then a bone cracked in his neck, which seemed to give him pleasure. 'The things that are wrong with you, are wrong with this whole godforsaken pisspot of an island.'

'Wait a minute,' I said. 'Wait a full, well-rounded minute. This can't be right. This can't be a fucking American, telling me what's wrong with this country.'

'Got no balls, Thomas. You ain't got them. This country ain't got them. Maybe you had them once, and you lost them. I don't know, and I don't care so much.'

'Now Rusty, be careful,' I said. 'I ought to warn you that over here, people take the word "balls" to mean courage. We don't understand the American meaning, of having a big mouth and getting an erection every time you say "Delta" and "strike" and "kick ass". Important cultural difference there. And by cultural difference,' I added, because the blood was running a bit hot I must admit, 'we don't mean a divergence of values. We mean fuck you up the arse with a wire brush.'

He laughed at that. Which was not the reaction I'd been hoping for. Quite a large part of me had hoped that he'd try and hit me, so that I'd be able to punch him in the throat and ride off into the night with an easy mind.

'Well, Thomas,' he said, 'I hope we've cleared some air there. Hope you feel better now.'

'Much better, thank you,' I said.

'Me too.'

He got up to refill my glass, and then dropped the cigarettes and lighter in my lap.

'Thomas, I'll be straight. You can't see, or speak to, Sarah Woolf right now. Just ain't possible. But at the same time, I won't expect you to lift a finger for me until you have seen her. How's that? Sound fair enough to you?'

I sipped at the whisky and eased a cigarette from the packet.

'You haven't got her, have you?'

He laughed again. I was going to have to put a stop to this somehow.

'I never said we did, Thomas. What did you think, that we had her chained to a bedpost somewhere? Come on, give us a little credit, will you? We do this for a living, you know. We're not right off the boat here.' He dropped back into his chair and resumed his neck-stretching, and I wished I could have helped. 'Sarah is where we can reach her if we need to. Right now, seeing as how you're being such a nice little English boy, we don't need to. Okay?'

'No, not okay.' I stubbed out the cigarette and got to my feet. It didn't seem to bother Barnes. 'I see her, make sure she's all right, or I don't do this. Not only don't I do this, I might even kill you just to prove exactly how much I'm not going do it. Okay?'

I started slowly to move towards him. I thought he might cry out to the Carls, but that didn't worry me. If it came to it, I only needed a few seconds – whereas the Carls would take about an hour to get those ridiculous bodies kick-started into action. Then I realised why he was so relaxed.

He'd dropped his hand into the briefcase at his side, and there was a glint of grey metal as the hand emerged. It was a big gun, and he held it loosely over his crotch, aimed at my midriff, range about eight feet.

'Well Jiminy Cricket,' I said. 'You're about to get an erection, Mr Barnes. Isn't that a Colt Delta Elite you've got there in your lap?'

He didn't answer this time. Just looked.

'Ten millimetre,' I said. 'A gun for people who've either got a small penis or little faith in their ability to hit the middle of the target.' I was wondering how to cover those eight feet without him hitting me with a decent body shot. It wasn't going to be easy, but it was possible. Provided one had balls. Before and after the event.

He must have sensed what I was thinking, because he cocked the hammer. Very slowly. It did make a satisfying click, I must admit.

'You know what a Glaser slug is, Thomas?' He spoke softly, almost dreamily.

'No, Rusty,' I said, 'I don't know what a Glaser slug is. Sounds like it's a chance for you to bore me to death instead of shoot me. Off you go.'

'The bullet of the Glaser Safety Slug, Thomas, is a small cup made of copper. Filled with fine lead shot in liquid teflon.' He waited for me to take this in, knowing I would know what it meant. 'On impact, the Glaser is guaranteed to dump ninety-five per cent of its energy on the target. No shoot-throughs, no ricochets, just a lot of knocking down.' He paused, and took a sip of whisky. 'Big, big holes in your body.'

We must have stayed like that for quite a while. Barnes tasting whisky, me tasting life. I could feel myself sweating and my shoulder blades started to itch.

'Okay,' I said. 'Maybe I won't try and kill you just at the moment.'

'Glad to hear it,' said Barnes after a long while, but the Colt didn't move.

'Putting a big hole in my body isn't going to help you much.'

'Ain't gonna hurt me much either.'

'I need to speak to her, Barnes,' I said. 'She's why I'm here. If I don't speak to her, there's no point to any of this.'

Another couple of hundred years went by, and then I

started thinking that Barnes was smiling. But I didn't know why, or when he'd begun. It was like sitting in a cinema before the main feature, trying to work out whether the lights really were going down.

And then it hit me. Or caressed me, rather. Nina Ricci's Fleur de Fleurs, one part per billion.

We were down on the river bank. Just the two of us. The Carls paced somewhere, but Barnes had told them to keep their distance and they did. The moon was out and it spilt across the water towards where we sat, lighting her face with a milky glow.

Sarah looked terrible and wonderful. She'd lost some weight, and she'd been crying more than was good for her. They'd told her that her father was dead twelve hours before, and at that moment I wanted to put my arm round her more than I've ever wanted to do anything. But it wouldn't have been right. I don't know why.

We sat in silence for a while, looking out over the water. The cabin-cruisers had switched off their lights, and the ducks had turned in long ago. Either side of the moon stain, the river was black and quiet.

'So,' she said.

'Yeah,' I said.

There was another long silence, as we thought about what had to be said. It was like a big concrete ball that you know you've got to lift. You can walk round and round looking for a place to take hold of it, but it just isn't there.

Sarah had the first try.

'Be honest. You didn't believe us, did you?'

She nearly laughed, so I nearly answered by saying that she hadn't believed that I wasn't trying to kill her father. I stopped myself in time.

'No, I didn't,' I said.

'You thought we were a joke. Mad pair of Americans seeing ghosts in the night.'

'Something like that.'

She started to cry again, and I sat and waited until the squall passed. When it did, I lit a couple of cigarettes and handed her one. She drew on it heavily, and then flicked non-existent ash into the river every few seconds. I watched her and pretended not to.

'Sarah,' I said. 'I'm very sorry. For everything. For what's happened. And for you. I want . . . ' I couldn't for the life of me think of the right thing to say. I just felt I ought to be saying something. 'I want to put things right, somehow. I mean, I know that your father . . . '

She looked up at me and smiled, to tell me not to worry.

'But there's always a choice,' I blundered on, 'between doing the right thing or the wrong thing, no matter what's happened. And I want to do the right thing. Do you understand?'

She nodded. Which was damn good of her, because I hadn't the faintest idea what I meant. I had too many things to say, and too small a brain to sort them out with. Post Office, three days before Christmas, that was my head.

She sighed.

'He was a good man, Thomas.'

Well, what do you say?

'I'm sure he was,' I said. 'I liked him.' That was true.

'Didn't really know it until a year ago,' she said. 'You kind of don't think of your parents as being anything, do you? Good or bad. They're just there.' She paused. 'Until they're not.'

We stared at the river for a while.

'Your parents alive?'

'No,' I said. 'My father died when I was thirteen. Heart attack. My mother four years ago.'

'I'm sorry.' I couldn't believe it. She was being polite, in the middle of all this.

'That's all right,' I said. 'She was sixty-eight.'

Sarah leaned towards me and I realised I'd been speaking very softly. I'm not sure why. Maybe it was respect for her grief, or perhaps I didn't want my voice to puncture the little

201

composure she had.

'What's your favourite memory of your mother?'

It wasn't a sad question. It really sounded as if she wanted to know, as if she was getting ready to enjoy some story of my childhood.

'Favourite memory.' I thought for a moment. 'Every day, between seven and eight o'clock in the evening.'

'Why?'

'She'd have a gin and tonic. Seven o'clock on the dot. Just one. And for that hour she became the happiest, funniest woman I've ever known.'

'What about afterwards?'

'Sad,' I said. 'No other word for it. She was a very sad woman, my mother. Sad about my father, and about herself. If I'd been her doctor, I'd have prescribed gin six times a day.' For a moment, I felt like I wanted to cry. It passed. 'What about you?'

She didn't have to think very hard for hers, but she waited anyway, playing it over in her mind and making herself smile.

'I don't have any happy memories of my mother. She started fucking her tennis coach when I was twelve and disappeared the next summer. Best thing that ever happened to us. My father,' and she closed her eyes at the warmth of the memory, 'taught my brother and me to play chess. When we were eight or nine. Michael was good, took it up real quick. I was pretty good, too, but Michael was better. But when we were learning, my dad used to play us without his queen. He'd always take the black pieces and he'd always play without the queen. And as Michael and me got better and better, he never took the piece back. Kept playing without his queen, even when Michael was beating him in ten moves. Got to the point where Michael could have played without his own queen and still won. But my dad just kept on, losing game after game, and never once played with a full set of pieces.'

She laughed, and the movement of it stretched her out until she was lying back, resting on her elbows.

'On Dad's fiftieth birthday, Michael gave him a black queen, in a little wooden box. He cried. Weird, seeing your dad cry. But I think it just gave him so much pleasure to see us learn, and get strong, that he never wanted to lose the feeling of it. He wanted us to win.'

And then, suddenly, the tears arrived in a huge wave, crashing over her and shaking her thin body until she could hardly breathe. I lay down and put my arms around her, squeezing her tight to shield her from everything.

'It's all right,' I said. 'Everything is all right.'

But of course it wasn't all right. Not by miles.

Sixteen

With skill she vibrates her eternal tongue,
For ever most divinely in the wrong.

EDWARD YOUNG

There was a bomb scare on the flight out to Prague. No bomb, but lots of scare.

We were just settling ourselves into our seats when the pilot's voice came over the intercom, telling us to deplane with all possible speed. No 'ladies and gentlemen, on behalf of British Airways,' or anything like that. Just get off the plane now.

We hung around in a lilac-painted room, with ten fewer chairs than there were passengers and no music to play by, and you weren't allowed to smoke. I was, though. A uniformed woman with a lot of make-up told me to put it out, but I explained that I was asthmatic and the cigarette was a herbal dilation remedy I had to take whenever I was under stress. Everybody hated me for that, the smokers even more than the non-smokers.

When we finally shuffled back on to the aircraft, we all looked under our seats, worried that the sniffer dog might have had a cold that day, and that somewhere there was a little black hold-all that all the searchers had missed.

There once was a man who went to see a psychiatrist, crippled by a fear of flying. His phobia was based on the belief that there would be a bomb on any plane he boarded. The psychiatrist tried to shift the phobia but couldn't, so he sent his patient to a statistician. The statistician prodded a calculator and informed the man that the odds against there being a bomb on board the next flight he took were half a million to one. The man still wasn't happy, and sat there convinced that he'd be on that one plane out of half a million. So the statistician prodded the calculator again and said 'all right, would you feel safer if the odds were ten million to one against?' The man said, yes, of course he would. So the statistician said 'the odds against there being two, separate, unrelated bombs on board your next flight are exactly ten million to one against.' The man looked puzzled, and said 'that's all well and good, but how does it help me?' The statistician replied: 'It's very simple. You take a bomb on board with you.'

I told this to a grey-suited businessman from Leicester, sitting in the seat next to me, but he didn't laugh at all. Instead, he called a stewardess and said he thought I had a bomb in my luggage. I had to tell the story again to the stewardess, and a third time to the co-pilot who came back and squatted at my feet with a scowl on his face. I'm never going to make polite conversation ever again.

Perhaps I'd misjudged how people feel about bombs on aeroplanes. That's possible. A more likely explanation is that I was the only person on the flight who knew where the hoax bomb call had come from, and what it meant.

It was the first, lumbering, scene-setting move of Operation Dead Wood.

Prague airport is slightly smaller than the sign which says 'Prague Airport', at the front of the terminal building. The thumping Stalinist scale of it made me wonder whether the sign had been built before radio navigation, so that pilots could read it while still only half-way across the Atlantic.

Inside, well, an airport is an airport is an airport. It doesn't matter where you are in the world, you have to have stone floors for the luggage trolleys, you have to have luggage trolleys, and you have to have glass cases displaying crocodile skin belts that no one will ever want to buy in a thousand years of civilisation.

News of Czecho's escape from the Soviet maw hadn't reached the immigration officials, who sat in their glass boxes and re-fought the Cold War with every disgusted flick of their eyes from passport photograph to decadent imperialist standing before them. I was that imperialist, and I'd made the mistake of wearing a Hawaiian shirt, which, I suppose, emphasised my decadence. I'll know better next time. Except that maybe by next time, someone will have found the key to the glass boxes and told these poor buggers that they're now sharing cultural and economic floorspace with Euro-Disney. I decided to try and learn the Czech for 'missing you already'.

I changed some money and went outside to hail a taxi. It was a cool evening, and the broad, Stalinist puddles in the car-park, splashing blue and grey reflections of the newly-built neon advertisements around the sky, made it seem even cooler. I rounded the corner of the terminal building and the wind bounded up to greet me, licking at my face with diesel-flavoured rain and then skipping playfully around my shins, tugging at my trousers. I stood there for a moment, soaking up the strangeness of the place, heavily conscious that I had, in all kinds of ways, gone from one state to another.

I found a cab eventually, and told the driver in fluent English that I wanted Wenceslas Square. This request, I now know, is phonically identical to the Czech phrase for 'I am an air-brained tourist, please take everything I have'. The car was a Tatra, and the driver was a bastard; he drove fast and well, humming happily to himself, like a man who's just won the pools.

*

*

It was one of the most beautiful sights I've ever seen in any city. Wenceslas Square is not a square at all, but a double avenue, running down a slope from the massive National Museum which overlooks it. Even if I'd known nothing of the place, I would have felt that this was important. History ancient and modern had happened in large dollops over this half-mile of grey and yellow stone, and it had left a smell. *L'Air Du Temps de Praha*. Prague Springs, Summers, Winters and Autumns had come and gone, and would probably come again.

When the driver told me how much money he wanted, I had to spend a few minutes explaining that I didn't actually want to buy the cab, I just wanted to settle up for the fifteen minutes I'd spent in it. He told me that it was a limousine service, or at least he said 'limousine' and shrugged a lot, and after a while agreed to reduce his demands to the merely astronomical. I hefted my bag and started to walk.

The Americans had told me to find my own digs, and the only sure way to look like a man who's spent a long time looking for somewhere to stay is to spend a long time looking for somewhere to stay. So I settled into a comfortable march and did Prague One, which is the central district of the old city, in about two hours. Twenty-six churches, fourteen galleries and museums, an opera house – where the boy Mozart had staged his first-ever performance of *Don Giovanni* – eight theatres, and a McDonald's. One of the above had a fifty-yard queue outside it.

I stopped in a few bars to soak up some ambience, which came in tall, straight glasses with 'Budweiser' written on the side, and watched to see how the modern Czech walks, talks, dresses and disports himself. Most of the waiters assumed I was German, which was a fair enough mistake to make considering the city was heaving with them. They travelled in groups of twelve, with back-packs and huge thighs, and strung themselves out across the street when they walked. But then of course, for most Germans, Prague is only a few hours away by fast tank, so it's hardly surprising that they treat the place like the end of their garden.

I had a plate of boiled pork and dumplings in a café by the river and, on the advice of a Welsh couple at the next table, took a stroll across the Charles Bridge. Mr and Mrs Welsh had assured me that it was a spectacular construction, but thanks to the thousand buskers draped over every yard of parapet, all of them singing Dylan songs, I never saw any of it.

I found lodgings eventually at the Zlata Praha, a tatty boarding-house on the hill near the castle. The landlady gave me a choice between a big dirty room or a small clean one, and I chose the big dirty one, thinking I could clean it myself. After she'd gone I realised how silly that was. I've never even cleaned my own flat.

I unpacked my things, lay down on the bed and smoked. I thought about Sarah, and her father, and Barnes. I thought about my own parents, and Ronnie, and helicopters and motorcycles and Germans and McDonald's hamburgers.

I thought about a lot of things.

I woke at eight, and listened to the sounds of the city hauling itself up and taking itself to work. The only unfamiliar noise came from the trams, clattering and hissing their way across cobbled streets and over the bridges. I wondered whether I should stay with the Hawaiian shirt or not.

By nine o'clock I was in the town square, being pestered by a short man with a moustache offering me a tour of the city by horse-drawn carriage. I was supposed to be swayed by the quaint authenticity of his conveyance, but on casual inspection it looked to me extremely like the bottom-half of a Mini Moke, with the engine taken out and shafts for the horse where the headlights used to be. I said no thank you a dozen times, and fuck off once.

I was looking for a café with Coca-Cola umbrellas over its

tables. That was what they'd said. Tom, when you get there, you'll see a café with Coca-Cola shades over the tables. What they hadn't said, or hadn't realised, was that the Coca-Cola rep had been quite fantastically conscientious around these parts, unloading his umbrellas on twenty or so establishments in a hundred yard radius of the square. The Camel Cigarettes rep had only scored twice, so he was presumably dead in a ditch somewhere while the Coca-Cola man was receiving brass plaques and a personalised car-parking space at headquarters in Utah.

I found it after twenty minutes. The Nicholas. Two pounds for a cup of coffee.

They'd told me to go indoors, but it was a beautiful morning and I felt like not doing what I was told, so I sat outside with a view of the square and the passing Germans. I ordered coffee, and as I did so I saw two men emerge from the café and sit down at a nearby table. They were both young and fit-looking, and both wore sunglasses. Neither of them looked in my direction. They'd probably been inside for an hour, getting themselves nicely positioned for the meeting, and I'd gone and spoilt everything.

Excellent.

I adjusted the position of my chair and closed my eyes for a while, letting the sun get in amongst the crow's feet.

'Master,' said a voice, 'a rare and special pleasure.'

I looked round and saw a figure in a brown raincoat squinting down at me.

'This seat taken?' said Solomon. He sat in it without waiting for an answer.

I stared at him.

'Hello, David,' I said eventually.

I knocked a cigarette out of its packet while he signalled a waiter. I glanced over at the two Sunglasses, but they were looking as far away from me as possible every time I turned.

'*Kava, prosim,*' said Solomon, in what seemed like a pretty handy accent. He turned to me. 'Good coffee, terrible food.

209

That's what I've been putting on my postcards.'

'It's not you,' I said.

'Isn't it? Who is it then?'

I kept on staring. It was all most unexpected.

'Let me put it this way,' I said. 'Is it you?'

'Do you mean is it me sitting here, or is it me you're supposed to be meeting?'

'David.'

'It's both, sir.' Solomon leaned back to let the waiter unload the coffee. He took a sip and smacked his lips with approval. 'I have the honour to be acting as trainer for the duration of your stay in this territory. I trust you will find the relationship a profitable one.'

I nodded my head in the direction of the Sunglasses.

'They with you?'

'That's the idea, master. Not one that they like very much, but that's all right.'

'American?'

He nodded.

'As apple pie. This operation is very, very joint. Much jointer than we've had it for a long time, as a matter of fact. A good thing, all in all.'

I thought for a while.

'But why didn't they tell me?' I said. 'I mean, they knew I knew you, so why didn't they tell me?'

He shrugged.

'Are we not but teeth on the cogs of a gigantic machine, sir?'

Well, quite.

Of course, I wanted to ask Solomon everything.

I wanted to take him right back to the beginning – to reconstruct all that we knew about Barnes, and O'Neal, and Murdah, and Dead Wood and Graduate Studies – so that between us we'd be able to triangulate some kind of position in this mess, and perhaps even plot a course out of it.

But there were reasons why I couldn't. Big, strapping

reasons that stuck their hands up at the back of the class and wriggled about in their seats, forcing me to listen to them. If I told him what I thought I knew, Solomon would either do the right thing or the wrong thing. The right thing would, very possibly, get Sarah and me killed, and, very certainly, wouldn't stop what was coming. It might postpone it, get it replayed on another pitch at another time, but it wouldn't stop it. The wrong thing didn't bear thinking about. Because the wrong thing would mean that Solomon was on the other team, and when you come right down to it, nobody knows anybody.

So, for the time being, I shut up and listened while Solomon ran over the fine print on how I was expected to pass the next forty-eight hours. He spoke fast but calmly, and we covered a lot of ground in ninety minutes, thanks to him not having to say 'this is real important' every other sentence, as the Americans had done.

The Sunglasses drank Coke.

I had the afternoon to myself, and as it looked like being the last one I'd get for a while, I wasted it extravagantly. I drank wine, read old newspapers, listened to an open-air performance of some Mahler, and generally sported myself as a gentleman of leisure.

I met a French woman in a bar who said she worked for a computer software company, and I asked her if she'd have sex with me. She just shrugged, Frenchly, which I took to mean no.

Eight o'clock was the appointed hour, so I dawdled in a café until ten past, pushing another helping of boiled pork and dumplings around the plate and smoking immoderately. I paid the bill and walked out into the cool evening, at last feeling my pulse shake itself up at the prospect of action.

I knew I had no reason to feel good. I knew that the job was almost impossible, that the road ahead was long, rocky, and had very few petrol stations, and that my chances of making three score years and ten had dropped through the floor.

But, for whatever reason, good is what I felt.

*

Solomon was waiting for me at the rendezvous with one of the Sunglasses. One of the pairs of sunglasses, I mean. Although of course he wasn't wearing sunglasses now, it being dark, so I quickly had to concoct a new name for him. After a few moments thought, I came up with No Sunglasses. I think there may be a touch of Cree Indian in me.

I apologised for being late, and Solomon smiled and said I wasn't, which was irritating, and then all three of us climbed into a dirty, grey diesel Mercedes, with No Sunglasses at the wheel, and set off on the main road out of the east of the city.

After half-an-hour we'd cleared the outskirts of Prague, and the road had narrowed to two fastish lanes, which we took at an easy pace. Just about the worst way to fuck up a covert operation on foreign soil is to get a speeding ticket, and No Sunglasses seemed to have learnt this lesson well enough. Solomon and I passed the occasional remark about the countryside, how green it was, how parts of it looked a bit like Wales – although I'm not sure if either of us had ever been there – but otherwise we didn't talk much. Instead, we drew pictures on the steamed-up rear windows while Europe unfolded outside, Solomon doing flowers and me doing happy faces.

After an hour the signs started showing for Brno, which never looks right written down, and never sounds right said, either, but I knew we weren't going that far. We turned north towards Kostelec, and then almost immediately east again, on an even narrower road, with no signs at all. Which just about summed things up.

We wound through a few miles of black pine forest, and then No Sunglasses went on to side-lights, which cut our speed down. After a few miles of that, he doused the lights altogether, and told me to put out my cigarette because it was 'fucking with his night vision'.

And then, all of a sudden, we were there.

They'd been keeping him in the basement of a farm house. For how long, I couldn't tell – I only knew that it wasn't going to be for much longer. He was about my age, about my height, probably had been about my weight before they'd stopped feeding him. They said his name was Ricky, and that he came from Minnesota. They didn't say that he was scared out of his wits and wanted to go back to Minnesota as soon as he could, because they didn't have to. It was in his eyes, as clearly as anything has ever been in anyone's eyes.

Ricky had dropped out at the age of seventeen. Dropped out of school, dropped out of his family, dropped out of just about everything that a young man can drop out of – but then, pretty soon, he'd dropped into some other things, alternative things, and they'd made him feel better about himself. For a while, anyway.

Ricky felt a lot worse about himself at this moment; most probably because he'd managed to get himself into one of those situations where you're naked in the cellar of a strange building, in a strange country, with strangers staring at you, some of whom have obviously been hurting you for a while, and others of whom are just waiting to take their turn. Flickering across the back of Ricky's mind, I knew, were images from a thousand films, in which the hero, trussed-up in the same predicament, throws back his head with an insolent sneer and tells his tormentors to go screw themselves. And Ricky had sat in the dark, along with millions of other teenage boys, and duly absorbed the lesson that this is how men are supposed to behave in adversity. They endure, first of all; then they avenge.

But not being all that bright – being two balls short of a pig-fuck, or whatever they say in Minnesota – Ricky had neglected to notice the important advantages that these celluloid gods had over him. In fact, there really is only one advantage, but it is a very important one. The advantage is that films aren't real. Honestly. They're not.

In real life, and I'm sorry if I'm shattering some deeply

213

cherished illusions here, men in Ricky's situation don't tell anyone to go and screw themselves. They don't sneer insolently, they don't spit in anyone's eye, and they certainly, definitely, categorically don't free themselves in a single bound. What they actually do is stand stock still, and shiver, and cry, and beg, literally beg, for their mother. Their nose runs, their legs shake, and they whimper. That is what men, all men, are like, and that is what real life is like.

Sorry, but there it is.

My father used to grow strawberries under a net. Every now and then, a bird, seeing some fat, red, sweet things on the ground, decided to try and get under the net, steal the fruit therefrom, and clear off. And every now and then, that bird would get the first two things right – no sweat, they'd go like clockwork – and then he or she would make a complete dog's breakfast of the third. They would get stuck in the fine mesh, and there'd be a lot of squawking and flapping, and my father would look up from the potato trench, whistle me over, and tell me to get the bird out. Carefully. Get hold of it, untangle it, set it free.

This was the job I hated more than any other in the whole universe of childhood.

Fear is frightening. It is the most frightening of all the emotions to behold. An animal in a state of rage is one thing, often a pretty alarming one thing, but an animal in a state of terror – that juddering, staring, skittering bundle of feathered panic – is something I never wanted to see again.

And yet, here I was, seeing it.

'Piece a fuckin' shit,' said one of the Americans, coming into the kitchen and immediately busying himself with a kettle.

Solomon and I looked at each other. We'd sat at the table for twenty minutes after they'd taken Ricky away, without exchanging a word. I knew that he'd been as shaken as I was, and he knew I knew, so we'd just sat there, me staring at the wall, him scratching lines on the side of his chair with

214

his thumbnail.

'What happens to him now?' I asked, still staring at the wall.

'Not your problem,' said the American, as he spooned coffee grounds into a jug. 'Not anybody's problem, after today.' I think he laughed as he said that, but I couldn't be sure.

Ricky was a terrorist. That was how the Americans thought of him, and that was why they hated him. They hated all terrorists anyway, but what made Ricky special, what made them hate him more than most, was the fact that he was an American terrorist. And that just didn't seem right. Until Oklahoma City, the average American had looked upon the letting-off of bombs in public places as a quaint, European tradition, like bull-fighting or Morris dancing. And if it ever spread out of Europe, it surely went east, to the camel jockeys, the goddamn towel-heads, the sons and daughters of Islam. Blowing-up shopping malls and embassies, sniping at elected officers of the government, hijacking 747s in the name of anything other than money, was downright un-American and un-Minnesotan. But Oklahoma City changed a lot of things, all of them for the worse, and, as a result, Ricky was being made to pay top dollar for his ideology.

Ricky was an American terrorist, and he'd let the side down.

I was back in Prague by dawn, but I didn't go to bed. Or at least, I went to bed, but I didn't get in. I sat on the edge, with a filling ashtray and an emptying packet of Marlboro, and stared at the wall. If there'd been a television in the room, I might have watched that. Or I might not. A ten-year-old episode of *Magnum*, dubbed into German, isn't much more interesting than a wall.

They'd told me that the police would come at eight, but in the event it was only a few minutes after seven when I heard the first boot on the first step. That little ruse was presumably meant to guarantee bleary-eyed surprise on my part, in case I was unable to affect it convincingly. No faith, these people.

They numbered about a dozen, all of them in uniform, and they made an over-cooked meal of the whole business, kicking in the door, shouting and knocking things over. The head-boy spoke some English, but not enough, apparently, to understand 'that hurts'. They dragged me down the stairs past the white-faced landlady – who probably hoped that the days of tenants being hauled off at dawn by police vans were gone for good – while other tousled heads peeked nervously at me through the cracks of doors.

At the station, I was held in a room for a while – no coffee, no cigarettes, no friendly faces – and then, after some more shouting, a few slaps and pokes in the chest, I was chucked in a cell; *sans* belt, *sans* bootlaces.

On the whole, they were pretty efficient.

There were two other occupants of the cell, both male, and they didn't get up when I came in. One of them probably couldn't have got up if he'd wanted to, seeing as how he was drunker than I think I've ever been in my entire life. He was sixty and unconscious, with alcohol seeping from every part of his body, and his head hung so low on his chest you almost couldn't believe that there was a spine in there, holding him together.

The other man was younger, darker, wearing a tee-shirt and khaki trousers. He looked at me once, head to toe and back again, and then carried on cracking the bones in his wrists and fingers while I lifted the drunk out of his chair and laid him, not too gently, in the corner. I sat down opposite the tee-shirt and closed my eyes.

'Deutsch?'

I couldn't tell how long I'd been asleep because they'd taken my watch as well – in case I managed to work out a way of hanging myself with it, presumably – but the numbness of my buttocks suggested at least a couple of hours.

The drunk had gone, and the tee-shirt was now squatting at my side.

'Deutsch?' he said.

216

I shook my head and closed my eyes again, taking one last draught of myself before stepping into another person.

I heard the tee-shirt scratching at himself. Long, slow, thoughtful scratches.

'American?' he said.

I nodded, still with my eyes closed, and felt a strange moment of peace. So much easier to be someone else.

They kept the tee-shirt for four days, and me for ten. I wasn't allowed to shave or smoke, and eating was actively discouraged by whoever cooked the food. They questioned me once or twice about the bomb scare on the flight from London, and asked me to look at photographs – two or three in particular to begin with, and then, when they started to lose interest, whole directories of wrong-doers – but I made a big point of not focusing on them, and tried to yawn whenever they slapped me.

On the tenth night, they took me to a white room and photographed me from a hundred different angles, then gave me back my belt, laces and watch. They even offered me a razor. But as the handle looked rather sharper than the blade, and my beard seemed to be helping me towards metamorphosis, I turned it down.

It was dark outside, cold and dark, and it was trying to rain in a feeble, oh-I-can't-really-be-bothered-with-this sort of a way. I walked slowly, as if I didn't care about the rain, or much else that life on this earth had to offer, and hoped that I wouldn't have to wait long.

I didn't have to wait at all.

It was a Porsche 911, in dark-green, and there was nothing particularly clever about spotting it, because Porsches were as rare on the streets of Prague as I was. It trickled along beside me for a hundred yards, then made up its mind, spurted ahead to the end of the street and stopped. As I got to within ten yards or so, the passenger door was pushed open. I slowed down, checked behind and in front, and ducked my head to

217

look at the driver.

He was in his mid-forties, with a square jaw and successfully greying hair, and Porsche marketing men would happily have pushed him forward as 'a typical owner' – if he really was the owner, which was sort of unlikely, considering his occupation.

Of course, at that moment, I wasn't supposed to know his occupation.

'Want a lift?' he said. Could have been from anywhere, and probably was. He saw me thinking about his offer, or thinking about him, so he added a smile to close the deal. Very good teeth.

I glanced behind him to where the tee-shirt sat, folded up on the tiny rear seat. He wasn't wearing a tee-shirt now, of course, but a lurid purple thing that had no creases in it. He enjoyed my expression of surprise for a few moments, then nodded at me – part hello, part get in – and when I did so, the driver blipped the throttle and let out the clutch all in a playful rush, so that I had to scrabble to close the door. The two of them seemed to find this very entertaining. The tee-shirt, whose real name was most definitely not and never had been Hugo, shoved a packet of Dunhill in front of my nose, and I took one and pressed the dashboard lighter home.

'Where are you headed?' said the driver.

I shrugged and said maybe the centre, but it didn't really matter. He nodded and carried on humming to himself. Puccini, I think. Or it might have been Take That. I sat and smoked, and said nothing, as if I was used to this kind of thing happening.

'By the way,' said the driver eventually, 'I'm Greg.' He smiled, and I thought to myself, well of course you are.

He took a hand off the wheel and held it out to me. We shook, short but friendly, and then I left a pause, just to show that I was my own man and that I spoke when I felt like it, not before.

After a while, he turned to look at me. A firmer look. Not so friendly. So I answered him.

'My name is Ricky,' I said.

PART TWO

PART TWO

Seventeen

You cannot be serious.
JOHN MCENROE

I'm part of a team now. A cast. And a caste. We are drawn from six nations, three continents, four religions, and two genders. We are a happy band of brothers, with one sister, who's also happy and gets her own bathroom.

We work hard, play hard, drink hard, even sleep hard. In fact, we are hard. We handle weapons in a way that says we know how to handle weapons, and we discuss politics in a way that says we have taken the bigger view.

We are The Sword Of Justice.

The camp changes every couple of weeks, and so far has drawn its water from the rivers of Libya, Bulgaria, South Carolina and Surinam. Not its drinking water, of course; that comes in plastic bottles, flown in twice a week along with the chocolate and the cigarettes. At this moment, The Sword Of Justice seems to have come down in favour of Badoit, because it's 'gently carbonated', and therefore accommodates, more or less, the fizzy and the flat factions.

The last few months, I can't deny, have wrought a change in all of us. The burdens of physical training, unarmed combat, communications drills, weapons practice, tactical and strategic planning, all these were borne at first in a grim spirit of suspicion and competitiveness. That has now gone, I'm glad to say, and in its place blooms a genuine and formidable *esprit de corps*. There are jokes that we all finally understand, after the thousandth repetition; there have been love affairs that have amicably fizzled out; and we share the cooking, complimenting each other in a chorus of nods and mmmms on our various specialities. Mine, which I do believe is one of the most popular, is hamburgers with potato salad. The secret is the raw egg.

It is the middle of December now, and we are about to travel to Switzerland – where we plan to ski a little, relax a little, and shoot a Dutch politician a little.

We are having fun, living well, and feeling important. What more can one possibly ask from life?

Our leader, inasmuch as we acknowledge the concept of leadership, is Francisco; Francis to some, Cisco to others, and The Keeper to me, in my covert messages to Solomon. Francisco says that he was born in Venezuela, the fifth of eight children, and that he suffered from polio as a child. I've no reason to doubt him on any of this. The polio is supposed to account for the withered right leg and the theatrical limp, which seems to come and go depending on his mood and how much he is asking you to do or give. Latifa says he is beautiful and I suppose she may have a point, if three-foot-long eyelashes and olive skin are your thing. He is small and muscular, and if I were casting the part of Byron, I would probably give Francisco a call; not least because he is an absolutely fantastic actor.

To Latifa, Francisco is the heroic elder brother – wise, sensitive, and forgiving. To Bernhard, he is a grim, unflappable professional. To Cyrus and Hugo, he is the fiery idealist, for whom nothing of anything is enough. To Benjamin, he is the tentative scholar, because Benjamin believes in God and wants to be sure of every step. And to Ricky, the Minnesotan anarchist with the beard and the accent, Francisco is a back-slapping, beer-drinking, rock 'n' roll adventurer, who knows a lot of Bruce Springsteen lyrics. He really can play all the parts.

If there is a real Francisco, then I think I saw him one day on a flight from Marseille to Paris. The system is that we travel in pairs but sit separately, and I was half a dozen rows behind Francisco on an aisle seat, when a boy of about five, sitting up at the front of the cabin, started crying and moaning. His mother unhitched the lad from his seat and was starting to lead him down the aisle towards the lavatory, when the aircraft pitched slightly to one side, and the boy stumbled against Francisco's shoulder.

Francisco hit him.

Not hard. And not with a fist. If I was a lawyer in the case, I might even be able to make out that it was nothing more than a firm push, to try and help the boy get upright again. But I'm not a lawyer, and Francisco definitely hit him. I don't think anyone saw it but me, and the boy himself was so startled that he stopped crying; but that instinctive, fuck off reaction, to a five-year-old child, told me rather a lot about Francisco.

Apart from that, and God knows we all have our bad days, the seven of us get on pretty well with each other. We really do. We whistle while we work.

The one thing that I thought might prove our undoing, as it has proved the undoing of almost every co-operative venture in human history, simply hasn't materialised. Because we, The Sword Of Justice, architects of a new world order and standard bearers for the cause of freedom, actually, genuinely, share the washing-up.

I've never known it happen before.

The village of Mürren – no cars, no litter, no late payment of bills – lies in the shadow of three great and famous mountains: the Jungfrau, the Monke, and the Eiger. If you're interested in things of a legendary nature, you may like to know that the Monk is said to spend his time defending the virtue of the Young Woman from the predations of the Ogre – a job he has carried out successfully and with very little apparent effort since the Oligocene period, when these three lumps of rock were, with relentless geologic, wrenched and pummelled into being.

Mürren is a small village, with very little prospect of getting any bigger. Being accessible only by helicopter or funicular railway, there is a limit to the quantity of sausage and beer that can be got up the hill to sustain its residents and visitors and, by and large, the locals like it that way. There are three big hotels, a dozen or so smaller boarding houses, and a hundred scattered farm houses and chalets, all built with that exaggeratedly tall pitched roof that makes every Swiss building look as if most of it is buried underground. Which, given their fetish for nuclear shelters, it probably is.

Although the village was conceived and built by an Englishman, it's not a particularly English resort nowadays. Germans and Austrians come to walk and cycle in the summer, and Italians, French, Japanese, Americans – anyone, basically, who speaks the international language of brightly-coloured leisure fabrics – come to ski in the winter.

The Swiss come all year round to make money. The money-making conditions are famously excellent from November to April, with several off-piste retail sites and *bureau de change* facilities, and hopes are high that next year – and about time too – money-making will become an Olympic sport. The Swiss are quietly fancying their chances.

But there is one feature in particular that has made Mürren especially attractive to Francisco, because this is our first outing and we've all got a few butterflies. Even Cyrus, and he's hard as nails. Owing to the fact that it's small, Swiss, law-abiding, and hard to get to, the village of Mürren has no police force.

Not even part-time.

*

Bernhard and I arrived this morning, and checked into our hotels; he in The Jungfrau, me for The Eiger.

The girl at reception examined my passport as if she'd never seen one before, and took twenty minutes to go through the phenomenal list of things that Swiss hoteliers like to know about you before they'll let you sleep in one of their beds. I think I may have got stuck for a moment on the middle name of my geography teacher, and I definitely hesitated on the postal code of the midwife who attended the birth of my great-grandmother, but otherwise I sailed through it without a hitch.

I unpacked, and changed into a day-glo orange, yellow and lilac windcheater, which is the sort of thing you have to wear in a ski resort if you don't want to be conspicuous, then ambled out of the hotel, up the hill into the village.

It was a beautiful afternoon; one to make you realise that God really can be very good sometimes with weather and scenery. The nursery slopes were almost empty at this time of day, there being a good hour of skiing time left before the sun dipped behind the Schilthorn and people suddenly remembered that they were seven thousand feet above sea level in the middle of December.

I sat outside a bar for a while and pretended to write postcards, every now and then casting an eye towards a herd of quite fantastically young French children who were following a female instructor down the slopes in crocodile formation. Each one about the size of a fire extinguisher, and dressed in three hundred pounds' worth of Gortex and duck-down, they slithered and snaked behind their Amazon leader, some of them upright, some bent double, and some even too small for you to be able to tell whether they were upright or bent double.

I started wondering how long it would be before pregnant mothers started appearing on ski slopes, sliding down on their stomachs, yelling technical instructions and whistling Mozart.

*

Dirk Van Der Hoewe, in the company of his Scottish wife Rhona and their two teenage daughters, arrived at The Edelweiss at eight o'clock the same evening. They'd had a long journey, six hours door to door, and Dirk was tired, irritable, and fat.

Politicians aren't usually fat nowadays – either because they work harder than they used to, or because modern electorates have expressed a preference for being able to see both sides of the person they're voting for without having to lean over – but Dirk looked like he'd bucked the trend. He was a physical reminder of an earlier century, when politics was something you did between two and four in the afternoon, before squeezing into some fancy trousers for an evening of piquet and foie gras. He wore a tracksuit and furry boots, which is not considered unusual if you're Dutch, and a pair of spectacles bounced around his breasts on a loop of pink string.

He and Rhona stood in the middle of the foyer directing their sumptuous luggage, which had Louis Vuitton written all over it, while their daughters scowled and kicked at the floor, deep in their furious, adolescent hell.

I watched from the bar. Bernhard watched from the newspaper stand.

The next day was a technical rehearsal, Francisco had said. Take everything at half-speed, quarter-speed even, and if there's a problem, or anything that looks like it might become one, stop and check it out. The day after would be dress rehearsal, at full-speed, using a ski pole as the rifle, but today was technical.

The team was me, Bernhard and Hugo, with Latifa as back-up; which we hoped we wouldn't have to use, because she couldn't ski. Neither could Dirk – there being very few hills in Holland larger than a packet of cigarettes – but he had paid for his holiday, had arranged for a news photographer to be there to catch the care-worn statesman at play, and all in all was damned if he wasn't going to give it a try.

We watched Dirk and Rhona as they hired their equipment, grunting and clumping with the boots; we watched them as they trudged fifty yards up the nursery slopes, stopping every now and then to admire the view and muck about with the gear; we watched as Rhona got herself ready to point downhill, and Dirk found a hundred and fifty reasons not to go anywhere; and then, finally, when we were all starting to feel itchy at having to stand still doing nothing for so long, we saw the Dutch Deputy Minister of Finance, white-faced with the stress of it all, slither ten feet down the hill and sit down.

Bernhard and I exchanged a look. The only one we'd allowed ourselves since we arrived, and I had to turn away and scratch my knee.

By the time I looked back at Dirk, he too was laughing. It was a laugh that said I am an adrenalin-maddened speed freak, who craves danger the way other men crave women and wine. I take fantastic risks, and by rights I shouldn't still be alive. I am living on borrowed time.

They repeated the exercise three times, stepping an extra yard up the hill for each run, before fatness got the better of Dirk, and they retired to a café for lunch. As the two of them stumped off across the snow, I turned back to the mountain for a glimpse of the daughters, hoping to judge how good they were on skis, and therefore how far afield they'd be likely to go on an average day. If they were gangly and awkward, I reckoned they'd probably hang about the lower slopes, within reach of their parents. If they were any good, and if they hated Dirk and Rhona even half as much as they seemed to, they would be in Hungary by now.

I could see no sign of them, and was about to turn back down the slope when I caught sight of a man, standing on a crest above me, looking down into the valley. He was too far away for me to be able to read his features, but even so, he was absurdly conspicuous. And not just because he had neither skis, poles, boots, sunglasses, nor even a woolly hat.

What made him conspicuous was the brown raincoat, bought from the back pages of the *Sunday Express*.

Eighteen

This night methinks is but the daylight sick,
THE MERCHANT OF VENICE

'Who pulls the trigger?'

Solomon had to wait for an answer.

In fact he had to wait for every answer, because I was on a skating-rink, skating, and he wasn't. It took me roughly thirty seconds to complete a circuit and drop off a reply, so I had lots of scope to be irritating. Not that I need lots of scope, you understand. Give me just an eency-weency bit of scope, and I'll madden you to death.

'Do you mean the metaphorical trigger?' I said, as I passed.

I glanced over my shoulder and saw that Solomon had smiled and lifted his chin a little, like an indulgent parent, and then turned back to the game of curling he was supposed to be watching.

Another lap. Speakers blared out some jolly Swiss oom-pah music.

'I mean the trigger trigger, sir. The actual . . .'

'Me.' And I was off again.

I was definitely getting the hang of this skating thing. I'd started to copy a fancy cross-over turn from a German girl in front of me, and it was working pretty well. I was just about keeping up with her too, which was pleasing. She must have been about six.

'The rifle?' This was Solomon again, speaking through cupped hands, as if he was blowing on them for warmth.

He had to wait longer for this reply, because I fell over on the far side of the rink, and for a moment or two managed to convince myself that I'd broken my pelvis. But I hadn't. Which was a shame, because it would have solved all sorts of problems.

I finally got round to him again.

'Arrives tomorrow,' I said.

That wasn't strictly true, as it happens. But in the circumstances of this particular de-briefing, the truth was going to take about a week and a half to deliver.

The rifle wasn't arriving tomorrow. Bits of it were already here.

With a lot of prompting from me, Francisco had agreed to go with the PM L96A1. It's not a pretty name, I know, nor even a very memorable one; but the PM, nicknamed 'the Green Thing' by the British Army – on the basis, presumably, that it is both green and a thing – does its job well enough; that job being to fire a 7.62 millimetre round with sufficient accuracy to give the competent recreational shooter, which was definitely me, a guaranteed hit at six hundred yards.

Manufacturers' guarantees being what they are, I'd told Francisco that if the shot was an inch over two hundred yards – less, if there was a cross-wind – I wasn't taking it.

He'd managed to get hold of a Green Thing in take-down format; or, as the makers would have you have it, a 'covert sniper rifle system'. It comes in pieces, in other words, and most of those pieces had already arrived in the village. The compressed sniper-scope had come in as a 200 millimetre lens on the front of Bernhard's camera, with the mount hidden inside; the bolt was doing service as the handle of Hugo's razor, while Latifa had managed to get two rounds of Remington Magnum ammunition into each heel of a stupidly expensive pair of patent-leather shoes. All we lacked was a barrel, and that was coming into Wengen on the roof of Francisco's Alfa Romeo – together with a lot of other long metal things that people use for winter sports.

I'd brought the trigger myself, in my trouser pocket. Perhaps I'm just not the creative type.

We had decided to do without the stock and fore-end, as both of them are hard to disguise and, frankly, inessential. Likewise the bipod. A firearm, when all is said and done, is nothing more than a tube, a piece of lead, and some gunpowder. Putting a lot of carbon-fibre bits on it, and a go-faster stripe down the side, won't make the person you hit any deader. The only extra ingredient you need to make a weapon meaningfully lethal – and, thankfully, it's a thing that's still pretty hard to come by, even in this wicked old world – is someone with the will to point and fire it.

Someone like me.

Solomon had told me nothing about Sarah. Nothing at all. How she was, where she was – I could even have made do with what he'd last seen her wearing, but he hadn't said a word.

Perhaps the Americans had told him to say nothing. Good or bad. 'Hear this, David, and hear it good. Our analysis of Lang indicates a negatory response profile to incoming amatory data.' Something like that. With a few 'now let's kick ass' phrases thrown in. But then, Solomon knew me well enough to make his own decisions about what he told me or didn't tell me. And he didn't tell me. So either he didn't have any news about Sarah, or the news he did have wasn't good. Or then again, perhaps the best reason of all for not telling me, because the simplest is often the best, was that I hadn't asked.

230

I don't know why.

I lay in my bath at The Eiger, turning the taps with my feet and adding a pint or two of hot water every quarter of an hour, and thought about it afterwards. Perhaps I was scared of what I'd hear. That was possible. Perhaps I was thinking about the risk of my covert meetings with Solomon; that by extending them, with a lot of chat about the folks back home, I was putting his life at risk as well as my own. That was also possible, if a touch shaky.

Or perhaps – and this was the explanation I came to last, moving cautiously around it, peering at it, prodding it with a sharp stick every now and then to see if it'd get up and bite me – perhaps I'd stopped caring. Perhaps I'd just been pretending to myself that Sarah was the reason I was going through with all of this when, in actual fact, now would be a good time to admit that I had made better friends, discovered a deeper purpose, had more reasons to get out of bed in the mornings, since I joined The Sword Of Justice.

Obviously, that just wasn't possible at all.

That was absurd.

I climbed into bed and slept the sleep of the tired.

It was cold. That was the first thing I noticed as I pulled back the curtains. A dry, grey, just-remember-you're-in-the-Alps-sonny kind of cold, and that worried me a little. True, it might keep some of the more reluctant skiers in their beds, which would be useful; but it would also slow my fingers to 33rpm and make good marksmanship extremely difficult, if not impossible. Worse still, it would make the sound of the shot travel further.

As rifles go, the Green Thing isn't a particularly noisy instrument – nothing like an M16, which frightens people to death fractionally before the bullet hits them – but even so, when you happened to be the one holding the thing, and you're busy lining up your cross-hairs on an eminent European statesman, you tend to get a little self-conscious about things like noise. About things like everything, in fact.

You want people to look the other way for a moment, if they wouldn't mind. Knowing, as you squeeze the trigger, that half-a-mile away, cups would stop on their way to lips, ears would cock, eyebrows would raise, and 'what the fuck was that?' would come tumbling out of a few hundred mouths in a few dozen languages, just cramps your style ever so slightly. In tennis, they call it choking on the shot. I don't know what they call it in assassination. Choking on the shot, probably.

I breakfasted well, laying down calories against the possibility that my diet might change radically in the next twenty-four hours, and remain changed until my beard turned grey, and then I headed down to the ski room in the basement. A French family were falling about down there, arguing over who had whose gloves, where the sun cream had gone, why ski-boots hurt as much as they do – so I settled down on the farthest bench I could find and resolved to take my time gathering the gear.

Bernhard's camera was heavy and awkward, clunking painfully about my chest and feeling twice as phoney as it was. The rifle bolt and one round of ammunition were stowed in a nylon bum-bag, strapped round my waist, and the barrel nestled inside one of the ski poles – red dot on the handle, in case I couldn't tell the difference between a pole that weighed six ounces and one that weighed near enough four pounds. I'd thrown the other three rounds of ammunition out of the bathroom window, reasoning that one round had better be enough because if it wasn't, I was going to be in even bigger trouble – and I just didn't think I could face bigger trouble right at that moment. I wasted a minute cleaning my fingernails with the end of the trigger, then carefully folded the tiny sliver of metal in a paper napkin and stuffed it into my pocket.

I stood up, took a deep breath, and clumped past *la famille* to the lavatory.

The condemned man threw up a hearty breakfast.

Latifa had her sunglasses propped up on top of her head,

which meant stand by, which meant nothing. No sunglasses, and the Van Der Hoewes were staying indoors to play tiddlywinks. Sunglasses over the eyes meant they were headed for the slopes.

On top of the head meant they might, you might, I might, anything might.

I stumped across the foot of the nursery slopes, heading for the funicular railway station. Hugo was already there, dressed in orange and turquoise, and he too had his sunglasses perched on top of his head.

The first thing he did was look at me.

In spite of all our lectures, all our training, all our grim nods of agreement at Francisco's coaching tips – in spite of all of that, Hugo was looking straight at me. I knew immediately that he would keep looking at me until our eyes met, so I stared back at him, hoping to get it over with.

His eyes were shining. There's no other word for it. Shining with fun and excitement and let's go, like a child on Christmas morning.

He reached a gloved hand to his ear and adjusted the Walkman headphones. An average ski-bum, you would have tutted to yourself if you'd seen him; it's not enough to be gliding through the most beautiful scenery on God's earth, he has to go and put Guns 'N' Roses over the top of it. I'd probably have got annoyed by those headphones myself, if I hadn't known that they were actually connected to a short wave receiver at his hip, and that Bernhard was broadcasting his own particular shipping forecast from the other end.

It had been agreed that I would carry no radio. The reasoning went that in the event of my capture – Latifa had actually reached across and squeezed my arm when Francisco said this – nobody would have any immediate reason to think of accomplices.

So all I had was Hugo and his shining eyes.

At the top of the Schilthorn mountain, at an altitude of a little over three thousand metres, stands, or sits, the Piz Gloria

233

restaurant; an astonishing confection of glass and steel where, for the price of a pretty decent sports car, you can sit, and drink coffee, and take in a view of no less than six countries on a clear day.

If you're anything like me, it might take you most of that clear day to work out which six countries they might be, but if you have any time left over, you're liable to spend it wondering how on earth the Mürrenians got the building up there and how many of them must have died in the course of its assembly. When you've seen a construction like that, and reflected on how long it takes the average British builder to send you an estimate for a kitchen extension, you end up quite admiring the Swiss.

The restaurant's other claim to fame is that it once served as a location in a James Bond film; its stage name of Piz Gloria has clung to the place ever since, along with the operator's right to sell 007 memorabilia to anyone who hasn't been bankrupted by the cup of coffee.

In short, it was a place that any visitor to Mürren just had to visit if they got the chance, and the Van Der Hoewes had decided, over a supper of *boeuf en croûte* the previous evening, that they definitely had the chance.

Hugo and I dismounted at the top cable-car station and split up. I went inside, and gasped and pointed and shook my head at how really neat all this mountain stuff was, while Hugo hung around outside, smoking and fiddling with his bindings. He was trying to cultivate the look of the serious skier, who wanted steep hills and fine powder, and anyway, don't talk to me because the bass solo on this track is just awesome. I was happy to play the gawping idiot.

I wrote some more postcards – all of them to a man called Colin, for some reason – and every now and then glanced down at Austria, or Italy, or France, or some other place with snow in it, until the waiters started to get peeved. I was just beginning to wonder whether The Sword Of Justice budget could stretch to a second cup, when a movement of bright colour caught my eye. I looked up and saw that Hugo was waving from the gantry outside.

Everyone else in the restaurant noticed him too. Probably thousands of people in Austria, Italy and France noticed him. All in all, it was a hopeless piece of amateurism, and if Francisco had been there he would have slapped Hugo hard, the way he'd had to do many times during training. But Francisco wasn't there, and Hugo was making a multicoloured arse of himself, and a gibbering wreck of me, for no good reason. The only saving grace was that none of the many curious onlookers would have been able to tell exactly who or what he was waving at.

Because he was wearing sunglasses over his eyes.

I took the first part of the run at a gentle pace, for two reasons: firstly, because I wanted my breathing to be as even as possible when the time came for the shot; secondly, and more importantly, because I didn't want – with a passion, I didn't want – to break my leg and have to be stretchered off the mountain with a lot of rifle parts concealed about my person.

So I side-slipped and edged, making the turns as big and slow as possible, gently traversing the blackest part of the run until I came to the tree-line. The severity of the slope was something of a worry. Any fool could have seen that Dirk and Rhona were, frankly, not good enough to manage it without a great deal of falling over, and possibly even some notgetting-up-again. If I'd been Dirk, or a friend of Dirk, or even just an interested skier-by, I'd have said forget it. Take the cable-car back down again and find something gentler.

But Francisco was confident about Dirk. He felt he knew his man. Francisco's analysis said that Dirk was careful with money – which, I suppose, is one of the qualities you look for in a Minister of Finance – and if Dirk and Rhona decided to scratch, they'd have to pay a hefty penalty for the cable-car ride back down.

Francisco was prepared to bet my life that Dirk would ski it. Just to make sure, he'd popped Latifa into the bar of The

Edelweiss the night before, while Dirk was spilling a couple of brandies down the inside of his throat, and made her bill and coo at the bravery of any man prepared to tackle the Schilthorn. Dirk had looked a little worried at first, but Latifa's batting eyelashes and heaving bosom had finally pulled him round, and he'd promised to buy her a drink the following evening if he made it down in one piece.

Latifa crossed her fingers behind her back, and promised to be there on the dot of nine.

Hugo had marked the spot, and he stood there now, smoking, and grinning, and generally having a hell of a time. I skied past him and came to rest ten yards further into the trees, just to remind myself, and Hugo, that I still knew how to make decisions. I turned and looked back up at the mountain, checking the position, the angles, the cover – then jerked my head at Hugo.

He tossed his cigarette away, shrugged, and set off down the mountain, turning a tiny mogul into a needlessly spectacular jump, and then sending a plume of powder into the air as he paralleled a perfect stop on the other side of the run, about a hundred yards further down. He turned away from me, unzipped his suit, and started to urinate against a rock.

I wanted to urinate too. But I had the feeling that if I started, I'd never stop; I'd just keep on pissing away, until there was nothing left of me but a pile of clothes.

I unhitched the lens from the front of the camera, removed the cap, and trained it on the mountain, squinting through the eyepiece. The image was thick with condensation, so I unzipped my jacket and slipped the scope inside, trying to warm it against my body.

It was cold and quiet, and I could hear my fingers shaking as I started to assemble the rifle.

I had him now. Perhaps half-a-mile away. He was as fat as ever, with the kind of silhouette that snipers dream about. If

236

they dream about anything.

Even at that distance, I could tell that Dirk was having a horrible time. His body language came across in short, simple sentences. I. Am. Going. To. Die. His bottom was stuck out, his chest was forward, legs rigid with fear and exhaustion, and he was moving with glacial slowness.

Rhona was making a slightly better job of the descent, but not by much. Awkwardly, jerkily, but making progress of a kind, she trickled down the slope as slowly as she could, trying not to get too far ahead of her miserable husband.

I waited.

At six hundred yards, I started to over-breathe, charging the blood with oxygen so I'd be ready to switch off the tap, and keep it switched off, from three hundred. I exhaled through the side of the mouth, gently blowing away from the scope.

At four hundred yards, Dirk fell for about the fifteenth time, and didn't look in any hurry to get up. As I watched him panting for breath, I pulled back on the knurled grip of the bolt, and heard the firing-pin cock with a shatteringly loud click. Jesus, this shot was going to be noisy. I suddenly found myself wondering about avalanches, and had to stop myself from spinning into a wild fantasy of being buried under a thousand tons of snow. What if my body wasn't found for a couple of years? What if this anorak was desperately unfashionable by the time they hauled me out? I blinked five times, trying to steady my breath, my vision, my panic. It was too cold for avalanches. For avalanches, you need a lot of snow, then a lot of sun. We had neither. Get a grip. I squinted through the scope, and saw that Dirk was on his feet again.

On his feet, and looking at me.

Or at least, he was looking towards me, peering down into the trees while he scraped snow out of his goggles.

He couldn't have seen me. It wasn't possible. I had buried myself behind a drift, digging out the narrowest possible channel in which to rest the rifle, and whatever shape he was trying to make out would have been disguised by the irregular jumble of trees. He couldn't have seen me.

So what was he looking at?

I gently eased my head down below the level of the drift and twisted round, checking for some solitary langlaufer, or an errant chamois, or the chorus-line of *No, No Nanette* – anything that might have caught Dirk's eye. I held my breath and turned my head slowly from left to right, sweeping the hill for sounds.

Nothing.

I inched back up to the top of the drift, and squinted through the scope again. Left, right, up, down.

No Dirk.

I bobbed my head up, the way they tell you never to do, and desperately searched the stinging, blurring whiteness for some glimpse of him. My mouth suddenly seemed to taste of blood, and my heart was hammering on the inside of my chest, frantic to get out.

There. Three hundred yards. Moving faster. He was having a go at a schuss, on a flatter part of the slope, and it had carried him over to the far side of the piste. I blinked again, settled my right eye to the scope, and closed my left.

At two hundred yards, I drew in a long, steady breath, pinched it off when my lungs reached three-quarters full, and held it.

Dirk was traversing now. Traversing the slope, and my line of fire. I held him easily in the sight – could have fired at any time – but I knew that this just had to be the surest shot of my life. I nestled my finger on the trigger, taking up the slack of the mechanism, the slack of the flesh between my second and third joint, and waited.

He stopped at about a hundred and fifty yards. Looked up at the mountain. Down the mountain. Then turned his body towards me. He was sweating heavily, gasping with the effort, with the fear, with the knowledge. I settled the cross-hairs on the exact centre of his chest. As I'd promised Francisco. As I'd promised everyone.

Squeeze it. Never pull. Squeeze it as slowly and as lovingly as you know how.

Nineteen

Good evening. This is the
nine o'clock news from the BBC.

PETER SISSONS

We didn't leave Mürren for another thirty-six hours. That was my idea.

I told Francisco that the first thing they'd do would be to check the train departures. Anybody who left, or tried to leave, within twelve hours of the shooting, would be in for a hell of a time, guilty or innocent.

Francisco had chewed his lip for a while, before gently smiling his agreement. I think that staying in the village struck him as the cooler, more daring option, and coolness and daring were qualities that Francisco definitely hoped to see one day, attached to his name in a *Newsweek* profile. A moody picture, with the caption: 'Francisco: cool and daring'. Something like that.

The real reason I wanted to stay in Mürren was so that I could get a chance to speak to Solomon, but I thought it probably best not to tell Francisco that.

So we hung about, separately, and gawped along with everyone else as the helicopters arrived. First police, then Red Cross, then, inevitably, the television crews. Word of the shooting was round the village in fifteen minutes, but most of the tourists seemed to be too stunned to talk to each other about it. They wandered here and there, watching, frowning, keeping their children close.

The Swiss sat in bars and murmured to each other; either they were upset, or they were worried about the effect on business. It was hard to tell. They needn't have worried, of course. By nightfall, the bars and restaurants were fuller than I'd ever seen them. Nobody wanted to miss out on an opinion, on a rumour, on any shred of interpretation they could hang on this ghastly, terrible event.

First of all, they blamed the Iraqis, which seems to be standard procedure nowadays. The theory lasted for an hour or so, until wise heads began to suggest that Iraqis couldn't have done it, couldn't even have got into the village without people noticing. Accent, skin-colour, kneeling down and facing Mecca. These were things that just didn't get past the nose of your average canny Swiss without attracting attention.

Next came an out-of-control pentathlete; exhausted after twenty miles of cross-country skiing, our man stumbles and falls, causing his .22 target rifle to discharge, killing Herr Van Der Hoewe in an accident of astronomical unlikelihood. Weird though this theory was, it attracted a considerable amount of support; mainly because it involved no malice, and malice was something that the Swiss simply did not want to countenance in their snow-capped paradise.

For a while, the two rumours lay down with each other, giving birth, after a time, to a truly bizarre hybrid: it was an Iraqi pentathlete, said the not-at-all-wise heads. Maddened with envy at the success of the Scandinavians in the last winter Olympics, an Iraqi pentathlete (someone knew someone who had heard the name Mustapha mentioned) had run amok; in fact, was probably still out there somewhere,

240

stalking the mountain in search of tall, blond skiers.

And then there was a lull. The bars began to empty, the cafés closed down for the night, and the waiters found themselves exchanging mystified looks as they cleared away plate after plate of uneaten food.

It took me a while to realise what was happening too.

The tourists, finding nothing very satisfactory in most of the explanations being trafficked about the town, had retreated to their hotel rooms to kneel, in ones and twos, before the all-powerful, all-seeing CNN, whose Man On The Spot, Tom Hamilton, was, even now, giving the world the benefit of 'the very latest reports, just in'.

Gathered around the television in the bar of Züm Wilden Hirsch, Latifa and I, wearing a dozen slightly drunk Germans about our shoulders, heard Tom expound the idea that 'the killing was possibly the work of activists' – for which, I would guess, Tom gets paid around $200,000 a year. I wanted to ask him how he had managed so ruthlessly to exclude the possibility that it was the work of passivists; in fact, I could easily have done so, since Tom was plying his trade, in a pool of flaring tungsten light, not two hundred yards from where we were trying to stand up. Only twenty minutes before, I had stood and watched while a CNN technician buttoned a radio microphone into Tom's tie, and Tom had waved him away and said he'd do it himself, because he didn't want anyone spoiling the knot.

The statement was due to have been released at ten o'clock, local time. If Cyrus had done his job, and the statement had reached them as planned, then CNN were taking their time verifying it. More likely, if the rest of the staff were anything like Tom, they were taking their time reading it. Francisco had insisted on using the word 'hegemony', and that had probably knocked them back a bit.

It finally came on the air at twenty-five past eleven, delivered slowly and clearly, and with a hefty sub-text of 'God these guys make me sick' by the CNN anchorman, Doug Rose.

The Sword Of Justice.

Mum, come quick. That's us. The man's talking about us.

I think, if I'd wanted to, I could probably have slept with Latifa that night.

The rest of the CNN coverage consisted of a lot of library footage concerning terrorism through the ages, stretching the viewer's memory all the way back to the beginning of last week, when a group of Basque separatists had bombed a government building in Barcelona. A man with a beard came on and tried to flog copies of a book he'd written about fanaticism, and then we were back to CNN's main agenda: telling people who are watching CNN that what they really ought to be doing is watching CNN. Preferably in a different fine hotel to the one they're in.

I lay on my bed at The Eiger, alone, feeding whisky and nicotine into myself with alternate hands, and started to wonder what would happen to you if you were ever actually *in* the fine hotel they were advertising, at the time they advertised it. Would it mean that you had died? Or gone to a parallel universe? Or that time had started to go backwards?

I was getting drunk, you see, which was why I didn't hear the knock at first. Or if I did hear it at first, I just convinced myself that I didn't, and that the knocking had been going on for ten minutes, possibly ten hours, while my brain yanked itself from its CNN torpor. I hauled myself off the bed.

'Who is it?'

Silence.

I had no weapon, nor any particular desire to use one, so I opened the door wide and stuck my head out. What will be will be.

A very short man stood in the corridor. Short enough to really hate someone of my height.

'Herr Balfour?'

I had a moment of complete blankness. The kind of blankness that often descends on agents working under cover – when the plates come spinning off the poles and they lose track of who they're supposed to be, who they really are, which hand they hold a pen with, or how door handles work. Drinking whisky, I've found, tends to increase the frequency of these episodes.

I was aware of him staring at me, so I pretended to cough while I struggled to get a hold of myself. Balfour, yes or no. Balfour was a name I was using, but with whom? I was Lang to Solomon, Ricky to Francisco, Durrell to most of the Americans, and Balfour . . . that's it. I was Balfour to the hotel; and therefore, if they so chose, and I had no doubt that they had so chosen, I was Balfour to the police, too.

I nodded.

'You will come with me.'

He turned on his heel and marched off down the corridor. I grabbed my jacket and room key and followed him, because Herr Balfour was a good citizen, who abided by every law he could find and expected others to do the same. As we walked to the lift, I looked down at his feet and saw that he was wearing platform shoes. He really was enormously short.

It was snowing outside (which, I grant you, is where it usually snows, but remember that I was only just starting to sober up) and huge discs of white were fluttering to the ground, like the debris from some celestial pillow-fight, covering everything, softening everything, making everything matter less.

We walked for about ten minutes, him taking seven paces to my one, until we reached a small building out on the edge of the village. It was a wooden, single-storey affair, and it might have been very old, or it might not. It had loose-fitting shutters over the windows, and the marks in the snow said that a lot of people had been paying calls recently. Or perhaps it was one person, who kept forgetting something.

It was a strange experience, walking into that house, and I think it would have been just as strange if I'd been sober. I felt like I should have brought something; gold or frankincense, at the very least. I didn't feel so bad about the myrrh, because I've never been quite certain what it is.

The Very Short Man stopped at a side door, glanced over his shoulder at me, then knocked once. After what seemed like a while, a bolt was shot somewhere, then another, and another, and another, and at last the door swung open. A grey-haired woman peered at the Very Short Man for a moment, at me for three moments, nodded, and stood aside to let us through.

Dirk Van Der Hoewe sat on the only chair in the room, polishing his glasses. He wore a heavy overcoat, with a scarf tucked in at the neck, and his fat feet bulged out of the side of his shoes. They were expensive shoes, black Oxfords with leather laces. I only noticed this because he seemed to be studying them so closely himself.

'Minister, this is Thomas Lang,' said Solomon, stepping out of the shadows, looking more at me than at Dirk.

Dirk took his time polishing his glasses, then stared at the floor while he slid them delicately on to his nose. At last, he lifted his head and looked at me. Not a friendly look. He was breathing through his mouth, like a child trying hard not to taste the broccoli.

'How do you do?' I said, holding out my hand.

Dirk looked at Solomon, as if no one had warned him that he might have to touch me as well, and then grudgingly offered me a limp wet thing with fingers on it.

We stared at each other for a while.

'May I go now?' he said.

Solomon paused for a moment, sadly, as if he'd been hoping that the three of us might stick around for a while and play some whist.

'Of course, sir,' he said.

It wasn't until Dirk stood up that I saw that although he was fat – oh by golly yes, he was definitely fat – he was still nothing like the size he'd been when he arrived in Mürren.

That's the thing about Life-Tec body armour, you see. It's wonderful stuff, and does everything you hope it will do in

244

the line of keeping you alive. But it's not flattering. To the figure, I mean. Worn with skiing clothes, it can make a slightly fat man look very fat, while a man like Dirk ends up as a barrage balloon.

I couldn't begin to guess what sort of a deal they'd struck with him. Or with the Dutch government, come to that. Certainly no one was going to put themselves out telling me. Maybe he'd been coming up for his sabbatical, or his retirement, or his sacking – or maybe they'd caught him in bed with a dozen ten-year-old girls. Or perhaps they'd just given him a lot of money. I understand that sometimes works with people.

However they did it, Dirk was going to have to lie pretty low for the next couple of months, for his sake as well as mine. If he popped up at an international conference next week, pronouncing on the need for a flexible exchange-rate mechanism amongst the north European states, it was going to look distinctly odd, and cause questions to be asked. Even CNN might have followed that one up.

Dirk didn't make his apologies, and left. The grey-haired woman squeezed him out through the door, and he and the Very Short Man disappeared into the night together.

'How are you feeling, sir?'

It was me on the chair now, and Solomon was pacing slowly round me after our de-briefing, measuring my morale, my fibre, my drunkenness. He had one finger held to his lips, and pretended not to be watching me.

'I'm fine, thank you, David. How are you?'

'Relieved, master. I would say. Yes. Definitely relieved.' There was a pause. He was doing a lot more thinking than talking. 'By the way,' he said at last, 'I am to congratulate you on a very fine shot, sir. My American colleagues want you to know.'

Solomon smiled at me, in a slightly sickly way, as if he'd now reached the bottom of the Nice Things To Say Box and was about to have to open the other one.

'Well, I'm delighted to have given satisfaction,' I said. 'What now?'

I lit a cigarette and tried to blow rings, but Solomon's pacing was spoiling the playing surface. I watched the smoke drift away, streaky and mis-shapen, and eventually realised that Solomon hadn't answered me.

'David?'

'Well yes, master,' he said, after a pause. 'What now? That's certainly an intelligent, pertinent question, and one that deserves the fullest kind of answer.'

Something was definitely wrong. Solomon didn't normally talk like this. I talk like this, when I'm drunk, but Solomon never does.

'Well?' I said. 'Do we wrap it up? Job done, bad guys caught with their hands in the till, scones and knighthoods all round?'

He stopped, somewhere behind my right shoulder.

'The truth, master, is that things get a little awkward from now on.'

I turned to look at him. And tried to smile. He didn't smile back.

'So what would be the adjective to describe the way things have been up to now, do you think? I mean, if trying to hit someone in the middle of a flak jacket isn't awkward . . . '

But he wasn't listening to me. That wasn't like him either.

'They want you to go on,' he said.

Well, of course they did. I knew that. Catching terrorists was not the object of this exercise and never had been. They wanted me to go on, they wanted it all to go on, until the setting was right for the big demonstration. CNN right there on the spot, cameras rolling – not arriving four hours after the event.

'Master,' said Solomon, after a while, 'I have to ask you a question, and I need you to answer me honestly.'

I didn't like the sound of this. This was all horribly wrong. This was red wine with fish. This was a man wearing a dinner jacket and brown shoes. This was as wrong as things get.

'Fire away,' I said.

He really did look worried.

'Will you answer me honestly? I need to know before I ask the question.'

'David, I can't tell you that.' I laughed, hoping he'd drop his shoulders, relax, stop frightening me. 'If you ask me to tell you whether or not you've got bad breath, I will answer you honestly. If you ask me . . . I don't know, practically anything else, then yes, I will probably lie.'

This didn't seem to satisfy him much. There was no reason why it should have done, of course, but what else could I say?

He cleared his throat, slowly and deliberately, as if he might not get the chance to do it again for some time.

'What precisely is your relationship with Sarah Woolf?'

I was really thrown now. Couldn't make head or tail of this. So I watched while Solomon walked slowly backwards and forwards, pursing his lips and frowning at the floor, like someone trying to broach the subject of masturbation with his teenage son. Not that I've ever been present at such a session, but I imagine that it involves a lot of blushing and fidgeting, and the discovery of microscopic specks of dust on sleeves of jackets that suddenly require a huge amount of attention.

'Why are you asking me, David?'

'Please, master. Just . . . ' This was not Solomon's best day, I could tell. He took a deep breath. 'Just answer. Please.'

I watched him for a while, feeling angry with him and sorry for him in just about equal parts.

'"For old times' sake," were you about to say?'

'For the sake of anything,' he said, 'that will make you answer the question, master. Old times, new times, just tell me.'

I lit another cigarette and looked at my hands, trying, as I'd tried many times before, to answer the question for myself, before I answered it for him.

Sarah Woolf. Grey eyes, with a streak of green. Nice tendons. Yes, I remember her.

What did I really feel? Love? Well, I couldn't answer that, could I? Just not familiar enough with the condition to be able to pin it on myself like that. Love is a word. A sound. Its association with a particular feeling is arbitrary, unmeasurable, and ultimately meaningless. No, I'll have to come back to that one, if you don't mind.

What about pity? I pity Sarah Woolf because . . . because what? She lost her brother, then her father, and now she's locked in the dark tower while Childe Roland fumbles about with a collapsible step-ladder. I could pity her for that, I suppose; for the fact that she gets me as a rescuer.

Friendship? For God's sake, I hardly know the woman.

Well what was it, then?

'I'm in love with her,' I heard someone say, and then realised it was me.

Solomon closed his eyes for a second, as if that was the wrong answer, *again* – then moved slowly, reluctantly, to a table by the wall, where he picked up a small plastic box. He weighed it in his hand for a moment, as if contemplating whether to give it to me or hurl it out of the door into the snow; and then he started rummaging in his pocket. Whatever he was looking for was in the last pocket he tried, and I was just thinking how nice it was to see this happening to someone else for a change, when he produced a pencil torch. He gave me the torch and the box, then turned his back and drifted away, leaving me to get on with it.

Well, I opened the box. Of course I did. That's what you do with closed boxes that people give you. You open them. So I lifted the yellow plastic lid, actually and metaphorically, and straight away my heart sank a little lower still.

The box contained slide photographs, and I knew, absolutely knew, that I wasn't going to like whatever was in them.

I plucked out the first one, and held it up in front of the torch.

Sarah Woolf. No mistake there.

A sunny day, a black dress, getting out of a London taxi.

248

Good. Fair enough. Nothing wrong with that. She was smiling – a big, happy smile – but that's allowed. That's okay. I didn't expect her to be sobbing into her pillow twenty-four hours a day. So. Next.

Paying the driver. Again, nothing wrong with that. You ride in a cab, you have to pay the driver. This is life. The photograph was taken with a long lens, at least a 135, probably more. And the closeness of the sequence meant a motor-drive. Why would anyone bother to take . . .

Moving away from the cab towards the kerb, now. Laughing. The cab driver's watching her bottom, which I would do if I was a cab driver. She'd watched the back of his neck, he was watching her bottom. A fair exchange. Well not quite fair, perhaps, but no one ever said it was a perfect world.

I glanced up at Solomon's back. His head was bowed.

And the next one, please.

A man's arm. Arm and shoulder, in fact, in a dark-grey suit. Reaching out for her waist, while she tilts her head back, ready for a kiss. The smile is bigger still. Again, who's worrying? We're not puritans. A woman can go out for lunch with somebody, can be polite, pleased to see him – doesn't mean we have to call the police, for fuck's sake.

Arms round each other now. Her head is camera-side, so his face is obscured, but they're definitely hugging. A proper, full-on hug. So he's probably not her bank manager. So what?

This one's almost the same, but they've started to turn. His head lifting away from her neck.

They're coming towards us now, arms still round each other. Can't see his face, because a passer-by is passing-by, close to the camera, blurred. But her face. Her face is what? Heaven? Bliss? Joy? Rapture? Or just politeness. Next and final slide.

Oh, hello, I thought to myself. This is the one.

'Oh, hello,' I said aloud. 'This is the one.'

Solomon didn't turn.

A man and a woman are coming towards us, and I know

249

them both. I've just owned up to being in love with the woman, although I'm not really sure if that's true, and I'm getting less sure by the second, while the man . . . yeah, right.

He's tall. He's good-looking, in a weathered kind of a way. He's dressed in an expensive suit. And he's smiling too. They're both smiling. Smiling on a big scale. Smiling so hard, it looks like the tops of their heads are about to fall off.

Of course I'd like to know what the fuck the two of them are so happy about. If it's a joke, I'd like to hear it – judge for myself whether it's worth rupturing your pancreas over, whether it's the kind of joke that would make you want to take hold of the person next to you and squeeze them like that. Or squeeze them at all.

Obviously, I don't know the joke, I'm just sure that it wouldn't make me laugh. Incredibly sure.

The man in the photograph, with his arm round my mistress of the dark tower, making her laugh – filling her with laughter, filling her with pleasure, filling her with bits of himself, for all I know – is Russell P. Barnes.

We're going to take a break there. Join us after I've thrown the box of slides across the room.

Twenty

Life is made up of sobs,
sniffles, and smiles,
with sniffles predominating.

O. HENRY

I told Solomon everything. I had to.

Because, you see, he is a clever man, one of the cleverest I've ever known, and it would have been silly to try and stagger on without making use of his intellect. Until I saw these photographs, I'd been pretty much on my own, ploughing a lonely furrow, but now was the time to admit that the plough had wobbled off at right angles and run into the side of the barn.

It was four o'clock in the morning by the time I finished, and long before then Solomon had broken open his knapsack and pulled out the kind of things that the Solomons of this world never seem to be without. We had a thermos of tea, with two plastic cups; an orange each, and a knife to peel them with; and a half-pound of Cadbury's milk chocolate.

So, as we ate, and drank, and smoked, and disapproved of smoking, I laid out the story of Graduate Studies from beginning to middle: that I was not where I was, doing what I was doing, for the good of democracy; I was not keeping anyone safe in their beds at night, or making the world a freer, happier place; all I was doing – all I'd ever been doing since the whole thing started – was selling guns.

Which meant that Solomon was selling them too. I was the gun seller, the sales rep, and Solomon was something in the marketing department. I knew he wouldn't like that feeling much.

Solomon listened, and nodded, and asked the right questions, in the right order, at the right time. I couldn't tell whether or not he believed me; but then, I'd never been able to do that with Solomon, and probably never would.

When I'd finished, I sat back and toyed with a couple of squares of chocolate, and wondered whether bringing Cadbury's to Switzerland was the same as bringing coals to Newcastle, and decided it wasn't. Swiss chocolate has gone badly downhill since I was a lad, and nowadays is only fit for giving to aunts. And all the while, Cadbury's chocolate plods on and on, better and cheaper than any other chocolate in the world. That's my view, anyway.

'That's a heck of a story, master, if you don't mind me saying.' Solomon was standing, staring at the wall. If there'd been a window, he'd probably have stared out of that, but there wasn't.

'Yup,' I agreed.

So we came back to the photographs, and we thought about what they might mean. We supposed and we postulated; we maybeed, and what-iffed, and how-aboutted; until eventually, when the snow was just beginning to gather some light from somewhere and bounce it in through the shutters and under the door, we decided that we'd at last covered all the angles.

There were three possibilities.

Quite a lot of sub-possibilities, obviously, but at that moment we felt like we wanted to deal in broad strokes, so we swept up the sub-possibilities into three main piles, which ran like this: he was bullshitting her; she was bullshitting him;

neither one of them was bullshitting the other, they'd simply fallen in love with each other – fellow Americans, passing the long afternoons together in a strange city.

'If she's bullshitting him,' I began, for about the hundredth time, 'it's to what purpose? I mean, what is she hoping to gain by it?'

Solomon nodded, then quickly rubbed his face, squeezing his eyes shut.

'A post-coital confession?' He winced at the sound of his own words. 'She records it, films it or whatever, sends it to the Washington *Post*?'

I didn't like that much, and neither did he.

'Pretty feeble, I'd say.'

Solomon nodded again. He was still agreeing with me rather more than I deserved – probably because he was relieved that I hadn't gone to pieces altogether, what with one thing and about a million others, and wanted to massage me back into a reasonable and optimistic frame of mind.

'So he's bullshitting her?' he said, putting his head on one side, eyebrows raised, ushering me through the gate like a subtle sheepdog.

'Maybe,' I said. 'A willing captive is less trouble than an unwilling one. Or maybe he's spun her some yarn, told her it'll all be taken care of. He has the ear of the President himself, something like that.'

That didn't sound too good either.

Which left us with possibility number three.

Now why would a woman like Sarah Woolf want to get together with a man like Russell P. Barnes? Why would she walk with him, laugh with him, make the beast with four buttocks with him? If that's actually what she was doing, and there wasn't much doubt in my mind about it.

All right, he was handsome. He was fit. He was intelligent, in a stupid sort of a way. He had power. He dressed well. But apart from all that, what was in it for her? I mean, for Christ's sake, he was old enough to be a corrupt representative of her government.

I deliberated on the sexual charms of Russell P. Barnes as I trudged back to the hotel. Dawn was definitely pulling into the station by now, and the snow had begun to throb with an electric, new-fallen whiteness. It climbed the inside of my trousers, and clung, squeakily, to the soles of my boots, and the bit just in front seemed to say 'don't walk on me, please don't walk . . . oh.'

Russell arsing Barnes.

I got back to the hotel and made for my room as quietly as I could. I unlocked the door, slipped inside and then, immediately, stopped: froze, with my windcheater half off. After the journey through the snow, with nothing but alpine air moving around my system, I was tuned to pick up all the nuances of indoor smells – the stale beer from the bar, the shampoo in the carpet, the chlorine from the basement swimming pool, the beachy sun-cream smell from just about everywhere – and now this new smell. A smell of something that really shouldn't have been in the room.

It shouldn't have been there because I was only paying for a single, and Swiss hotels are notoriously strict about this kind of thing.

Latifa was stretched out on my bed, asleep, the top sheet coiled around her naked body like a Rubens pastiche.

'Where the fuck have you been?'

She was sitting up now, the sheet tight round her chin, while I sat on the end of the bed and pulled off my boots.

'For a walk,' I said.

'For a walk where?' snapped Latifa, still crumpled with sleep, and angry with me for seeing her that way. 'It's fucking snow. Where do you walk in fucking snow? What have you been doing?'

I yanked off the last boot and slowly turned to look at her.

'I shot a man today, Latifa.' Except I was Ricky to her, so I pronounced it Laddifa. 'I pulled the trigger and shot a man down.' I turned away and stared at the floor, the soldier-poet,

254

sickened by the ugliness of battle.

I felt the sheet relax under me. Slightly. She watched me for a while.

'You walked all night?'

I sighed. 'I walked. I sat. I thought. You know, a human life . . . '

Ricky, as I'd painted him, was a man not wholly at ease with the business of talking, so this answer took some time to get out. We let a human life hang in the air for a while.

'A lot of people die, Rick,' said Latifa. 'There is death everywhere. Murder everywhere.' The sheet relaxed a little more, and I saw her hand move gently to the side of the bed, next to mine.

Why was it that I kept on hearing this argument wherever I went? Everybody's doing it, so you'd be a square not to join in and help the whole business along. I suddenly wanted to slap her, and tell her who I was, and what I really thought; that killing Dirk, killing anybody, was not going to change anything apart from Francisco's fucking ego, which was already large enough to house the world's poor twice over, with a few million bourgeoisie in the spare-room.

Fortunately, I am the consummate professional, so I just nodded and hung my head, and sighed some more, and watched her hand creep nearer and nearer to mine.

'It's good that you feel bad,' she said, after some thought. Not much thought, obviously, but some. 'If you felt nothing, it would mean there was no love, no passion. And we are nothing without passion.'

We're not a great deal with it, I thought, and started to pull off my shirt.

Things were changing, you see. In my head.

It was the photographs that had finally done it – had made me realise that I had been bouncing around inside other people's arguments for so long that I'd reached the point of not caring. I didn't care about Murdah and his helicopters; I didn't care about Sarah Woolf and Barnes; I didn't care about O'Neal and Solomon, or Francisco and The Sword Of fucking

Justice. I didn't care who won the argument, or who won the war.

I particularly didn't care about myself.

Latifa's fingers brushed against the back of my hand.

When it comes to sex, it seems to me, men really are caught between a rock and a soft, limp, apologetic place.

The sexual mechanisms of the two genders are just not compatible, that's the horrible truth of it. One is a runabout, suitable for shopping, quick journeys about town, and extremely easy parking; the other is an estate, designed for long distances, with heavy loads – altogether larger, more complex, and more difficult to maintain. You wouldn't buy a Fiat Panda to move antiques from Bristol to Norwich, and you wouldn't buy a Volvo for any other reason. It's not that one is better than the other. They're just different, that's all.

This is a truth we dare not acknowledge these days – because sameness is our religion and heretics are no more welcome now than they ever were – but I'm going to acknowledge it, because I've always felt that humility before the facts is the only thing that keeps a rational man together. Be humble in the face of facts, and proud in the face of opinions, as George Bernard Shaw once said.

He didn't, actually. I just wanted to put some authority behind this observation of mine, because I know you're not going to like it.

If a man gives himself up to the sexual moment, then, well, that's all it is. A moment. A spasm. An event without duration. If, on the other hand, he holds back, by trying to remember as many names as he can from the Dulux colour chart, or whatever happens to be his chosen method of deferment, then he's accused of being coldly technical. Either way, if you're a heterosexual man, emerging from a modern sexual encounter with any kind of credit is a fiendishly difficult thing to do.

Yes, of course, credit is not the point of the exercise. But then again, it's easy to say that when you've got some. Credit,

I mean. And men just don't get any these days. In the sexual arena, men are judged by female standards. You may hiss and tut and draw in your breath as sharply as you like, but it's true. (Yes, obviously, men judge women in other spheres – patronise them, tyrannise them, exclude them, oppress them, make them utterly miserable – but in matters of a writhing nature, the mark on the bench was put down by women. It is for the Fiat Panda to try and be like the Volvo, not the other way round.) You just don't hear men criticising women for taking fifteen minutes to reach a climax; and if you do, it's not with any implied accusation of weakness, or arrogance, or self-centredness. Men, generally, just hang their heads and say yes, that's the way her body is, that's what she needed from me, and I couldn't deliver it. I'm crap and I'll leave at once, as soon as I can find my other sock.

Which, to be honest, is unfair, bordering on the ridiculous. In the same way that it would be ridiculous to call a Fiat Panda a crap car, just because you can't fit a wardrobe in the back. It might be crap for all sorts of other reasons – it breaks down, or it uses a lot of oil, or it's lime-green with the word 'turbo' written pathetically across the back window – but it's not crap because of the one characteristic that it was specifically designed to have: smallness. Neither is a Volvo a crap car, simply because it won't squeeze past the barrier in the Safeways car-park and allow you to get out without paying.

Burn me on a mound of faggots if you like, but the two machines are just plain different, and that's that. Designed to do different things, at different speeds, on different types of roads. They're different. Not the same. Unalike.

There, I've said it. And I don't feel any better.

Latifa and I made love twice before breakfast, and once afterwards, and by mid-morning I'd managed to remember Burnt Umber, which made thirty-one, something of a personal record.

'Cisco,' I said, 'tell me something.'

'Sure, Rick. Go ahead.'

He glanced across at me, then reached down to the dashboard and popped the cigarette lighter.

I thought, for a long, slow, Minnesotan moment.

'Where does the money come from?'

We travelled about two kilometres before he answered.

We were in Francisco's Alfa Romeo, just the two of us, gradually reeling in the Autoroute de Soleil from Marseille to Paris, and if he let 'Born In The USA' go round just once more on the tape-deck, I was probably going to have a nosebleed.

Three days had passed since the shooting of Dirk Van Der Hoewe, and The Sword Of Justice was feeling pretty invincible by now, because the newspapers had started to discuss other matters and the police were scratching their computerised, intelligence-gathering heads at the lack of any firm leads.

'Where does the money come from,' Francisco repeated eventually, drumming the steering-wheel with his fingers.

'Yeah,' I said.

The motorway hummed by. Wide, straight, French.

'Why do you want to know?'

I shrugged.

'Just . . . you know . . . just thinking.'

He laughed like a crazy rock 'n' roll thing.

'Don't you think, Ricky, my friend. You just do. You good at doing. Stick with that.'

I laughed too, because this was Francisco's way of making me feel good. If he'd been six inches taller, he'd have ruffled my hair like a big-hearted older brother.

'Yeah. I was just thinking, though . . . '

I stopped. For thirty seconds we both sat a little straighter in our seats as a dark-blue *Gendarme* Peugeot cruised past. Francisco eased fractionally off the accelerator and let it go.

'I was thinking,' I said, 'like when I paid the check at the hotel, you know . . . and I thought, like, that's a lot of money . . . you know . . . like six of us . . . hotels and stuff . . . plane tickets . . . lots of money. And I thought . . . like, where's it coming from? You know, somebody's paying, right?'

Francisco nodded wisely, as if he was trying to help me with a complicated problem involving girlfriends.

'Sure, Ricky. Somebody's paying. Somebody's got to pay, all the time.'

'Right,' I said. 'That's what I thought. Somebody's got to pay. So, like, I thought . . . you know . . . who?'

He kept his eyes to the front for a while, then slowly turned and looked at me. For a long time. So long, that I had to keep flicking my eyes to the road in front to make sure there wasn't a fleet of jack-knifing lorries ahead of us.

In between these glances, I shone back at him with as much innocent stupidity as I could manage. Ricky's not dangerous, I was trying to say. Ricky's an honest infantryman. Ricky's a simple soul who just wants to know who's paying his wages. Ricky is not – never has been, and never will be – a threat.

I chuckled, nervously.

'You going to watch the road?' I said. 'I mean, like . . . you know.'

Francisco chewed his lip for a moment, then suddenly laughed with me and turned back to face the front.

'You remember Greg?' he said, in a happy, sing-song way.

I frowned, heavily, because unless a thing happened in the last few hours, Ricky's not sure he can remember it too well.

'Greg,' he said again. 'With the Porsche. With the cigars. Took your picture for the passport.'

I waited a while, and then nodded vigorously.

'Greg, sure, I remember him,' I said. 'Drove a Porsche.'

Francisco smiled. Maybe he was thinking that it didn't matter what he told me, because I'd have forgotten it all by the time we got to Paris.

'That's him. Well now, Greg, he is a clever guy.'

'Yeah?' I said, as if this was a new concept to me.

'Oh sure,' said Francisco. 'Real clever. Clever guy with money. Clever guy with a lot of things.'

I thought about this for a while.

'Seemed like an asshole to me,' I said.

Francisco looked at me in surprise, then let out a yell of

259

delighted laughter, and hammered the steering-wheel with his fist.

'Sure he's an asshole,' he shouted. 'A fucking asshole, yeah.'

I laughed along with him, glowing with pride at having said something to please the master. Eventually, gradually, we both calmed down, and then he reached out a hand and turned off the Bruce Springsteen. I could have kissed him.

'Greg works with another guy,' said Francisco, his face becoming suddenly serious. 'Zurich. They are like finance people. They move money around, do deals, handle a lot of big stuff. Varied stuff. You know?' He looked across at me, and I frowned dutifully back, showing some hard concentration. That seemed to be what he wanted. 'Anyhow, Greg gets a call. Money coming in. Do this with it, do that with it. Sit on it. Lose it. Whatever.'

'You mean, like, we got a bank account?' I said, grinning.

Francisco grinned too.

'Sure, we got a bank account, Ricky. We got a lot of bank accounts.'

I shook my head in wonder at the ingenuity of this, and then frowned again.

'So Greg pays money for us, right? But not his money?'

'No, not his money. He deals with it, takes his cut. Big cut, I think, seeing as how he drives a Porsche, and all I got is this fucking Alfa. But it ain't his money.'

'So who?' I said. Probably too quickly. 'I mean, like one guy? Or a lot of guys, or what?'

'One guy,' said Francisco, then took a last, long, deciding look at me – auditing me, weighing me up – trying to remember all the times I'd annoyed him, all the times I'd pleased him; figuring out whether I'd done enough to earn this one piece of information that I had no right or reason to know. Then he sniffed, which is a thing Francisco always did when he was getting ready to say something important.

'I don't know his name,' he said. 'His real name, I mean. But he uses a name for the money. For the banks.'

'Yeah?' I said.

I was trying to make it look as if I wasn't holding my breath. Cisco was teasing me now, drawing the whole thing out for fun.

'Yeah?' I said again.

'The name is Lucas,' he said at last. 'Michael Lucas.'

I nodded.

'Cool,' I said.

After a while I settled my head back against the window, and pretended to sleep.

There's a thing, I thought, as we thrummed along towards Paris, and Christ knew what. There's a strange piece of philosophy in action. I just hadn't realised that before.

Thou Shalt Not Kill, I'd always assumed, was top of the list. The Big One. Coveting neighbour's asses, obviously, was a thing to avoid; likewise, committing adultery, not honouring thy father and thy mother, and bowing down before graven images.

But Thou Shalt Not Kill. Now that is a Commandment. That's the one everyone can remember, because it seems the rightest, the truest, the most absolute.

The one that everyone forgets is the one about not bearing false witness against thy neighbour. It seems paltry by comparison to Thou Shalt Not Kill. Nit-picking. A parking offence.

But when it's thrust in your face, and when your gut reacts to it seconds before you brain has had a chance even to digest what it's heard, you realise that life, morality, values – they just don't seem to work the way you thought they did.

Murdah shot Mike Lucas through the throat, and that was one of the wickedest things I'd ever seen, in a life not unmarked by the seeing of wicked things. But when Murdah decided, for reasons of convenience, or amusement, or administrative neatness, to bear false witness against the man he'd killed – to take away not just his physical life, but his moral life too; his existence, his memory, his reputation; using his name, blackening it, just to cover his own tracks – so that he could hang the blame for what was to come on a twenty-eight-year-old CIA man who went a little funny in the head, well, that was the point when things started to change for me.

That was the point when I started to get really angry.

Twenty-one

I think I bust a button on my trousers.
MICK JAGGER

Francisco gave us ten days' leave for rest and recreation.

Bernhard said he was going to spend it in Hamburg, and he had a look on his face that seemed to indicate some kind of sexual thing might be involved; Cyrus went to Evian Les Bains, because his mother was dying – although it later turned out that she was dying in Lisbon, and Cyrus simply wanted to be as far away from her as possible when she finally went; Benjamin and Hugo flew to Haifa, for a little scuba diving; and Francisco hung around at the Paris house, acting up the loneliness-of-command role.

I said I was going to London, and Latifa said she'd come with me.

'We have a fucking good time in London. I'll show you things. London is a great town.' She grinned at me, and threw her eyelashes about the place.

'Fuck you,' I said. 'I don't want you hanging off my fucking elbow.'

These were harsh words, obviously, and I really wished I

263

hadn't had to put it like that. But the risk of being in London with Latifa at my side, and some twerp yelling at me in the street, 'Thomas, long time no see, who's the bird?' was just too awful to contemplate. I needed to be able to move freely, and ditching Latifa was the only way I could manage it.

Of course, I could have made up some story about having to visit my grandparents, or my seven children, or my venereal disease counsellor, but in the end I decided that fuck off was less complicated.

I flew from Paris to Amsterdam on the Balfour passport, and then spent an hour trying to shed any Americans who might have been keen enough to follow me. Not that they had any particular reason to. The shooting in Mürren had satisfied most of them that I was a solid team player, and anyway, Solomon had recommended a long leash until the next contact.

Even so, I wanted every pair of eyebrows to be straight and level for the next few days, with nobody, on any side, saying 'hello, what's this?' over something I did or somewhere I went. So at Schiphol airport, I bought a ticket to Oslo and threw it away, then bought a change of clothes and a new pair of sunglasses, and dithered around in the lavatory for a while, before emerging as Thomas Lang, the well-known non-entity.

I arrived at Heathrow at six o'clock in the evening and checked into the Post House hotel; which is a handy place, because it's so close to the airport; and a horrible place, because it's so close to the airport.

I had a long bath, then flopped on to the bed with a packet of cigarettes and an ashtray, and dialled Ronnie's number. I had to ask her for a favour, you see – the kind of favour that you need to take a while to get round to – so I was settling in for a big session.

We talked for a long time, which was nice; nice anyway, but particularly nice because Murdah was, in the very long run, going to have to pay for the call. Just like he was going to have to pay for the champagne and steak I ordered from room service, and the lamp I broke when I tripped on the edge of the bed. I knew, of course, that it would probably take him something like a hundredth of a second to earn enough money to cover it all – but then, when you go to war, you have to be ready to live off small triumphs like this.

While you wait for the big one.

'Mr Collins. Do take a seat.'

The receptionist flicked a switch and spoke into thin air.

'Mr Collins to see Mr Barraclough.'

Of course it wasn't thin air. It was, instead, a wire-thin microphone attached to a headset, buried somewhere inside a big hair-do. But it took me a good five minutes to realise this, during which time I wanted to call somebody and tell them that the receptionist was hallucinating quite seriously.

'Won't be a minute,' she said. To me or the microphone, I'm not sure.

She and I were in the offices of Smeets Velde Kerkplein, which, if nothing else, would presumably score you something pretty decent in a game of Scrabble; and I was Arthur Collins, a painter from Taunton.

I wasn't sure if Philip would remember Arthur Collins, and it didn't really matter if he didn't; but I'd needed some tiny purchase to get me up here to the twelfth floor, and Collins had seemed like the best bet. An improvement, anyway, on Some Bloke Who Once Slept With Your Fiancée.

I got up and paced slowly around the room, cocking my head to one side in a painterly fashion at the various chunks of corporate art that covered the walls. They were, for the most part, huge daubs of grey and turquoise, with the odd – the very odd – streak of scarlet. They looked as if they'd been designed in a laboratory, and probably had, specifically to maximise feelings of confidence and optimism in the breast of the first-time SVK investor. They didn't work for me, but then I was here for other reasons.

A yellow oak door swung open down the corridor and Philip stuck his head out. He squinted at me for a moment, then stepped out and held the door wide.

'Arthur,' he said, a little hesitantly. 'How's it going?'

He was wearing bright yellow braces.

Philip had his back to me, and was half-way through pouring me a cup of coffee.

'My name isn't Arthur,' I said, as I slumped back into a chair.

His head shot round, then shot back again.

'Shit,' he said, and started to suck the cuff of his shirt. Then he turned and shouted towards the open door. 'Jane, darling, get us a cloth, will you?' He looked down at the mess of coffee, milk, and sodden biscuits, and decided that he couldn't be bothered.

'Sorry,' he said, still licking his shirt, 'you were saying?' He sauntered round behind me, making for the sanctuary of his desk. When he got there, he sat down very slowly. Either because he was haemorrhoidal, or because there was a chance that I might do something dangerous. I smiled, to show him that he was haemorrhoidal.

'My name isn't Arthur,' I said again.

There was a pause, and a thousand possible responses clattered through Philip's brain, spinning across his eyes like a fruit-machine.

'Oh?' he said, at last.

Two lemons and a bunch of cherries. Press restart.

'I'm afraid Ronnie lied to you that day,' I said, apologetically.

He tipped himself back in his chair, his face fixed into a cool, pleasant, nothing-you-can-say-will-ruffle-me smile.

'Did she now?' A pause. 'That was very naughty of her.'

'It wasn't out of guilt. I mean, you must understand, nothing had happened between us.' I left a pause – about the length of time it would take to say 'I left a pause' – and then delivered the punch line. 'At that stage.'

He flinched. Visibly.

Well of course it was visibly. Because I wouldn't have

266

known about it otherwise. What I mean is, it was a big flinch, almost a jump. Big enough, certainly, to satisfy the square leg umpire.

He looked down at his braces and scraped at one of the brass adjusters with his fingernail.

'At that stage. I see.' Then he looked up at me. 'I'm sorry,' said Philip, 'but I feel as if I should ask you for your real name, before we go any further. I mean, if you're not Arthur Collins, you know . . . ' He trailed off, desperate and panicky, but not wanting to show it. Not in front of me, anyway.

'My name is Lang,' I said. 'Thomas Lang. And let me say first of all that I absolutely realise how much of a shock this will be to you.'

He waved away my attempt at an apology, and sat there for a moment, chewing his knuckle while he thought about what he was going to do next.

He was still sitting like that five minutes later, when the door opened, and a girl in a stripy shirt, presumably Jane, stood there with a tea-towel and Ronnie.

The two women paused in the doorway, eyes flitting here and there, while Philip and I got to our feet and did our own lot of flitting. If you'd been a film director, you'd have had a heck of a job deciding where to put the camera. The tableau stayed as it was, with all of us writhing in the same social hell, until Ronnie broke the silence.

'Darling,' she said.

Philip, the poor dope, took a step forward at this.

But Ronnie was now heading for my side of the desk, and so Philip had to turn his step into a vague gesture towards Jane, and what happened with the coffee was this, and the biscuits got all like that, and would you mind awfully much being a love?

By the time he'd finished, and turned back to us, Ronnie was in my arms, hugging me like an express train. I hugged her back, because the occasion seemed to demand it, and also because I wanted to. She smelled very nice.

After a while, Ronnie disengaged slightly, and leaned back

to look at me. I think maybe there were tears in her eyes, so she was definitely throwing herself into it. Then she turned towards Philip.

'Philip . . . what can I say?' she said, which was about all she could say.

Philip scratched the back of his neck, blushed a little, and then got back to the coffee stain on his shirt cuff. He was an Englishman, all right.

'Leave that for a moment, Jane, will you?' he said, without looking up. This was music to Jane's ears, and she was out of the door in a second. Philip tried a gallant laugh.

'So,' he said.

'Yeah,' I said. 'So.' I laughed too, just as awkwardly. 'I guess that's about it, really. I'm sorry, Philip. You know . . . '

We stood like that, the three of us, for another age, waiting for someone to whisper the next line from the prompt corner. Then Ronnie turned to me, and her eyes said do it now.

I took a deep breath.

'Philip, by the way,' I said, unhooking myself from Ronnie and stepping up to his desk, 'I wondered if I could ask you . . . you know . . . if you'd do me a favour.'

Philip looked as if I'd just hit him with a building.

'A favour?' he said, and I could tell that he was weighing up the pros and cons of getting very cross.

Ronnie tutted behind me.

'Thomas, don't do this,' she said. Philip looked at her and frowned very slightly, but she didn't pay any attention. 'You promised not to do this,' she whispered.

It was beautifully judged.

Philip sniffed the air and found it, if not sweet, certainly less sour than it had been, because within thirty seconds of us telling him that we were the only happy couple in the room, it now looked as if Ronnie and I were about to have an argument.

'What kind of favour?' he asked, folding his arms across his chest.

'Thomas, I said no.' Ronnie again, really quite angry now.

I half-turned, speaking to her, but looking at the door, as if we'd had this argument a few times before.

'Look, he can say no, can't he?' I said. 'I mean, Christ, I'm only asking.'

Ronnie took a couple of steps forward, edging slightly round the corner of the desk, until she was nearly half-way between us. Philip looked down at her thighs, and I could see him judging our relative positions. I'm not out of this yet, he was thinking.

'You're not to take advantage of him, Thomas,' said Ronnie, moving a little further round the desk. 'You're just not. It isn't fair. Not now.'

'Oh for God's sake,' I said, hanging my head.

'What kind of favour?' said Philip again, and I sensed the hope rising in him.

Ronnie moved closer still.

'No, don't, Philip,' she said. 'Don't do this. We'll go, we'll let you . . . '

'Look,' I said, still with my head down, 'I may not get a chance like this ever again. I have to ask him. This is my job, remember? Asking people.' I was starting to get sarcastic and nasty, and Philip was loving every second of it.

'Please don't listen, Philip, I'm sorry . . . ' Ronnie shot me an angry look.

'No, that's all right,' said Philip. He looked back at me, taking his time, thinking that all he had to do now was not make a mistake. 'What is your job, Thomas, by the way?'

That was nice, the Thomas. A sweet, friendly, rock-solid way to address the man who's just stolen your fiancée.

'He's a journalist,' said Ronnie, before I had a chance to answer. The word 'journalist' came out as if it was a pretty horrible occupation. Which, let's face it . . .

'You're a journalist, and you want to ask me something?' said Philip. 'Well, fire away.' Philip was smiling now. Gracious in defeat. A gentleman.

'Thomas, if you ask him, at a time like this, after what we agreed . . . ' She let it hang in the air. Philip wanted her to finish it.

'What?' I said, with a load of truculence.

Ronnie stared at me furiously, then spun on her heel to face the wall. As she did so, she brushed against Philip's elbow, and I saw him arch slightly. It was beautifully done. I'm very close now, he was thinking. Easy does it.

'Doing a piece on the breakdown of the nation-state,' I said wearily, almost drunkenly. The few journalists I've spoken to in my life all seemed to have this in common: an attitude of perpetual exhaustion, brought on by dealing with people who just aren't quite as fantastic as they are. I was trying to duplicate it now, and it seemed to be coming out pretty well. 'Economic supremacy of multinationals over governments,' I slurred, as if every dolt in the land ought to know by now that this was the hot issue.

'For what paper would that be, Thomas?'

I slumped back down in the chair. Now the two of them were standing, together, on the far side of the desk, while I slouched away on my own. All I needed to do was burp a few times and start picking spinach out of my teeth, and Philip would know he was on to a winner.

'Any paper that'll have it, basically,' I said, with a grumpy shrug.

Philip was pitying me now, wondering how he could ever have believed that I was a threat.

'And you want some . . . what, information?' Coasting down the final straight to victory.

'Yeah, right,' I said. 'Just about the movement of money, really. How people get around various currency laws, sling money about the place without anyone ever knowing. Most of it's general background stuff really, but there are one or two actual cases that interest me.'

I did actually burp slightly as I said that. Ronnie heard it and turned to face me.

'Oh tell him to get lost, Philip, for goodness' sake,' she said. She glared at me. It was a bit frightening. 'He's barged in here . . .'

'Look, mind your own business, can't you?' I said. I was glaring oafishly back at her, and you could have sworn the two of us had been unhappily married for years. 'Philip doesn't mind, do you, Phil?'

Philip was about to say that he didn't mind at all, that all this was going splendidly from his point of view, but Ronnie wouldn't let him. She was spitting fire.

'He's being polite, you numbskull,' she shouted. 'Philip has got manners.'

'Unlike me?'

'You said it.'

'You didn't have to.'

'Oh, you're just so sensitive.'

Hammer and tongs, we were going. And we'd hardly had any rehearsal.

There was a long, nasty pause, and perhaps Philip started to think that it all might slip away from him at the last moment, because he said:

'Did you want to trace specific movements of money, Thomas? Or was it, generally, the mechanisms people might use?'

Bingo.

'Ideally both, Phil,' I said.

After an hour-and-a-half I left Philip with his computer terminal and a list of 'really good mates who owed him one', and made my way across the City of London to Whitehall, where I had an absolutely revolting lunch with O'Neal. Although the food was pretty good.

We talked of cabbages and kings for a while, and then I watched O'Neal's colour gradually change from pink, to white, to green, as I recapped the story so far. When I laid out what I thought might be a reasonably zingy finish to the whole thing, he turned grey.

'Lang,' he croaked, over the coffee, 'you can't . . . I mean . . . I can't possibly contemplate your having anything . . . '

'Mr O'Neal,' I said, 'I'm not asking for your permission.'

He stopped croaking, and just sat there, his mouth flapping vaguely. 'I'm telling you what I think is going to happen. As a courtesy.' Which, I admit, was an odd word to use in a situation like this. 'I want you, and Solomon, and your department, to be able to get out of this without too much egg down the front of your shirt. Use it, or don't use it. It's up to you.'

'But . . . ' he floundered, 'you can't . . . I mean . . . I could have you reported to the police.' I think even he realised how feeble that sounded.

'Of course you could,' I said. 'If you wanted your department to be closed down within forty-eight hours, and its offices turned into a crêche facility for the Ministry of Agriculture and Fisheries, then yes, reporting me to the police would certainly be an excellent way of going about it. Now, do you have that address?'

He flapped his mouth some more, and then shook himself awake, came to a decision, and started sneaking huge, theatrical looks around the restaurant, as a way of telling all the other lunchers that I Am Now Going To Give This Man An Important Piece Of Paper.

I took the address from him, bolted my coffee, and got up from the table. When I glanced back from the door, I had the very strong feeling that O'Neal was wondering how he could arrange to be on holiday for the next month.

The address was in Kentish Town, and turned out to be one of a clutch of low-rise sixties council blocks, with freshly-painted woodwork, window-boxes, trimmed hedges and a pebble-dashed row of garages to one side. The lift even worked.

I stood and waited on the open second-floor landing, and tried to imagine what appalling series of bureaucratic errors had led to this estate being so well looked after. In most parts of London, they collect the dustbins from the middle-class streets and empty them into the council estates, before setting fire to a couple of Ford Cortinas on the pavement. But not here, obviously. Here, there was a building that worked, where people could actually live with a degree of dignity, and not feel as if the rest of society was disappearing over the horizon in a Butlins charabanc. I felt like writing a stiff letter to somebody. And then tearing it up and throwing the bits on to the lawn below.

The glass-panelled door of number fourteen swung open, and a woman stood there.

'Hello,' I said. 'My name is Thomas Lang. I'm here to see Mr Rayner.'

Bob Rayner fed goldfish while I told him what I wanted.

This time, he wore glasses and a yellow golfing sweater, which I suppose hard men are allowed to do on their days off, and he got his wife to bring me tea and biscuits. We had an awkward ten minutes while I enquired after his head, and he told me that he still got the odd headache, and I said I was sorry about that, and he said not to worry, because he used to get them before I hit him.

And that seemed to be that. Water under the bridge. Bob was a professional, you see.

'Do you think you can get it?' I asked.

He tapped on the side of the aquarium, which didn't seem to impress the fish in the slightest.

'Cost you,' he said, after a while.

'That's fine,' I said.

Which it was. Because Murdah would be paying.

Twenty-two

The clever men at Oxford
Know all that there is to be knowed
But they none of them know one half as much
As intelligent Mr Toad.

KENNETH GRAHAME

The remainder of my London excursion was taken up with preparations of one sort or another.

I typed a long and incomprehensible statement, describing only those parts of my adventure in which I had behaved like a good and clever man, and deposited it with Mr Halkerston at the National Westminster Bank in Swiss Cottage. It was long because I didn't have time to do a short one, and incomprehensible because my typewriter has no letter 'd'.

Halkerston looked worried; whether by me, or by the fat brown envelope I gave him, I couldn't tell. He asked if I had any special instructions as to the circumstances under which it should be opened, and when I told him to use his judgement, he quickly put the envelope down and asked someone else to come and take it to the strong room.

I also converted the balance of Woolf's original payment to me into traveller's cheques.

Feeling flush, I then went back to Blitz Electronics on Tottenham Court Road, where I spent an hour with a very nice man in a turban, talking about radio frequencies. He assured me that the Sennheiser Mikroport SK 2012 was absolutely the thing, and that I should accept no substitutes, so I didn't.

I then headed east to Islington to see my solicitor, who pumped my hand and spent fifteen minutes telling me that we must play golf again. I told him that was a splendid idea, but, strictly speaking, we would need to play golf before we'd be able to play it again, at which he blushed and said he must have been thinking of a Robert Lang. I said yes, he must have been, and proceeded to dictate and sign a will, in which I bequeathed all my estate and chattels to The Save The Children Fund.

And then, with only forty-eight hours to go before I was due back in the trenches, I ran into Sarah Woolf.

When I say ran into her, I do actually mean I ran into her.

I'd hired a Ford Fiesta for a couple of days, to take me about London while I made a final peace with my Creator and my Creditors, and the course of my errands took me within yearning distance of Cork Street. So, for no reason that I'm prepared to own up to, I took a left, and a right, and a left again, and found myself tooling past the mostly shuttered galleries, thinking of happier days. Of course, they hadn't really been happier at all. But they'd been days, and they'd had Sarah in them, and that was near enough.

The sun was low and bright, and I think 'Isn't She Lovely?' was dribbling from the radio as I turned my head, for the tiniest of instants, towards the Glass building. I turned back, just as a flash of blue darted out in front of me from behind a van.

Darted, at least, is the word I'd have used on the claim form. But I suppose stepped, strolled, ambled, even walked – any of those would have been nearer the truth.

I stamped on the brake pedal, far too late, and watched in stiff-armed horror as the blue flash first backed away from me, then held its ground, then slammed its fists down on to

275

the bonnet of the Fiesta as the front bumper slid towards its shins.

There was nothing to spare. Absolutely nothing. If the bumper had been dirty, I would have touched her. But it wasn't, and I didn't, which allowed me to become immediately furious. I'd thrown open the door and got half-way out of the car, meaning to say what the fuck's the matter with you, when I realised that the legs I'd nearly broken were familiar. I looked up and saw that the blue flash had a face, and the sort of startling grey eyes that make men talk gibberish, and excellent teeth, quite a few of which were showing now.

'Jesus,' I said. 'Sarah.'

She stared at me, white-faced. Half in shock, and the other half in shock.

'Thomas?'

We looked at each other.

And as we looked at each other, standing there in Cork Street, London, England, in bright sunshine, with Stevie Wonder being sentimental in the car, things around us seemed to change somehow.

I don't know how it happened, but in those few seconds, all the shoppers, and businessmen, and builders, and tourists, and traffic wardens, with all their shoes and shirts and trousers and dresses and socks and bags and watches and houses and cars and mortgages and marriages and appetites and ambitions . . . they all just faded away.

Leaving Sarah and me, standing there, in a very quiet world.

'Are you all right?' I said, about a thousand years later.

It was just something to say. I don't really know what I meant by it. Did I mean was she all right because I hadn't hurt her, or was she all right because a lot of other people hadn't hurt her?

Sarah looked at me as if she didn't know either, but after a while I think we decided to go with the former.

'I'm fine,' she said.

And then, as if they were arriving back from their lunch hour, the extras in our film began to move again, to make noise. Chattering, shuffling, coughing, dropping things. Sarah was gently wringing her hands. I turned to look at the bonnet of the Ford. She'd made an impression.

'Are you sure?' I said. 'I mean, you must have . . .'

'Really, Thomas, I'm fine.' There was a pause, which she spent straightening her dress, and I spent watching her do it. Then she looked up at me. 'What about you?'

'Me?' I said. 'I'm . . .'

Well, I mean to say. Where was I supposed to begin?

We went to a pub. The Duke Of Somewhereshire, tucked into the corner of a mews near Berkeley Square.

Sarah sat down at a table and opened her handbag, and while she fiddled around inside it, doing that woman thing, I asked her if she wanted a drink. She said a large whisky. I couldn't remember whether you're supposed to give alcohol to people who've just had a shock, but I knew I wasn't up to asking for hot, sweet tea in a London pub, so I made my way to the bar and ordered two double Macallans.

I watched her, the windows, and the door.

They had to have been following her. Had to.

With the stakes as they were, it was inconceivable that they would let her wander round unattended. I was the lion, if you can believe that for a moment, and she was the tethered goat. It would have been madness to let her roam.

Unless.

Nobody came in, nobody peered in, nobody wandered past and sneaked a sideways look in. Nothing. I looked at Sarah.

She'd finished with her handbag, and now sat, looking towards the middle of the room, her face a complete blank. She was in a daze, thinking of nothing. Or she was in a jam, thinking of everything. I couldn't tell. I was pretty sure that she knew I was looking at her, so the fact that she didn't look back was odd. But then odd isn't a crime.

I collected the drinks and made my way back towards her table.

'Thanks,' she said, taking the glass from me and throwing its contents down her throat in one go.

'Steady,' I said.

She looked at me for a moment with real aggression, as if I was just one more person at the end of a long line, getting in her way, telling her what to do. And then she remembered who I was – or remembered to pretend to remember who I was – and smiled. I smiled back.

'Twelve years ageing in a sherry cask,' I said cheerfully, 'stuck out on a Highland hillside, waiting for its big moment – and then bang, doesn't even get to touch the sides. Who'd be a single malt whisky?'

I was wittering, obviously. But under the circumstances, I felt entitled to do a bit of that. I had been shot, beaten, knocked off my bike, imprisoned, lied to, threatened, slept with, patronised, and made to shoot at people I'd never met. I had risked my life for months, and was hours away from having to risk it again, along with a lot of other lives, some of which belonged to people I quite liked.

And the reason for it all – the prize at the end of this Japanese quiz show I'd been living in for as long as I could remember – was sitting in front of me now, in a safe, warm, London pub, having a drink. While outside, people strolled up and down, buying cuff-links and remarking on the uncommonly fine weather.

I think you'd have wittered too.

We got back into the Ford, and I drove us around.

Sarah still hadn't really said much, except that she was sure there was nobody following her, and I'd said good, that's a relief, and hadn't believed it for a second. So I drove around, and watched the rear-view mirror. I took us down narrow one-way streets, up leafy, car-free avenues, jinked from lane to lane on the Westway, and saw nothing. I thought hang the expense, and drove into, and straight out of, two multi-storey car-parks, which is always a nightmare for the following vehicle. Nothing.

I left Sarah in the car while I got out and checked for a magnetic transmitter, running my fingers under the bumpers and wheel arches for fifteen minutes until I was sure. I even pulled over a couple of times, and scanned the skies above for a clattering police helicopter.

Nothing.

If I'd been a betting man, and I'd had something to bet with, I'd have put it all on us being clean, untailed, and unwatched.

Alone in a quiet world.

People talk about nightfall, or night falling, or dusk falling, and it's never seemed right to me. Perhaps they once meant befalling. As in night befalls. As in night happens. Perhaps they, whoever they were, thought of a falling sun. That might be it, except that that ought to give us dayfall. Day fell on Rupert the Bear. And we know, if we've ever read a book, that day doesn't fall or rise. It breaks. In books, day breaks, and night falls.

In life, night rises from the ground. The day hangs on for as long as it can, bright and eager, absolutely and positively the last guest to leave the party, while the ground darkens, oozing night around your ankles, swallowing for ever that dropped contact lens, making you miss that low catch in the gully on the last ball of the last over.

Night rose on Hampstead Heath as Sarah and I walked together, sometimes holding hands, sometimes not.

We walked in silence mostly, just listening to the sounds of our feet on the grass, the mud, the stones. Swallows flitted here and there, darting in and out of the trees and bushes like furtive homosexuals, while the furtive homosexuals flitted here and there, pretty much like swallows. There was a lot of activity on the Heath that night. Or perhaps it's every night. Men seemed to be everywhere, in ones, and twos, and threes and mores, appraising, signalling, negotiating, getting it done:

plugging into each other to give, or receive, that microsecond of electric charge that would allow them to go back home and concentrate on the plot of an Inspector Morse without getting restless.

This is what men are like, I thought. This is unfettered male sexuality. Not without love, but separate from love. Short, neat, efficient. The Fiat Panda, in fact.

'What are you thinking about?' asked Sarah, staring hard at the ground as she walked.

'About you,' I said, with hardly a stumble.

'Me?' she said, and we strolled for a while. 'Good or bad?'

'Oh good, definitely.' I looked at her, but she was frowning, still staring downwards. 'Definitely good,' I said again.

We came to a pond, and stood by it, and stared at it, and threw stones in it, and generally gave thanks for it according to whatever ancient mechanism it is that draws people to water. I thought back to the last time we had been alone together, on the banks of the river at Henley. Before Prague, before the Sword, before all kinds of other things.

'Thomas,' she said.

I turned and looked at her head on, because I suddenly had the feeling that she'd been rehearsing something in her mind and now wanted to get it out in a hurry.

'Sarah,' I said.

She kept looking down.

'Thomas, what do you say we make a run for it?'

She paused for a while, and then, at last, raised her eyes to me – those beautiful, huge, grey eyes – and I could see desperation in them, deep and on the surface. 'I mean, together,' she said. 'Just get the hell out.'

I looked at her and sighed. In another world, I thought to myself, it might have worked. In another world, in another universe, in another time, as two quite different people, we really might have been able to put all of this behind us, take off to some sun-drenched Caribbean island, and have sex and pineapple juice, non-stop, for a year.

But now, it wasn't going to work. Things I'd thought for a long time, I now knew; and things I'd known for a long time, I now hated knowing.

I took a deep breath.

'How well do you know Russell Barnes?' I said.

She blinked.

'What?'

'I asked you how well you knew Russell Barnes.'

She stared at me for a moment, then let out a kind of laugh; the way I do, when I realise I'm in big trouble.

'Barnes,' she said, looking away and shaking her head, trying to behave as if I'd just asked her whether she preferred Coke or Pepsi. 'What the hell has that . . . '

I took hold of her by the elbow and squeezed, jerking her round to face me again.

'Will you answer the fucking question, please?'

The desperation in her eyes was changing to panic. I was scaring her. To be honest, I was scaring myself.

'Thomas, I don't know what you're talking about.'

Well, that was it.

That was the last glimmer of hope gone. When she lied to me, standing there by the water in the rising night, I knew what I knew.

'It was you who called them, wasn't it?'

She struggled against my grip for a moment, and then laughed again.

'Thomas, you're . . . what the hell is the matter with you?'

'Please, Sarah,' I said, keeping hold of her elbow, 'don't act.'

She was getting really frightened now, and started to try and pull away. I hung on.

'Jesus Christ . . . ' she began, but I shook my head and she stopped. I shook my head when she frowned at me, and I shook my head when she tried to look scared. I waited until she'd stopped all those things.

'Sarah,' I said eventually, 'listen to me. You know who Meg Ryan is, don't you?' She nodded. 'Well, Meg Ryan gets paid

281

millions of dollars to do what you're trying to do now. Tens of millions. Do you know why?' She stared back at me. 'Because it's a very difficult thing to do well, and there aren't more than about a dozen people in the world who can pull it off at this distance. So don't act, don't pretend, don't lie.'

She closed her mouth and seemed suddenly to relax, so I eased my grip on her elbow, and then let go altogether. We stood there like grown-ups.

'It was you who called them,' I said again. 'You called them the first night I came to your house. You called them from the restaurant, the night they took me off the bike.'

I didn't want to have to say the last bit, but somebody had to.

'You called them,' I said, 'and they came to kill your father.'

She cried for about an hour, on Hampstead Heath, on a bench, in the moonlight, in my arms. All the tears in the world ran down her face and soaked into the earth.

At one point the crying became so violent, and so loud, that we began to gather a distant, scattered audience, who muttered to each other about calling the police, and then thought better of it. Why did I put my arms around her? Why did I hold a woman who'd betrayed her own father, and who'd used me like a piece of paper-towel?

Beats me.

When at last the crying started to ease, I kept on holding her, and felt her body jerk and shudder with those after-tears hiccups that children get.

'He wasn't meant to die,' she said suddenly, with a clear, strong voice, which made me wonder if it was coming from somewhere else. Maybe it was. 'That wasn't meant to happen. In fact,' she wiped at her nose with her sleeve, 'they actually promised me he'd be okay. They said as long as he was stopped, then nothing would happen. We'd both be safe, and we'd both be . . . '

She faltered, and for all the calm in her voice, I could tell

282

that she was dying from the guilt.

'You'd both be what?' I said.

She bent her head back, stretching her long neck, offering her throat to someone who wasn't me.

Then she laughed.

'Rich,' she said.

For a moment, I was tempted to laugh too. It sounded like such a ridiculous word. Such a ridiculous thing to be. It sounded like a name, or a country, or a kind of salad. Whatever the word was, it surely couldn't mean having a lot of money. It was just, simply, too ridiculous.

'They promised you'd be rich?' I said.

She took a deep breath and sighed, and her laughter faded away so quickly it might never have happened.

'Yup,' she said. 'Rich. Money. They said we'd have money.'

'Said it to who? Both of you?'

'Oh God, no. Dad wouldn't have . . . ' She stopped for a moment, and a violent shiver ran over her body. Then she tilted her chin upwards, and closed her eyes. 'He was way, way past listening to that kind of stuff.'

I saw his face. The eager, determined, born-again look. The look of a man who'd spent his life making money, making his way, paying his bills, and then, just in time, he'd discovered that wasn't the point of the game after all. He'd seen a chance to put it right.

Are you a good man, Thomas?

'So they offered you money,' I said.

She opened her eyes and smiled, quickly, and then wiped her nose again.

'They offered me all kinds of things. Everything a girl could want. Everything a girl already had, in fact, until her father decided he was going to take it away.'

We sat like that for a while, holding hands, thinking and talking about what she'd done. But we didn't get very far.

When we began, both of us thought that this was going to be the biggest, deepest, longest talk either of us had ever had with another human being. Almost immediately, we realised it wasn't. Because there was no point. There was so much to be said, such a huge mound of explanation to be gone through, and yet somehow, none of it really needed to be said at all.

So I'll say it.

Under Alexander Woolf's leadership, the company of Gaine Parker Inc made springs, levers, door catches, carpet grips, belt buckles, and a thousand other bits and pieces of Western life. They made plastic things, and metal things, and electronic things, and mechanical things, some of them for retailers, some of them for other manufacturers, and some for the United States government.

This, in the beginning, was good for Gaine Parker. If you can make a lavatory seat that pleases the head Woolworths buyer, you're quids in. If you can make one that pleases the US government, by conforming to the specifications demanded of a military lavatory seat – and I assure you that there is such a thing, and it has specifications, and at a guess I'd say those specifications probably cover thirty sides of A4 paper – if you can do that, well, then you're quids in, out, round to the front and in again, a million times over.

As it happened, Gaine Parker didn't make lavatory seats. They made an electronic switch that was very small and did something clever with semi-conductors. As well as being indispensable to the manufacturers of air-conditioning thermostats, the switch also found a home in the cooling mechanism of a new kind of military-specification diesel generator. And so it came to pass, in February of 1972, that Gaine Parker and Alexander Woolf became sub-contractors to the US Department of Defense.

The blessings of this contract were without number. Besides allowing, or even encouraging, Gaine Parker to charge eighty dollars for an item that elsewhere in the market would be lucky to fetch five, the contract served as a stamp of guaranteed, no nonsense, blue-chip quality, causing the world's customers for small, clever, switchy things to beat a wide gravel drive to Woolf's door.

From that moment, nothing could go wrong, and nothing did. Woolf's standing in the *matériel* business grew and grew, and his access to the very important people who run that world – and who therefore could safely be said to run *the* world – grew with it. They smiled at him, and joked with him and put him up for membership of the St Regis golf club on Long Island. They called him at midnight for long chats about this and that. They asked him to go sailing with them in the Hamptons, and, more importantly, accepted his return invitation. They sent his family Christmas cards, and then Christmas presents, and, eventually, they began to wine him at two hundred-seat Republican party dinners, where much talk was exchanged on the subject of the budget deficit and America's economic regeneration. And the higher he rose, the more contracts came his way, and the smaller, and more intimate, the dinners became. Until, finally, they stopped having much to do with party politics at all. They had more to do with the politics of common sense, if you follow me.

It was at the end of one of these dinners that a fellow admiral of industry, his judgement skewed by a couple of pints of claret, told Woolf about a rumour he had come across. The rumour was a fantastic one, and Woolf, of course, didn't believe it. In fact, he found it funny. So funny, that he decided to share the laugh with one of the very important people, during one of their regular late-night phone-calls – and found that the line had gone dead before he'd reached the punch line.

The day Alexander Woolf decided to take on the military-industrial complex was the day everything changed. For him, for his family, for his business. Things changed quickly, and they changed for good. Roused from its slumber, the military-industrial complex lifted a great, lazy paw, and swatted him away, as if he were no more than a human being.

They cancelled his existing contracts and withdrew possible future ones. They bankrupted his suppliers, disrupted his labour force, and investigated him for tax evasion. They bought his company's stock in a few months and sold it in a few hours, and when that didn't do the trick, they accused him of trading in narcotics. They even had him thrown out of the St Regis, for not replacing a fairway divot.

None of which bothered Alexander Woolf one bit, because he knew that he'd seen the light, and the light was green. But it did bother his daughter, and the beast knew this. The beast knew that Alexander Woolf had started out in life with German as his first language, and America as his first religion; that at seventeen, he was selling coat-hangers out of the back of a van, living alone in one basement room in Lowes, New Hampshire, with both parents dead and not ten dollars to his name. That was what Alexander Woolf had come from, and that was what he was prepared to go back to, if going back was what it took. To Alexander Woolf, poverty was not the dark, or the unknown, or a thing to be feared in any way. At any time of life.

But his daughter was different. His daughter had experienced nothing but big houses, and big swimming pools, and big cars, and big orthodontistry treatments, and poverty frightened her to death. The fear of the unknown was what made her vulnerable, and the beast knew that too.

A man had made her a proposition.

'So,' she said.

'Well quite,' I said.

Her teeth were chattering, which made me realise how long we'd been sitting there. And how much I still had left to do.

'I'd better take you home,' I said, getting to my feet.

Instead of getting up with me, she curled tighter to the bench, her arms folded across her stomach as if she was in pain. Because she was in pain. When she spoke, her voice was incredibly quiet, and I had to squat down at her feet to hear. The lower I got, the more she bowed her head to avoid my eyes.

'Don't punish me,' she said. 'Don't punish me for my

father's death, Thomas, because I can do that without your help.'

'I'm not punishing you, Sarah,' I said. 'I'm just going to take you home, that's all.'

She lifted her head and looked at me again, and I saw a new fear sliding into her eyes.

'But why?' she said. 'I mean, we're here, now. Together. We can do anything. Go anywhere.'

I looked down at the ground. She hadn't got it yet.

'And where do you want to go?' I asked.

'Well it doesn't matter, does it?' she said, her voice getting louder as the desperation grew. 'The point is we can go. I mean, Christ, Thomas, you know . . . they controlled you because they threatened me, and they controlled me because they threatened you. That's how they did it. And that's over now. We can go. Take off.'

I shook my head.

'I'm afraid it's not that simple now,' I said. 'If it ever was.'

I stopped and thought for a moment, wondering how much I ought to tell her. Nothing, is what I really ought to tell her. But fuck it.

'This thing isn't just about us,' I said. 'If we just walk away, other people are going to die. Because of us.'

'Other people?' said Sarah. 'What are you talking about? What other people?'

I smiled at her, because I wanted her to feel better, and not so scared, and also because I was remembering them all.

'Sarah,' I said. 'You and I . . . '

I faltered.

'What?' she said.

I took a deep breath. There was no other way of saying it.

'We have to do the right thing,' I said.

Twenty-three

But there is neither East nor West, Border, nor Breed, nor Birth,
When two strong men stand face to face, though they come from
the ends of the earth.

RUDYARD KIPLING

Don't go to Casablanca expecting it to be like the film.

In fact, if you're not too busy, and your schedule allows it, don't go to Casablanca at all.

People often refer to Nigeria and its neighbouring coastal states as the armpit of Africa; which is unfair, because the people, culture, landscape, and beer of that part of the world are, in my experience, first rate. However, it is true that when you look at a map, through half-closed eyes, in a darkened room, in the middle of a game of What Does That Bit Of Coastline Remind You Of, you *might* find yourself saying yes, all right, Nigeria does have a vaguely armpitty kind of shape to it.

Bad luck Nigeria.

But if Nigeria is the armpit, Morocco is the shoulder. And if Morocco is the shoulder, Casablanca is a large, red, unsightly spot on that shoulder, of the kind that appears on the actual morning of the day that you and your intended have decided to head for the beach. The sort of spot that chafes painfully against your bra strap or braces, depending on your gender preference, and makes you promise that from now on you're definitely going to eat more fresh vegetables.

Casablanca is fat, sprawling, and industrial; a city of concrete-dust and diesel fumes, where sunlight seems to bleach out colour, instead of pouring it in. It hasn't a sight worth seeing, unless half-a-million poor people struggling to stay alive in a shanty-town warren of cardboard and corrugated iron is what makes you want to pack a bag and jump on a plane. As far as I know, it hasn't even got a museum.

You may be getting the idea that I don't like Casablanca. You may be feeling that I'm trying to talk you out of it, or make your mind up for you; but it really isn't my place to do that. It's just that, if you're anything like me – and your entire life has been spent watching the door of whatever bar, café, pub, hotel, or dentist's surgery you happen to be sitting in, in the hope that Ingrid Bergman will come wafting through in a cream frock, and look straight at you, and blush, and heave her bosom about the place in a way that says thank God, life does have some meaning after all – if any of that strikes a chord with you, then Casablanca is going to be a big fucking disappointment.

We had divided ourselves into two teams. Fair skin, and olive skin.

Francisco, Latifa, Benjamin and Hugo were the Olives, while Bernhard, Cyrus and I made up the Fairs.

This may sound unfashionable. Even shocking. Perhaps you were busy imagining that terrorist organisations are equal opportunities employers, and that distinctions based on skin colour simply have no place in our work. Well, in an ideal world, perhaps, that's how terrorists would be. But in Casablanca, things are different.

You cannot walk the streets of Casablanca with fair skin.

Or, at least, you can, but only if you're prepared to do it at the head of a crowd of fifty scampering children, who call, and shout, and point, and laugh, and try and sell you American dollars, good price, best price, and hashish likewise.

If you're a tourist with fair skin, you take this as it comes. Obviously. You smile back, and shake your head, and say *la, shokran* – which causes even more laughter, and shouting, and pointing, which in turn causes another fifty children to come and follow your pied pipe, all of whom, strangely, have also got the best price for American dollars – and, generally, you do your best to enjoy the experience. After all, you're a visitor, you look strange and exotic, you're probably wearing shorts and a ridiculous Hawaiian shirt, so why the hell shouldn't they point at you? Why shouldn't a fifty yard journey to the tobacconist's take three-quarters of an hour, and stop traffic in all directions, and just about make the late editions of the Moroccan evening papers? This is why you went abroad, after all. To be abroad.

That's if you're a tourist.

If, on the other hand, you went abroad in order to take over an American consulate building with automatic weapons, so that you could hold the consul and his staff to ransom, demand ten million dollars and the immediate release of two hundred and thirty prisoners of conscience, and then leave by private jet, having mined the building with sixty kilos of C4 plastic explosive – if that's what you nearly put in the Purpose Of Visit box on the immigration form but didn't, because you're a highly-trained professional who doesn't make slips like that – then frankly you can do without the staring and pointing stuff from kids on the street.

So the Olives were to work the surveillance, while the Fairs prepared for the assault.

We had taken over an abandoned school building in the Hay Mohammedia district. It might once have been a classy, grassy suburb, but not any more. The grass had long since been laid over by the corrugated iron house-builders, the drains were ditches by the side of the road, and the road was something that might get built eventually. Inshallah.

This was a poor place, full of poor people, where food was bad and scarce, and fresh water was something that old people told their grandchildren about on long winter evenings. Not that there were many old people in Hay Mohammedia. Here, the part of an old person was usually played by a forty-five year old with no teeth, courtesy of the achingly-sweet mint tea that stood in for a standard of living.

The school was a large building. Two storeys high on three sides, built round a cement courtyard, where children must once have played football, or said prayers, or had lessons in how to bother Europeans; and round the outside there was a fifteen foot wall, broken only by a single, iron-sheeted gate that led into the courtyard.

It was a place where we could plan, and train, and relax.

And have violent arguments with each other.

They began as small, trifling things. Sudden irritations over smoking, and who had the last of the coffee, and who's going to sit in the front of the Land Rover today. But they seemed, gradually, to be getting worse.

At first, I put them down to straightforward nerves, because the game we were playing here was bigger, much bigger, than anything we'd tried so far. It made Mürren seem like a piece of cake, without marzipan.

The marzipan in Casablanca was the police, and maybe they had something to do with the increasing tension, and the sulks, and the arguments. Because they were everywhere. They came in dozens of shapes and sizes, with dozens of different uniforms that signified dozens of different powers and authorities, most of which boiled down to the fact that, if you so much as glanced at them in a way they didn't like, they could fuck up your life for ever.

At the entrance to every police station in Casablanca, for example, stood two men with machine pistols.

Two men. Machine pistols. Why?

You could stand there all day, and you could watch these men as they conspicuously caught not one criminal, quelled not one riot, beat off not one invasion by a hostile foreign power – did not do, in fact, one thing that made the average Moroccan's life better in any way.

Of course, whoever decided to spend the money on these men – whoever decreed that their uniforms should be designed by a Milanese fashion-house, and that their sunglasses should be of the wrap-around type – would probably say 'well of course we haven't been invaded, because we have two men outside every police station with machine pistols and shirts that are two sizes too small for them'. And you'd have to bow your head and leave the office, walking backwards, because there's no dealing with logic like that.

The Moroccan police are an expression of the state. Picture the state as a larger bloke in a bar, and picture the populace as a small bloke in the same bar. The large bloke bares a tattooed bicep, and says to the small bloke 'did you spill my beer?'

The Moroccan police are the tattoo.

And for us, they were definitely a problem. Too many brands of them, too many of each brand, too heavily-armed, too everything.

So maybe that's why we're getting jumpy. Maybe that's why, five days ago, Benjamin – softly spoken Benjamin, who loves chess, and once thought he would become a rabbi – maybe that's why Benjamin called me a fucking shit bastard.

We were sitting round the trestle table in the dining-hall, chewing our way through a tajine stew, cooked by Cyrus and Latifa, and nobody was feeling much like talking. The Fairs had spent the day constructing a full scale mock-up of the front part of the consulate offices, and we were tired, and smelt of timber.

The model stood behind us now, like the set of a school pantomime, and every now and then somebody would look

292

up from their food and examine it, wondering whether they'd ever get to see the real thing. Or, having seen it, whether they'd ever get to see anything else.

'You're a fucking shit bastard,' said Benjamin, leaping to his feet and standing there, clenching and unclenching his fists.

There was a pause. It took a while for everyone to realise who he was looking at.

'What did you call me?' said Ricky, straightening slightly in his chair – a man slow to anger, but a terrible enemy once he got there.

'You heard,' said Benjamin.

For a moment I wasn't sure whether he was going to hit me or cry.

I looked at Francisco, expecting him to tell Benjamin to sit down, or get out, or do something, but Francisco just looked back at me and kept on chewing.

'The fuck I do to you?' said Ricky, turning back to Benjamin.

But he just kept on standing there, staring, clenching his fists, until Hugo piped up, and said that the stew was great. Everyone fell on this gratefully, and said yes, wasn't it fantastic, and no, it definitely wasn't too salty. Everyone, that is, except me and Benjamin. He stared at me, and I stared back, and only he seemed to know what this was about.

Then he turned on his heel and marched out of the hall, and after a while we heard the scrape of the iron gate opening, and then the Land Rover's motor grinding into life.

Francisco kept on looking at me.

Five days have passed since then, Benjamin has managed to smile at me a couple of times, and now we're all set to go.

We have dismantled the model, packed our bags, burnt our bridges and said our prayers. It's really quite exciting.

Tomorrow morning, at nine thirty-five, Latifa will enquire about a visa application at the American consulate. At nine forty, Bernhard and I will present ourselves for an appointment with Mr Roger Buchanan, the commercial attaché. At nine forty-seven, Francisco and Hugo will arrive with a trolley bearing four plastic barrels of mineral water, and an invoice made out to Sylvie Horvath of the consular section.

Sylvie has actually ordered the water – but not the six cardboard boxes on which the barrels will be resting.

And at nine fifty-five, give or take a second, Cyrus and Benjamin will crash the Land Rover into the west wall of the consulate.

'What's that for?' asked Solomon.

'What's what for?' I said.

'The Land Rover.' He took the pencil out of his mouth and pointed at the drawings. 'You're not going to get through the wall like that. It's two feet thick, reinforced concrete, and you've got those bollards along the side as well. Even if you get through them, it'll take your speed right down.'

I shook my head.

'It's just a noise,' I said. 'They make a big noise, jam the horn down, Benjamin falls out of the driver's door with blood all over his shirt, and Cyrus screams for some first aid. We get as many people as we can into the west side of the building, finding out what the noise is about.'

'Do they have first aid?' said Solomon.

'Ground floor. Store-room next to the staircase.'

'Anyone qualified to give it?'

'All the American staff have taken a course, but Jack's the most likely.'

'Jack?'

'Webber,' I said. 'Consular guard. Eighteen years in the US Marine Corps. Carries a standard 9mm Beretta at his right hip.'

I stopped. I knew what Solomon was thinking.

'So?' he said.

'Latifa has a Mace canister,' I said.

He jotted something down – but slowly, as if he knew that

what he was writing wasn't going to make a lot of difference.

I knew it too.

'She'll also be carrying a Micro Uzi in her shoulder bag,' I said.

We were sitting in Solomon's hired Peugeot, parked on some high ground near La Squala – a crumbling, eighteenth-century edifice that once housed the main artillery position overlooking the port. It was as nice a view as you can find in Casablanca, but neither of us was enjoying it all that much.

'So what happens now?' I said, as I lit a cigarette with Solomon's dashboard. I say the dashboard, because most of it came away with the cigarette lighter when I pulled, and it took a moment to put the whole thing back together. Then I inhaled, and tried, without much success, to blow the smoke out through the open window.

Solomon kept on staring at his notes.

'Well, presumably,' I prompted him, 'there will be a brigade of Moroccan police and CIA men hidden in the ventilator shafts. And presumably, when we walk in, they will pop out and say you're under arrest. And presumably, The Sword Of Justice and anyone who's ever had dealings with it will shortly be appearing in a court just two hundred yards from this cinema. And presumably, all of this will happen without anyone so much as grazing their elbow.'

Solomon took a deep breath, and let it out slowly. Then he started to rub his stomach, the way I hadn't seen him do for ten years. Solomon's duodenal ulcer was the only thing that could make him stop thinking about work.

He turned and looked at me.

'I'm being sent home,' he said.

We stared at each other for a while. And then I started to laugh. The situation wasn't funny, exactly – laughing just happened to be what came out of my mouth.

'Of course you are,' I said, eventually. 'Of course you're being sent home. That makes perfect sense.'

'Look, Thomas,' he began, and I could see in his face how much he was hating this.

'"Thank you for a very fine piece of work, Mr Solomon,"' I said, in my Russell Barnes voice. '"We surely want to thank you for your professionalism, and your commitment, but we'll take it from here, if you don't mind." Oh, that is just perfect.'

'Thomas, listen to me.' He'd called me Thomas twice in thirty seconds. 'Just get out. Run for it, will you?'

I smiled at him, which made him talk faster.

'I can take you up to Tangier,' he said. 'You get yourself into Ceuta, and then a ferry to Spain. I'll call the local police, get them to park a van outside the consulate, the whole thing blows over. None of it ever happened.'

I looked into Solomon's eyes, and saw all the trouble that was in them. I saw his guilt, and his shame – I saw a duodenal ulcer in his eyes.

I tossed the cigarette out of the window.

'Funny,' I said. 'That's what Sarah Woolf wanted me to do. Take off, she said. Sun-kissed beaches, far from the madding CIA.'

He didn't ask me when I'd seen her, or why I hadn't listened to what she'd said. He was too busy with his own problem. Which was me.

'Well?' he said. 'Do it, Thomas, for God's sake.' He reached across and took hold of my arm. 'This is crazy, this whole thing. If you walk into that building, you're not coming out alive. You know that.' I just sat there, which infuriated him. 'Jesus Christ, you're the one who's been saying it all along. You're the one who's known it all along.'

'Oh, come on, David. You knew it too.'

I watched his face as I spoke. He had about a hundredth of a second in which to frown, or open his mouth in amazement, or say what are you talking about, and he missed it. As soon as that hundredth of a second was gone, I knew, and he knew I knew.

'The photograph of Sarah and Barnes together,' I said, and Solomon's face stayed blank. 'You knew what it meant. You knew there was only one explanation for it.'

At last, he dipped his eyes, and loosened his grip on my arm.

'How did the two of them come to be together, after what had happened?' I said. 'Only explanation. It wasn't after. It was before. That picture was taken *before* Alexander Woolf was shot. You knew what Barnes was doing, and you knew, or probably guessed, what Sarah was doing. You just didn't tell me.'

He closed his eyes. If he was asking for forgiveness, it wasn't out loud, and it wasn't from me.

'Where is UCLA now?' I said, after a while.

Solomon shook his head gently.

'I don't know of any such device,' he said, still with his eyes closed.

'David . . . ' I began, but Solomon cut me off.

'Please,' he said.

So I let him think whatever he had to think, and decide whatever he had to decide.

'All I know, master,' Solomon said at last, and suddenly it sounded like the old days again, 'is that a US military transport aircraft landed at the Gibraltar RAF base at noon today, and off-loaded a quantity of mechanical spares.'

I nodded. Solomon had opened his eyes.

'How big a quantity?'

Solomon took another deep breath, wanting to get the whole thing out at once.

'A friend of a friend of a friend who was there, said it was two crates, each one roughly twenty feet by ten by ten, that they were accompanied by sixteen male passengers, nine of whom were in uniform, and that these men immediately took charge of the crates, and removed them to a hangar by the perimeter fence, set aside for their exclusive use.'

'Barnes?' I said.

Solomon thought for a moment.

'I couldn't say, master. But the friend thought he might just have recognised an American diplomat among the party.'

Diplomat, my arse. Diplomat, his arse, come to that.

'According to the friend,' Solomon continued, 'there was also a man in distinctive civilian clothes.'

I sat up, feeling sweat shoot from the palms of my hands.

'Distinctive how?' I said.

Solomon put his head on one side, trying hard to remember the exact details. As if he had to.

'Black jacket, black striped trousers,' he said. 'The friend reckoned he looked like a hotel waiter.'

And that sheen to the skin. The sheen of money. The sheen of Murdah.

Yip, I thought. The gang's all here.

As we drove back towards the centre of the city, I described to Solomon what I was going to do, and what I needed him to do.

He nodded every now and then, not liking a single moment of it, although he must have noticed that I wasn't actually blowing party streamers either.

When we reached the consulate building, Solomon slowed right down, and then eased the Peugeot round the block, until we came level with the monkey-puzzle tree. We looked up into its high, sweeping branches for a while, then I nodded to Solomon, and he got out and unlocked the boot of the car.

Inside there were two packages. One rectangular, about the size of a shoe-box, the other tubular, nearly five feet long. Both of them were wrapped in brown grease-proof paper. There were no marks, no serial numbers, no best before dates.

I could tell that Solomon didn't really want to touch them, so I leaned in and hauled the packages out myself.

He slammed the car door and started the engine as I walked towards the wall of the consulate.

Twenty-four

But hark! My pulse like a soft drum
Beats my approach, tells thee I come.

BISHOP HENRY KING

The American consulate in Casablanca stands half-way down the leafy boulevard Moulay Yousses, a thoroughly minuscule enclave of nineteenth-century French grandeur, built to help the weary colonialist unwind after a hard day's infrastructure-designing.

The French came to Morocco to build roads, railways, hospitals, schools, fashion sense – all the things that the average Frenchman knows to be indispensable to a modern civilization – and when five o'clock came, and the French looked upon their works and saw that they were good, they reckoned they had bloody well earned the right to live like Maharajahs. Which, for a time, they did.

But when neighbouring Algeria blew up in their faces, the French realised that, sometimes, it's better to leave them wanting more; so they opened their Louis Vuittons, and packed their bottles of aftershave, and their other bottles of aftershave, and that extra bottle that had slid down behind the lavatory cistern, that turned out, on closer inspection, to contain aftershave, and stole away into the night.

The inheritors of the vast, stuccoed palaces that the French left behind were not princes, or sultans, or millionaire industrialists. They were not nightclub singers, or footballers, or gangsters, or television soap stars. They were, by an amazing chance, diplomats.

I call it an amazing chance, because that now makes a clean sweep. In every city, in every country in the world, diplomats live and work in the most valuable and desirable real estate there is to be found. Mansions, castles, palaces, ten-up-ten-downs with ensuite deer park: whatever and wherever it may be, diplomats walk in, look around, and say yes, I think I can bear this.

Bernhard and I straightened our ties, checked our watches, and trotted up the steps to the main entrance.

'So now, what can I do for you two gentlemen?'

Call-Me-Roger Buchanan was in his early fifties, and he had risen as high in the American diplomatic service as he was ever going to get. Casablanca was his final posting, he'd been here three years, and sure, he liked it just fine. Great people, great country, food's a little too oil-based, but otherwise just grand.

The oil in the food didn't seem to have slowed Call-Me-Roger down all that much, because he must have been pushing at least sixteen stone, which, at five feet nine, is quite a push.

Bernhard and I looked at each other, with eyebrows raised, as if it didn't really matter which one of us spoke first.

'Mr Buchanan,' I said gravely, 'as my colleague and I explained in our letter, we manufacture what we believe to be the finest kitchen gloves presently coming out of the North African region.'

Bernhard nodded, slowly, as if he might have gone further and said the world, but no matter.

300

'We have facilities,' I continued, 'in Fez, Rabat, and we're shortly to be opening a plant just outside Marrakech. Our product is a fine product. We're sure of that. It's one you may have heard of, one you may even have used, if you're what they call a "New Man".'

I chortled like a numbskull, and Bernhard and Roger joined in. Men. Using kitchen gloves. That's a good one. Bernhard took up the story, leaning forward in his chair and speaking with sombre, respectable Germanicism.

'Our scale of production,' he said, 'has now reached a point where we'd be very interested in considering a licence to export to the North American market. And I think what we would like from you, sir, is a little help through the many mechanisms we would need to have in place.'

Call-Me-Roger nodded, and jotted something down on a pad of paper. I could see that he had our letter in front of him on the desk, and it looked as if he'd drawn a ring round the word 'rubber'. I would have liked to have asked him why, but this wasn't the moment.

'Roger,' I said, getting to my feet, 'before we get started in depth.'

Roger looked up from his pad.

'Down the hall, second door on the right.'

'Thanks,' I said.

The lavatory was empty, and smelled of pine. I locked the door, checked my watch, then climbed up on to the seat and eased open the window.

To the left, a sprinkler tossed graceful arcs of water across an expanse of well-tended lawn. A woman in a print-dress was standing by the wall, picking at her fingernails, while a few yards away, a small dog defecated intensely. In the far corner, a gardener in shorts and a yellow tee-shirt knelt and fiddled with some shrubs.

To the right, nothing.

More wall. More lawn. More flower beds.

And a monkey-puzzle tree.

I jumped down from the lavatory, looked at my watch again, unlocked the door and stepped out into the corridor.

It was empty.

I walked quickly to the staircase and bounced merrily down, two steps at a time, drumming my hand on the banister to no particular tune. I passed a man in shirt-sleeves carrying paper, but I said a loud 'morning' before he could say anything.

I reached the first floor and turned right, and saw that the corridor was busier.

Two women were standing half-way down, deep in conversation, and a man on my left was locking, or unlocking, an office door.

I glanced at my watch and started to ease up, feeling in my pockets for something that, maybe, I'd left somewhere, or if not there, somewhere else, but then again, maybe I never had it, but if I had, should I go back and look for it? I stood in the corridor, frowning, and the man on the left had opened the office door and was looking at me, about to ask me if I was lost.

I pulled my hand out of my pocket and smiled at him, holding up a key ring.

'Got it,' I said, and he gave me a small, uncertain nod as I walked on.

A bell pinged at the end of the corridor and I speeded up a little, jangling the keys in my right hand. The lift doors slid open, and a low trolley started to nose its way out into the corridor.

Francisco and Hugo, in their neat blue overalls, carefully shepherded the trolley out of the lift; Francisco pushing, Hugo resting both his hands on the water barrels. Relax, I wanted to say to him, as I slowed down to let the trolley go ahead of me. It's only water, for Christ's sake. You're following it as if it's your wife on her way to the delivery room.

Francisco was moving slowly, checking the numbers on the office doors, looking very good indeed, while Hugo kept turning and licking his lips.

I stopped at a notice-board and examined it. I tore down three pieces of paper, two of them being the fire drill, and one, an open invitation to a barbecue at Bob and Tina's, Sunday at noon. I stood there, reading them as if they needed to be read, and then looked at my watch.

They were late.

Forty-five seconds late.

I couldn't believe it. After everything we'd agreed, and practised, and sworn about, and practised again, the little fuckers were late.

'Yes?' said a voice.

Fifty-five seconds.

I looked down the corridor, and saw that Francisco and Hugo had reached the open reception area. A woman sat at a desk, peering at them over big glasses.

Sixty-five fucking seconds.

'*Salem alicoum*,' said Francisco, in a soft voice.

'*Alicoum salem*,' said the woman.

Seventy.

Hugo banged his hand on the top of the water barrels, then turned and looked at me.

I started to walk forwards, took two steps, and then I heard it.

Heard it and felt it. It was like a bomb.

When you watch cars crashing on television, you're fed a certain level of sound by the dubbing mixers, and you probably think to yourself that's it, that's what a car crash sounds like. You forget, or, with a bit of luck, you never know, how much energy is being released when half-a-ton of metal hits another half-a-ton of metal. Or the side of a building. Vast amounts of energy, capable of shaking your body from head to toe, even though you're a hundred yards away.

The Land Rover's horn, jammed down with Cyrus's knife, cut through the silence like the wail of an animal. And then it quickly faded away, swamped by the sounds of doors opening, chairs being pushed back, bodies scuffling into doorways – looking at each other, looking back down the corridor.

Then they were all talking, and most of them were saying Jesus, and goddamn, and the fuck was that, and suddenly I was watching a dozen backs, scurrying away from us, tripping, skipping, tumbling over each other to get to the stairwell.

'You think we should see?' said Francisco to the woman behind the desk.

She looked at him, then squinted down the corridor.

'I can't . . . you know . . . ' she said, and her hand moved towards the telephone. I don't know who she thought she was going to call.

Francisco and I looked at each other for about a hundredth of a second.

'Was that . . . ' I began, staring nervously at the woman, 'I mean, did that sound like a bomb?'

She put one hand on the phone and the other out in front, palm towards the window, asking the world to just stop and wait a moment while she got herself together.

There was a scream from somewhere.

Somebody had seen the blood on Benjamin's shirt, or fallen over, or just felt like screaming, and it got the woman half on to her feet.

'What could that be?' said Francisco, as Hugo started to move round the edge of her desk.

This time she didn't look at him.

'They'll tell us,' she said, peering past me down the corridor. 'We stay where we are, and they'll tell us what to do.'

As she said it, there was a metallic click, and the woman instantly knew that it was out of place, was terribly wrong; because there are good clicks and bad clicks, and this was definitely one of the worst.

She swung round to look at Hugo.

'Lady,' he said, his eyes shining, 'you had your chance.'

So here we are.

Sitting pretty, feeling good.

We have had control of the building for thirty-five minutes now and, all in all, it could have been a lot worse.

The Moroccan staff have gone from the ground floor, and Hugo and Cyrus have cleared the second and third floors from end to end, herding men and women down the main staircase and out into the street with a lot of unnecessary shouts of 'let's go' and 'move it'.

Benjamin and Latifa are installed in the lobby, where they can move quickly from the front of the building to the back if they need to. Although we all know they won't need to. Not for a while, anyway.

The police have turned up. First in cars, then in jeeps, now by the truckload. They are scattered around outside in tight shirts, yelling and moving vehicles, and they haven't yet decided whether to walk nonchalantly across the street, or scuttle across with their heads dipped low to avoid sniper fire. They can probably see Bernhard on the roof, but they don't yet know who he is, or what he's doing there.

Francisco and I are in the consul's office.

We have a total of eight prisoners here – five men and three women, bound together with Bernhard's job-lot of police handcuffs – and we have asked them if they wouldn't mind sitting on the very impressive Kelim rug. If any of them moves off the rug, we have explained, they do it at the risk of being shot dead by Francisco or myself, with the help of a pair of Steyr AUG sub-machine guns that we cleverly remembered to bring with us.

The only exception we have made is for the consul himself, because we are not animals – we have an awareness of rank and protocol, and we don't want to make an important man sit cross-legged on the floor – and anyway, he needs to be able to speak on the phone.

Benjamin has been playing with the telephone exchange, and has promised us that any call, to any number in the building, will come through to this office.

*

305

So Mr James Beamon, being the duly appointed representative of the United States government in Casablanca, second in command on Moroccan soil only to the ambassador in Rabat, is sitting at his desk now, staring at Francisco with a look of cool appraisal.

Beamon, as we know well from our researches, is a career diplomat. He is not the retired shoe-salesman you might expect to find in such a post – a man who has given fifty million dollars to the President's election campaign fund, and been rewarded with a big desk and three hundred free lunches a year. Beamon is in his late-fifties, tall and heavily built, and he has a very quick brain. He will handle this situation well and wisely.

Which is exactly what we want.

'What about the rest-room?' Beamon says.

'One person, every half an hour,' says Francisco. 'You decide the order among yourselves, you go with one of us, you do not lock the door.' Francisco moves to the window and looks out into the street. He raises a pair of binoculars to his eyes.

I look at my watch. Ten forty-one.

They will come at dawn, I think to myself. The way attackers have done since attacking was first invented.

Dawn. When we're tired, hungry, bored, scared.

They will come at dawn, and they will come in from the east, with a low sun behind them.

At eleven twenty, the consul had his first call.

Wafiq Hassan, Inspector of Police, introduced himself to Francisco, then said hello to Beamon. He had nothing specific to relate, except that he hoped everybody would act with good sense, and that this whole thing could be sorted out without any trouble. Francisco said afterwards that he spoke good English, and Beamon said he'd been to Hassan's house for dinner two nights ago. The two of them had talked about how quiet Casablanca was.

At eleven forty, it was the press. Sorry to bother us,

306

obviously, but did we have a statement to make? Francisco spelt his name, twice, and said we would be delivering a written statement to a representative of CNN, just as soon as they got here.

At five to twelve, the phone rang again. Beamon answered it and said he couldn't talk just at the moment, would it be possible to call back tomorrow, or maybe the day after? Francisco took the receiver from him and listened for a moment, and then burst out laughing at the tourist from North Carolina, who wanted to know whether the consulate could guarantee the drinking water in the Regency Hotel.

Even Beamon smiled at that.

At two fifteen, they sent us lunch. A stew of mutton and vegetables, with a vast pot of couscous. Benjamin collected it from the front steps, while Latifa nervously waved her Uzi back and forth in the doorway.

Cyrus found some paper plates somewhere, but no cutlery, so we sat and let the food cool, before scooping it up with our fingers.

It was very nice, considering.

At ten past three, we heard the trucks starting to move, and Francisco ran to the window.

The two of us watched as police drivers revved and ground gears, shunting backwards and forwards in ten-point turns.

'Why are they moving?' said Francisco, squinting through the binoculars.

I shrugged.

'Traffic warden?'

He looked at me angrily.

'Fuck, I don't know,' I said. 'It's something to do. Maybe they want to make some noise while they dig a tunnel. Nothing we can do about it.'

Francisco chewed his lip for a second, and then moved to the desk. He picked up the phone and dialled the lobby. Latifa must have answered.

'Lat, stay ready,' said Francisco. 'You hear anything, see anything, call me.'

He slammed the phone down, a little too hard.

You were never as cool as you pretended, I thought.

By four o'clock the phone had started to get very busy, with Moroccans and Americans ringing at five minute intervals, and always demanding to speak to someone other than the person who'd answered.

Francisco decided it was time to switch us round, so he called Cyrus and Benjamin up to the first floor, and I went down to join Latifa.

She was standing in the middle of the hall, peering through the windows and hopping from foot to foot, throwing the baby Uzi from hand to hand.

'What's the matter?' I said. 'You want to take a piss?'

She looked at me and nodded, and I told her to go and do it, and not worry so much.

'Sun's going down,' said Latifa, half a packet of cigarettes later.

I looked at my watch, then out through the rear windows, and sure enough, there was that falling sun, that rising night.

'Yeah,' I said.

Latifa started adjusting her hair, using the reflection from the glass window at the reception desk.

'I'm going outside,' I said.

She looked round, startled.

'What? You crazy?'

'I just want to take a look, that's all.'

'Look at what?' said Latifa, and I could see she was furious with me, as if I really was deserting her for good. 'Bernhard's on the roof, he can see better than anybody. What you want to go outside for?'

I sucked at my teeth for a moment, and checked my watch again.

'That tree's bothering me,' I said.

'You want to look at a fucking tree?' said Latifa.

'Branches go over the wall. I just want to take a look.'

She came to my shoulder and peered out through the window. The sprinkler was still going.

'Which tree?'

'That one there,' I said. 'The monkey-puzzle tree.'

Ten minutes past five.

The sun about half-way through its descent.

Latifa was sitting at the foot of the main staircase, scuffing the marble floor with her boot and toying with the Uzi.

I looked at her and thought, obviously, of the sex we'd had together – but also of the laughs, and the frustrations, and the spaghetti. Latifa could be maddening at times. She was definitely fucked up and hopeless in just about every conceivable way. But she was also great.

'It's going to be okay.' I said.

She lifted her head and looked back at me.

I wondered whether she was remembering the same things.

'Who the fuck said it wasn't?' she said, and ran her fingers through her hair, dragging a slice of it down over her face to shut me out.

I laughed.

'Ricky,' shouted Cyrus, leaning over the banister from the first floor.

'What?' I said.

'Up here. Cisco wants you.'

The hostages were spread out on the rug now, heads in laps, back against back. Discipline had relaxed enough for some of them to stretch their legs out over the edge of the rug. Three or four of them were singing 'Swannee River' in a quiet, half-hearted way.

'What?' I said.

Francisco gestured towards Beamon, who held out the phone to me. I frowned and waved it away, as if it was probably my wife and I'd be home in half-an-hour anyway. But Beamon kept holding out the receiver.

'They know you're an American,' he said.

309

I shrugged a so what.

'Talk to them, Ricky,' said Francisco. 'Why not?'

So I shrugged again, sulkily, Jesus, what a waste of time, and ambled up to the desk. Beamon glared up at me as I took the phone.

'A goddamn American,' he whispered.

'Kiss my ass,' I said, and put the receiver to my ear. 'Yeah?'

There was a click, and a buzz, and another click.

'Lang,' said a voice.

Here we go, I thought.

'Yeah,' said Ricky.

'How you doing?'

It was the voice of Russell P. Barnes, arsehole of this parish, and even through the fizzing interference, his voice was back-slappingly confident.

'The fuck do you want?' said Ricky.

'Wave, Thomas,' said Barnes.

I signalled to Francisco for the binoculars, and he handed them across the desk to me. I moved to the window.

'You want to look to your left,' said Barnes.

I didn't, actually.

On the corner of the block, in a corral of jeeps and army trucks, stood a clutch of men. Some in uniform, some not.

I lifted the binoculars, and saw trees and houses leaping about in the magnified scale, and then Barnes shot across the lens. I went back, and steadied, and there he was, a phone at his ear, and binoculars at his eyes. He did actually wave.

I checked the rest of the group, but couldn't see any striped grey trousers.

'Just sayin' hello, Tom,' said Barnes.

'Sure,' said Ricky.

The line crackled away as we waited for each other. I knew I could wait longer than him.

'So, Tom,' said Barnes, eventually, 'when can we expect you out of there?'

I looked away from the binoculars, and glanced at Francisco, and at Beamon, and at the hostages. I looked at them, and thought of the others.

'We ain't comin' out,' said Ricky, and Francisco nodded slowly.

I looked through the binoculars and saw Barnes laugh. I didn't hear it, because he held the receiver away from his face, but I saw him throw back his head and bare his teeth. Then he turned to the group of men round him and said something, and some of them laughed too.

'Sure, Tom. When you . . . '

'I mean it,' said Ricky, and Barnes kept on smiling. 'Whoever you are, nothing you try is going to work.'

Barnes shook his head, enjoying my performance.

'You may be a clever guy,' I said, and saw him nod. 'You may be an educated man. Maybe you're even a college graduate.'

The laugh faded a little from Barnes' face. That was nice.

'But nothing you try is going to work.' He dropped the binoculars and stared. Not because he wanted to see me, but because he wanted me to see him. His face was like stone. 'Believe me, Mr Graduate,' I said.

He stayed stock-still, his eyes lasering across the two hundred yards between us. And then I saw him shout something, and he put the receiver back to his ear.

'Listen, you piece of shit, I don't care whether you come out of there or not. And if you do come out, I don't care whether it's walking, or in a big rubber bag, or in a lot of little rubber bags. But I got to warn you Lang . . . ' He pressed the phone tighter to his mouth, and I could hear spittle in his voice. 'You better not mess with progress. Do you understand me? Progress is something you've just got to let happen.'

'Sure,' said Ricky.

'Sure,' said Barnes.

I saw him look off to the side and nod.

'Take a look to the right, Lang. Blue Toyota.'

I did as I was told, and a windscreen skidded through the image in the binoculars. I steadied on it.

Naimh Murdah and Sarah Woolf, side-by-side in the front of the Toyota, drinking something hot from plastic beakers.

Waiting for the Cup Final kick-off. Sarah was looking down at something, or at nothing, and Murdah was examining himself in the rear-view mirror. He didn't seem to mind what he saw.

'Progress, Lang,' said the voice of Barnes. 'Progress is good for everybody.'

He paused and I slid the binoculars left again, just in time to see him smile.

'Look,' I said, putting some worry into my voice, 'just let me talk to her, will you?'

Out of the corner of my eye, I saw Francisco straighten in his chair. I had to deal with him, keep him straight, so I held the phone away from my face and threw an embarrassed grin over my shoulder.

'It's my mom,' I said. 'Worried about me.'

We both laughed a little at that.

I squinted through the binoculars again, and saw that Barnes was now standing by the Toyota. Inside the car, Sarah had the phone to her mouth, and Murdah had turned sideways in his seat to watch her.

'Thomas?' she said. Her voice sounded low and raw.

'Hi,' I said.

There was a pause, while we exchanged one or two interesting thoughts across the fizzing line, and then she said, 'I'm waiting for you.'

That's what I wanted to hear.

Murdah said something I didn't catch, and then Barnes reached in through the window and took the phone from Sarah.

'No time for all this, Tom. You can talk all you want, once you're out of there.' He smiled. 'So, any thoughts you'd like to share at this time, Thomas? A word, maybe? Little word, like yes or no?'

I stood there, watching Barnes watching me, and I waited as long as I dared. I wanted him to feel the size of my decision. Sarah was waiting for me.

Please, God, this had better work.

'Yes,' I said.

Twenty-five

Do be careful with this stuff,
because it's extremely sticky.

<small>VALERIE SINGLETON</small>

I persuaded Francisco to hold off with the statement for a while.

He wanted to get it out straight away, but I said a few more hours of uncertainty wouldn't do us any harm. Once they knew who we were, and could put a name to us, the story would cool a little. Even if there were fireworks afterwards, the mystery would have gone.

Just a few more hours, I said.

And so we waited through the night, taking our turns in the different positions.

The roof was the least popular, because it was cold and lonely, and nobody took that for more than an hour. Otherwise, we ate, and chatted, and didn't chat, and thought about our lives and how they'd brought us to this. Whether we were captors or captives.

They didn't send us any more food that night, but Hugo found some frozen hamburger buns in the canteen, and we laid them out on Beamon's desk to thaw and prodded them whenever we couldn't think of anything else to do.

The hostages dozed and held hands most of the time. Francisco had thought about splitting them up and scattering them over the building, but in the end he'd decided that they'd just take more guarding that way, and he was probably right. Francisco was being right about quite a lot of things. Taking advice, too, which made a nice change. I suppose there aren't many terrorists in the world who are so familiar with hostage situations that they can afford to be dogmatic, and say nah, the way you do it is this. Francisco was in uncharted waters just as much as the rest of us, and it made him nicer somehow.

It was just after four, and I had fixed it so that I was down in the lobby with Latifa when Francisco hobbled down the stairs with the statement for the press.

'Lat,' he said, with a charming smile, 'go tell the world for us.'

Latifa smiled back at him, thrilled that the wise elder brother had conferred this honour upon her, but not wanting to show it too much. She took the envelope from him and watched, lovingly, as he limped back to the staircase.

'They're waiting for you now,' he said, without turning round. 'Give it to them, tell them it goes straight to CNN, nobody else, and if they don't read it, word for word, they got dead Americans in here.' He stopped as he reached the half-landing, and turned to us. 'You cover her good, Ricky.'

I nodded and we watched him go, and then Latifa sighed. What a guy, she was thinking. My hero, and he chose me.

The real reason Francisco had chosen Latifa, of course, was that he reckoned it might make an armed assault by the gallant Moroccans fractionally less likely if they knew we had women in the team. But I didn't want to spoil her moment by saying that.

Latifa turned and looked out through the main doors, clutching the envelope and squinting into the bright lights of the television crews. She put a hand up to her hair.

314

'Fame at last,' I said, and she made a face at me.

She moved across to the reception desk and started to fiddle with her shirt in the reflection of the glass. I followed.

'Here,' I said, and I took the envelope from her and helped arrange the collar of the shirt in a cool way. I fluffed her hair out from behind her ears, and wiped a smudge of something off her cheek. She stood there and let me do it. Not as an intimacy. More like a boxer in his corner, getting set for the next round while the seconds squirt and rub and rinse and primp.

I reached into my pocket, took out the envelope, and handed it to her, while she took some deep breaths.

I gave her shoulder a squeeze.

'You'll be okay,' I said.

'Never been on TV before,' she said.

Dawn. Sunrise. Daybreak. Whatever.

There is still a gloom over the horizon, but it has an orange smear to it. The night is shrinking back into the ground, as the sun scrabbles for a finger-hold on the edge of the skyline.

The hostages are mostly asleep. They have drawn closer together in the night, because it has been colder than anyone thought it would be, and legs are no longer lolling over the edge of the rug.

Francisco looks tired as he holds out the phone for me. He has his feet propped up on the side of Beamon's desk, and he is watching CNN with the sound turned down, as a kindness to the sleeping Beamon.

I'm tired too, of course, but maybe I've got a little more adrenalin in my blood at this moment. I take the phone from Francisco.

'Yeah.'

Some popping, electronic noises. Then Barnes.

'Your five-thirty alarm call,' he says, with a smile in his voice.

'What do you want?' And I realise immediately that I have said this with an English accent. I look across at Francisco,

315

but he doesn't seem to have noticed. So I turn back to the window and listen to Barnes for a while, and when he's finished I take a deep breath, hoping desperately and not caring at all, both at the same time.

'When?' I say.

Barnes chuckles. I laugh too, in no particular accent.

'Fifty minutes,' he says, and hangs up.

When I turn back from the window, Francisco is watching me. His eyelashes seem longer than ever.

Sarah is waiting for me.

'They're bringing us breakfast,' I say, bending my Minnesotan vowels this time.

Francisco nods.

The sun is going to be clambering up soon, gradually heaving itself over the window sill. I leave the hostages, and Beamon, and Francisco, dozing in front of CNN. I walk out of the office and take the lift to the roof.

Three minutes later, forty-seven to go, and things are about as ready as they're going to be. I take the stairs down to the lobby.

Empty corridor, empty stairwell, empty stomach. The blood in my ears is loud, much louder than the sound of my feet on the carpet. I stop at the second floor landing, and look out into the street.

Decent crowd, for this time of the morning.

I was thinking ahead, that's why I forgot the present. The present hasn't happened, isn't happening, there is only the future. Life and death. Life or death. These, you see, are big things. Much bigger than footsteps. Footsteps are tiny things, compared to oblivion.

I had dropped down half a flight, just turned the corner on to the mezzanine, before I heard them and realised how wrong they were – wrong because they were running footsteps, and nobody should have been running in this building. Not now. Not with forty-six minutes to go.

Benjamin rounded the corner and stopped.

'What's up, Benj?' I said, as coolly as I could.

He stared at me for a moment. Breathing hard.

'The fuck have you been?' he said.

I frowned.

'On the roof,' I said. 'I was . . . '

'Latifa's on the roof,' he snapped.

We stared at each other. He was blowing through his mouth, partly from exertion, partly from anger.

'Well, Benj, I told her to go down to the lobby. There's going to be breakfast . . . '

And then, in a rush of angry movement, Benjamin lifted the Steyr to his shoulder and jammed his cheek against the stock, his fists clenching and unclenching around the grips.

And the barrel of the weapon had disappeared.

Now, how could that be? I thought to myself. How could the barrel of a Steyr, four hundred and twenty millimetres long, six grooves, right hand twist – how could that just disappear?

Well of course it couldn't, and it hadn't.

It was just my point of view.

'You fucking shit bastard,' says Benjamin.

I stand there, staring into a black hole.

Forty-five minutes to go, and this, let's face it, is about the worst possible time for Benjamin to bring up a subject as big, as broad, as many-headed as Betrayal. I suggest to him, politely I hope, that we might deal with it later; but Benjamin thinks now would be better.

'You fucking shit bastard,' is the way he puts it.

Part of the problem is that Benjamin has never trusted me. That's really the gist of it. Benjamin has had his suspicions right from the start, and he wants me to know about them now, in case I feel like trying to argue with him.

It all began, he tells me, with my military training.

Oh really, Benj?

Yes really.

Benjamin had lain awake at night, staring at the roof of his tent, wondering where and how a retarded Minnesotan had learnt to strip an M16, blindfold, in half the time it took everyone else. From there, apparently, he'd gone on to wonder about my accent, and my taste in clothes and music. And how come I put so many miles on the Land Rover when I was only going out for some beer?

This is all trifling stuff, of course, and, until now, Ricky could have batted it back without any trouble.

But the other part of the problem – the bigger part, frankly, right at this moment – is that Benjamin was fooling around with the telephone exchange during my conversation with Barnes.

Forty-one minutes.

'So what's it to be, Benj?' I say.

He presses his cheek harder against the stock, and I think I can see his finger turning white on the trigger.

'You going to shoot me?' I say. 'Now? Going to pull that trigger?'

He licks his lips. He knows what I'm thinking.

He twitches slightly, then pulls his face away from the Steyr, keeping his huge eyes on me.

'Latifa,' he calls over his shoulder. Loud. But not loud enough. He seems to be having trouble with his voice.

'They hear gunshots, Benj,' I say, 'they're going to think you've killed a hostage. They're going to storm the building. Kill us all.'

The word 'kill' hits him, and for an instant I think he might fire.

'Latifa,' he says again. Louder this time, and that has to be it. I can't let him shout a third time. I start to move, very slowly, towards him. My left hand is as loose as a hand can be.

'For a lot of guys out there, Benj,' I say, moving, 'a gunshot is just what they want to hear right now. You going to give them that?'

He licks his lips again. Once. Twice. Turns his head

towards the stairs.

I grab the barrel with my left hand, and push it back into his shoulder. No choice. If I pull the weapon away from him, the trigger's depressed, and so am I. So I push it back and to the side, and as his face comes further away from the stock I drive the heel of my right hand up under Benjamin's nose.

He drops like a stone – faster than a stone, as if some massive force is pushing him down to the floor – and for a moment I think I may have killed him. But then his head starts to move from side to side, and I can see the blood bubbling away from his lips.

I ease the Steyr out of his hands and flick down the safety catch, just as Latifa shouts up from the stairwell.

'Yeah?'

I can hear her feet on the stairs now. Not fast, but not slow.

I look down at Benjamin.

That's democracy, Benj. One man against many.

Latifa rounds the corner of the lower flight, the Uzi still slung at her shoulder.

'Jesus,' she says, when she sees the blood. 'What happened?'

'I don't know,' I say. I'm not looking at her. I'm bending over Benjamin, peering anxiously into his face. 'Guess he fell.'

Latifa brushes past me and squats at Benjamin's side, and as she does so, I glance at my watch.

Thirty-nine minutes.

Latifa turns and looks up at me.

'I'll do this,' she says. 'Take the lobby, Rick.'

So I do.

I take the lobby, and the front entrance, and the steps, and the hundred and sixty-seven yards from the steps to the police cordon.

My head feels hot by the time I get there, because I have my hands clasped on top of it.

Not surprisingly, they frisked me like they were taking a frisking exam. To get into the Royal College of Frisking. Five

319

times, head to toe, mouth, ears, crotch, soles of shoes. They tore most of my clothes from my body, and left me looking like an opened Christmas present.

It took them sixteen minutes.

They left me for another five, leaning against the side of a police van, arms and legs spread, while they shouted and pushed past each other. I stared at the ground. Sarah is waiting for me.

Christ, she'd better be.

Another minute went by, more shouting, more pushing, and I started to look around, thinking that if something didn't happen soon, I'd have to make it happen. Bloody Benjamin. My shoulders started to ache from the weight of my leaning.

'Good job, Thomas,' said a voice.

I looked to my left, under my arm, and saw a pair of scuffed Red Wing boots. One flat on the ground, the other cocked at a right angle, with the toe buried in the dust. I slowly tilted up to find the rest of Russell Barnes.

He was leaning against the door of the van, smiling, holding out his packet of Marlboro to me. He wore a leather flight jacket, with the name Connor stitched over his left breast. Who the fuck was Connor?

The friskers had fallen back a little, but only a little, out of an apparent respect for Barnes. Plenty of them kept on watching me, thinking maybe they'd missed a bit.

I shook my head at the cigarettes.

'Let me see her,' I said.

Because she's waiting for me.

Barnes watched me for a moment, then smiled again. He was feeling good, and relaxed, and loose. Game over, for him.

He looked to his left.

'Sure,' he said.

He bounced himself casually away from the van, making the metal skin of the door pop, and gestured for me to follow him. The sea of tight shirts and wrap-around sunglasses parted as we walked slowly across towards the blue Toyota.

To our right, behind a steel barrier, stood the television

crews, their cables coiled about their feet and their blue-white lights puncturing the remains of the night. Some of the cameras trained on me as I walked, but most of them stuck to the building.

CNN seemed to have the best position.

Murdah got out of the car first, while Sarah just sat and waited, staring ahead through the windscreen, her hands clasped between her thighs. We had got to within a couple of yards before she turned to look at me, and tried to smile.

I'm waiting for you, Thomas.

'Mr Lang,' said Murdah, coming round the back of the car, stepping between me and Sarah. He was wearing a dark-grey overcoat, and a white shirt with no tie. The sheen of his forehead seemed a little duller than I remembered, and there were a few hours' worth of stubble around his jaw, but otherwise he looked well.

And why wouldn't he?

He stared into my face for a second or two, then gave a brief, satisfied nod. As if I'd done nothing more than mow his lawn to a reasonable standard.

'Good,' he said eventually.

I stared back at him. A blank stare, because I didn't really want to give him anything right now.

'What's good?' I said.

But Murdah was looking over my shoulder, signalling something, and I felt movement behind me.

'See you around, Tom,' said Barnes.

I turned and saw that he had started to move away, walking slowly backwards in a casual, loose-limbed, gonna-miss-you style. As our eyes met, he gave me a small, ironic salute, then wheeled round and headed off towards an army Jeep, parked near the back of the mess of vehicles. A blond man in plain clothes started the engine as Barnes approached, then tooted his horn twice to clear the crowd from around the front of the Jeep. I turned back to Murdah.

He was examining my face now, a little closer, a little more professional. Like a plastic surgeon.

'What's good?' I said again, and waited while my question travelled the immense distance between our two worlds.

'You have done as I wished,' said Murdah at last. 'As I predicted.'

He nodded again. A bit of a snip here, a tuck there – yes, I think we can do something with this face.

'Some people, Mr Lang,' he went on, 'some friends of mine, told me that you would be a problem. You were a man who might try and kick off the traces.' He took a deeper breath. 'But I was right. And that is good.'

Then, still looking into my face, he stepped to one side and opened the passenger door of the Toyota.

I watched as Sarah twisted slowly round in her seat and climbed out. She straightened up, her arms crossed in front of her as if warding off the cold of the dawn, and lifted her face to me.

We were so close.

'Thomas,' she said, and for a second I allowed myself to plunge into those eyes, deep down, and touch whatever it was that had brought me here. I would never forget that kiss.

'Sarah,' I said.

I reached out and put both my arms around her – shielding her, enveloping her, hiding her from everything and everyone – and she just stood there, keeping her hands in front of her body.

So I dropped my right hand to my side, and slid it between our bodies, across our stomachs, feeling, searching for contact.

I touched it. Took hold of it.

'Goodbye,' I whispered.

She looked up at me.

'Goodbye,' she said.

The metal was warm from her body.

I let her go, and turned, slowly, to face Murdah.

He was talking softly into a mobile phone, looking back at me, smiling, his head cocked slightly to one side. And when he took in my expression he knew that something was wrong. He glanced down at my hand, and the smile tumbled away from his face like orange-peel from a speeding car.

'Jesus Christ,' said a voice behind me, and I suppose that meant that someone else must have seen the gun too. I couldn't be sure, because I was staring hard into Murdah's eyes.

'It's over,' I said.

Murdah stared back at me, the mobile phone dropping down from his mouth.

'It's over,' I said again. 'Not off.'

'What . . . what are you talking about?' he said.

Murdah stood watching the gun, and the knowledge of it, the beauty of our little tableau, rippled outwards through the sea of tight shirts.

'The expression is,' I said, 'to kick *over* the traces.'

Twenty-six

The sun has got his hat on,
Hip hip hip hooray,

L. ARTHUR ROSE AND DOUGLAS FURBER

We're back on the roof of the consulate now. Just so as you know.

The sun is already bobbing its head along the horizon, evaporating the sky-line of dark tiles into a misty strip of whiteness, and I think to myself that if it was up to me, I'd have the helicopter airborne by now. The sun is so strong, so bright, so hopelessly blinding that, for all I know, the helicopter might already be there – there might be fifty helicopters, hovering twenty yards up-sun of me, watching me unwrap my two packets of brown, grease-proof paper.

Except, of course, I'd hear them.

I hope.

'What do you want?' says Murdah.

He is behind me, perhaps twenty feet away. I have handcuffed him to the fire escape while I get on with my chores, and he doesn't seem to like that very much. He seems agitated.

324

'What do you want?' he screams.

I don't answer, so he goes on screaming. Not words, exactly. Or, at least, none that I recognise. I whistle a few bars of something to block out the noise, and continue attaching clip A to retaining lug B, while making sure that cable C is not fouling bracket D.

'What I want,' I say eventually, 'is for you to see it coming. That's all.'

I turn to look at him now, to see how bad he's feeling. It's very bad, and I find I don't mind all that much.

'You are insane,' he shouts, tugging at his wrists. 'I am here. Do you see?' He laughs, or almost laughs, because he can't believe how stupid I am. 'I am here. The Graduate will not come, because I am here.'

I turn away again, and squint into the low wall of sunlight.

'Well I hope so, Naimh,' I say. 'I really do. I hope you still have more than one vote.'

There is a pause, and when I turn back to him, I find that the sheen has folded itself into a frown.

'Vote,' he says eventually, in a soft voice.

'Vote,' I say again.

Murdah watches me carefully.

'I don't understand you,' he says.

So I take a deep breath, and try and lay it out for him.

'You're not an arms dealer, Naimh,' I say. 'Not any more. I've taken that privilege away from you. For your sins. You're not rich, you're not powerful, you're not connected, you're not a member of the Garrick.' That doesn't register with him, so maybe he never was anyway. 'All you are, at this moment, is a man. Like the rest of us. And as a man, you only get one vote. Sometimes not even that.'

He thinks carefully before he answers. He knows I'm mad, and that he must go gently with me.

'I don't know what you're saying,' he says.

'Yes you do,' I say. 'You just don't know whether *I* know what I'm saying.' The sun inches a little higher, straining on its tip-toes to get a better view of us. 'I'm talking about the

325

twenty-six other people who stand to gain directly from the success of The Graduate, and the hundreds, maybe thousands, of people who will gain indirectly. People who have worked, and lobbied, and bribed, and threatened, and even killed, just to get this close. They all have votes too. Barnes will be talking to them at this moment, asking for a yes or no answer, and who's to say how the numbers will come out?'

Murdah is very still now. His eyes are wide and his mouth is open, as if he's not enjoying the taste of something.

'Twenty-six,' he says, very quietly. 'How do you know twenty-six? How do you know this?'

I make a modest face.

'I used to be a financial journalist,' I say. 'For about an hour. A man at Smeets Velde Kerplein followed your money for me. Told me a lot of things.'

He drops his gaze, concentrating hard. His brain has got him here, so his brain must get him out.

'Of course,' I say, forcing him back on to the track, 'you may be right. Maybe the twenty-six will all rally round, call it off, write it off, whatever. I just wouldn't stake my life on it.'

I leave a pause, because I feel that, one way and another, I've earned the right to it.

'But I'm very happy to stake yours,' I say.

This shakes him. Knocks him out of his stupor.

'You are insane,' he shouts. 'Do you know that? Do you know that you are insane?'

'Right,' I say. 'So call them. Call Barnes, tell him to stop it. You're on the roof with a madman, and the party is off. Use your one vote.'

He shakes his head.

'They will not come,' he says. And then, in a much quieter voice, 'They will not come, because I am here.'

I shrug, because it's all I can think of. I'm feeling very shruggy at this moment. The way I used to feel before parachute jumps.

'Tell me what you want,' screams Murdah, suddenly, and

he starts to rattle the iron of the fire-escape with his handcuffs. When I look across again, I can see bright, wet blood on his wrists.

Diddums.

'I want to watch the sun rise,' I say.

Francisco, Cyrus, Latifa, Bernhard, and a bloody Benjamin have joined us up here on the roof, because this seems to be where the interesting people are at the moment. They are variously scared and confused, unable to get a grip on what is happening; they have lost their place in the script, and are hoping that somebody will call out a page number very soon.

Benjamin, needless to say, has done his best to poison the others against me. But his best stopped being good enough the moment they saw me coming back into the consulate, holding a gun to Murdah's neck. They found that strange. Peculiar. Not consistent with Benjamin's wild theories of Betrayal.

So they stand before me now, eyes flitting between me and Murdah; they are sniffing the wind, while Benjamin trembles with the strain of not shooting me.

'Ricky, what the fuck is happening here?' says Francisco.

I stand up slowly, feeling things crack in my knees, and step back to admire the result of my labours.

Then I turn away, and wave a hand towards Murdah. I have rehearsed this speech a few times, and I think I've got most of it down.

'This man,' I tell them, 'used to be an arms dealer.' I move a little closer to the fire-escape, because I want everyone to be able to hear me clearly. 'His name is Naimh Murdah, he is the chief executive officer of seven separate companies, and the majority shareholder in a further forty-one. He has homes in London, New York, California, the south of France, the west of Scotland, the north of anywhere with a swimming pool. He has a total net worth of just over a billion dollars,' which makes me turn to look at Murdah, 'and that must have been an exciting moment, Naimh. Big cake on that day, I would imagine.' I look back at my audience. 'More importantly, from our point of view, he is the sole signatory to over ninety separate bank accounts, one of which has been paying our wages for the last six months.'

Nobody seems ready to jump in here, so I press on for the coup.

'This is the man who conceived, organised, supplied and financed The Sword Of Justice.'

There is a pause.

Only Latifa makes a sound; a little snort of disbelief, or fear, or anger. Otherwise, they are silent.

They stare at Murdah for a long time, and so do I. I notice now that he also has some blood on his neck – perhaps I was a little rough getting him up the stairs – but apart from that, he looks well. And why wouldn't he?

'Bullshit,' says Latifa eventually.

'Right,' I say. 'Bullshit. Mr Murdah, it's bullshit. Would you go along with that?'

Murdah stares back, trying desperately to judge which of us is the least mad.

'Would you go along with that?' I say again.

'We are a revolutionary movement,' says Cyrus suddenly, which makes me look at Francisco – because really it was his job to say that. But Francisco is frowning, and looking around, and I know he's thinking about the difference between planned action and real action. It was nothing like this in the brochure, is Francisco's complaint.

'Of course we are,' I say. 'We are a revolutionary movement, with a commercial sponsor. That's all. This man,' and I point at Murdah as dramatically as I can, 'has set you up, has set all of us up, has set the world up, to buy his guns.' They shift about a little. 'It's called marketing. Aggressive marketing. Creating a demand for a product, in a place where once only daffodils grew. That's what this man does.'

I turn and look at this man, hoping that he's going to chip in and say yes, it's all true, every word of it. But Murdah

328

doesn't seem to want to talk, and instead we have a long pause. A lot of Brownian thoughts rushing about, colliding with each other.

'Guns,' says Francisco eventually. His voice is low and soft, and he might be calling from miles away. 'What guns?'

This is it. The moment when I have to make them understand. And believe.

'A helicopter,' I say, and they all look at me now. Murdah too. 'They are sending a helicopter here to kill us.'

Murdah clears his throat.

'It will not come,' he says, and I can't really tell whether he's trying to persuade me or himself. 'I am here, and it will not come.'

I turn back to the others.

'Any time now,' I say, 'a helicopter is going to appear, from that direction.' I point into the sun, and notice that Bernhard is the only one who turns. The rest of them keep on watching me. 'A helicopter that is smaller, faster, and better-armed than anything you have ever seen in your lives. It is going to come here, very soon, and take us all off the roof of this building. It is probably going to take the roof as well, and the next two floors, because this is a machine of unbelievable power.'

There is a pause, and some of them look down at their feet. Benjamin opens his mouth to say something, or, more probably, shout something, but Francisco stretches out a hand and rests it on Benjamin's shoulder. Then looks at me.

'We know they are sending a helicopter, Rick,' he says.

Whoa.

That doesn't sound right. That doesn't sound remotely right. I look around the other faces, and when I make contact with Benjamin, he can't control himself any longer.

'Can't you see, you fucking shit?' he screams, and he's almost laughing, he hates me so much. 'We've done it.' He starts to jump up and down on the spot, and I can see that his nose has started to bleed again. 'We've done it, and your treachery has been for nothing.'

I look back to Francisco.

329

'They called us, Rick,' he says, his voice still soft and distant. 'Ten minutes ago.'

'Yes?' I say.

They're all watching me now, as Francisco speaks.

'They're sending a helicopter,' he says. 'To take us to the airport.' He lets out a sigh, and his shoulders drop a little. 'We've won.'

Oh for fuck's sake, I think to myself.

So here we stand, in a desert of gritty asphalt, with a few air-conditioning vents standing in as palm trees, while we wait for life or death. A place in the sun, or a place in the dark.

I have to speak now. I've tried a couple of times already to get myself heard, but there was some loose, foolish talk among the comrades of throwing me off the roof, so I held back. But now, the sun is perfect. God has reached down, placed the sun on the tee, and is, at this moment, rummaging in his bag for the driver. This is the perfect time, and I have to speak.

'So what happens?' I say.

Nobody answers, for the simple reason that nobody can. We all know what we want to happen, of course, but wanting is not enough any more. Between the idea and the reality falls the shadow, and all that. I take some looks from all quarters. Absorb them.

'We're just going to hang about here, is that it?'

'Shut the fuck up,' says Benjamin.

I ignore him. I have to.

'We wait here, on the roof, for a helicopter. That's what they said?' Still nobody answers. 'Did they by any chance suggest we stand in a line, with bright orange circles round us?' Silence. 'I mean, I'm just wondering how we could make this any easier for them.'

I direct most of this towards Bernhard, because I have the feeling that he's the only one who isn't sure. The rest of them have clutched at the straw. They're excited, hopeful, busy deciding whether or not they're going to sit by the window,

330

and if there'll be time to get duty frees – but, like me, Bernhard has been turning every now and then, squinting into the sun, and perhaps he's also thinking that this would be a good time to attack someone. This is the perfect time, and Bernhard is feeling vulnerable up here on the roof.

I turn to Murdah.

'Tell them,' I say.

He shakes his head. Not a refusal. Just confusion, and fear, and some other things. I take a few steps towards him, which makes Benjamin jab the air with his Steyr.

I have to keep going.

'Tell them what I've said is true,' I say. 'Tell them who you are.'

Murdah closes his eyes for a moment, then opens them wide. Perhaps he was hoping to find kempt lawns and white-jacketed waiters, or the ceiling of one of his bedrooms; when all he sees is a handful of dirty, hungry, scared people with guns, he slumps down against the parapet.

'You know I'm right,' I say. 'The helicopter that comes here, you know what it's for. What it's going to do. You have to tell them.' I take a few more steps. 'Tell them what has happened, and why they're going to die. Use your vote.'

But Murdah is spent. His chin is down on his chest, and his eyes have closed again.

'Murdah . . . ' I say, and then stop, because someone has made a short, hissing sound. It's Bernhard, and he is standing still, looking down at the roof, his head cocked to one side.

'I hear it,' he says.

Nobody moves. We are frozen.

And then I hear it too. And then Latifa, and then Francisco.

A distant fly in a distant bottle.

Murdah has either heard it, or believed that the rest of us have heard it. His chin has lifted from his chest, and his eyes are wide open.

But I can't wait for him. I walk over to the parapet.

'What are you doing?' says Francisco.

'This thing is going to kill us,' I say.

'It's here to save us, Ricky.'

'Kill us, Francisco.'

'You fucking shit,' screams Benjamin. 'What the fuck are you doing?'

They're all watching me now. Listening and watching. Because I have reached down to my little tent of brown grease-proof paper, and laid bare the treasures therein.

The British-made Javelin is a light-weight, supersonic, self-contained surface-to-air missile system. It has a two-stage solid-fuel rocket motor, giving an effective range of between five and six kilometres, it weighs sixty-odd pounds in all, and it comes in any colour you want, so long as it's olive green.

The system is made up of two handy units, the first being a sealed launch canister, containing the missile, and the second being the semi-automatic-line-of-sight-guidance system, which has a lot of very small, very clever, very expensive electronic stuff inside it. Once assembled, the Javelin is capable of performing one job supremely well.

It shoots down helicopters.

That's why I'd asked for it, you see. Bob Rayner would have got me a teasmaid, or a hair-dryer, or a BMW convertible, if I'd paid the right money.

But I'd said no, Bob. Put away those tempting things. I want a big toy. I want a Javelin.

This particular model, according to Bob, had fallen onto the back of a lorry leaving an Army Ordnance depot near Colchester. You may wonder how such a thing can happen in the modern age, what with computerised inventories, and receipts, and armed men standing at gates – but, believe me, the army is no different from Harrods. Stock shrinkage is a constant problem.

The Javelin had been carefully removed from the lorry by some friends of Rayner's, who had transferred it to the underside of a VW minibus, where it had stayed, thank God, the course of its twelve hundred mile journey to Tangier.

I don't know if the couple driving the bus knew it was there. I only know that they were New Zealanders.

'You put that down,' screams Benjamin.

'Or what?' I say.

'I'll fucking kill you,' he yells, moving closer to the edge of the roof.

There is a pause, and it's filled by buzzing. The fly in the bottle is angry.

'I don't care,' I say. 'I really don't. If I put this down, I'm dead anyway. So I'll hang on to it, thanks.'

'Cisco,' shouts Benjamin in desperation. 'We've won. You said we've won.' Nobody answers him, so Benjamin starts his jumping again. 'If he shoots at the helicopter, they will kill us.'

There's some more shouting now. A lot more. But it's getting harder to tell where the shouting is coming from, because the buzz is gradually turning into a clatter. A clatter from the sun.

'Ricky,' says Francisco, and I realise that he is standing right behind me now. 'You put it down.'

'It's going to kill us, Francisco,' I say.

'Put it down, Ricky. I count to five. You put it down, or I shoot you. I mean it.'

And I think he probably does mean it. I think he really believes that this sound, this beating of wings, is Mercy, not Death.

'One,' he says.

'Up to you, Naimh,' I say, adjusting my eye to the rubber collar on the sight. 'Tell them the truth now. Tell them what this machine is, and what it's going to do.'

'He's going to kill us,' screams Benjamin, and I think I can see him leaping around somewhere on my left.

'Two,' says Francisco. I switch on the guidance system. The buzzing has gone, drowned out by the lower frequencies of the helicopter's noise. Bass notes. Beating of wings.

'Tell them, Naimh. If they shoot me, everybody dies. Tell them the truth.'

The sun covers the sky, blank and pitiless. There is only sun and clatter.

'Three,' says Francisco, and suddenly there's some metal behind my left ear. It might be a spoon, but I don't think so.

'Yes or no, Naimh? What is it to be?'

'Four,' says Francisco.

The noise is big now. As big as the sun.

'Kill it,' says Francisco.

But it isn't Francisco. It's Murdah. And he's not saying, he's screaming. Going mad. He is ripping at the handcuffs, bleeding, shouting, thrashing, kicking grit across the roof. And now I think Francisco has started shouting back at him, telling him to shut up, while Bernhard and Latifa scream at each other, or at me.

I think, but I'm not sure. They have all begun to disappear, you see. Fading away, leaving me in a very quiet world.

Because now I can see it.

Small, black, fast. It could be a bug on the front of the sight.

The Graduate.

Hydra rockets. Hellfire air-to-ground missiles. .50 cannons. Four hundred miles an hour, if it needs to. One chance only.

It will come in and pick its targets. It has nothing to fear from us. Bunch of crazy terrorists with automatic rifles, popping away. Couldn't hit a barn door.

Whereas the Graduate can punch a whole room out of a building with one press of a button.

One chance only.

This fucking sun. Blazing at me, burning out the image on the sight.

Tears started in my eyes from the brightness of the picture, but I held my eye open.

Put it down, Benjamin is saying. Screaming it in my ear, from a thousand miles away. Put it down.

Jesus, it's fast. It jinks along the rooftops, maybe half a mile.

You fucking shit bastard.

Cold and hard on my neck. Somebody is definitely trying to put me off. Pushing a barrel through my neck.

I'll shoot you dead, screams Benjamin.

Remove the safety cover, and flick down the trigger. Your Javelin is now armed, gentlemen.

Choking on the shot.

Put it down.

The roof exploded. Just disintegrated. And then, a fraction of a second later, the sound of the cannon fire. An incredible, deafening, body-shaking noise. Chunks of stone flew up and sideways, every piece as deadly as the shells that caused it. Dust and violence and destruction. I winced and turned away, and the tears ran down my face as the sun let me go.

It had made its first pass. At incredible speed. Faster than anything I'd seen, anything but a fighter. And its turn was unbelievable. It just dropped an elbow and spun. Flat out one way, spin, flat out the other. Nothing in between.

I could taste the fumes from its exhaust.

I raised the Javelin again, and as I did so, I saw Benjamin's head and shoulders thirty feet away. The rest of him, fuck knows where.

Francisco was screaming at me again, but this time it was in Spanish, and I'll never know what that was about.

Here it comes. Quarter of a mile.

And this time I really could see it.

The sun was behind me now, rising, getting up to speed, shining its full force on this little black bundle of hatred coming towards me.

Cross-wires. Black dot.

Flying a straight course. No evasion. Why bother? Bunch of crazy terrorists, nothing to fear from them.

I can see the pilot's face. Not in the sight, but in my mind. From the first pass, the image of the pilot's face has come into my mind.

Let's go.

I pulled the trigger, firing up the thermal battery, and braced myself as the first stage motor shoved me back towards the parapet with the force of the missile's launch.

Newton, I thought.

Coming in now. Fast as ever, fast as anything, but I can see you.

I can see you, you fucking shit bastard.

The second stage motor ignited, kicking the Javelin forward, keen and eager. Let the dog see the rabbit.

I just hold it. That's all I do. Hold it in the cross-wires.

The camera in the aiming unit tracks the flare from the missile tail, compares it with signals from the sight – any mismatch, and an error correction signal is sent to the missile.

All I have to do is hold it in the cross-wires.

Two seconds.

One second.

Latifa's cheek had been cut by flying masonry, and it was bleeding badly.

We sat in Beamon's office, and I tried to staunch the wound with a towel, while Beamon covered us with Hugo's Steyr.

Some of the other hostages had got hold of weapons too, and they were scattered over the room, peering nervously out of the windows. I looked around the room at the nervous faces, and suddenly felt exhausted. And hungry. Ravenously hungry.

There was some noise in the corridor. Footsteps. Shouts in Arabic, and French, and then English.

'Turn that up, will you?' I said to Beamon.

He glanced over his shoulder at the television, where a blonde woman was mouthing at us. The caption underneath said 'Connie Fairfax – Casablanca'. She was reading something.

Beamon stepped forward and twisted up the volume.

Connie had a nice voice.

336

Latifa had a nice face. The blood from her cut was starting to thicken.

'. . . issued three hours ago to CNN, by a young woman of Arab appearance,' said Connie, and then the picture cut to footage of a small, black helicopter, apparently getting into serious difficulties. Connie kept reading.

'My name is Thomas Lang,' she said. 'I have been coerced into this action by officers of the American intelligence services, ostensibly to penetrate a terrorist organisation, The Sword Of Justice.' The picture cut back to Connie as she looked up and pressed at her earpiece.

A man's voice said: 'Connie, weren't they responsible for the shooting in Austria?'

Connie said yes, that was absolutely right. Except it was Switzerland.

Then she looked down at the piece of paper.

'The Sword Of Justice is, in reality, being financed by a western arms dealer, in conjunction with renegade elements of the American CIA.'

The shouts in the corridor had subsided, and when I looked over to the doorway, I saw that Solomon was standing there, watching me. He nodded, once, and then slowly advanced into the room, picking his way through the wreck of furniture. A clutch of tight shirts appeared behind him.

'It's the truth,' screamed Murdah, and I turned to the television to see what kind of footage they'd got of his rooftop confession. It wasn't great, to be honest. The tops of a couple of heads, moving about occasionally. Murdah's voice was distorted, layered with background noise, because I hadn't been able to position the radio microphone near enough to the fire-escape. But I'd have known it was him, all the same, which meant that others would too.

'Mr Lang closed his statement,' said Connie, 'by giving CNN a wavelength of 254.125 megahertz, the VHF frequency from which this recording was made. No one has yet identified the voices involved, but it appears . . .'

I gestured at Beamon.

'You can turn it off, if you want,' I said. But he left it on, and I wasn't going to argue with him.

Solomon perched himself on the edge of Beamon's desk. He looked at Latifa for a moment, then at me.

'Shouldn't you be rounding up some suspects?' I said.

Solomon smiled a little.

'Mr Murdah is very rounded up indeed, at the moment,' he said. 'And Miss Woolf is in good hands. As for Mr Russell P. Barnes . . . '

'He was flying The Graduate,' I said.

Solomon raised an eyebrow. Or rather, he left it where it was and dropped his body slightly. He looked as if he didn't want to be surprised any more today.

'Rusty used to fly helicopters for the Marines,' I said. 'That's how he got involved in the first place.' I eased the towel gently away from Latifa's face, and saw that the bleeding had stopped. 'Do you think I can make a phone call from here?'

We flew back to England ten days later in an RAF Hercules. The seats were hard, the cabin was noisy, and there was no film. But I was happy.

I was happy watching Solomon sleep, slumped on the other side of the cabin, his brown raincoat folded behind his head and his hands clasped across his stomach. Solomon was a good friend at any time, but asleep, I felt like I almost loved him.

Or maybe I was just getting my loving mechanism warmed up, ready for someone else.

Yes, that was probably it.

We touched down at RAF Coltishall just after midnight, and a gaggle of cars followed as we taxied to the hangar. After a while, the door clanged open and some cold Norfolk air climbed aboard. I took a deep breath of it.

O'Neal was waiting outside, hands thrust deep into the pockets of his overcoat, shoulders bunched around his ears. He jerked his chin at me, and Solomon and I followed him to a Rover.

O'Neal and Solomon got in the front, and I slid in behind them, slowly, wanting to enjoy this moment.

'Hello,' I said.

'Hello,' said Ronnie.

There was a pause of the better sort, and Ronnie and I smiled at each other and nodded.

'Miss Crichton wanted very much to be here on your return,' said O'Neal, wiping condensation off the windscreen with his glove.

'Really?' I said.

'Really,' said Ronnie.

O'Neal started the engine, while Solomon fiddled with the de-mister.

'Well,' I said, 'whatever Miss Crichton wants, she must definitely have.'

Ronnie and I kept on smiling as the Rover swept out of the base, and into the Norfolk night.

In the six months that followed, overseas sales of the Javelin surface-to-air missile increased by a little over forty per cent.

THE END

Moab is my Washpot

Stephen Fry

'Stephen Fry is one of the great originals . . . This autobiography of his first twenty years is a pleasure to read, mixing outrageous acts with sensible opinions in bewildering confusion . . . That so much outward charm, self-awareness and intellect should exist alongside behaviour that threatened to ruin the lives of innocent victims, noble parents and Fry himself, gives the book a tragic grandeur that lifts it to classic status.'
Financial Times

'A remarkable, perhaps even unique, exercise in autobiography . . . that aroma of authenticity that is the point of all great autobiographies; of which, I rather think, this is one.'
Evening Standard

'He writes superbly about his family, about his homosexuality, about the agonies of childhood . . . some of his bursts of simile take the breath away . . . his most satisfying and appealing book so far.'
Observer

'This is one of the most extraordinary and affecting biographies I have read . . . Stephen is . . . painfully honest when trying to grapple with his ever-present demons, and often, as you might expect, very funny . . . I hope to goodness there'll be a sequel. I can't wait for more.'
Daily Mail

arrow books

Also available in Arrow

Thank You, Jeeves

P.G. Wodehouse

A Jeeves and Wooster novel

Thank You, Jeeves is the first novel to feature the incomparable
valet Jeeves and his hapless charge Bertie Wooster – and
you've hardly started to turn the pages when Jeeves resigns
over Bertie's dedicated but somewhat untuneful playing of the
banjo. In high dudgeon, Bertie disappears to the country as a
guest of his chum Chuffy – only to find his peace shattered by
the arrival of his ex-fiancée Pauline Stoker, her formidable
father and the eminent loony-doctor Sir Roderick Glossop.
When Chuffy falls in love with Pauline and Bertie seems to be
caught in flagrante, a situation boils up which only Jeeves
(whether employed or not) can simmer down . . .

arrow books

Also available in Arrow

Carry On, Jeeves

P.G. Wodehouse

A Jeeves and Wooster collection

These marvellous stories introduce us to Jeeves, whose first ever duty is to cure Bertie's raging hangover ('If you would drink this, sir . . . it is a little preparation of my own invention. It is the Worcester Sauce that gives it its colour. The raw egg makes it nutritious. The red pepper gives it its bite. Gentlemen have told me they have found it extremely invigorating after a late evening.')

And from that moment, one of the funniest, sharpest and most touching partnerships in English literature never looks back . . .

arrow books

THE POWER OF READING

Visit the Random House website and get connected with information on all our books and authors

EXTRACTS from our recently published books and selected backlist titles

COMPETITIONS AND PRIZE DRAWS Win signed books, audiobooks and more

AUTHOR EVENTS Find out which of our authors are on tour and where you can meet them

LATEST NEWS on bestsellers, awards and new publications

MINISITES with exclusive special features dedicated to our authors and their titles

READING GROUPS Reading guides, special features and all the information you need for your reading group

LISTEN to extracts from the latest audiobook publications

WATCH video clips of interviews and readings with our authors

RANDOM HOUSE INFORMATION including advice for writers, job vacancies and all your general queries answered

Come home to Random House

www.rbooks.co.uk